You better believe it

Black Verse in English from Africa, the West Indies and the United States

Selected and annotated by Paul Breman

Penguin Books

Penguin Books Ltd, Harmondsworth,
Middlesex, England
Penguin Books Inc., 7110 Ambassador Road,
Baltimore, Maryland 21207, U.S.A.
Penguin Books Australia Ltd, Ringwood,
Victoria, Australia

This selection published by Penguin Books 1973
Copyright © Paul Breman, 1973

Printed in the United States of America by
Kingsport Press, Inc., Kingsport, Tennessee
Set in Monotype Bembo

for rosey pool and robert hayden

for harold jackman, ray durem, langston hughes,
and conrad kent rivers

for nan, jill, remco and marc

Maldigo la poesía concebida como un lujo cultural por los
  neutrales
que, lavándose las manos, se desentienden y evaden.
Maldigo la poesía de quien no toma partido, partido hasta
  mancharse.*

GABRIEL CELAYA

*I detest the kind of poetry which is nothing but an intellectual
pastime for the middle-of-the-roaders, who wash their hands and
split hairs to evade the issues. I detest poetry written by those who
do not take sides, do not commit themselves for fear the dirt might
stick.

Contents

9 *Contents*

12   *Contents*

17 Contents

Introduction

This anthology contains poems written in English by 'black' writers from Africa, the West Indies, and the United States of America.

The order is chronological. Since it is impossible to achieve the ideal arrangement (which would be by the date of each individual poem) I have compromised by using the writers' year of birth instead. This may be awkward in a few isolated cases, but on the whole it affords a useful pattern of generations, which emerges from even a cursory look at the table of contents.

The chronological order deliberately upsets the more obvious geographical one. It is no longer useful, I think, to present the literary development that took place in different parts of the black world as so many entirely separate streams: they are coming together, and the time has come to see the unity in their variety. I hope that, later, it will become necessary to cut across the language barriers in a similar way – but for this, now is not yet the time.

The main theme of the collection is: how have black writers, from different geographical and social backgrounds, reacted to what has become known as 'the black experience'? This is a question to which there is no one general answer, therefore I have selected two hundred specific answers that appealed to me, and I have tried to include with them enough of my reasons and enough basic information to enable an interested reader to set out on a further quest of his own.

Perhaps I might have been expected, instead, to have written a substantial introduction deftly explaining what it is all about. I feel that too often such introductions negate the purpose of an anthology. Canonizing one's own views too easily reduces the contents to literary history, which is convenient only to those who have no wish to read the poems. More important still, it robs the reader of the joy of discovery, the fun of one's own mistakes, and the warmth of a growing personal relationship with the material and its creators.

To me, this joy and this fun and this warmth have remained the ultimate reasons, from the early days when, by chance, I started collecting Negro verse to the much later ones when, deliberately, I began to publish black poetry. This anthology just takes the process one step further, and actively tries to communicate the joy, share the fun and spread the warmth.

At the same time, of course, when one sets out to compile an anthology one wants to make it different from any other in the field. In the case of black poetry, two things seemed never to have been seriously attempted: the integration of expressions from different continents, and the application of poem-content, rather than mere author-skin, as a selection principle.

The only other thing I would like to elaborate on is the dedication. Rosey Pool, who died just when the final draft of this book was ready, was the first to make material which I only knew about by hearsay actually available – way back in 1947. Because of Robert Hayden my interest as a collector developed into commitment as a publisher: his *Ballad of Remembrance* inaugurated the series of black poetry books which I have been issuing since 1962. The year before that, Harold Jackman asked the question which I have been trying, once again, to answer here: what excuse do you have for compiling yet another anthology? Langston Hughes was the first black writer I knew, first through correspondence and much later as a friend – indefatigable, loyal, and adept at hiding the axes he kept ready for grinding. Ray Durem was the discovery Langston and I shared, which weighed on both our consciences because at the time there was nothing either of us could do for him. Conrad Kent Rivers was one of the most rewarding people I have ever known, and the living embodiment of all the dilemmas adherent to being 'black and bid to sing'. I wish the five who died were still here, with Bob Hayden, to laugh or curse and to tell me if this is black enough.

George Moses Horton

stands out as the only pre-Civil War poet whose life and work retain any validity in present-day terms. Born in 1797 in Northampton County, North Carolina, into slavery for the Horton family, he was eventually allotted to one of the sons who brought him, in 1815, to a plantation very near Chapel Hill, already renowned for its university. Here George Moses taught himself (and his brother) to read by a unique, self-invented method: he learned the methodist hymnal by heart, then compared the words with those in a spelling book. Permitted to hire himself out to work for others, he served in the house of the university president where students became aware of his ability to handle words and rhyme – soon he was doing a reasonably lucrative trade in love poems which sold for about half a dollar a piece. His customers included at least one future president (James Polk) and it is fascinating to think how many white southern families may owe their beginnings to a slave-engineered courtship: the poems written for William Sheppard Pettigrew survive in the family archive, but what about the score of other buyers George Moses recalled in his autobiography?

In 1829 a collection of less occasional poetry appeared under the title *The hope of liberty*, a very literal hope, for the author dreamed of buying his freedom with the proceeds and of going to Liberia. But the sales were negligible, and the reissue of 1837, appended to the poems of Phyllis Wheatley, is tellingly titled *Poems by a slave*. Meanwhile George Moses had been befriended by novelist Caroline Lee Hertz (see her *Lovell's folly* of 1833), who had his poem 'On liberty' published in the recently founded *Lancaster Gazette* in April 1828. It was taken over by William Lloyd Garrison, who reprinted it in his *Liberator* on 29 March 1834. In poems like this, and in his letters asking various people for grants and help, it becomes quite clear that George Moses was nobody's abject house-nigger: he had a clear idea of his capabilities, used them very professionally to a specific end, and took an outspoken and straightforward stand on civil and personal liberty. His

'Feeble petition' was accompanied by a letter to Horace Grealey, editor of the *New York Tribune*, dated 11 September 1852 and saying: 'It is evident that you have heard of me by the fame of my work in poetry, much of which I am now too closely confined to carry out and which I feel a warm interest to do; and, sir, by favouring me with a bounty of 175 dollars, I will endeavour to reward your generosity with my productions as soon as possible.' The letter never reached Grealey, it was found unposted in the files of George Moses's chief 'benefactor'.

In 1845, George Moses prefaced his *Poetical works* with an autobiographical sketch up to 1831, carefully omitting any reference to attempts at buying his freedom. When the war reached North Carolina he escaped to the northern lines, thus gaining freedom at last by a voluntary act, and later in the same year (1865) he brought out another volume of poetry, *Naked genius*. His object had been achieved, the dark phase of his life neatly wound up; as far as one knows, George Moses never set pen to paper again in all his further life, which seems to have been spent around Philadelphia and to have lasted probably until 1883.

There are two studies of George Moses Horton: an unpublished master thesis by M. T. T. Lakum (1951) at North Carolina College, Durham, deals mainly with his poetry, while Richard Walser's *The black poet* (1967) recounts his life from a diligent search among contemporary documents.

On liberty and slavery

Alas! and am I born for this,
    To wear this slavish chain?
Deprived of all created bliss,
    Through hardship, toil and pain!

How long have I in bondage lain,
  And languished to be free!
Alas! and must I still complain –
  Deprived of liberty.

Oh, Heaven! and is there no relief
  This side the silent grave –
To soothe the pain – to quell the grief
  And anguish of a slave?

Come, Liberty, thou cheerful sound,
  Roll through my ravished ears!
Come, let my grief in joys be drowned,
  And drive away my fears.

Say unto foul oppression, Cease:
  Ye tyrants rage no more,
And let the joyful trump of peace,
  Now bid the vassal soar.

Soar on the pinions of that dove
  Which long has cooed for thee,
And breathed her notes from Afric's grove,
  The sound of Liberty.

Oh, Liberty! thou golden prize,
  So often sought by blood –
We crave thy sacred sun to rise,
  The gift of nature's God!

Bid Slavery hide her haggard face,
  And barbarism fly:
I scorn to see the sad disgrace
  In which enslaved I lie.

Dear Liberty! upon thy breast,
   I languish to respire;
And like the Swan unto her nest,
   I'd to thy smiles retire.

Oh, blest asylum – heavenly balm!
   Unto thy boughs I flee –
And in thy shades the storm shall calm,
   With songs of Liberty!

The poet's feeble petition

Bewailing mid the ruthless wave,
   I lift my feeble hand to thee.
Let me no longer live a slave
   But drop these fetters and be free.

Why will regardless fortune sleep
   Deaf to my penitential prayer,
Or leave the struggling Bard to weep,
   Alas, and languish in despair?

He is an eagle void of wings
   Aspiring to the mountain's height;
Yet in the vale aloud he sings
   For Pity's aid to give him flight.

Then listen all who never felt
   For fettered genius heretofore –
Let hearts of petrifaction melt
   And bid the gifted Negro soar.

William Edward Burghardt DuBois

was a continent unto himself, of a size and a scope that reduce a thumbnail sketch of his life to mere statistics. Born 23 February 1868 at Great Bassington, Mass., he was educated at Fisk (B.A. 1888), Harvard (B.A. 1890, M.A. 1891), and during a year in Berlin. He taught first at Wilberforce for two years, then at the University of Pennsylvania for a year, finally at Atlanta: economics and history, 1896–1910. He obtained a Ph.D. from Harvard in 1895 on *The suppression of the African slave trade to America*. He founded and edited the eighteen Atlanta University studies of the Negro problem, 1897–1910, arising out of his own independent pioneer study *The Philadelphia Negro* of 1896. In 1905 he initiated the Niagara Movement which, in 1908, led to the National Association for the Advancement of Coloured People (N.A.A.C.P.) of which he was a co-founder and for which he became director of research and publicity in 1910, founding its magazine *The Crisis* and editing it from 1910 to 1933.

During this period he published a number of books, essays and articles which have proved to be of increasing importance even to this day, but which in their own time gained him more enemies than friends. His quarrels were famous and influential: with Booker T. Washington on the importance of higher education, with Marcus Garvey on the question of integration (in later life he would not have taken the same stand, but for personal reasons would still have detested Garvey). His style is precise, his opinions are totally uncompromising; he has a biting wit and is unsparing in his criticism. Reserved in personal life, his prose can soar into passionate poetry and contains total dictums of more than prophetic quality: 'The problem of the twentieth century is the problem of the colour-line' (*The souls of black folk*, 1903). Similar prose, and prose-poems like the famous 'Litany of Atlanta' written in 1906 on a train taking him towards the riot city, is found in *The quest of the silver fleece* (1911), *Darkwater* (1920), and *Dark princess* (1928). His other works include *John Brown* (1909), *The Negro* (1915), and *The gift of black folk* (1924). Key sentence of this period was 'Courage God, I come!' in *The Crisis* of July 1917. The poem included here, 'I am the smoke king', first appeared in *The Horizon* in 1899: it is the earliest positive assertion of blackness I have so far come across – like the 'Litany' was one of the earliest free-verse exercises by a black poet.

In 1933 he left the N.A.A.C.P. to go back to Atlanta, initiate and edit the *Encyclopedia of the Negro*, and in 1940 to found *Phylon* (still going as the Atlanta University review of race and culture). During the war years the Pan-African movement, founded by DuBois with his counter-conference during the Versailles peace talks in 1919 and last convened in New York in 1927, entered another active stage which proved decisive: the Fifth Congress, held in Manchester, in 1945, with George Padmore and Kwame Nkrumah as joint secretaries, became the basis of the African liberation movement, its militant leadership at last in close contact with trade unions, farmers' movements and radical students. DuBois at this time was again head of special research for the N.A.A.C.P. (1944–8) but became vice-president of the new Council on African Affairs in 1949 following a final row over N.A.A.C.P. policy. The books of this period reflect the main preoccupations: *Black reconstruction* (1935), *Black folk, then and now* (1939), *Dusk of dawn: autobiography of a race concept* (1940), *Color and democracy* (1945), *The world and Africa* (1947).

His work for the Council on African Affairs and his activities at the peace conferences in New York, Paris and Moscow made his life in the United States increasingly difficult; his participation in the Peace Information Center (required to register as a 'foreign agent') and his nomination (at eighty-two!) to run for Senator resulted in active opposition, like being arrested on his eighty-third birthday, and being refused a passport until 1957. In 1959 DuBois is given the Lenin Peace Prize, in 1961 he leaves the United States for good, to settle in Ghana at Nkrumah's invitation, there to head the ambitious Encyclopedia Africana project. In a characteristic gesture of defiance his last act in America was to enroll as a member of the Communist Party – which he had never been before, simply because he had little sympathy for the party however much he may have been persecuted for his 'communist

views'. His poem 'Ghana calls' appeared in *Présence Africaine*
New Series 34–5 – together with his relatively few other poems
it was collected in *Selected poems*, published at Accra shortly after
his death which occurred there on 27 August 1963.

Several books have since appeared about DuBois, often on a
thesis level, but the ultimate biography remains to be written,
despite *His day is marching on* written by novelist Shirley Graham
whom he married in 1952. *Cheer the lonesome traveller* by Leslie
Alexander Lacy (1970) is the nearest thing so far. Other recent
additions to the DuBois canon are *The seventh son: the thought and
writings of W. E. B. DuBois* edited with an introduction by Julius
Lester (2 vols, 1971) and *W. E. B. DuBois: a profile* edited by
Rayford Logan (1972). The DuBois archives are now at Fisk
University.

A Folkways record, FH 5511, contains a 'recorded autobio-
graphy' edited by Moses Asch from readings and conversations.

The song of the smoke

I am the smoke king,
I am black.
I am swinging in the sky,
I am ringing worlds on high;
I am the thought of the throbbing mills,
I am the soul of the soul toil kills,
I am the ripple of trading rills,

Up I'm curling from the sod,
I am whirling home to God.
I am the smoke king,
I am black.

I am the smoke king,
I am black.

I am wreathing broken hearts,
I am sheathing devils' darts;
Dark inspiration of iron times,
Wedding the toil of toiling climes
Shedding the blood of bloodless crimes,

Down I lower in the blue,
Up I tower toward the true,
I am the smoke king,
I am black.

I am the smoke king,
I am black.

I am darkening with song,
I am hearkening to wrong;
I will be black as blackness can,
The blacker the mantle the mightier the man,
My purpl'ing midnights no day dawn may ban.

I am carving God in night,
I am painting hell in white.
I am the smoke king,
I am black.

I am the smoke king,
I am black.

I am cursing ruddy morn,
I am nursing hearts unborn;
Souls unto me are as mists in the night,
I whiten my blackmen, I blacken my white,
What's the hue of a hide to a man in his might!

Hail, then, grilly, grimy hands,
Sweet Christ, pity toiling lands!
Hail to the smoke king,
Hail to the black!

James Weldon Johnson

was born James William Johnson, on 17 June 1871 in Jacksonville, Florida, where he attended the coloured grammar school before going to Atlanta University (B.A. 1894). He returned to his native town to teach in, take over and become principal of his old school, and to turn it into the first coloured high school. In 1897 he became the first black man to be admitted to the Florida bar, and practised law for several years. In 1901 he moved to New York, where he joined his brother James Rosamund and Bob Cole to write successful musicals for the Broadway stage. At the same time, he put in three years of graduate work at Columbia, and obtained his M.A. from Atlanta in 1904. He then entered the consular service, in Venezuela from 1906, in Nicaragua from 1909, and finally for a year in the Azores from 1912. In Venezuela, he also wrote his first book, *The autobiography of an ex-colored man*, which was published anonymously in 1912 and caused a mild sensation by treating a strictly taboo subject ('passing') in its widest implications and, to use DuBois's phrase, 'from within the veil'. Much later, in his real autobiography *Along this way* (1933), Johnson recalled with amusement 'being introduced to and talking with one man who tacitly admitted to those present that he was the author of the book' – it was not until 1927 that Johnson put his name to the new edition done by Knopf with a preface by Carl van Vechten.

Back in New York in 1914 he first took up his musical past, translated Goyescas for the Metropolitan Opera in 1915, and became contributing editor to the *New York Age*, the older of the New York negro newspapers. In 1916 he became field secretary to the N.A.A.C.P., a task he fulfilled with such vigour that his Haitian mission resulted in a congressional investigation. From 1919 to 1930 he served the organization as general secretary, and it is during this period that most of his writing was done. His *Book of American Negro poetry*, the first anthology of its kind, appeared in 1922 with an essay on 'The negro's creative genius'; the *Books of American Negro spirituals* followed in 1925 and 1926, the first

one prefaced by his much-anthologized poem 'Black and un-
known bards' written around 1907. His first collection of poems
appeared in 1917 as *Fifty years and other poems*: the title poem alone
first appeared as 'Atlanta University leaflet no. 27' in 1913. *God's
trombones*, the instantly popular 'negro sermons in verse' followed
in 1927 – it is astonishing how much vitality these poems have
retained, as witness Woodie King's remarkable production of
them for Concept East in Detroit in 1966. *Saint Peter relates an
incident of the Resurrection day* appeared in 1930, and in 1935
is used also for the main title of Johnson's selected poems. The
poem included here, 'The white witch', first appeared in *The
Crisis* in the early war years. Ostensibly a rather Keatsian ballad
of fairly traditional imagery, it has puzzled many of its readers but
Johnson said, 'I consider its meaning quite plain' – and I agree.
Perhaps one should remember that Johnson also wrote the *Ex-
colored man*, and that he was the first to state that 'sex has gone to
the white man's head, transferred its seat to the imagination' (in
Negro Americans: what now? 1934 – thirty years before Hernton's
Sex and racism).

In 1930 Johnson left the N.A.A.C.P. to become professor of
creative literature at Fisk, a post which, alternating with a visiting
professorship at New York University from 1934, he held until
his untimely death in a car crash on 26 June 1938. Recently Miles
Jackson junior has done much to rescue Johnson's memory from
temporary oblivion. Jackson also edited the correspondence with
George L. Towns (in *Phylon*, summer 1968).

The white witch

O brothers mine, take care! Take care!
The great white witch rides out tonight,
Trust not your prowess nor your strength;
Your only safety lies in flight;
For in her glance there is a snare,
And in her smile there is a blight.

The great white witch you have not seen?
Then, younger brothers mine, forsooth,
Like nursery children you have looked
For ancient hag and snaggle-tooth;
But no, not so; the witch appears
In all the glowing charms of youth.

Her lips are like carnations red,
Her face like new-born lilies fair,
Her eyes like ocean waters blue,
She moves with subtle grace and air,
And all about her head there floats
The golden glory of her hair.

But though she always thus appears
In form of youth and mood of mirth,
Unnumbered centuries are hers,
The infant planets saw her birth;
The child of throbbing Life is she,
Twin sister to the greedy Earth.

And back behind those smiling lips,
And down within those laughing eyes,
And underneath the soft caress
Of hand and voice and purring sighs,
The shadow of the panther lurks,
The spirit of the vampire lies.

For I have seen the great white witch,
And she has led me to her lair,
And I have kissed her red, red lips
And cruel face so white and fair;
Around me she has twined her arms,
And bound me with her yellow hair.

I felt those red lips burn and sear
My body like a living coal;
Obeyed the power of those eyes
As the needle trembles to the pole;
And did not care although I felt
The strength go ebbing from my soul.

Oh! she has seen your strong young limbs,
And heard your laughter loud and gay,
And in your voices she has caught
The echo of a far-off day,
When man was closer to the earth;
And she has marked you for her prey.

She feels the old Antæan strength
In you, the great dynamic beat
Of primal passions, and she sees
In you the last besieged retreat
Of love relentless, lusty, fierce,
Love pain-ecstatic, cruel-sweet.

O, brothers mine, take care! Take care!
The great white witch rides out tonight.
O, younger brothers mine, beware!
Look not upon her beauty bright;
For in her glance there is a snare,
And in her smile there is a blight.

Paul Laurence Dunbar

was the first black writer to make his living as a professional in his chosen craft. Born 27 June 1872, he began writing poetry while still in grammar school in his native Dayton, Ohio, where he also edited the school paper. Graduating from high school in 1891 he took up the standard employment of a coloured high school graduate: he became an elevator operator. He produced his first collection of poetry, *Oak and ivy*, privately in 1893, and followed it in 1895 with *Majors and minors*. The books sold badly, but did arouse a certain amount of interest. Dunbar's break came in 1897, when William Dean Howells wrote him up in *Harper's Weekly* (27 June) and also contributed a preface to a new book of poems, *Lyrics of lowly life*, which was largely edited out of the two previous collections. Howells unfortunately greatly stressed 'those pieces of his where he studies the moods and traits of his race in its own accent of our English', that is, those poems which have rather misleadingly become known as 'dialect verse'. Dunbar suffered greatly from this type-casting, although it undoubtedly helped his career. Looking at the large volume of his work today, it is surprising to see how little of it is 'in dialect', and even more so to realize what outspoken or insinuated comment Dunbar was able to get away with (and obviously wanted to express) under the accepted image of being a good darkey. Obviously, once the mask had been established, the world no longer looked for the face.

After the publication of *Lyrics of lowly life* (in which both the 'Ante-bellum sermon' and 'We wear the mask' had appeared) Dunbar held only one more non-literary job, a sinecure in the Library of Congress from 1897 to 1899. His output in these last ten years of his life was quite large: four books of short stories, four novels, several librettos for musicals (of which *Clorinda* is the better known), and three more collections of poetry. *Lyrics of the hearthside* appeared in 1899, *Lyrics of love and laughter* (another 'mask', this title – it was in this volume that Dunbar published 'The haunted oak', the earliest poem describing a lynching) came in 1903, and his last, *Lyrics of sunshine and shadow*, in 1905. During these last years a number of his poems were regrouped into smaller volumes illustrated with photographs by the Hampton Institute Camera Club, more specifically by Leigh Richmond Miner. These books are intriguing period documents, both for their early art-nouveau design and for their record of vanishing rural life. The best is *Poems of cabin and field* of 1899, earliest of them all.

Dunbar died 9 February 1906 of tuberculosis, still in his native Dayton. He had paid a brief visit to England in 1897, but on the whole travelled little, apart from short trips to promote his work or see his friend Booker T. Washington at Tuskegee. The son of former slaves (his father escaped via the 'underground railroad') had become one of America's most popular writers, but his personal life was intensely unhappy: ill health, a miserable marriage, and the conviction that whatever civic acclaim he won was based on the least valuable part of his production, threw a heavy shadow over his thirty-four short years. His work is only now beginning to be re-evaluated in terms which would have pleased the poet, the turning point in the ebb of his reputation as a Tom-poet probably being marked by Pauline Myers's magnificent readings around 1965. Young Sidney Poitier had earlier done some remarkable readings on the Glory album GLP1 'Poetry of the Negro', which included both 'An ante-bellum sermon' and the inevitable 'We wear the mask'.

An ante-bellum sermon

We is gathahed hyeah, my brothahs,
  In dis howlin' wildaness,
Fu' to speak some words of comfo't
  To each othah in distress.
An' we chooses fu' ouah subjic'
  Dis – we'll 'splain it by an' by;
'An' de Lawd said, "Moses, Moses,"
  An' de man said, "Hyeah am I."'

Now ole Pher'oh, down in Egypt,
  Was de wuss man evah bo'n,
An' he had de Hebrew chillun
  Down dah wukin' in his co'n;
'Twell de Lawd got tiahed o' his foolin',
  An' sez he: 'I'll let him know –
Look hyeah, Moses, go tell Pher'oh
  Fu' to let dem chillun go.'

'An' ef he refuse to do it,
  I will make him rue de houah,
Fu' I'll empty down on Egypt
  All de vials of my powah.'
Yes, he did – an' Pher'oh's ahmy
  Wasn't wuth a ha'f a dime;
Fu' de Lawd will he'p his chillun,
  You kin trust him evah time.

An' yo' enemies may 'sail you
  In de back an' in de front;
But de Lawd is all aroun' you,
  Fu' to ba' de battle's brunt.
Dey kin fo'ge yo' chains an' shackles
  F'om de mountains to de sea;
But de Lawd will sen' some Moses
  Fu' to set his chillun free.

An' de lan' shall hyeah his thundah,
  Lak a blas' f'om Gab'el's ho'n,
Fu' de Lawd of hosts is mighty
  When he girds his ahmor on.
But fu' feah some one mistakes me,
  I will pause right hyeah to say,
Dat I'm still a-preachin' ancient,
  I ain't talkin' 'bout to-day.

But I tell you, fellah christuns,
   Things'll happen mighty strange;
Now, de Lawd done dis fu' Isrul,
   An' his ways don't nevah change,
An' de love he showed to Isrul
   Wasn't all on Isrul spent;
Now don't run an' tell yo' mastahs
   Dat I's preachin' discontent.

'Cause I isn't; I'se a-judgin'
   Bible people by deir ac's;
I'se a-givin' you de Scriptuah,
   I'se a-handin' you de fac's.
Cose ole Pher'oh b'lieved in slav'ry,
   But de Lawd he let him see,
Dat de people he put bref in, –
   Evah mothah's son was free.

An' dah's othahs thinks lak Pher'oh,
   But dey calls de Scriptuah liar,
Fu' de Bible says, 'a servant
   Is a-worthy of his hire.'
An' you cain't git roun' nor thoo dat,
   An' you cain't git ovah it,
Fu' whatevah place you git in,
   Dis hyeah Bible too'll fit.

So you see de Lawd's intention,
   Evah sence de worl' began,
Was dat his almighty freedom
   Should belong to evah man,
But I think it would be bettah,
   Ef I'd pause agin to say,
Dat I'm talkin' 'bout ouah freedom
   In a Bibleistic way.

But de Moses is a-comin',
    An' he's comin' suah and fas':
We kin hyeah his feet a-trompin',
    We kin hyeah his trumpit blas'.
But I want to wa'n you people,
    Don't you git too brigity;
An' don't you git to braggin'
    'Bout dese things, you wait an' see.

But when Moses wif his powah
    Comes an' sets us chillun free,
We will praise de gracious Mastah
    Dat has gin us liberty;
An' we'll shout ouah halleluyahs,
    On dat mighty reck'nin' day,
When we'se reco'nized ez citiz' –
    Huh uh! Chillun, let us pray!

The haunted oak

Pray why are you so bare, so bare,
    Oh, bough of the old oak-tree;
And why, when I go through the shade you throw,
    Runs a shudder over me?

My leaves were green as the best, I trow,
    And sap ran free in my veins,
But I saw in the moonlight dim and weird
    A guiltless victim's pains.

I bent me down to hear his sigh;
    I shook with his gurgling moan,
And I trembled sore when they rode away,
    And left him here alone.

They'd charged him with the old, old crime,
   And set him fast in jail:
Oh, why does the dog howl all night long,
   And why does the night wind wail?

He prayed his prayer and he swore his oath,
   And he raised his hand to the sky;
But the beat of hoofs smote on his ear,
   And the steady tread drew nigh.

Who is it rides by night, by night,
   Over the moonlit road?
And what is the spur that keeps the pace,
   What is the galling goad?

And now they beat at the prison door,
   'Ho, keeper, do not stay!
We are friends of him whom you hold within,
   And we fain would take him away

'From those who ride fast on our heels
   With mind to do him wrong;
They have no care for his innocence,
   And the rope they bear is long.'

They have fooled the jailer with lying words,
   They have fooled the man with lies;
The bolts unbar, the locks are drawn,
   And the great door open flies.

Now they have taken him from the jail,
   And hard and fast they ride,
And the leader laughs low down in his throat,
   As they halt my trunk beside.

Oh, the judge, he wore a mask of black,
  And the doctor one of white,
And the minister, with his oldest son,
  Was curiously bedight.

Oh, foolish man, why weep you now?
  'Tis but a little space,
And the time will come when these shall dread
  The mem'ry of your face.

I feel the rope against my bark,
  And the weight of him in my grain,
I feel in the throe of his final woe
  The touch of my own last pain.

And never more shall leaves come forth
  On a bough that bears the ban;
I am burned with dread, I am dried and dead,
  From the curse of a guiltless man.

And ever the judge rides by, rides by,
  And goes to hunt the deer,
And ever another rides his soul
  In the guise of a mortal fear.

And ever the man he rides me hard,
  And never a night stays he;
For I feel his curse as a haunted bough,
  On the trunk of a haunted tree.

We wear the mask

We wear the mask that grins and lies,
It hides our cheeks and shades our eyes,
This debt we pay to human guile;
With torn and bleeding hearts we smile,
And mouth with myriad subtleties.
Why should the world be overwise,
In counting all our tears and sighs?
Nay, let them only see us, while
    We wear the mask.

We smile, but, O great Christ, our cries
To thee from tortured souls arise.
We sing, but oh the clay is vile
Beneath our feet, and long the mile;
But let the world dream otherwise,
    We wear the mask!

Bruce Grit

may or may not be the real name of the author of the following poem, and we will probably never know much more about him. Arna Bontemps told me that he was a New York newspaper man, but did not have any further details. 'The black man's burden' appeared on page 291 of an anthology called *Cullings from Zion's poets*, edited by Benjamin F. Wheeler D.D., dedicated 'to the worn out ministers of the African Methodist Episcopal Zion Church' and published without place or imprint in 1907. I find the rhyme irresistible, if only because it introduces a sense of humour and the explicit use of the black-white antithesis into the over-careful, totally predictable rubbish of the Booker Washington period.

Perhaps not *totally* predictable, for this 382-page volume which originates from Mobile, Alabama, instead of the usual northern towns, contains a few more surprises which historians of 'negro poetry' could well note. There is, for instance, a remarkable long poem written by the later Bishop Hood in 1859 when he was twenty-eight, very much in the style of the camp-meeting versions of Wesley hymns. Among the eighty-nine contributors, sixty-one of whom have their portraits and biographies included, there are various other authors from the still badly documented Reconstruction period just after the Civil War.

The black man's burden

Why speak of the white man's burden;
    What burden hath he borne?
That has not been shared by the black man
    From the day creation dawned?

Why talk of the white man's burden,
   Why boast of the white man's power,
When the black man's load is heavier,
   And increasing every hour?

Why taunt us with our weakness,
   Why boast of your brutal strength?
Know you not that the children of meekness
   Shall inherit the earth at length?

'Take up the white man's burden!'
   What burdens doth he bear,
That have not been borne with courage
   By brave men everywhere?

Then why the white man's burden?
   What more doth he bare then we,
The victims of his power and greed,
   From the great lakes to the sea?

James Edward McCall

born 2 September 1880, educated at Alabama State Normal and Industrial School in his native Montgomery and at Howard (medicine, briefly, until blindness resulting from typhoid cut his studies short), turned to writing at the instigation of his sister who also guided his further training in this field (Albion College 1905–7) until he married in 1914. A regular contributor to various dailies, McCall became city editor of the *Detroit Independent* when he moved to that city in 1920, having previously published a 'race weekly' called *The Emancipator* in Montgomery from 1916 to 1919.

An occasional poet at best, but one who happened to write one of the key poems of an era in 'The new Negro'. Taking its title from the Alain Locke anthology of 1925 (I cannot find any evidence that the poem was written earlier), the poem sums up exactly what the Negro Renaissance stood for. When McCall died, 26 July 1963, his total poetic output ran to about a hundred poems – most of them quite rightly unpublished. He had by that time long retired from business, having earlier become part owner of the *Independent*'s printing works and later the owner and editor of its successor, the *Detroit Tribune*.

The new Negro

He scans the world with calm and fearless eyes,
    Conscious within of powers long since forgot;
At every step, new man-made barriers rise
    To bar his progress – but he heeds them not.
He stands erect, though tempests round him crash,
    Though thunder bursts and billows surge and roll;
He laughs and forges on, while lightnings flash

Along the rocky pathway to his goal.
Impassive as a Sphinx, he stares ahead –
　Foresees new empires rise and old ones fall;
While caste-mad nations lust for blood to shed,
　He sees God's finger writing on the wall.
With soul awakened, wise and strong he stands,
　Holding his destiny within his hands.

Raymond Garfield Dandridge

was born in Cincinnati, Ohio, in 1882, and attended the grammar and high school there before going into business as a painter-decorator; he suffered a stroke very early in life (1911) which left him paralysed in both legs as well as the right arm until his death in 1930. He started writing when he became an invalid, under the influence of Dunbar, the only black model available to an aspiring poet at that time, but developed a strong and personal line of protest poetry which puts him on a par with McKay's work of the same period. His *Penciled poems* appeared as early as 1917, followed by *The poet and other poems* in 1920, and finally by *Zalka Peetruza and other poems* in 1928. No anthology after 1924 included any of his work, not even *Caroling Dusk*, the anthology edited by Countee Cullen; the honour of having revived his reputation goes to the *Journal of Black Poetry* which printed 'Time to die' in its third issue, late in 1966.

Time to die

Black brother, think you life so sweet
That you would live at any price?
Does mere existence balance with
The weight of your great sacrifice?
Or can it be you fear the grave
Enough to live and die a slave?
O Brother! be it better said,
When you are gone and tears are shed,
That your death was the stepping stone
Your children's children cross'd upon.
Men have died that men might live:
Look every foeman in the eye!
If necessary, your life give
For something, ere in vain you die.

Fenton Johnson

was a Chicagoan born and bred, who lived on State Street and drew most of his material from observations of the street life around him. Born 7 May 1888, he started writing at the age of nine. He attended Chicago University, then 'taught school one year and repented', became a journalist, and edited a succession of little magazines of which only *The Favorite Magazine* is at all remembered. At nineteen he produced some of his own plays at the Pekin Theatre in Chicago, and soon after his verse started appearing in magazines like *Others* (edited by Alfred Kreymborg) and *Poetry* (alongside early Marianne Moore and William Carlos Williams). His techniques fitted in with this particular stage of development in American poetry (as does the fact that around 1910 he drove his own electric automobile around Chicago), but his first book, *A little dreaming* (1913), consisted curiously of dialect verse offset by a 300-line free-verse poem called 'The vision of Lazarus'. Two other collections of poetry followed shortly after: *Visions of the dusk* in 1915 and *Songs of the soil* in 1916. A collection of short stories called *Tales of darkest America* appeared in 1920, and his last book, *For the highest good*, consisted of essays on American politics.

Little is known of his later life. During the thirties he worked on one of the W.P.A. writers' projects in a group directed by Arna Bontemps. At that time he again wrote poetry, the typescript of which Bontemps has preserved at Fisk. In 1963, Arna and I planned an edition of forty-two of the W.P.A. poems under the title *The daily grind*, but this never materialized – five of the poems, including the title one, were printed in Bontemps's anthology *American Negro poetry* in 1963. Fenton Johnson died in 1958 and some time before his death all his remaining work was destroyed by a flood in the cellar where it had been stored.

Tired

I am tired of work; I am tired of building up somebody
   else's civilization.

Let us take a rest, M'Lissy Jane.

I will go down to the Last Chance Saloon, drink a gallon or
   two of gin, shoot a game or two of dice and sleep the
   rest of the night on one of Mike's barrels.

You will let the old shanty go to rot, the white people's
   clothes turn to dust, and the Calvary Baptist Church
   sink to the bottomless pit.

You will spend your days forgetting you married me and
   your nights hunting the warm gin Mike serves the
   ladies in the rear of the Last Chance Saloon.

Throw the children into the river; civilization has given us
   too many. It is better to die than to grow up and find
   that you are colored.

Pluck the stars out of the heavens. The stars mark our
   destiny. The stars marked my destiny.

I am tired of civilization.

Claude McKay

was born on Sunny Ville farm in the Clarendon Hills of Jamaica, on 15 September – his own notes and his various biographers have put the year as 1889, 1890, and 1891 (even his *Selected poems* (1953) manage to have two conflicting dates), but the earliest date seems the most probable and occurs in the older sources. Educated by his freethinking schoolmaster brother, McKay was at seventeen apprenticed to a wheelwright and cabinet-maker, but left this trade at nineteen to become a police constable. His first collection of verse was called *Constab ballads*; it appeared around 1911, and was followed in 1912 by *Songs of Jamaica*, which was dedicated to the Governor of the island. *Songs* included both 'dialect' and 'straight' verse and had six tunes at the end composed by the author. McKay's work at this stage was easy, fluent, humorous, and rather facile; it is easy to see why this dark, handsome, uniformed boy became a popular success. However, the year *Songs* appeared, McKay went to the United States, where his life changed completely and (I think) disastrously – even if it did make him a better writer, for a brief but important while. He went to study agriculture, attended Tuskegee for three months, then went to Kansas State College until 1914. A small legacy brought him further north to New York, to Harlem. The city fascinated him, he quickly lost his money but stayed on, and from 1915 to 1918 held the usual succession of menial jobs. These years saw the rise of Harlem, the economic boom of the war, and the Russian revolution – McKay's work is impregnated with the new spirit and the social upheaval, but his yearning for the World to Come is always tempered by a nostalgia for the one that was, for the soil, the sun, and the life on his tropical island.

After the war, McKay spent two years in Europe, mostly in France, then came back to New York to become associate editor on Max Eastman's *Liberator* magazine. His work had by then attracted wide attention in America, but the first book of his new poetry appeared in London in 1920: *Spring in New Hampshire* contained both 'The tropics in New York' and 'The Harlem dancer'; it also had 'The lynching' and a longer poem, the much-anthologized 'Flame-heart', which in later years contributed greatly to the liberation of a new generation of West Indian writers. In 1922 McKay and Eastman went to Russia, where they stayed for almost a year, and afterwards McKay decided to remain in Europe. He spent most of the twenties in France and in Morocco, living quietly, and turning to prose. *Harlem shadows* (1922) remained his last volume of verse, but six years later his first novel, *Home to Harlem*, burst on the Harlem scene and became a sensation equalled only by Van Vechten's *Nigger heaven*. *Home to Harlem* is a well-written, fast, irreverent book which tried to portray life as most black people lived it – which meant that nice negroes didn't like it, whites did, and the book was a national bestseller. *Banjo* (1929) depicted life in Marseilles, showed the freedom a coloured man could find outside the United States, and found few readers. *Banana bottom* (1933) was set in Jamaica at the time of the author's own youth and *Gingertown* (1932) was a collection of stories ranging over the whole of McKay's interests.

Increasingly disillusioned with the practical outcome of the communist revolution, and desperately needing something to cling to (his 'Prayer' to Max Eastman had expressed this need at a very early date), McKay grew more and more despondent during the later thirties, producing only his autobiography *A long way from home* in 1937 and the documentary *Harlem: Negro metropolis* in 1940. By that time he was back in New York, where in 1942 he completed his conversion to Roman Catholicism. His later years were plagued by ill health, he wrote little or nothing, his conversion had lost him what old friends he still had, and he lived in increasing poverty, teaching at Catholic schools in Chicago until his death on 22 May 1948.

The autobiography of brown childhood planned by McKay and Cedric Dover under the title *East Indian, West Indian* remains unpublished except for an extract in *Phylon* (second quarter 1953). Wayne Cooper and Robert C. Reinders contributed a well-documented account of *Claude McKay in England, 1920* to the *New Beacon reviews* edited by John La Rose in 1968. Addison Gayle has recently published *Claude McKay, the black poet at war*, which relates his work to the later concepts of négritude and pan-africanism.

As a black writer, McKay is best remembered for single lines which must have been very startling in their day – which, it should be remembered, was before the Harlem Renaissance. 'The white man is a tiger at my throat.' 'The Negroes need salvation from within.' 'There is no white man who could write my book.' Some of his most-reprinted work contains no direct reference to any particular environment or situation at all: the sonnet 'If we must die' could equally well have come out of the Spanish civil war, or been translated from the Vietnamese.

The tropics in New York

Bananas ripe and green, and ginger-root,
   Cocoa in pods and alligator pears,
And tangerines and mangoes and grape fruit,
   Fit for the highest prize at parish fairs,

Set in the window, bringing memories
   Of fruit-trees laden by low-singing rills,
And dewy dawns, and mystical blue skies
   In benediction over nun-like hills.

My eyes grew dim, and I could no more gaze;
   A wave of longing through my body swept,
And, hungry for the old, familiar ways,
   I turned aside and bowed my head and wept.

The Harlem dancer

Applauding youths laughed with young prostitutes
And watched her perfect, half-clothed body sway;
Her voice was like the sound of blended flutes
Blown by black players upon a picnic day.
She sang and danced on gracefully and calm,
The light gauze hanging loose about her form;
To me she seemed a proudly-swaying palm
Grown lovelier for passing through a storm.
Upon her swarthy neck black shiny curls
Luxuriant fell; and tossing coins in praise,
The wine-flushed, bold-eyed boys, and even the girls,
Devoured her shape with eager, passionate gaze;
But looking at her falsely-smiling face,
I knew her self was not in that strange place.

Outcast

For the dim regions whence my fathers came
My spirit, bondaged by the body, longs.
Words felt, but never heard, my lips would frame;
My soul would sing forgotten jungle songs.
I would go back to darkness and to peace,
But the great western world holds me in fee,
And I may never hope for full release
While to its alien gods I bend my knee.
Something in me is lost, forever lost,
Some vital thing has gone out of my heart,
And I must walk the way of life a ghost
Among the sons of earth, a thing apart;
For I was born, far from my native clime,
Under the white man's menace, out of time.

Jean Toomer

had a brief, distinguished and lastingly influential spell as a black author, before opting out voluntarily while in his early thirties. Born in 1894 in Washington, D.C., he was educated through the public schools of that city and Dunbar High, then read law at the University of Wisconsin (1914–15) and the College of the City of New York. His literary career started in 1918, his first works were published in the New Orleans *Double dealer* in September 1922, the same issue in which Thornton Wilder made his debut. Toomer was teaching at Sparta in Georgia at that time, and his exposure to the South had a profound impact on his work: 'Georgia opened me. There one finds soil, soil in the sense the Russians know it – the soil every art and literature that is to live must be embedded in.' And so in 1923 his one book *Cane* appeared, an unprecedented 'personal anthology' of stories, sketches, poems and a play, half of which were based on his Georgia experiences (which lasted less than a year), the other half dealing with Washington. The book was probably the highlight of the whole Renaissance period, but it also showed clearly the limitations of what Alain Locke called 'being racial for the sake of art' – and nowhere more clearly than in his often reprinted 'Song of the son'.

Through the Renaissance years, Toomer published a few poems and stories, in *The Little Review*, *Opportunity*, *Broom*, and *Secession*, and at least one more play, *Balo*, in Locke's collection of *Plays of Negro life*. After that, Toomer, whose portrait by Winold Reiss shows him to be more than light enough to pass as a non-black, withdrew from black life. After fairly brief stops at the fashionable Gurdjieff Institute in Paris in 1926, and at the even more fashionable artists' colonies of the period (Carmel and Taos), he lived with his wife, the novelist Margery Latimer whom he married in 1932 but soon lost in childbirth. After his second marriage in November 1943, Toomer settled in a Quaker community at Bucks County, Pennsylvania, where he worked as a teacher and spiritualist. He wrote little and published less: a short novel, *York Beach*, in the *New American Caravan* in 1929, a collection of aphorisms in 1931 under the title *Essentials*, and an occasional poem in the *Caravan*. Toomer died 30 March 1967 in a rest home near Philadelphia.

Cane was reprinted by Walter Goldwater in New York in 1967, and has been the start of a general re-evaluation of Toomer's work and position in black American letters: it has appeared in a paperback edition with an introduction by Arna Bontemps, and the original publishers, who left the book dormant since its second printing in 1927, have decided not to renew Goldwater's licence but to cash in on the boom. Recently, *Black Scholar* magazine printed part of his early autobiography *Earth-being*. The book opens with this illuminating statement: 'It is our task to suffer a conscious apprenticeship in the stupidities and abnormalities of mankind.' Fisk University, that mausoleum of inaccessible treasures, houses Toomer's literary legacy. In 1972 Darwin D. Turner discussed Toomer, Countee Cullen and Zora Neale Hurston in *In a minor key: three Afro-American writers and their search for identity*.

Reapers

Black reapers with the sound of steel on stones
Are sharpening scythes. I see them place the hones
In their hip-pocket as a thing that's done,
And start their silent swinging, one by one.
Black horses drive a mower through the weeds,
And there, a field rat, startled, squealing bleeds,
His belly close to ground. I see the blade,
Blood-stained, continue cutting weeds and shade.

November cotton flower

Boll-weevil's coming, and the winter's cold,
Made cotton-stalks look rusty, seasons old,
And cotton, scarce as any southern snow,
Was vanishing; the branch, so pinched and slow,
Failed in its function as the autumn rake;
Drouth fighting soil had caused the soil to take
All water from the streams; dead birds were found
In wells a hundred feet below the ground –
Such was the season when the flower bloomed.
Old folks were startled, and it soon assumed
Significance. Superstition saw
Something it had never seen before:
Brown eyes that loved without a trace of fear,
Beauty so sudden for that time of year.

Melvin Beaunorus Tolson

was born 6 February 1900 (according to the publishers of *Harlem gallery*, but in 1898 according to all earlier sources) at Moberly in Missouri. He went through the public schools of Kansas and Missouri (where he edited various high school and college newspapers), then through Fisk, Lincoln (B.A.) and Columbia (M.A.). A gift for rhetoric and a fascination for un-essential facts or references determined part of his life and a good deal of his work. He taught for twenty-two years at Wiley College, Marshall, Texas, then became professor of creative literature at Langston in Oklahoma; here he trained and led debating teams to victory in nation-wide contests, directed the Dust Bowl Theater, and served four terms as mayor.

His first book of poetry, *Rendez-vous with America* (including the much-anthologized 'Dark symphony'), appeared in 1944, curiously late for an author who, in age and to some extent in spirit, belonged to the Renaissance generation. He dramatized Walter White's novel *Fire in the flint*, and wrote several original plays: *The Moses of Beale Street* is 'a negro miracle play', *Southern front* dealt with Arkansas sharecroppers. Commissioned to write a work for Liberia's centenary, he produced his *Libretto for the Republic of Liberia*, a poem of 770 lines somewhat sparingly explained in 194 footnotes. Its seventh section appeared separately in *Poetry* magazine in 1950 (the whole was not published until 1953) with a preface by Allen Tate; Tolson had fun doing quietly and unobtrusively what no black author had yet succeeded in, that is breaking into the white poetry syndicate. Once in, there was no stopping: soon Seldon Rodman, Roethke and Robert Frost took up the cause, the *Prairie Schooner* followed suit, and eventually its editor Karl Shapiro gave the final blessing in his preface to Tolson's last book, *Harlem gallery. Book I: The curator*, 1965. Tolson found the formula to what whitey wants; he is 'intricate, erudite and obscure', but skilfully, imaginatively, and with a wicked sense of storyteller's humour. He was probably closer to Sterling Brown than to anybody else in black letters, but had chosen a

totally different road which enabled him to keep writing where
Brown had been silent for all of three decades. Tolson died 28
August 1966, after a long battle with cancer; at the time of his
death he was writer-in-residence at the Tuskegee Institute.

from Harlem gallery

Mu

Hideho Heights
and I, like the brims of old hats,
slouched at a sepulchered table in the Zulu Club.
Frog Legs Lux and his Indigo Combo
spoke with tongues that sent their devotees
out of this world!

Black and brown and yellow fingers flashed,
like mirrored sunrays of a heliograph,
on clarinet and piano keys, on cornet valves.

Effervescing like acid on limestone,
Hideho said:
'O White Folks, O Black Folks,
the dinosaur imagined its extinction meant
the death of the piss ants.'

Cigarette smoke
– opaque veins in Carrara marble –
magicked the habitués into
humoresques and grotesques.
Lurid lights
spraying African figures on the walls
ecstasied maids and waiters,
pickups and stevedores –

with delusions
of Park Avenue grandeur.

Once, twice,
Hideho sneaked a swig.
'On the house,' he said, proffering the bottle
as he lorded it under the table.
Glimpsing the harpy eagle at the bar,
I grimaced,
'I'm not the house snake of the Zulu Club.'

A willow of a woman,
bronze as knife money,
executed, near our table, the Lenox Avenue Quake.
Hideho winked at me and poked
that which
her tight Park Avenue skirt vociferously advertized.
Peacocking herself, she turned like a ballerina,
her eyes blazing drops of rum on a crêpe suzette.
'Why, you –'
A sanitary decree, I thought. 'Don't *you* me!' he fumed.
The lips of a vixen exhibited a picadill flare.
'*What* you smell isn't cooking,' she said.
Hideho sniffed.
'Chanel No. 5,' he scoffed,
'from Sugar Hill.'
I laughed and clapped him on the shoulder.
'A bad metaphor, *poet*.'
His jaws closed
like an alligator squeezer.
'She's a willow,' I emphasized,
'a willow by a cesspool.'
Hideho mused aloud,
'Do I hear The Curator rattle Eliotic bones?'

Out of the Indigo Combo
flowed rich and complex polyrhythms.
Like surfacing bass,
exotic swells and softenings
of the veld vibrato
emerged.

Was that Snakehips Briskie
gliding out of the aurora australis of the Zulu Club
into the kaleidoscopic circle?

Etnean gasps!
Vesuvian acclamations!

Snakehips poised himself –
Giovanni Gabrieli's
single violin against his massed horns.

The silence of the revelers was the arrested
hemorrhage of an artery
grasped by bull forceps.
I felt Hideho's breath against my ear.
'The penis act in the Garden of Eden,' he confided.

Convulsively, unexampledly,
Snakehips' body and soul
began to twist and untwist like a gyrating rawhide –
began to coil, to writhe
like a prismatic-hued python
in the throes of copulation.

Eyes bright as the light
at Eddystone Rock,
an ebony Penthesilea

grabbed her tiger's-eye yellow-brown
beanpole Sir Testiculus of the evening
and gave him an Amazonian hug.
He wilted in her arms
like a limp morning-glory.
'The Zulu Club is in the groove,' chanted Hideho,
'and the cats, the black cats, are *gone*!'

In the *ostinato*
of stamping feet and clapping hands,
the Promethean bard of Lenox Avenue became a
lost loose-leaf
as memory vignetted
Rabelaisian I's of the Boogie-Woogie dynasty
in barrel houses, at rent parties,
on riverboats, at wakes:
The Toothpick, Funky Five, and Tippling Tom!
Ma Rainey, Countess Willie V., and Aunt Harriet!
Speckled Red, Skinny Head Pete, and Stormy Weather!
Listen, Black Boy.
Did the High Priestess at 27 rue de Fleurus
assert, 'The Negro suffers from nothingness'?
Hideho confided like a neophyte on The Walk,
'Jazz is the marijuana of the Blacks.'
In the *tribulum* of dialects, I juggled the idea;
then I observed,
'Jazz is the philosophers' egg of the Whites.'

Hideho laughed from below the Daniel Boone rawhide belt
he'd redeemed, in a Dallas pawn shop,
with part of the black-market
loot set loose
in a crap game
by a Yangtze ex-coolie who,

in a Latin Quarter dive below Telegraph Hill,
out-Harvarded his Alma Mater.

Frog Legs Lux and his Indigo Combo
let go
with a wailing pedal point
that slid into
Basin Street Blues
like Ty Cobb stealing second base:
Zulu,
King of the Africans,
arrives on Mardi Gras morning;
the veld drum of Baby Dodds'
great-grandfather
in Congo Square
pancakes the first blue note
in a callithump of the USA.
And now comes the eve of Ash Wednesday.
Comus on parade!
All God's children revel
like a post-Valley Forge
charivari in Boston celebrating the nuptials of
a gay-old-dog minuteman with a lusty maid.

Just as
the bourgeois adopted
the lyric-winged piano of Liszt in the court at Weimar
for the solitude of his
aeried apartment,
Harlem chose
for its cold-water flat
the hot-blues cornet of King Oliver
in his cart
under the
El pillars of the Loop.

The yanking fishing rod
of Hideho's voice
jerked me out of my bird's-foot violet romanticism.
He mixed Shakespeare's image with his own
and caricatured me:
'Yonder Curator has a lean and hungry look;
he thinks too much.
Such blackamoors are dangerous to
the Great White World!'

With a dissonance
from the Weird Sisters,
the jazz diablerie
boiled down and away
in the vacuum pan
of the Indigo Combo.

Sterling Brown

born Sterling Allan Brown, 1 May 1901 in Washington, D.C., attended city schools and from 1918 Williams College, where he married in 1919 and obtained his B.A. in 1922 – following with an M.A. from Harvard in 1923. His further life has largely been spent in teaching literature, at Manassas summer school in Virginia in 1923, Virginia Seminary at Lynchburo 1923–6, at Lincoln (Jefferson City, Missouri) 1926–8, Fisk the next year, and from 1929 onwards at Howard in Washington, D.C. He served as editor for 'negro materials' in the Federal Writers' Project from 1936 to 1939, was a member of the Carnegie-Myrdal 'American dilemma' research commission in 1939, and held visiting professorships at Vassar, the University of Minnesota and the New York School for Social Research. His published works consist of *Southern road*, a collection of poems published in 1932 with an introduction by James Weldon Johnson; and two long and very important essays on *The Negro in American fiction* and *Negro poetry and drama*, published in 1937 and 1938 as numbers six and seven in the 'Bronze booklets' series of the Associates in Negro Folk Education in Washington. During the thirties he wrote a literary criticism column for *Opportunity*, and in 1941 he was the main editor of *The Negro caravan*, which is still the best and most balanced anthology in its field.

Since then, nothing. True, he wrote to Countee Cullen as early as 1927: 'I have published nothing of the voluminous works cluttering my desk,' but that was not quite the same. His one volume of verse which has appeared since then is probably the most important single volume any black writer in America has produced – but the second, to be called *No hiding place* and announced for 1938, never appeared – not necessarily for lack of interest by publishers. Fortunately, Brown continues to write, and he reads his ballads (superbly) for his many friends in Washington, Chicago and other places – but I have tried in vain to get him to publish them for many years now, and each year the problem seems more insurmountable. Which is a pity, for Sterling Brown singlehandedly changed the concept of 'dialect verse' from the largely literary plantation school of Dunbar's day through poems like 'Ma Rainey' and 'Long gone' to observations of folk life recorded with a keen ear, a genuine personal interest, and unobtrusive but all-important technical virtuosity. What Brown did for the country was only partly duplicated by Langston Hughes for the town, for Langston lacked both the ear and the technique. The true measure of Sterling Brown as a writer and as a superb storyteller can be found on two Folkways albums: 'Long gone' and 'Ma Rainey' recorded in 1940 on FP 91-1; 'Old Lem' and five other poems on FL 9790.

Old Lem

I talked to old Lem
And old Lem said:

    'They weigh the cotton
    They store the corn
        We only good enough
        To work the rows;
    They run the commissary
    They keep the books
        We gotta be grateful
        For being cheated;
    Whippersnapper clerks
    Call us out of our name
        We got to say mister
        To spindling boys
    They make our figgers
    Turn somersets
        We buck in the middle
        Say, "Thankyuh, sah."

They don't come by ones
They don't come by twos
But they come by tens.

'They got the judges
They got the lawyers
They got the jury-rolls
They got the law
          They don't come by ones
They got the sheriffs
They got the deputies
          They don't come by twos
They got the shotguns
They got the rope
     We git the justice
     In the end
          And they come by tens.

'Their fists stay closed
Their eyes look straight
     Our hands stay open
     Our eyes must fall
          They don't come by ones
They got the manhood
They got the courage
          They don't come by twos
     We got to slink around,
     Hangtailed hounds.
They burn us when we dogs
They burn us when we men
          They come by tens . . .

'I had a buddy
Six foot of man

Muscled up perfect
Game to the heart
> *They don't come by ones*

Outworked and outfought
Any man or two men
> *They don't come by twos*

He spoke out of turn
At the commissary
They gave him a day
To git out the county.
He didn't take it.
He said 'Come and get me.'
They came and got him.
> *And they came by tens.*

He stayed in the county –
He lays there dead.

> *They don't come by ones*
> *They don't come by twos*
> *But they come by tens.'*

An old woman remembers

Her eyes were gentle; her voice was for soft singing
In the stiff-backed pew, or on the porch when evening
Comes slowly over Atlanta. But she remembered.
She said: 'After they cleaned out the saloons and the dives
The drunks and the loafers, they thought that they had better
Clean out the rest of us. And it was awful.
They snatched men off of street-cars, beat up women.
Some of our men fought back, and killed too. Still
It wasn't their habit. And then the orders came
For the milishy, and the mob went home,

And dressed up in their soldiers' uniforms,
And rushed back shooting just as wild as ever.
Some leaders told us to keep faith in the law,
In the governor; some did not keep that faith,
Some never had it: he was white too, and the time
Was near election, and the rebs were mad.
He wasn't stopping hornets with his head bare.
The white folks at the big houses, some of them
Kept all their servants home under protection
But that was all the trouble they could stand.
And some were put out when their cooks and yard-boys
Were thrown from cars and beaten, and came late or not
      at all.
And the police they helped the mob, and the milishy
They helped the police. And it got worse and worse.

'They broke into groceries, drug-stores, barber shops,
It made no difference whether white or black.
They beat a lame bootblack until he died,
They cut an old man open with jack-knives –
The newspapers named us black brutes and mad dogs,
So they used a gun butt on the president
Of our seminary where a lot of folks
Had sat up praying prayers the whole night through.

'And then,' she said, 'our folks got sick and tired
Of being chased and beaten and shot down.
All of a sudden, one day, they all got sick and tired.
The servants they put down their mops and pans,
And brooms and hoes and rakes and coachman whips,
Bad niggers stopped their drinking Dago red,
Good Negroes figured they had prayed enough,
All came back home – they'd been too long away –
A lot of visitors had been looking for them.

'They sat on their front stoops and in their yards,
Not talking much, but ready; their welcome ready:
Their shotguns oiled and loaded on their knees.

'And then
There wasn't any riot any more.'

Long gone

I laks yo' kin' of lovin',
  Ain't never caught you wrong,
But it jes' ain' nachal
  Fo' to stay here long;

It jes' ain' nachal
  Fo' a railroad man,
With a itch fo' travelin'
  He cain't understan' . . .

I look at de rails,
  An' I looks at de ties,
An' I hears an ole freight
  Puffin' up de rise,

An' at nights on my pallet,
  When all is still,
I listens fo' de empties
  Bumpin' up de hill;

When I oughta be quiet,
  I is got a itch
Fo' to hear de whistle blow
  Fo' de crossin' or de switch,

An' I knows de time's a-nearin'
  When I got to ride,
Though it's homelike and happy
  At yo' side.

You is done all you could do
  To make me stay;
'Tain't no fault of yours I'se leavin' –
  I'se jes dataway.

I is got to see some people
  I ain't never seen,
Gotta highball thu some country
  Whah I never been.

I don't know which way I'm travelin' –
  Far or near,
All I knows fo' certain is
  I cain't stay here.

Ain't no call at all, sweet woman,
  Fo' to carry on –
Jes' my name and jes' my habit
  To be Long Gone . . .

Langston Hughes

is again a separate chapter; a continent, certainly not of the size and magnitude of DuBois's but warmer and more inhabitable. For most of his writing life, and that was all of his life, he just *was* 'negro poetry' whenever that nebulous concept was mentioned at home or abroad – and all the effect this had on him was a deepening sense of obligation towards those of his fellow-writers who had not achieved such public recognition, especially towards the young. 'To meet him is to come face to face with the essence of human goodness' said Mphahlele – and perhaps this tribute would have pleased Langston, because it comes from an African, and because as early as 1940 Langston wrote, 'I was only an American Negro – who had loved the surface of Africa and the rhythms of Africa – but I was not Africa. I was Chicago and Kansas City and Broadway and Harlem.' His first trip to Africa had already caused him to realize, with genuine regret, 'you see, unfortunately, I am not black'.

Hughes was born 1 February 1902 in Joplin, Missouri, but because of a broken family spent his early years with his grandmother in Lawrence, Kansas. This grandmother was the widow of Lewis Sheridan Leary, one of the five negroes who took part in John Brown's raid on the armoury at Harper's Ferry in 1859 – and Langston later treasured the shawl in which Leary died. He moved to Cleveland with his mother in 1916 and attended Central High from which he graduated in 1920. After that he spent a year with his father, a lawyer, in Mexico, and another year at Columbia University, cut short by the final break with his father and consequent lack of support. Soon after he went to sea as a cabin boy, and spent the next few years travelling, having his first glimpse of Africa, spending the winter of 1924 in Paris and the summer of 1925 in Italy. An unhappy year in Washington produced his engineered 'discovery' by Vachel Lindsay, his prize in the *Opportunity* contest, and eventually, through Carl van Vechten, the publication of his first book, *The weary blues*, in 1926, followed the next year by *Fine clothes to the Jew*. That latter year he also entered Lincoln University in Pennsylvania where he stayed until his graduation in 1929. In 1930 his first novel *Not without laughter* was published.

From 1930 on Langston Hughes made his home in Harlem and his living entirely from writing. Poems, songs, short stories, novels, plays, opera librettos, musicals, documentaries, anthologies and juveniles flowed from his pen with astonishing speed and regularity for almost four decades. One form sometimes eclipsed the other for a while, but the source never dried up and the level of writing never sagged too low. Coast-to-coast lecture tours, trips to Latin America and longer excursions into Europe (especially his long stay in Russia on a film project which never came off, and a spell in Spain as war correspondent together with Nicolas Guillén) further widened his outlook and his staggeringly large acquaintance. The list of his poetry books alone is impressive: *Dear lovely death* in 1931, *The dream keeper* and *Scottsboro Ltd* both in 1932, *A new song* in 1938 (his most 'proletarian' volume, in the communist sense), *Shakespeare in Harlem* 1942, two pamphlets the next year called *Freedom's plow* and *Jim Crow's last stand*. Three more collections followed before there was a temporary halt in the writing of poetry: *Fields of wonder* in 1947, *One way ticket* in 1949, and perhaps the best single volume of his whole career, *Montage of a dream deferred*, in 1951.

During the war Hughes wrote a weekly column for the *Chicago Defender* and out of these sketches grew the character that made him even more widely popular than his poetry had done, the delightful Jesse B. Simple, who would fill several volumes of stories, appear in a play, and from the play in a successful musical called *Simply Heavenly* which saw production on Broadway in 1957, and in Hollywood and London in 1958. Hughes's controversial play *Mulatto* had first introduced him to Broadway, when Rose McClendon played the leading role for two years (1935–6) until her untimely death. Meanwhile Hughes had also written the libretto for a William Grant Still opera, *Troubled island*, which the New York City Opera performed with a minuet by Balanchine and 'voodoo dances' by Jean-Leon Destine. *Tambourines to glory* (1958) was the next stage play, and late in life Hughes had truly amazing international success with the gospel song sequence *Black nativity*, the effect of which owed more to the skill of Vinette Carroll and the personalities of Marion Williams and Alex Bradford than to the quality of the linking lyrics.

In the 1950s Hughes wrote little or no poetry, but concentrated instead on documentaries like *A pictorial history of the Negro in America* (1956), juveniles like the four volumes in the 'First book' series (*First book of jazz, of negroes, of rhythms*, and *of the West Indies*), and on anthologies like the two he compiled with Arna Bontemps: *The poetry of the Negro 1746–1949*, and *The book of Negro folklore*. The latter trend he continued during the sixties with *An African treasury* (1960), *Poems from black Africa* (1963) and *New Negro poets: USA* (1964) in which he introduced to America its first generation of 'black poets', previously published only in two almost simultaneous anthologies from London: my own *Sixes and sevens* and Rosey Pool's *Beyond the blues*, both of 1962. *Something in common* (1963) was his last collection of short fiction – a neglected part of his voluminous corpus which had started as early as 1937 with one of his finest works, *The ways of white folks*, and continued in 1952 with the collection *Laughing to keep from crying*.

As important as his published work is in these later years Langston functioned as a self-appointed clearing house for information and advice for editors, anthologists, and (more important) for young writers in need of spiritual or often material encouragement. Generous to a fault, Langston Hughes really was what Senghor (at the New York ceremonies for the Dakar Festival prizegiving) jokingly called him, 'the daddy of them all'. He died 22 May 1967 in his home on 127th Street in Harlem, and for many people New York has never been the same since. James Emanuel's sympathetic study, *Langston Hughes*, appeared later the same year. Several recordings capture at least some of the Hughes personality, notably his reading of *Simple* stories on Folkways FL 9790 and of a large number of poems with a jazz backing on MGM E 3697. A number of magazines have devoted memorial issues to Langston Hughes – the most rewarding is perhaps *Freedomways* (spring 1968) which includes a useful bibliography. A full and exhaustively annotated bibliography has appeared in Donald C. Dickinson,

A bio-bibliography of Langston Hughes, his expanded doctoral dissertation. *Langston Hughes, black genius: a critical evaluation* (1972) is a collection of twelve essays on different aspects of his work and influence, edited by Therman B. O'Daniel for the College Language Association.

The poems chosen to represent Langston in this anthology range from his earliest to his last. 'The Negro speaks of rivers' was written in 1920, it was one of the first to be published (in *The Crisis*, 1921) and it is certainly the most reprinted – but somehow always without the original dedication. 'Red silk stockings' is from his second book, *Fine clothes to the Jew*: it carries more sting than the combined aesthetic poetry of the whole Renaissance, and was very much disliked by well-meaning members of the race – the title of the book had already caused a great deal of adverse comment, anyway. 'My People' appeared in *The Dream keeper*, and with some of the other poems in the last section of that book is among the earliest expressions of unequivocal 'black is beautiful'. 'Lennox Avenue mural' is a whole section of the *Montage of a dream deferred* – it is a total testament, summarizing most of Langston Hughes's themes and interests, it has some of his best poetry and some of his keenest observations, yet it is simple and direct and almost objective. Almost. 'Junior addict', finally, is from *The panther and the lash* (1967), Hughes's last book, in which he collected, very deliberately, all his most 'racial' verse from his previous books plus those written after *Ask your mama* of 1961. 'Junior addict' had previously appeared only in the *Liberator* in 1963.

My people

The night is beautiful,
So the faces of my people.

The stars are beautiful,
So the eyes of my people.

Beautiful, also, is the sun.
Beautiful, also, are the souls of my people.

The Negro speaks of rivers

for W. E. B. DuBois

I've known rivers:
I've known rivers ancient as the world and older than the
    flow of human blood in human veins.

My soul has grown deep like the rivers.

I bathed in the Euphrates when dawns were young.
I built my hut near the Congo and it lulled me to sleep.
I looked upon the Nile and raised the pyramids above it.
I heard the singing of the Mississippi when Abe Lincoln went
    down to New Orleans, and I've seen its muddy bosom
    turn all golden in the sunset.

I've known rivers:
Ancient, dusky rivers.

My soul has grown deep like the rivers.

Red silk stockings

Put on yo' red silk stockings,
Black gal.
Go out an' let de white boys
Look at yo' legs.

Ain't nothin' to do for you, nohow,
Round this town,
You's too pretty.
Put on yo' red silk stockings, gal,
An' tomorrow's chile'll
Be a high yaller.

Go out an' let de white boys
Look at yo' legs.

Lennox avenue mural

Harlem:

What happens to a dream deferred?
    Does it dry up
    like a raisin in the sun?
    Or fester like a sore —
    And then run?
    Does it stink like rotten meat?
    Or crust and sugar over —
    like a syrupy sweet?
    Maybe it just sags
    like a heavy load.

    Or does it explode?

Good morning:

Good morning, daddy!
I was born here, he said,

watched Harlem grow
until colored folks spread
from river to river
across the middle of Manhattan
out of Penn Station
dark tenth of a nation,
planes from Puerto Rico,
and holds of boats, chico,
up from Cuba Haiti Jamaica,
in busses marked NEW YORK
from Georgia Florida Louisiana
to Harlem Brooklyn the Bronx
but most of all to Harlem
dusky sash across Manhattan.
I've seen them come dark
    wondering
    wide-eyed
    dreaming
out of Penn Station –
but the trains are late.
The gates open –
but there're bars
at each gate.

    What happens
    to a dream deferred?

Daddy, ain't you heard?

Same in blues:

I said to my baby,
Baby, take it slow.
I can't, she said, I can't!
I got to go!

There's a certain
amount of traveling
in a dream deferred.

Lulu said to Leonard,
I want a diamond ring.
Leonard said to Lulu,
You won't get a goddamn thing!

A certain
amount of nothing
in a dream deferred.

Daddy, daddy, daddy,
All I want is you.
You can have me, baby –
but my lovin' days is through.

A certain
amount of impotence
in a dream deferred.

Three parties
On my party line –
But that third party,
Lord, ain't mine!

There's liable
to be confusion
in a dream deferred.

From river to river,
Uptown and down,
There's liable to be confusion
when a dream gets kicked around.

Comment on curb:

You talk like
they don't kick
dreams around
Downtown.

  I expect they do –
  But I'm talking about
  Harlem to you!

Letter:

Dear Mama,
    Time I pay rent and get my food
and laundry I don't have much left
but here is five dollars for you
to show you I still appreciates you.
My girl-friend send her love and say
she hopes to lay eyes on you sometime in life.
Mama, it has been raining cats and dogs up
here. Well, that is all so I will close.
      Your son baby
        Respectably as ever,
          Joe

Island:

Between two rivers,
North of the park,
Like darker rivers
The streets are dark.

Black and white,
Gold and brown –
Chocolate-custard
Pie of a town.

Dream within a dream,
Our dream deferred.

Good morning, daddy!

Ain't you heard?

Junior addict

The little boy
who sticks a needle in his arm
and seeks an out in other worldly dreams,
who seeks an out in eyes that droop
and ears that close to Harlem screams,
cannot know, of course,
(and has no way to understand)
a sunrise that he cannot see
beginning in some other land –
but destined sure to flood – and soon –
the very room in which he leaves
his needle and his spoon,
the very room in which today the air
is heavy with the drug
of his despair.

> (Yet little can
> tomorrow's sunshine give
> to one who will not live.)

Quick, sunrise, come –
Before the mushroom bomb
Pollutes his stinking air
With better death
Than is his living here,
With viler drugs
Than bring today's release
In poison from the fallout
Of our peace.

> *'It's easier to get dope
> than it is to get a job.'*

Yes, easier to get dope
than to get a job –
daytime or nightime job,
teen-age, pre-draft,
pre-lifetime job.

Quick, sunrise, come!
Sunrise out of Africa,
Quick, come!
Sunrise, please come!
Come! Come!

Arna Bontemps

Langston Hughes in *The big sea* says Bontemps, 'poet and coming novelist, quiet and scholarly, looking like a young edition of Dr DuBois, was the mysterious member of the Harlem literati, in that we knew he had recently married, but none of us had ever seen his wife. He never brought her with him to any of the parties, so she remained the mystery of the New Negro Renaissance. But I went with him once to his apartment to meet her, and found her a shy and charming girl, holding a golden baby on her lap. A year or two later there was another golden baby. And every time I went away to Haiti or Mexico or Europe and came back, there would be a new golden baby, each prettier than the last.'

Born 13 October 1902 at Alexandria in Louisiana, Bontemps has retained the same quiet and unassuming personality until this day; it pervades his work and his relations with other people, and it probably explains why one only now realizes how perfect a period expression the small body of his poetry is.

Educated in Los Angeles where his family settled when he was three, at San Fernando Academy (1917-20), and at Pacific Union College in Angwin, California (where 'it took him only a day or two to decide' that a medical training was not for him) up to his B.A. in 1923. Bontemps then moved to New York and taught at the Harlem Academy until 1931 (his marriage took place in 1926); he went to Alabama to teach at Oakwood Junior College in Huntsville until 1934, and finally to Shiloh Academy, Chicago, until 1938. In 1938, and again in 1942, he held a Rosenwald fellowship. In 1943 he obtained his M.A. in library science from the University of Chicago and became librarian of Fisk University at Nashville, Tennessee. This post he retained until 1965, when he went back to teaching, at the University of Illinois at Chicago Circle. In 1969 he became curator of the James Weldon Johnson Memorial Collection at Yale University – an increasingly important library including first rate source material like the Langston Hughes archives.

Bontemps's first poem appeared in *The Crisis* in 1924, and he won first prize in the contests offered by that magazine (1927) and by *Opportunity* (1926 and 1927). He never published a volume of poetry, however, until we did *Personals* in the Heritage series in 1963: the book is practically a 'collected poems', but even so only contains twenty-three titles. It also contains a very fine introduction by Bontemps which relates his generation's experience of Harlem, the cultural capital, to the later realization of Harlem the destructive ghetto. With the end of the Renaissance Bontemps turned to prose, and in this field became not only very successful but for a while almost prolific: *God sends Sunday* 1931, *Black thunder* 1936 and *Drums at dusk* 1939 are his novels; his juvenilia include *Popo and Fifina* (with Langston Hughes) in 1932, *You can't pet a possum* 1934, *Sad-faced boy* 1937, and two books in collaboration with Jack Conroy, *The fast sooner hound* 1942, and *Slappy Hooper* 1947. His last children's book, *Lonesome boy*, appeared in 1955. Also with Conroy: *They seek a city*, 1945, the first of his historical works which continued with *We have tomorrow* 1945, *The story of the Negro* 1948, *Chariot in the sky* (the story of the Jubilee Singers) 1951, to a biography of *Frederick Douglass* and *100 years of Negro freedom* in 1961. With Langston Hughes he edited two massive anthologies: *The poetry of the Negro 1746–1949* in 1949 and *The book of Negro folklore* in 1959. His edition of *Father of the blues* (the 'autobiography' of W. C. Handy), and the charming 'anthology of Negro poetry for young readers', *Golden slippers*, both appeared in 1941. *American Negro poetry* in 1963 included a fair number of discoveries among the younger contributors. Bontemps's latest anthology is *Hold fast to dreams* (1969).

Southern mansion

Poplars are standing there still as death
and ghosts of dead men
meet their ladies walking
two by two beneath the shade
and standing on the marble steps.

There is a sound of music echoing
through the open door
and in the field there is
another sound tinkling in the cotton:
chains of bondmen dragging on the ground.

The years go back with an iron clank,
a hand is on the gate,
a dry leaf trembles on the wall.
Ghosts are walking.
They have broken roses down
and poplars stand there still as death.

A black man talks of reaping

I have sown beside all waters in my day.
I planted deep, within my heart the fear
that wind or fowl would take the grain away.
I planted safe against this stark, lean year.

I scattered seed enough to plant the land
in rows from Canada to Mexico
but for my reaping only what the hand
can hold at once is all that I can show.

Yet what I sowed and what the orchard yields
my brother's sons are gathering stalk and root;
small wonder then my children glean in fields
they have not sown, and feed on bitter fruit.

Philip M. Sherlock

or, by his full title, Sir Philip Manderson Sherlock C.B.E., was born at Portland, Jamaica, in 1902, the son of a methodist minister. He was educated at Calabar High School and later in London, then embarked on a teaching career which lasted twenty years and ended in 1938 with the headmastership of Wolmer's. During the forties he was secretary and librarian to the Institute of Jamaica, then became professor of extra-mural studies at the University College of the West Indies, and from 1963 until 1969 was the vice-chancellor of that school, now called the University of the West Indies. In 1969 he became the secretary-general of the Association of Caribbean Universities.

Sherlock has always had a great interest in, and acquired a wide knowledge of, his island's history and folklore, and has done much to further the interests of others, especially schoolchildren. In this, he acknowledges a crucial debt to Claude McKay's 'Flame-heart': 'It was not great poetry, yet with what magic excitement I read "So much I have forgotten in ten years." This was the world I knew, where ground doves filled the noonday with their curious fluting and honey-fever grass sweetened the air. Here at last was a voice singing of the West Indian countryside as home, here at last an assertion of a West Indian way of life!'

Sherlock's own published poetry remains confined to a few magazines and anthologies, and one small book in the Miniature Poets series: *Ten poems*, January 1953. As editor (with Arthur J. Newman) of the New Age poetry books which began in 1932, and of the Caribbean Readers which started in 1937, he has contributed greatly to the appreciation of the true West Indian literature. Several collections of folk tales: *Annancy stories* 1936, *Anansi* 1956, *The man in the web* 1959, enlarged the corpus he was making available. From 1949 he edited *Caribbean Affairs* and in the next two decades he wrote several books on West Indian and Jamaican affairs: *Caribbean citizen* 1957, *Jamaica way* 1962, and a guide book called *This is Jamaica* which appeared in 1968. His latest book, *Iguana's tail*, appeared in 1969.

Jamaican fisherman

Across the sand I saw a black man stride
To fetch his fishing gear and broken things,
And silently that splendid body cried
Its proud descent from ancient chiefs and kings,
Across the sand I saw him naked stride;
Sang his black body in the sun's white light
The velvet coolness of dark forests wide,
The blackness of the jungle's starless night.
He stood beside the old canoe which lay
Upon the beach; swept up within his arms
The broken nets and careless lounged away
Towards his hut beneath the ragged palms . . .
Nor knew how fiercely spoke his body then
Of ancient wealth and freeborn regal men.

Countee Cullen

was born Countee Porter on 30 May 1903 in New York City. After the death of his mother, in 1914, he was adopted by a methodist preacher called Frederick Cullen – in his earliest magazine publications he still signs himself Countée P. Cullen. After attending public schools in New York he went to De Witt Clinton High School, New York University (B.A. 1925) and Harvard (M.A. 1926). His poetry began to attract attention while he was still in high school: he came second in the Witter Bynner national college-level poetry contest in 1923, again in 1924, and won it in 1925. His first book of poetry, *Color*, appeared in 1925 and gained a great deal of critical acclaim. It was followed in 1927 by *The ballad of the brown girl*, and by *Copper sun* which includes exercises in the different forms of English verse made at Harvard in the class of Robert Hillyer. The first four books all have stylish illustrations by Charles Cullen. Countee meanwhile became assistant editor of *Opportunity*, and was a central figure in the Harlem Renaissance of the later twenties. In 1927 he edited an anthology of his contemporaries, *Caroling dusk*, a model of balanced taste and judgement which has rightly remained in print ever since. A Guggenheim fellowship brought Cullen to Paris where he completed a new volume of verse, *The black Christ & other poems* (1929). His short-lived marriage to Yolande DuBois, daughter of W. E. B., had been celebrated with much pomp in 1928 but was lived out mostly with Countee in Europe, Yolande in Baltimore.

In the autumn of 1930 Cullen returned to New York. He was no longer married, and the Renaissance was becoming a memory rather than an active environment: he left for Paris before the next summer, to finish his studies at the Sorbonne. He also turned his attention to other forms of writing: a dramatization of Arna Bontemps's novel *God sends Sunday* and a novel of his own, *One way to heaven*, published in 1932. In 1935 his last book of verse appeared: *The Medea and some poems*. The depression made it increasingly difficult to gain a living from readings and writing, and in December 1934 Cullen took his first non-literary job, as a teacher of French in Frederick Douglass Junior High in Harlem. He remained a teacher until the end of his life, gradually becoming more interested in his pupils and their problems and in creative writing as a means of release: by 1940 he ran what must have been one of the first creative writing classes in Harlem for ninth-grade pupils.

In the autumn of 1940 he married again, and published his first book co-authored with his favourite cat, Christopher: *The lost zoo, a rhyme for the young, but not too young. by Christopher Cat and Countee Cullen, with illustrations by Charles Sebree* is one of the most charming and accomplished of pioneer children's books. In 1942 the same pair published *My nine lives and how I lost them*. These were the last books to appear in Cullen's lifetime. He died 9 January 1946. On 30 March, *St Louis woman*, his dramatization of Arna Bontemps's novel, finally opened with a musical score by Harold Arlen and Johnny Mercer, its cast headed by Pearl Bailey and Rex Ingram. (A revised version called *Free and easy*, with a Quincy Jones score and produced by Robert Breen as a follow-up to his phenomenal success with *Porgy and Bess* was tried out in Holland in 1962 but folded on the road.) In August 1946 *Theatre Arts* magazine published *The third fourth of July*, a play written by Cullen with his friend Owen Dodson, and in February 1947 *On these I stand* appeared, a 'selected poems', put together by the author shortly before his death. A Moses Asch recording of Cullen reading 'Heritage', made in the early forties, was released on Folkways FP 91-1.

In his own estimation, although not in that of later generations, Cullen was always very definitely a black poet within the accepted framework of the Harlem Renaissance, that is to say with complete adherence to 'correct English' and the standard verse forms, individuality asserting itself through the personal experiences that went into the writing and through the way these experiences were translated. This may not seem enough – Baldwin was very impatient with Cullen when sent, as a senior student at De Witt Clinton, to interview the school's only famous alumnus – but to Cullen it implied all that McKay expressed when he wrote:

'There is no white man who could write my book.' In fact, problems like the African heritage, the position of the black writer in a white society, interracial sexual relations, were treated in his work with greater honesty, more public soul-searching, and less aimless 'protest' than in the work of most of his contemporaries – and one can quite see why DuBois went to such length to engineer the marriage between Countee and Yolande, ill-advised as it may have been on a more personal level.

The one major study of Cullen's life, Blanche E. Ferguson's *Countee Cullen and the Negro Renaissance* (1966), is sloppily written, badly researched, and does its subject no justice whatsoever.

Heritage

for Harold Jackman

What is Africa to me:
Copper sun or scarlet sea,
Jungle star or jungle track,
Strong bronzed men, or regal black
Women from whose loins I sprang
When the birds of Eden sang?
One three centuries removed
From the scenes his fathers loved,
Spicy grove, cinnamon tree,
What is Africa to me?

So I lie, who all day long
Want no sound except the song
Sung by wild barbaric birds
Goading massive jungle herds,
Juggernauts of flesh that pass
Trampling tall defiant grass
Where young forest lovers lie,

Plighting troth beneath the sky.
So I lie, who always hear,
Though I cram against my ear
Both my thumbs, and keep them there,
Great drums throbbing through the air.
So I lie, whose fount of pride,
Dear distress, and joy allied,
Is my somber flesh and skin,
With the dark blood dammed within
Like great pulsing tides of wine
That, I fear, must burst the fine
Channels of the chafing net
Where they surge and foam and fret.

Africa? A book one thumbs
Listlessly, till slumber comes.
Unremembered are her bats
Circling through the night, her cats
Crouching in the river reeds,
Stalking gentle flesh that feeds
By the river brink; no more
Does the bugle-throated roar
Cry that monarch claws have leapt
From the scabbards where they slept.
Silver snakes that once a year
Doff the lovely coats you wear,
Seek no covert in your fear
Lest a mortal eye should see;
What's your nakedness to me?
Here no leprous flowers rear
Fierce corollas in the air;
Here no bodies sleek and wet,
Dripping mingled rain and sweat,
Tread the savage measures of

Jungle boys and girls in love.
What is last year's snow to me,
Last year's anything? The tree
Budding yearly must forget
How its past arose or set –
Bough and blossom, flower, fruit,
Even what shy bird with mute
Wonder at her travail there,
Meekly labored in its hair.
One three centuries removed
From the scenes his fathers loved,
Spicy grove, cinnamon tree,
What is Africa to me?
So I lie, who find no peace
Night or day, no slight release
From the unremittant beat
Made by cruel padded feet
Walking through my body's street.
Up and down they go, and back,
Treading out a jungle track.
So I lie, who never quite
Safely sleep from rain at night –
I can never rest at all
When the rain begins to fall;
Like a soul gone mad with pain
I must match its weird refrain;
Ever must I twist and squirm,
Writhing like a baited worm,
While its primal measures drip
Through my body, crying, 'Strip!
Doff this new exuberance.
Come and dance the Lover's Dance!'
In an old remembered way
Rain works on me night and day.

Quaint, outlandish heathen gods
Black men fashion out of rods,
Clay, and brittle bits of stone,
In a likeness like their own,
My conversion came high-priced;
I belong to Jesus Christ,
Preacher of humility;
Heathen gods are naught to me.

Father, Son, and Holy Ghost,
So I make an idle boast;
Jesus of the twice-turned cheek,
Lamb of God, although I speak
With my mouth thus, in my heart
Do I play a double part.
Ever at Thy glowing altar
Must my heart grow sick and falter,
Wishing He I served were black,
Thinking then it would not lack
Precedent of pain to guide it,
Let who would or might deride it;
Surely then this flesh would know
Yours had borne a kindred woe.
Lord, I fashion dark gods, too,
Daring even to give You
Dark despairing features where,
Crowned with dark rebellious hair,
Patience wavers just so much as
Mortal grief compels, while touches
Quick and hot, of anger, rise
To smitten cheek and weary eyes.
Lord, forgive me if my need
Sometimes shapes a human creed.

All day long and all night through,
One thing only must I do:
Quench my pride and cool my blood,
Lest I perish in the flood.
Lest a hidden ember set
Timber that I thought was wet
Burning like the dryest flax,
Melting like the merest wax,
Lest the grave restore its dead.
Not yet has my heart or head
In the least way realized
They and I are civilized.

Caprice

'I'll tell him, when he comes,' she said,
  'Body and baggage, to go,
Though the night be darker than my hair,
  And the ground be hard with snow.'

But when he came with his gay black head
  Thrown back, and his lips apart,
She flipped a light hair from his coat,
  And sobbed against his heart.

Roger Mais

was born at Kingston, Jamaica, in 1905, and spent his early boy-hood in that town. When he was seven, his family moved to Island Head, up in the Blue Mountains, and later to a more accessible property in St Thomas, an old stone house of slavery days. Schooled at Calabar, Mais had a 'varied and sometimes stormy career' as a civil servant and journalist, and worked with astonishing creativity, not only in all imaginable forms of writing but also as a painter and a photographer. His output in any of these fields is permeated with a searing lyric quality which makes much of the prose of his novels more 'poetic' than most of his poetry – comparable in this outward aspect to the work of DuBois.

Mais's first book, *And most of all man* (which included some poems), came out in Kingston in 1939. It was followed in 1942 by *Face and other stories*. The next year he became the centre of a violent controversy provoked by his article 'Now we know' which attacked colonial policy in a manner thought 'seditious' by the authorities ('there's a war on, you know') who jailed its author for eighteen months. During the later forties Mais seems to have written mostly plays (*Atlanta at Calydon*, a verse play, was performed in 1950) but in the early fifties he found his true form in a series of novels which lifted West Indian prose at once to total maturity. *The Hills were joyful together* appeared in 1953, *Brother man* in 1954, and *Black lightning* in 1955. 'Violence and an incredible tenderness lay at the twin poles of his being,' said Arthur Seymour. Perhaps it needed distance finally to channel his tumultuous creativity – he spent the early fifties in Europe, mostly in England – or perhaps it was the urgency of fading life that made him pour all his great gifts into one last outburst. He returned to Jamaica in 1954 and died the next year. The University of the West Indies library at Mona preserves a collection of his unpublished works, including at least five earlier novels, two of 1942–3, the others of 1950–52.

Men of ideas

Men of ideas outlive their times
An idea held by such a man does not end with his death
His life bleeding away goes down
Into the earth, and they grow like seed
The idea that is not lost with the waste of a single life
Like seed springing up a multitude.

They hanged Gordon from a boom
Rigged in front of the Court House
They hanged him with eighteen others for company
And Jesus had but two
But the ideas for which Gordon lived
Did not hang with him
And the great social revolution for which Jesus died
Did not die with him
Two men they nailed with Jesus side by side
Eighteen went to hang with Gordon from the new-rigged
    boom
But the idea of equality and justice with Gordon
Went into the ground and sprung up like seed, a multitude.

A hundred years the seed was a-growing in the ground
A hundred years is not too long
A hundred years is not too soon
A hundred years is a time and a season
And all things must wait a time and a season
And the time and the season for each growing thing
Is the way, and there is no other
The time and the season of its growing and bearing fruit
Are inherent in the nature of the seed
And inherent in it is its growth and its fruit
And this is the way and there is no other

A hundred years is not too long
For the seed to burst its husk under the ground
And cleave a path and press upward
And thrust a green blade in triumph at the sun
Do not be anxious for the house that is a-building
For the unsown acres under the plough
For all things await a time and a season.

The dream given to one man in the night
Not night nor darkness can call it back again
They hanged George William Gordon for the dream
He had been given in the night
That he carried in his breast
Thinking to put the dream to death
With the man they put to shameful death
But they give immortality to the dream
That time the man is put to death
For the dream is all
It is all of a man that there is and immortal
And all of immortality of a man there is.

A long time ago they hanged George William Gordon
But not so long
A long time ago
They put Jesus on the Cross
But not so long
For all things have a time and a season
A long time ago
The pea doves took the sweetwood seeds
And let them fall on the valley bottoms
That are now the virgin forest of the great backlands
Of new timber, a long time
Were the bare rock-spurs growing
That is now a matted forest floor

Where the wild birds took and dropped
The little sweet kernels of the tall timbers
A long time ago, but not so long
For all things have a time and a season
And a hundred years is not too long
And a hundred years is not too soon.
They hanged Gordon with eighteen others
They nailed Jesus between two thieves
But the ideas these men lived for did not die with them
A single grain of corn will yield an ear of corn
And an ear of corn in two generations will sow a field
And these things befall between a moon and a moon
All things await a time and a season
And twice a hundred years is not too long
Or twice a hundred years too soon.

Waring Cuney

was born in Washington, D.C., on 6 May 1906. After attending the public schools and Howard University in his native town he went to Lincoln (Pennsylvania) where he became a member of the Glee Club and decided to make singing his career. To this end he went to the New England Conservatory of Music in Boston and later to Rome. His twin brother also trained for a musical career (piano), but neither ever performed professionally: Waring switched to writing, Wright to typography (he teaches printing at Howard, and printed Gloria Douglas Johnson's annual poetry keepsakes). Cuney's poem 'No images' won the *Opportunity* poetry contest for 1926 – it is one of the most complete and most-reprinted pictures of the philosophy of the Renaissance, it was translated into more languages than even the work of Langston Hughes, and it firmly established Cuney's reputation as a 'one poem poet'.

This is far from true, for Cuney still continues to write his charming 'anecdotes' and 'observations'. Some of the poems written in the thirties and early forties were recorded by Josh White on the album *Southern exposure*: 'Hard time blues' is one of these. During the war Cuney served in the South Pacific as a technical sergeant in the army; his three and a half years of active service earned him several decorations. Ever since, he has lived in the Bronx district of New York, but since 1962 he has withdrawn from society and for at least six years not even his closest friends have been able to get in touch with him. As far as I can ascertain, Cuney's last appearance in print was the book we edited together for a Dutch bibliophile society (*Puzzles*, 1960, a handsome folio with eight two-colour woodcuts by Ru van Rossem) until a letter of his appeared in *Black World* (March 1971), slapping the wrists of John Oliver Killens for calling his early religious verse 'irreverent'. Since then Waring has emerged far enough to be actively engaged on a new volume of poetry, which will appear in the Heritage series under the title *Storefront church*.

No images

She does not know
Her beauty,
She thinks her brown body
Has no glory.

If she could dance
Naked
Under palm trees
And see her image in the river
She would know.

But there are no palm trees
On the street,
And dish water gives back
no images.

Hard time blues

Went down home 'bout a year ago
Things so bad, Lord, my heart was sore.
Folks had nothing was a sin and shame
Every-body said hard times was the blame.
Great God-a-mighty folks feeling bad
Lost every thing they ever had.

Sun was shining fourteen days and no rain
Hoeing and planting was all in vain.
Hard hard times, Lord, all around
Meal barrels empty crops burnt to the ground.
Great God-a-mighty folks feeling bad
Lost every thing they ever had.

Skinny looking children bellies poking out
That old pellagra without a doubt.
Old folks hanging 'round the cabin door
Ain't seen times this hard before.
Great God-a-mighty folks feeling bad
Lost every thing they ever had.

I went to the Boss at the Commissary store
Folks all starving please don't close your door,
Want more food a little more time to pay.
Boss Man laughed and walked away.
Great God-a-mighty folks feeling bad
Lost every thing they ever had.

Landlord coming 'round when the rent is due
You ain't got the money take your home from **you,**
take your mule and horse even take your cow
Get offa my land you ain't no good no how.
Great God-a-mighty folks feeling bad
Lost every thing they ever had.

Margaret Danner

was born Margaret Essie Cunningham, in Kentucky, from what has been intriguingly described as a 'poor mid-Chicago family'. Circumstantial evidence suggests that the date must lie shortly before 1910: Mrs Danner has never given out any information on the event, and probably regards Dudley Randall's 'broadside 35', which addresses her as 'granny blak poet', with severely mixed feelings. Her formal education took place in Chicago, where she has spent most of her life, and at Loyola and Roosevelt Universities.

Long before she ever published a book of her own, she had acquired a reputation among fellow-poets. In 1945 she won a prize in the Poetry Workshop of the Midwestern Writers Conference at Northwestern, and in 1951 she obtained a John Hay Whitney fellowship. *Poetry* magazine, that weighty pillar of the white poetry establishment, published her 'Far from Africa' series in 1952, and appointed her as assistant editor in 1956 – the first (and presumably only) negro to serve on its board. She had, of course, studied under Karl Shapiro, Paul Engle and other *Poetry* personnel. In 1960 Margaret Danner became the first writer-in-residence of Wayne State University, and at this time her first book, *Impressions of African art forms*, made its appearance. Its title adequately reflects the subject matter of much of Mrs Danner's work. 'The poet's love of African culture has resulted in poems whose engaging surface exoticism is balanced and enhanced by the depth of her insight into the universal meanings inherent in the products of that culture' – or so says the blurb for her second book, *To flower*, which, like all her later books, was published by another poet, in this case fellow Baha'i Robert Hayden (who probably wrote the blurb just quoted). Dudley Randall then published (and co-authored) *Poem counterpoem* at his Broadside Press in 1966, and in 1968 Diane Di Prima made *Iron lace* one of the last productions of her now unfortunately defunct Poets Press.

Meanwhile Margaret Danner had become the founder and director of Boone House, a centre for artists and writers in Detroit donated in 1962 by Dr Theodore S. Boone. In 1966 she went to

Africa where she took part in the Dakar Festival. The last few years have seen her as writer-in-residence at Virginia Union where she edited two anthologies of students' verse (*Brass horses* in 1968; *Regroup* in 1969), and at Le Moyne-Owen College (Memphis) since 1970.

The slave and the iron lace

The craving of Samuel Rouse for clearance to create
was surely as hot as the iron that buffeted him. His passion
for freedom so strong that it molded the smouldering
    fashions
he laced, for how also could a slave plot
or counterplot such incomparable shapes,

form or reform, for house after house,
the intricate Patio pattern, the delicate
Rose and Lyre, the Debutante Settee,
the complex but famous Grape; frame the classic vein
in an iron bench?

How could he turn an iron Venetian urn, wind the Grape
    Vine, chain
the trunk of a pine with a Round-the-Tree-settee,
mold a Floating Flower tray, a French chair – create all this
in such exquisite fairyland taste, that he'd be freed
and his skill would still resound a hundred years after?

And I wonder if I, with this thick asbestos glove of an
attitude could lace, forge and bend this ton of lead-chained
    spleen surrounding me?
Could I manifest and sustain it into a new free-form screen
of, not necessarily love, but (at the very least, for all
    concerned) grace.

Vera Bell

objects as strongly as Margaret Danner to being ranked in chronological sequence. Born in Jamaica 'during this century', she also objects to being included in a 'black' anthology. 'Difficult as it must be to classify literature according to the writers' skin colour, it should be even more so for a country like Jamaica where you may find every possible biological combination and a multiplicity of skin colours ranging from the purest white to ebony – not just the legendary two black, two white and one khaki. Even our folklore is a mixture of the African Annancy, the Brothers Grimm, Hans Andersen and a great hodge-podge of Irish folk tales. Biologically, I may give myself as an example – I am a mixture of Negro, English, Scottish and Irish, and there are others whose mixtures range over the whole wide world.' Why differentiate so carefully between countries in the British Isles and be at the same time so sweepingly general about one's black ancestry?

Vera Bell was educated at Wolmer's Girls' School. She has been a civil servant. She has edited a paper called *The welfare reporter* for the Jamaica Social Welfare Commission. She holds a diploma in archaeology from London University. She lives in England. She has contributed short stories to various magazines and anthologies from 1944 on, notably to Edna Manly's series of Focus anthologies. 'Ancestor' first appeared in the second of these, in 1948. Its theme has recently been taken up again, in a verse epic of which the first part, 'Ogog', was published in New York in 1971.

Ancestor on the auction block

Ancestor on the auction block
Across the years your eyes seek mine
Compelling me to look.

I see your shackled feet
Your primitive black face
I see your humiliation
And turn away
Ashamed.

Across the years your eyes seek mine
Compelling me to look
Is this mean creature that I see
Myself?
Ashamed to look
Because of myself ashamed
Shackled by my own ignorance
I stand
A slave.

Humiliated
I cry to the eternal abyss
For understanding
Ancestor on the auction block
Across the years your eyes meet mine
Electric
I am transformed
My freedom is within myself.

I look you in the eyes and see
The spirit of God eternal
Of this only need I be ashamed
Of blindness to the God within me
The same God who dwelt within you
The same eternal God
Who shall dwell
In generations yet unborn.

Ancestor on the auction block
Across the years
I look

I see you sweating, toiling, suffering
Within your loins I see the seed
Of multitudes
From your labour
Grow roads, aqueducts, cultivation
A new country is born
Yours was the task to clear the ground
Mine be the task to build.

Richard Wright

was born Richard Nathaniel Wright on 4 September 1908, on a plantation near Natchez, Mississippi. His family moved frequently from place to place and as a consequence Richard received little or no formal education. He left home at fifteen, went to Memphis, Tennessee, took his own schooling in hand, worked at any job he managed to find. At nineteen he went to Chicago where he stayed for the next ten years, living through the bleakest patch of the city's chequered history. He started to write, stories about his own experience mainly, his childhood in the South, manhood in the North. In 1935 he joined the Chicago Federal Writers' Project, in 1936 his story *Big boy leaves home* appeared in *The New Caravan* – it later became the first of the four (in subsequent editions five) novellas making up Wright's first book, *Uncle Tom's children* (1938), which won the *Story* magazine award. The year before Wright had moved to New York, to write for the *Daily Worker* and *New Masses*. In 1939 he received a Guggenheim, and in 1940 he published the startling novel, *Native son*, which was an instant best-seller, a Book of the Month Club selection, then a play by Wright himself and Paul Green, successfully directed on Broadway by Orson Welles, and later still an incredibly bad film made in Argentina in 1949 with the author and Canada Lee in the main roles. An explanatory essay entitled 'How bigger was born' first appeared separately in the same year, and was afterwards added to new editions of *Native son* in the same way as the *Children* had been introduced by the essay on 'The ethics of living Jim Crow'. In 1941 Wright's first book of non-fiction appeared, the grim 'folk history of the Negro in the United States' called *Twelve million black voices*. His next novel, the autobiographical *Black boy* (1945), repeated the success of *Native son*. In 1946 Wright left America for Europe, to settle in France – and stay there, as it turned out.

From the days of the Writers' Project to the years of his final emergence as a major writer, Richard Wright had been a member of the Communist party, but a more and more disillusioned one.

'I embraced Communism because I felt it was an instrumentality to help free the Negroes in America. But, in time, I found that instrumentality degrading. I dropped it of my own accord. I was not driven out; I was not frightened out of Communism by American government agents. I left under my own steam, I was prompted to leave by my love of freedom.'

The search for freedom occupied most of his later life – if he never found it, then the reason must lie in the human condition which does not allow absolutes, and nothing less than absolute freedom would do for Richard Wright. This for a long while alienated him from his black fellow-writers and from a black audience, and it is only in recent years that the dialogue about the black writer's responsibility and the problems of exile in its varied implications has brought a new awareness and appreciation of Wright's work. But long before all this his book about the emergence of Ghana as an independent state had coined the phrase 'Black power' (1954), and his book about the Bandung conference of Asian and African countries had twisted another phrase into *The color curtain* (1956). The latter book had been alone in recognizing the true significance of that almost totally ignored event. *Pagan Spain* and the essays in *White man, listen* (both 1957) had shown the width rather than the depth of Wright's interests, and it was left to the much neglected novels of his later years to express the philosophy behind the observations. *The Outsider* appeared in 1953, *Savage holiday* in 1954, and his last, *The long dream*, in 1958. Wright died in Paris on 28 November 1960. A few very beautiful fragments of the book he was then working on appeared in Herbert Hill's anthology *Soon one morning* in 1963. A collection of stories (including 'Silt' which had appeared in *New Masses* as early as 1937) came out in 1961. Another posthumous publication, *Lawd today* (1963), is in fact one of Wright's earliest works, written in and about Chicago during the depression.

Already there are several books on Wright. The biography *Richard Wright* by Constance Webb (1967) includes a bibliography compiled by Michel Fabre and Edward Margolies, published first in the *Bulletin of Bibliography* 24 (first quarter 1965), later reprinted in the *Negro Digest* for January 1969 as a supplement to their December 1968 Wright evaluation issue. Edward Margolies's *The art of Richard Wright* appeared in 1969. John A. Williams published a biography for younger readers in 1970 (*The most native of sons*). On the tenth anniversary of Wright's death *Studies in black literature* issued a special number with recollections and a long article by Michel Fabre on the poetry. Horace Cayton's biography, sure to outshine all others, is still in the making.

Between the world and me

And one morning while in the woods I stumbled suddenly
    upon the thing,
Stumbled upon it in a grassy clearing guarded by scaly oaks
    and elms.
And the sooty details of the scene rose, thrusting themselves
    between the world and me . . .

There was a design of white bones slumbering forgottenly
    upon a cushion of ashes.
There was a charred stump of a sapling pointing a blunt
    finger accusingly at the sky.
There were torn tree limbs, tiny veins of burnt leaves, and
    a scorched coil of greasy hemp;
A vacant shoe, an empty tie, a ripped shirt, a lonely hat, and
    a pair of trousers stiff with black blood.
And upon the trampled grass were buttons, dead matches,
    butt-ends of cigars and cigarettes, peanut shells, a
    drained gin-flask, and a whore's lipstick;
Scattered traces of tar, restless arrays of feathers, and the
    lingering smell of gasoline.
And through the morning air the sun poured yellow surprise
    into the eye sockets of a stony skull . . .
And while I stood my mind was frozen with a cold pity for
    the life that was gone.

The ground gripped my feet and my heart was circled by
    icy walls of fear –

The sun died in the sky; a night wind muttered in the grass
    and fumbled the leaves in the trees; the woods poured
    forth the hungry yelping of hounds; the darkness
    screamed with thirsty voices; and the witnesses rose and
    lived:

The dry bones stirred, rattled, lifted, melting themselves
    into my bones.

The grey ashes formed flesh firm and black, entering into
    my flesh.

The gin-flask passed from mouth to mouth; cigars and
    cigarettes glowed, the whore smeared the lipstick red
    upon her lips,

And a thousand faces swirled around me, clamoring that my
    life be burned . . .

And then they had me, stripped me, battering my teeth into
    my throat till I swallowed my own blood.

My voice was drowned in the roar of their voices, and my
    black wet body slipped and rolled in their hands as they
    bound me to the sapling.

And my skin clung to the bubbling hot tar, falling from me
    in limp patches.

And the down and quills of the white feathers sank into my
    raw flesh, and I moaned in my agony.

Then my blood was cooled mercifully, cooled by a baptism
    of gasoline.

And in a blaze of red I leaped to the sky as pain rose like
    water, boiling my limbs.

Panting, begging I clutched childlike, clutched to the hot
    sides of death.

Now I am dry bones and my face a stony skull staring in
    yellow surprise at the sun . . .

In the falling snow

In the falling snow
A laughing boy holds out his palms
Until they are white

Peter Blackman

was born in Barbados, 18 June 1909. He was educated partly in England, and in 1937 he went to West Africa as a missionary. Later he lived in England again, where *My song is for all men* (a long poem in four parts) was published in 1952. Around the same time he contributed an article to *Présence Africaine*, then a fairly rare thing for an English-writing author. It has proved impossible to obtain further details about Peter Blackman.

from My song is for all men

To all my wide continent I welcomed these they came to
    Africa
seized all they could lay hands upon
Took the best lands for their tilling to build them white
    houses
I pass them each day cool deep-shaded in green
Their dwelling places wanton in lovelinesses
Spread for their senses by sky river and sea

I am unlearned in philosophies of government
I may not govern myself children must learn of their elders
till they are elders themselves
I know nothing of science never created a great civilization
Poetry song music sculpture are alike foreign to my
    conceiving

I have never built a monument higher than a mudhut
Nor woven a covering for my body other than the passing
    leaves of the grass

I am the subman
My footprints are nowhere in history

This is your statement, remember, this your assessment
I merely repeat you
Remember this too, I do not ask you to pity me
Remember this always you cannot condescend to me
There are many other things I remember and would have
    you remember as well
I smelted iron in Nubia when your generations still ploughed
    with hardwood
I cast in bronze at Benin when London was marshland
I built Timbuctoo and made it a refuge for learning
When in the choirs of Oxford unlettered monks shivered
    unwashed

My faith in the living mounts like a flame in my story
I am Khama the Great
I helped Bolivar enfranchise the Americas
I am Omar and his thousands who brought Spain the light
    of the Prophet
I stood with my spear among the ranks of the Prempehs
And drove you far from Kumasi for more than a century
I kept you out of my coasts and not the mosquitoes

I have won many bitter battles against you and shall win
    them again
I am Toussaint who taught France there was no limit to
    liberty
I am Harriet Tubman flouting your torture to assert my
    faith in man's freedom
I am Nat Turner whose daring and strength always defied
    you
I have my yesterdays and shall open the future widely before
    me

Harold Minton Telemaque

is a Trinidadian by all but accident: only his father's profession as captain of an inter-island schooner let him be born at Plymouth on Tobago, 20 August 1910. Educated first of all by Moravian ministers at Bethesda, he later attended Bishop's High and then the government Training College for Teachers at Scarborough, Tobago. Teaching has been his profession ever since; from 1933 to 1939 back in Scarborough, then in Port-of-Spain. He also travelled quite extensively both in America and in Europe: 1949 saw him in London. He worked for the Ministry of Education at San Fernando, and from 1941 to 1953 was headmaster of the Intermediary School at Fyzabad, Trinidad. Since 1953 he has been schools inspector.

Telemaque has published two small collections of poetry: *Burnt bush* appeared in Trinidad in 1947, and *Scarlet* formed part of the Miniature Poets series edited by Arthur Seymour in British Guiana in April 1953. His often-quoted 'Poem' is an interesting paraphrase of Langston Hughes's 'The Negro speaks of rivers', illustrating how heavily the early black West Indian writers drew on the Harlem Renaissance in their efforts to break away from the deadly grip of w.a.s.p. English.

In our land

In our land,
Poppies do not spring
From atoms of young blood,
So gaudily where men have died:
In our land
Stiletto cane blades
Sink into our hearts,
And drink our blood.

In our land,
Sin is not deep,
And bends before the truth,
Asking repentently for pardon:
In our land
The ugly stain
That blotted Eden garden
Is sunk deep only.

In our land
Storms do not strike
For territory's fences,
Elbow room, nor breathing spaces:
In our land
The hurricane
Of clashes breaks our ranks
For tint of eye.

In our land
We do not breed
That taloned king, the eagle,
Nor make emblazonry of lions;
In our land,
The black birds
And the chickens of our mountains
Speak our dreams.

Dennis Chukude Osadebay

was born at Asaba in Nigeria on 29 June 1911 of mixed Ibo and Yoruba parentage. He went to the government school at Asaba, later to the Sacred Heart School and Hope Waddell Institute, both at Calabar in Eastern Nigeria. In 1929 he became a customs officer, serving at Calabar, Port Harcourt, in the Cameroons and Lagos until 1946 when he went to London to read law at Lincoln's Inn and at London University. Back in Nigeria he set up in private practice as a solicitor, but political activities soon took up most of his time. A founding member of Azikiwe's party in 1944, he was elected to the Western House of Assembly in 1951, served as opposition leader 1954–6 and was Deputy Speaker in 1958. Recognized leader of the Mid-West Movement, Osadebay was above all known for his strict impartiality in national affairs, a widely respected 'elder statesman' even when still in his forties – 'harmless, and as pious as a saint'. When Nigeria gained independence in October 1960 he became President of the Senate in succession to Azikiwe, but he resigned in 1963 to become the first President of the Mid-West Region.

With Osadebay, and a few strict contemporaries like Armattoe, we find the beginnings of an English-written literature that can be called African, in a hesitant way. Osadebay started writing poetry in the very early thirties, and some of his work of that period (like the two poems printed here) has become the classic expression of a continent awakening, not to the superficialities of an alien technocracy, but to a growing sense of its own values and possibilities. Nevertheless, Osadebay's collected poems, published as *Africa sings* in 1952, is largely filled with the gentle musings of an imperialist civil servant who can say with equal sincerity, 'Thank you, sons and daughters of Britannia', and, 'You bring your cross and make me dumb': this is at best abolitionist verse, and it is very sad to realize that *Africa sings*, as late as 1952, was the first published collection of English verse by a West African author.

Who buys my thoughts

Who buys my thoughts
Buys not a cup of honey
That sweetens every taste;
He buys the throb
Of Young Africa's soul,
The soul of teeming millions,
Hungry, naked, sick,
Yearning, pleading, waiting.

Who buys my thoughts
Buys not some false pretence
Of oracles and tin gods;
He buys the thoughts
Projected by the mass
Of restless youths who are born
Into deep and clashing cultures,
Sorting, questioning, watching.

Who buys my thoughts
Buys the spirit of the age,
The unquenching fire that smoulders
And smoulders
In every living heart
That's true and noble or suffering;
It burns all o'er the earth,
Destroying, chastening, cleansing.

Young Africa's plea

Don't preserve my customs
As some fine curios
To suit some white historian's tastes.
There's nothing artificial
That beats the natural way
In culture and ideals of life.
Let me play with the whiteman's ways
Let me work with the blackman's brains
Let my affairs themselves sort out.
Then in sweet rebirth
I'll rise a better man
Not ashamed to face the world.
Those who doubt my talents
In secret fear my strength
They know I am no less a man.
Let them bury their prejudice,
Let them show their noble sides,
Let me have untramelled growth,
My friends will never know regret
And I, I never once forget.

Israel Kafu Hoh

is a native of Ghana, born in 1912 at Afiadenyigba on the eastern coast. His father was an evangelist and Hoh's first schooling took place at the Evangelist Presbyterian Infant and Junior School, later the Senior School at Keta. From there he went to Teacher Training College at Akropong – it was there that he started writing poetry, about 1929. He finished his education at the Seminary at Ho in 1932, and from the next year on he has worked as a teacher at Amedzofe, Keta, Peki, Anloga and other places, often doubling as band master or scout leader, and becoming headmaster at the early age of thirty-three. In 1953 he 'retired' from active teaching to become education officer first at Abor, later at Aceloga and Dabala.

Hoh writes stage plays as well as poetry, has never published a book of his own, but is a frequent contributor to anthologies and small magazines.

Baby

A baby is a European,
He does not eat our food;
He drinks from his own water pot.

A baby is a European,
He does not speak our tongue;
He is cross when the mother understands him not.

A baby is a European,
He cares very little for others;
He forces his will upon its parents.

A baby is a European,
He is always very sensitive;
The slightest scratch on its skin results in an ulcer.

Robert Hayden

whose middle initial E, now discarded, stood for Earl, was born 4 August 1913 in Detroit, Michigan, went through the public school system of that town, and then attended Wayne University. From 1936 to 1938 he worked on a Federal Writers' Project, in charge of research into local negro history and folklore. His early poetry is very much of this period, in the same way as the work of Richard Wright and Margaret Walker: there is a small but distinguished number of poets whose work began to be published around 1940 who form a recognizable 'generation', the first major one after the Renaissance of the twenties. They have all quite obviously been shaped by the depressed thirties, and their work has none of the genteel aesthetics of the earlier poets: their sound is harsh, bitter, but assertive, positive in a very universal way: the depression has, for once, not only hit black America and for some 'the workers' and 'the people' have taken on International implications.

Hayden is the only one of this group who eventually escapes the limitations of subject and style, to forge a new poetic structure. Above all other black poets in the United States he has managed to create out of the painful reality of blackness, to transmute every aspect of it into sophisticated word-structures which are both intensely personal and completely universal: he uses the alien language which is also the native tongue in such a way as to bring out both the commonness of the unfamiliar and the specialness of the everyday. 'One needs psychic distance and emotional clarity in order to say anything beyond the obvious and rhetorical' – in the search for the former his Baha'i faith may have lent him strength, but the emotional clarity is a personal achievement which one associates more easily with Léon Damas or Aimé Césaire than with any of the anglophone black poets.

In 1938 Hayden went to the University of Michigan for graduate work, and afterwards he held various teaching posts, including a spell at Michigan itself, from 1944–6. He was also for a time the music critic of the *Michigan Chronicle*, and wrote a play called *Go down Moses*. His poetry received Hopwood Awards in 1938 and 1942, and he was Rosenwald fellow in 1947. A year earlier, he had been appointed associate professor of English at Fisk, where he eventually became professor of creative writing. In 1968 he finally left the stifling clique-ish atmosphere of Fisk, and he is again teaching at Michigan.

In 1940 his first small book of poems, *Heartshape in the dust*, appeared. While in Nashville he edited a privately printed series of poetry books, the Counterpoise series, which started in 1948 with *The lion and the archer*, co-authored by Hayden and Myron O'Higgins, and which later included Hayden's third book *Figure of time* (1955). His work of the fifties, including the masterly *Middle passage* and the Mexican poems written on a Ford Foundation grant in 1954, inaugurated my own Heritage series of poetry books: *A ballad of remembrance* appeared in April 1962, after three years of agonizing preparation. In 1966 it found belated recognition and justification when it won Hayden, through tireless promotion by Rosey Pool and Langston Hughes, the Grand Prix de la Poésie of the Dakar First World Festival of Negro Arts. In the same year *Selected poems* appeared as little more than an augmented version of 'Ballad'. Later poems appeared as *Words in the mourning time* in 1970. His next book, *The night-blooming cereus*, marked the tenth anniversary of the Heritage series. A seventy-six page interview in *How I write* (1972) contains the most comprehensive introduction to Hayden's rhyme and reason.

Hayden's verse has appeared in magazines like *Phylon*, *Poetry*, *Voices*, the *Midwest Journal* and the *Atlantic Monthly*. He is the editor of *Kaleidoscope: poems by American Negro poets* (1967) which showed a refreshingly original choice of material and unusually articulate and positive criticism of both individuals and trends.

Locus

Here redbuds like momentary trees
    of an illusionist;
here Cherokee rose, acacia and mimosa;
    here magnolia – totemic flower
whose redolence wreathes the legends of this place.
Here violent metamorphosis
    a look, a word, a gesture
may engender, with every blossom deadly
    and memorial sentinels,
their sabres drawn, storming firewood shacks,
apartheid streets. Here raw red earth and cotton-
    fields like palimpsests
new-scrawled with old embittering texts;
    rock hills where sachems counseled
or defied, where scouts gazed warily upon
the glittering death-march of De Soto. Here
    spareness, rankness, lush
brilliancies; beauty of outcropping
    stone, of what's hardbitten, sore-beset
yet flourishes, on thorny meagerness thrives,
twisting into grace. Here symbol houses
    built with an eternal summer
in mind, the swan-song houses where the brutal
    dream, companioned by its belles
and massas and avuncular crooning boys,
lives out its lengthy dying. Here guilt,
    here agenbite
and victimizer victimized by truth
    he dares not apprehend.
Here the past, adored and unforgiven,
its wrongs, denials, grievous loyalties
    alive in hard averted eyes –

the very structure of the bones; soul-scape;
   terrain
of warring shades whose guns are real.

A ballad of remembrance

Quadroon mermaids, afro angels, black saints
balanced upon the switchblades of that air
and sang. Tight streets unfolding to the eye
like fans of corrosion and elegiac lace
crackled with their singing: Shadow of time. Shadow of
   blood.

Shadow, echoed the Zulu king, dangling
from a cluster of balloons. Blood,
whined the gunmetal priestess, floating
over the courtyard where dead men diced.

What will you have? she inquired, the sallow vendeuse
of prepared tarnishes and jokes of nacre and ormolu,
what but those gleamings, oldrose graces,
manners like scented gloves? Contrived ghosts
rapped to metronome clack of lavalieres.

Contrived illuminations riding a threat
of river, masked Negroes wearing chameleon
satins gaudy now as a fortuneteller's
dream of disaster, lighted the crazy flopping
dance of love and hate among joys, rejections.

Accomodate, muttered the Zulu king,
toad on a throne of glaucous poison jewels.

Love, chimed the saints and the angels and the mermaids.
Hate, shrieked the gunmetal priestess
from her spiked bellcollar curved like a fleur-de-lys:

As well have a talon as a finger, a muzzle as a mouth,
as well have a hollow as a heart. And she pinwheeled
away in coruscations of laughter, scattering
those others before her like foil stars.

But the dance continued – now among metaphorical
doors, coffeecups floating poised
hysterias, decors of illusions; now among
mazurka dolls offering death's-heads
of cocaine roses and real violets.

Then you arrived, meditative, ironic,
richly human; and your presence was shore where I rested
released from the hoodoo of that dance, where I spoke
with my true voice again.

And therefore this is not only a ballad of remembrance
for the down-South arcane city with death
in its jaws like gold teeth and archaic cusswords;
not only a token for the troubled generous friends
held in the fists of that schizoid city like flowers,
but also, Mark Van Doren,
a poem of remembrance, a gift, a souvenir for you.

Middle Passage

i

Jesús, Estrella, Esperanza, Mercy:

Sails flashing to the wind like weapons,
sharks following the moans the fever and the dying;
horror the corposant and compass-rose.

Middle Passage:

> voyage through death
>
> > to life upon these
> > shores.

'10 April 1800 –
Blacks rebellious. Crew uneasy. Our linguist says
their moaning is a prayer for death,
ours and their own. Some try to starve themselves.
Lost three this morning leaped with crazy laughter
to the waiting sharks, sang as they went under.'

Desire, Adventure, Tartar, Ann:

Standing to America, bringing home
black gold, black ivory, black seed.

> *Deep in the festering hold thy father lies,*
> *of his bones New England pews are made,*
> *those are altar lights that were his eyes.*

Jesus Saviour Pilot Me
Over Life's Tempestuous Sea

We pray that Thou wilt grant, o Lord,
safe passage to our vessels bringing
heathen souls unto Thy chastening.

Jesus   Saviour

'8 bells. I cannot sleep, for I am sick
with fear, but writing eases fear a little
since still my eyes can see these words take shape
upon the page & so I write, as one
would turn to exorcism. 4 days scudding,
but now the sea is calm again. Misfortune
follows in our wake like sharks (our grinning
tutelary gods). Which one of us
has killed an albatross? A plague among
our blacks – Ophthalmia: blindness – & we
have jettisoned the blind to no avail.
It spreads, the terrifying sickness spreads.
Its claws have scratched sight from the Capt.'s eyes
 & there is blindness in the fo'c'sle
 & we must sail 3 weeks before we come
to port.'

> *What port awaits us, Davy Jones'*
> *or home? I've heard of slavers drifting, drifting,*
> *playthings of wind and storm and chance, their crews*
> *gone blind, the jungle hatred*
> *crawling up on deck.*

Thou   Who   Walked   On   Galilee

'Deponent further sayeth the *Bella J*
left the Guinea Coast
with cargo of five hundred blacks and odd
for the barracoons of Florida:

'that there was hardly room 'tween-decks for half
the sweltering cattle stowed spoon-fashion there;
that some went mad of thirst and tore their flesh
and sucked the blood:

'that Crew and Captain lusted with the comeliest
of the savage girls kept naked in the cabins;
that there was one they called the Guinea Rose
and they cast lots and fought to lie with her:

'that when the Bo's'n piped all hands, the flames
spreading from starboard already were beyond
control, the negroes howling and their chains
entangled with the flames:

'that the burning blacks could not be reached,
that the crew abandoned ship,
leaving their shrieking negresses behind;
that the Captain perished drunken with the wenches:

'further Deponent sayeth not.'

Pilot   O   Pilot   Me

ii

Aye, lad, and I have seen those factories,
Gambia, Rio Pongo, Calabar;
have watched the artful mongos baiting traps
of war wherein the victor and the vanquished

were caught as prizes for our barracoons.
Have seen the nigger kings whose vanity
and greed turned wild black hides of Fellatah,
Mandingo, Ibo, Kru to gold for us.

And there was one – King Anthracite we named him –
fetish face beneath French parasols
of brass and orange velvet, impudent mouth
whose cups were carven skulls of enemies:

he'd honor us with drum and feast and conjo
and palm-oil-glistening wenches deft in love,
and for tin crowns that shone with paste,
red calico and German-silver trinkets

would have the drums talk war and send
his warriors to burn the sleeping villages
and kill the sick and old and lead the young
in coffles to our factories.

Twenty years a trader, twenty years,
for there was wealth aplenty to be harvested
from those black fields, and I'd be trading still
but for the fevers melting down my bones.

iii

Shuttles in the rocking loom of history,
the dark ships move, the dark ships move,
their bright ironical names
like jests of kindness on a murderer's mouth;
plough through thrashing glister toward
fata morgana's lucent melting shore,
weave toward New World littorals that are
mirage and myth and actual shore.

Voyage through death,
                              voyage whose chartings are unlove.

A charnel stench, effluvium of living death,
spreads outward from the hold,
where the living and the dead, the horribly dying,
lie interlocked, lie foul with blood and excrement.

> *Deep in the festering hold thy father lies,*
> *the corpse of mercy rots with him,*
> *rats eat love's rotten gelid eyes.*

But oh the living look at you
with human eyes whose suffering accuses you,
whose hatred reaches through the swill of dark
to strike you like a leper's claw.

You cannot stare that hatred down
or chain the fear that stalks the watches
and breathes on you its fetid scorching breath;
cannot kill the deep immortal human wish,
the timeless will.

'But for the storm that flung up barriers
of wind and wave, The Amistad, señores,
would have reached the port of Príncipe in two,
three days at most; but for the storm we should
have been prepared for what befell.
Swift as the puma's leap it came. There was
that interval of moonless calm filled only
with the water's and the rigging's usual sounds,
then sudden movement, blows and snarling cries
and they had fallen on us with machete
and marlin-spike. It was as though the very
air, the night itself were striking us.
Exhausted by the rigors of the storm,
we were no match for them. Our men went down

before the murderous Africans. Our loyal
Celestino ran from below with gun
and lantern and I saw, before the cane-
knife's wounding flash, Cinquez,
that surly brute who calls himself a prince,
directing, urging on the ghastly work.
He hacked the poor mulatto down, and then
he turned on me. The decks were slippery
when daylight finally came. It sickens me
to think of what I saw, of how these apes
threw overboard the butchered bodies of
our men, true Christians all, like so much jetsam.
Enough, enough. The rest is quickly told:
Cinquez was forced to spare the two of us
you see to steer the ship to Africa,
and we like phantoms doomed to rove the sea
sailed east by day and west by night,
deceiving them, hoping for rescue,
prisoners on our own vessel, till
at length we drifted to the shores of this
your land, America, where we were freed
from our unspeakable misery. Now we
demand, good sirs, the extradition of
Cinquez and his accomplices to La
Havana. And it distresses us to know
there are so many here who seem inclined
to justify the mutiny of these blacks.
We find it paradoxical indeed
that you whose wealth, whose tree of liberty
are rooted in the labor of your slaves
should suffer the august John Quincy Adams
to speak with so much passion of the right
of chattel slaves to kill their lawful masters
and with his Roman rhetoric weave a hero's

garland for Cinquez. I tell you that
we are determined to return to Cuba
with our slaves and there see justice done. Cinquez –
or let us say "the Prince" – Cinquez shall die.'

The deep immortal human wish,
the timeless will:

Cinquez its deathless primaveral image,
life that transfigures many lives.

Voyage through death
                    to life upon these shores.

The ballad of Nat Turner

Then fled the mellows, the wicked juba
    and wandered wandered far
from curfew joys in the Dismal's night.
    Fool of St Elmo's fire

in scarey night I wandered, praying,
    Lord God my harshener,
speak to me now or let me die;
    speak, Lord, to this mourner.

And came at length to livid trees
    where Ibo warriors
hung shadowless, turning in wind
    that moaned like Africa,

their belltongue bodies dead, their eyes
   alive with the anger deep
in my own heart. Is this the sign,
   the sign forepromised me?

The spirits vanished. Afraid and lonely
   I wandered on in blackness.
Speak to me now or let me die.
   Die, whispered the blackness.

And wild things gasped and scuffled in
   the seething night; shapes
of evil writhed upon the air.
   I reeled with fear, I prayed.

Sudden brightness clove the preying
   darkness, brightness that was
itself a golden darkness, brightness
   so bright that it was darkness.

And there were angels, their faces hidden
   from me, angels at war
with one another, angels in dazzling
   battle. And oh the splendor

the fearful splendor of that warring.
   Hide me, I cried to rock and bramble.
Hide me, the rock, the bramble cried . . .
   How tell you of that holy battle?

The shock of wing on wing and sword
   on sword was the tumult of
a taken city burning. I cannot
   say how long they strove,

for the wheel in a turning wheel which is time
   in eternity had ceased
its whirling, and owl and moccasin,
   panther and nameless beast

and I were held like creatures fixed
   in flaming, in fiery amber.
But I saw I saw oh many of
   those mighty beings waver,

waver and fall, go streaking down
   into swamp water, and the water
hissed and steamed and bubbled and locked
   shuddering shuddering over

the fallen and soon was motionless.
   Then that massive light
began to fold fold slowly in
   upon itself, and I

beheld the conqueror faces and, lo,
   they were like mine, I saw
they were like mine and in joy and terror
   wept, praising praising Jehovah.

Oh praised my honer, harshener
   till a sleep came over me,
a sleep heavy as death. And when
   I awoke at last newborn

and purified, I rose and prayed
   and returned after a time
to the blazing fields, to the humbleness.
   And bided my time.

Frederick Douglass

When it is finally ours, this freedom, this liberty, this
        beautiful
and terrible thing, needful to man as air,
usable as earth; when it belongs at last to our children,
when it is truly instinct, brainmatter, diastole, systole,
reflex action; when it is finally won; when it is more
than the gaudy mumbo jumbo of politicians:
this man, this Douglass, this former slave, this Negro
beaten to his knees, exiled, visioning a world
where none is lonely, none hunted, alien,
this man, superb in love and logic, this man
shall be remembered. Oh not with statues' rhetoric,
not with legends and poems and wreaths of bronze alone,
but with the lives grown out of his life, the lives
fleshing his dream of the beautiful needful thing.

R. E. G. Armattoe

whose full names are Raphael Ernest Grail, was born 12 August 1913 at Denn in south-eastern Ghana. His father was an agent for a German firm in German Togoland, his mother came from Lome in French Togoland, and Raphael, attending Denn mission school, was completely trilingual. He graduated in 1929 from the Gold Coast's oldest secondary school, Mfantsipim in the West province, and went to Germany the next year where he first finished his secondary schooling in the Hamburg suburb of Wandsbeck, then started medical and anthropological studies at the University of Hamburg. From 1933 he continued his studies in France at the Sorbonne, at Besançon, and later at Lille (where he obtained his M.Litt.). In 1937 he came to England, studied medicine at Glasgow and Edinburgh, then anthropology in London. After his studies he founded the Lomeshic Research Institute of Anthropology and Racial Biology at Londonderry in Ulster: his work there made him a runner-up for the Nobel prize in 1949.

Armattoe had a marginal interest in politics and in the post-war development in the African countries. He spoke to the Pan-African Congress in Manchester in 1945; his support of a separatist movement for Togoland as well as his dislike for Nkrumah seem to stem from that occasion. Having returned 'home' (?) in 1948, he opposed Nkrumah's policy, and eventually became the acknowledged opposition leader. His quarrel over the 'cutting-out' policy for cocoa farms afflicted by the 'swollen foot' disease was a personal vendetta against Nkrumah, and his claim to have discovered a cure for the disease was never substantiated. On his return from a United Nations meeting where he had pleaded for the establishment of an independent Togo state, he was taken ill in London, and flown to Hamburg where he died 21 December 1953.

To include Armattoe as one of the 'pioneer poets' would be grossly misleading: he is interesting more as the last of the mission poets than as a 'father of African literature'. It is plain from his

poetry (if it wasn't already from his life) that he completely
accepted the white image of Africa. Certainly he glorified black
as a colour, but for the true Africans (those without the 'benefit'
of German, French and English brainwashing) he has nothing but
scorn – they are 'the lost dark people, sad and sullen', 'a servile
race' stemming 'from long lines of servile kings'. Armattoe
published one book of poetry, more or less his collected works,
which was roneod from typescript in 1950 under the title *Between
the forest and the sea*. This collection formed the basis, with but a
few exceptions and alterations, for the posthumous volume *Deep
down the blackman's mind* (1954), with its preposterous dedication
'to HS who will understand' in which HS stands for Homo
Sapiens! Ras Khan published a sympathetic study of Armattoe's
poetry in *Présence Africaine* NS12, 1957, pages 32–47.

Deep down the blackman's mind

Deep down the blackman's mind there's nothing new
Or bright, save midnight darkness and despair;
We tell you this, we are the ones who dare,
For we have learnt the magic spells that few

Have heard or known. There's horror stacked for you
Behind the blackman's mind. The brain that's there
The cruel homicidal sun flays bone bare,
Then chars the simple dreg an ashen hue.

Oh! If ours be the calm before the storm,
Then this dark sullen cloud may break with sun.
But not in our days. No, not in our days!
No mortal wit may change his shape or form,
Or make the blackman's thoughtless life of fun
Fit him to breed aught but a servile race.

A. J. Seymour

was born 12 January 1914 at Georgetown in Guyana and has lived pretty well all his life in 'B.G.' – but his influence has far exceeded provincial or parochial bounds and it is surely no exaggeration to say that without him the present state of West Indian poetry would be completely different and nowhere near as rich and impressive. His own work is usually described as 'transitional', which is a polite way of saying it is neither one thing nor yet another. He has, however, pioneered several strains of native subject matter, emphasizing the continuity of Caribbean history beyond European and African ancestry to Amerindian sources, and weaving a tapestry of mythological and natural motifs that is more individual than its rather stilted technique at first betrays.

After graduating from Queen's College in Georgetown, Seymour became a public information officer for the then colony. His only absence from Guyana came during 1962–4 when he was the development officer for information and culture of the Caribbean Organization in Puerto Rico. Since 1965 he has handled public relations for the Demarara Bauxite Company. But this 'official' part of his life is overshadowed by the more 'functional' aspect of Seymour the indefatigable furtherer of West Indian literature. As founder and editor of *Kyk-over-al*, a literary magazine published with fair regularity from 1945 to 1961, he published at least two generations of both prose and poetry and devoted three whole issues to some of the best early anthologies in the field: *An anthology of West Indian poetry* in 1952 (number 14), revised in 1957 (number 22), and an *Anthology of Guyanese poetry* in 1954. At the same time he published the Miniature Poets series, small collections of verse by Carter, Keane, McFarlane, Sherlock, Telemaque (to name but those who are included in this book as well). His own poetry has also largely appeared in these small private editions, but the first, *Verse*, and *More poems*, were published by the *Georgetown Daily Chronicle* in 1936 and 1937. These were followed by *Suns in my blood* (1940), *Over Guiana, clouds* (1944), *Six songs* (1946), *The Guiana book* (1948) and *Leaves from the tree*

(1951). After a long silence the series is continued in 1965 with the privately printed *Selected poems* and in 1968 with a group of nine poems called *Monologue*.

During the early fifties Seymour's weekly broadcasts spread the interest in Caribbean literature still further. Some of this material was collected in *A survey of West Indian literature* in 1950 and *Caribbean literature* in 1952. Sociological essays appeared in 1953 under the title *Window on the Caribbean*. In 1968 Seymour published a critical evaluation of *Edgar Mittelholzer: the man and his work*. Meanwhile he has himself been the subject of two critical studies: by Celeste Dolphin in the *New World Fortnightly* in 1965 and by Ed Brathwaite in *Contemporary poets of the English language* in 1970.

First of August

i

Gather into the mind
Over a hundred years of a people
Wearing a natural livery in the sun
And budding up in generations and dying
Upon a strip of South American coastland.

See a prostrate people
Straighten its knees and stand erect
And stare dark eyes against the sun.

Watch hidden power dome the brow
And lend a depth of vision to the eyes.

Gather into the mind
Over a hundred years of a people

Toiling against climate
Working against prejudice
Growing within an alien framework
Cramped, but stretching its limbs
And staring against the sun.

ii

Sometimes the blood forgets the flowering trees,
Red with flamboyants in the hard clear sun
And traces memories from hotter suns,
Other green-brilliant trees beneath a sky
That burns a deeper and more vital blue.

The blood goes back –

Coming across to land from Africa
The winds would close their mouths, the sea would smooth
And leave the little ships gasping, then the Sun
Would stand above and gaze right down the masts.

Children dying in dozens below the decks
The women drooping in clumps of flowers, the men
Standing about, with anger carved upon their foreheads.
A ferry of infamy from the heart of Africa
Roots torn and bleeding from their native soil,
A stain of race spreading across the ocean.

Then the new life of chains and stinging swamps
Whips flickering in the air in curling arabesques.

iii

Gather into the mind
Over a hundred years of a people
Wearing a natural livery in the sun
And budding up in generations and dying
Upon a strip of South American coastland.

Dudley Randall

was born in Washington, D.C., 14 January 1914 – just two days after Arthur Seymour: it is remarkable how closely their patterns (propagation of other people's work combined with a 'safe' basic profession) echo each other. Randall went through the public school system of Washington and St Louis, graduated in Detroit in 1930, then worked in the foundry of an automobile factory (he once wrote a proudly physical poem about that) and for a time as letter carrier for the U.S. Post Office. During the war he served in the South Pacific, and after that attended Wayne University from which he obtained his B.A. in 1949, and the University of Michigan where he ended up with an M.A. in library science in 1951. From that year on he has worked as a librarian first at Lincoln University in Missouri, later at Morgan State College in Baltimore, from 1958 in the Wayne County Federated Library Systems, and from 1963 as head of the reference interloan department. Since July 1969 he has been a librarian at the University of Detroit, doubling as poet-in-residence.

Randall's poems ('quiet, reflective, and somewhat formal in structure') are found in many of the new anthologies and magazines. 'Booker T. and W.E.B.' first appeared in 1952 in the *Midwest Journal*: poem and author were discovered years later by Rosey Pool, who set Randall writing again and made the poem an anthology favourite. The equally popular 'Ballad of Birmingham' opened a series of broadsides in September 1965, which has since grown to forty-five pieces by a large and varied number of (mainly young) black poets, and which has also become the foundation of Broadside Press, the most important black press in America, run by Randall from his home in Detroit. Randall's own account of the press's development can be found in the first issue of *Black Academy Review* (1970).

Broadside's first full-scale book was the remarkable anthology *For Malcolm: poems on the life and death of Malcolm X* (1967) which Dudley Randall edited with Margaret G. Burroughs. In 1969 he compiled an equally programmatic collection, called *Black poetry:*

a supplement to anthologies which exclude black poets. In addition to these, Randall has authored four books of poetry: *Poem counter-poem* (1966) together with Margaret Danner; *Cities burning* (1968) which, like many of the Broadside books, is also available on tape, in a complete reading by the author; *Love you* which in 1970 became volume ten in the Heritage series (for which he acts as American distributor), and *More to remember* which collected the 'poems of four decades' in 1972. An illuminating interview appeared in the December 1971 issue of *Black World*.

In 1966 Dudley Randall found time to visit Paris, Prague and the Soviet Union with a delegation of black artists (his trans-lations of Russian poetry have been praised) and in 1970 he went to Ghana, Togo and Dahomey.

The southern road

There the black river, boundary to hell,
And here the iron bridge, the ancient car,
And grim conductor, who with surly yell
Forbids white soldiers where the black ones are.
And I re-live the enforced avatar
Of desperate journey to a savage abode
Made by my sires before another war;
And I set forth upon the southern road.

To a land where shadowed songs like flowers swell
And where the earth is scarlet as a scar
Friezed by the bleeding lash that fell (O fell)
Upon my fathers' flesh. O far, far, far
And deep my blood has drenched it. None can bar
My birthright to the loveliness bestowed
Upon this country haughty as a star.
And I set forth upon the southern road.

This darkness and these mountains loom a spell
Of peak-roofed town where yearning steeples soar
And the holy holy chanting of a bell
Shakes human incense on the throbbing air
Where bonfires blaze and quivering bodies char.
Whose is the hair that crisped, and fiercely glowed?
I know it; and my entrails melt like tar
And I set forth upon the southern road.

O fertile hillsides where my fathers are,
From which my griefs like troubled streams have flowed,
I have to love you, though they sweep me far.
And I set forth upon the southern road.

Owen Dodson

was born in 1914 in Brooklyn, N.Y., where he attended school before going to Bates College (D.Litt. 1967) and finally Yale, where two of his early plays, *Divine comedy* and *Garden of time*, were first produced. The theatre has remained his first interest ever since: he has taught drama at Spelman, was commissioned to write a play on the Amistad mutiny for Talladega, directed summer theatre at Hampton Institute, the Theatre Lobby Washington and at Lincoln University in Missouri, then joined the staff of Howard, taking the Howard Players on a successful Scandinavian–German tour in 1949. Eventually he became head of Howard's drama department, where he remained until 1969 when he moved back to New York and produced a multi-media 'cultural history of the black presence in America' called *The dream awake* (Spoken Arts 1969).

Dodson's two books of poetry are *Powerful long ladder* in 1946, reprinted in 1970, and *The confession stone* (volume 13 in the Heritage series, 1970). He also writes short stories, verse plays (including one in collaboration with his great friend Countee Cullen), and novels (*Boy at the window* was published in 1951). With Mark Fax as composer he also wrote two operas, *A Christmas miracle* and the abandoned Howard Centenary opera. Both his poetry and his theatre work show a keen ear for speech patterns, but Dodson remains a rather isolated loner who wrestles with strong personal emotions rather than be tempted to voice mass conflict in a folk idiom.

For Edwin R. Embree

In countries where no birds are alive
Time bleeds into dreams children have
Of green sweet days of spring,
Of lollypops and kites.

In towns where all the shadows
Are in different places and the seasons
Of our thoughts have changed, killing
Whatever bloomed before in freedom and love,
Men hug blighted night:
Night covers their own damage:
They dream with torn blankets over their heads.

In a cabin where her sons are represented
By gold stars,
A black mother hears the present circumstance
In Tennessee or Georgia,
Sits in her rocking chair
And cracks her knuckles while she prays.

Time bleeds, shadows shift, knuckles crack.
Winter cancels spring, summer and fall.
Despair rises first thing every morning
And goes about his business
Ringing doorbells, calling: Howdy-do!

What we answer is our salvation or our end:
Some cry: I've been expecting you,
                    the coffee's on the stove.
                    The children are washing
                    behind their ears.
                    Take a seat; sit down.

They are lost before the first shine of the new sun.

Time bleeds, shadows shift, knuckles crack –
But there is a time of healing coming
When shadows will shift to normal,
A time of bright birds

And children without blood spotting their dreams:
Because there are still men whose hearts
Bear the large optimistic burden of freedom and peace:
Men who rise up early
And labor through the day for other men.

Time bleeds, shadows shift
But there is a time of healing coming
Because these men of strength are with us.

Ray Durem

was born in Seattle on 30 January 1915, received little formal
education, ran away from home at fourteen and joined the Navy
while well under age for admittance. He came of age in Spain in
1937, during the civil war, as a member of the International
Brigade. He started writing in the late forties, and some of his
work appeared a little later in the *Crusader*, whose editor Robert
Williams had not yet been driven from Monroe into Cuban, and
eventually Chinese, exile. Langston Hughes sent me a batch of
Ray's poems in 1953, thinking England might be a safer climate
for a forerunner of the 'black poetry' of the early sixties. Mean-
while Ray worked in factories, shops, warehouses and the like all
over the West Coast. He enlarged a bit on his education at the
University of California, and was a voracious reader anyway.
Sometimes he worked at his real profession as a television tech-
nician (there was a long spell in Phoenix, Arizona, together with
Chuck Anderson), but around the time his first daughter, Kenya,
was born in 1954, he had moved his family to Mexico to spare his
children the devastating experience of the United States. But one
does not 'commute' between Los Angeles and Guadalajara for
long, and at the time the first major group of Durem's poems
appeared (August 1962, in the anthology *Sixes and sevens*), the
family was back in Los Angeles, where Ray died on 17 December
1963 of a lingering and painful cancer.

The irony of Durem's life was that, descended from what one
can only describe as a mixed family, his appearance was that of a
'white' man – he could not only have 'passed', he was in a way
doing just that by insisting on living black and raising a black
family: his early experiences in Europe and America, and his
belief that indeed 'the hands of history' were about to 'strike
midnight' made it impossible for him to act otherwise. 'The
white man is my brother – his name is Cain.' And in another
much-quoted passage about his own life: 'When I was ten years
   used my fists. When I was thirty-five I used the pen. I hope
   to use the machine-gun.'

Ray Durem wrote well in advance of his generation and the trends of his time: it is sad that he died so much in advance of his own fulfilment. He left a tape recording of his poetry called 'Only their eyes'. The book *Take no prisoners* (Heritage series, volume 17), which very belatedly appeared in 1971, is a sort of 'selected poems' containing nearly all of his best work.

To all the nice white people

This pale skin lets me walk with you,
talk with you,
seduce your women,
listen to your witless conversations,
your cheap and banal music.

Cursed with your hue,
these eyes blue as the blue you worship
watch you with deadly venom,
waiting for a weakness!

Relax, eat well, and chuckle, fat white man.
Rest a little, cushioned by your own
and God's superiority.
Then,
while you sleep and bubble with contentment,
the hands of history strike midnight,
my blue eyes turn to sable,
my black hand reaches for your throat.

The saddest tears . . .

The saddest tears
are a brown girl's tears.
It takes so much to make her cry.

Take her son away,
get him on dope.
Work him in the fields.
Kill him in Korea.
Make him a waiter with a Ph.D.

She'll smile that special, bitter smile,
through the brown mask she uses for a shield,
and the tears will flow, but deep inside,
and blood red.

Take her man away,
work her in your big house.
Let her ride the streetcars.
Make her share her kitchen.
Give her a mortgage, takes a thousand days to pay.
She'll pay it.
Give her a sentence, takes a thousand nights to serve.
She'll serve it.

Paddy, you'll never wring a tear from her,
'cause she's the Queen
of Misery!

She won't cry for you,
but she'll weep for me.

Broadminded

Some of my best friends are white boys.
When I meet 'em,
I treat 'em
just the same as if they was people.

Margaret Walker

(or, in full, Margaret Abigail Walker Alexander) was born in Birmingham, Alabama, on 7 July 1915 and has remained in the Deep South practically all her life. A minister's daughter, she attended methodist church schools in Meridian, Mississippi, and in her native town. She graduated from Gilbert Academy in New Orleans in 1930, then attended Northwestern University. In the late thirties she was a member of the Chicago Writers' Project (at the same time as Richard Wright). In 1940 she obtained her M.A. at Iowa State, where she attended Paul Engle's workshop. Apart from some time spent on social work in New Orleans, Miss Walker has always been in teaching. She started at Livingstone College, Salisbury, North Carolina in 1940, and published her first book *For my people* in 1942 at the end of her two-year stay there. The book appeared in the Yale Series of Younger Poets, had a preface by Stephen Vincent Benét who was then editor of the series, and met with a great deal of critical acclaim. Although Margaret Walker has been writing since she was about thirteen, she has published little. Occasionally a poem appeared in *Poetry*, *Opportunity* or the *Negro Digest*. *Poetry* had published the title poem of her first book as early as 1937.

From 1942, for one year, Margaret Walker taught at West Virginia State College, following this by a year on a Rosenwald Fellowship. Since 1945 she has been on the staff of the Jackson (Mississippi) State College. She is married, and has four children, evenly divided over the sexes. Bringing up a black family in the South and coping with the demands of running English courses in what is still the most backward state of the nation at the same time, is a formidable task for anyone – but frail and fragile looking Margaret Walker is a formidable woman, and the voice with which she reads some of her poems (including 'For my people') on Folkways FP 91-1 packs a lot of power behind its deceptive high pitch. Her tribute to Mary McLeod Bethune, founder of e-Cookman College and of the National Council of Women, which dates from the late forties, is clearly a reflection on militant black womanhood in general, and Margaret Walker, in a less flamboyant way, is as much its representative as was Ms Bethune.

The grand-scale epic novel *Jubilee*, which appeared in 1966, was written 'in lieu of a dissertation' for a Ph.D. *Come down from yonder mountain* had preceded it in 1962. In 1970 Broadside Press brought out a new book of poetry called *Prophets for a new day*. Paula Giddings wrote a sympathetic essay on Margaret Walker for the December 1971 issue of *Black World*: 'A shoulder hunched against a sharp concern'.

For my people

For my people everywhere singing their slave songs repeat-
edly: their dirges and their ditties and their blues and
jubilees, praying their prayers nightly to an unknown
god, bending their knees humbly to an unseen power;

For my people lending their strength to the years, to the gone
years and the now years and the maybe years, washing
ironing cooking scrubbing sewing mending hoeing
plowing digging planting pruning patching dragging
along never gaining never reaping never knowing
and never understanding;

For my playmates in the clay and dust and sand of Alabama
backyards playing baptizing and preaching and doc-
tor and jail and soldier and school and mama and
cooking and playhouse and concert and store and hair
and Miss Choomby and company;

For the cramped bewildered years we went to school to learn
to know the reasons why and the answers to and the

people who and the places where and the days when, in memory of the bitter hours when we discovered we were black and poor and small and different and nobody cared and nobody wondered and nobody understood;

For the boys and girls who grew in spite of these things to be man and woman, to laugh and dance and sing and play and drink their wine and religion and success, to marry their playmates and bear children and then die of consumption and anemia and lynching;

For my people thronging 47th Street in Chicago and Lenox Avenue in New York and Rampart Street in New Orleans, lost disinherited dispossessed and happy people filling the cabarets and taverns and other people's pockets needing bread and shoes and milk and land and money and something – something all our own;

For my people walking blindly spreading joy, losing time being lazy, sleeping when hungry, shouting when burdened, drinking when hopeless, tied and shackled and tangled among ourselves by the unseen creatures who tower over us omnisciently and laugh;

For my people blundering and groping and floundering in the dark of churches and schools and clubs and societies, associations and councils and committees and conventions, distressed and disturbed and deceived and devoured by money-hungry glory-craving leeches, preyed on by facile force of state and fad and novelty, by false prophet and holy believer;

For my people standing staring trying to fashion a better
        way from confusion, from hypocrisy and misunder-
        standing, trying to fashion a world that will hold all
        the people, all the faces, all the adams and eves and
        their countless generations;

Let a new earth rise. Let another world be born. Let a bloody
        peace be written in the sky. Let a second generation
        full of courage issue forth; let a people loving free-
        dom come to growth. Let a beauty full of healing
        and strength of final clenching be the pulsing in our
        spirits and our blood. Let the martial songs be written,
        let the dirges disappear. Let a race of men now rise
        and take control.

For Mary McLeod Bethune

Great Amazon of God behold your bread
washed home again from many distant seas.
The cup of life you lift contains no less,
no bitterness to mock you. In its stead
this sparkling chalice many souls has fed,
and broken hearted people on their knees
lift up their eyes and suddenly they seize
on living faith, and they are comforted.

Believing in the people who are free,
who walk, uplifted in an honest way,
you look at last upon another day
that you have fought with God and men to see.
Great Amazon of God behold your bread.
We walk with you and we are comforted.

Eric M. Roach

was born on Tobago in 1915. After his studies he became a teacher, but military service during the Second World War interrupted this career and after the war he changed to the civil service in his native Tobago, then switched to journalism in Trinidad during the 1960s. He has never published a volume of his own, but was a regular contributor to *Bim* and the *Caribbean Quarterly* until about 1962. His work appears in most of the West Indian anthologies.

'I am the archipelago' remains one of the most complete expressions of the middle generation of West Indian writers, intensely preoccupied with their middle position in both time and place, and in the case of Roach especially with the intricate complications of race and ancestry: 'My whole history is my immediate family, and dimly seen behind the parents, the generations of heavy slave folk trampled into the clay where the sweet cane prospered in our bitter sweat.'

I am the archipelago

I am the archipelago hope
Would mould into dominion; each hot green island
Buffeted, broken by the press of tides
And all the tales come mocking me
Out of the slave plantations where I grubbed
Yam and cane; where heat and hate sprawled down
Among the cane – my sister sired without
Love or law. In that gross bed was bred
The third estate of colour. And now
My language, history and my names are dead
And buried with my tribal soul. And now
I drown in the groundswell of poverty

No love will quell. I am the shanty town,
Banana, sugarcane and cotton man;
Economies are soldered with my sweat
Here, everywhere; in hate's dominion;
In Congo, Kenya, in free, unfree America.

I herd in my divided skin
Under a monomaniac sullen sun
Disnomia deep in artery and marrow.
I burn the tropic texture from my hair;
Marry the mongrel woman or the white;
Let my black spinster sisters tend the church,
Earn meagre wages, mate illegally,
Breed secret bastards, murder them in womb;
Their fate is written in unwritten law,
The vogue of colour hardened into custom
In the tradition of the slave plantation.
The cock, the totem of his craft, his luck,
The obeahman infects me to my heart
Although I wear my Jesus on my breast
And burn a holy candle for my saint.
I am a shaker and a shouter and a myal man;
My voodoo passion swings sweet chariots low.

My manhood died on the imperial wheels
That bound and ground too many generations;
From pain and terror and ignominy
I cower in the island of my skin,
The hot unhappy jungle of my spirit
Broken by my haunting foe my fear,
The jackal after centuries of subjection.
But now the intellect must outrun time
Out of my lost, through all man's future years,
Challenging Atalanta for my life,

To die or live a man in history,
My totem also on the human earth.
O drummers, fall to silence in my blood
You thrum against the moon; break up the rhetoric
Of these poems I must speak. O seas,
O Trades, drive wrath from destinations.

Samuel W. Allen

was born in 1917, at Columbus in Ohio. He studied creative writing at Fisk under James Weldon Johnson, then went to the Harvard Law School. His wartime military service brought him to Europe after the war, under the terms of the G.I. Bill. In Paris, where he attended the Sorbonne, he became a friend of Richard Wright, who introduced him to the *Présence Africaine* circle. His first published poems appeared in *Présence Africaine* in 1949 (two poems in issue number 6, and three in number 7), and his unusually early awareness of what Senghor dubbed 'négritude' dates from this early exposure.

Back in the States, Allen went to the New School for Social Research in New York, then embarked on a long legal career in New York, where he was an assistant District Attorney, and then in Washington, D.C., first for the United States Information Agency, later with the Community Relations Service of the Department of Justice. His interest in Pan-Africa and négritude remained: he translated Sartre's 'Orphée nègre' essay into English in 1951, and wrote an article on 'Tendencies in African poetry' (*Présence Africaine* special, 'Africa seen by American Negroes', 1958) which is almost wholly devoted to francophone poetry. In 1962 he edited *Pan-Africanism reconsidered* for the same publishers. In 1968 Sam Allen left the law for literature; for two years he was poet-in-residence at Tuskegee, then went to Boston University.

His published poems are few. One of the earliest ones ('A moment please') has become an anthology classic, and his first book of poems was something of a 'cause célèbre' as one of the earliest collections of black poetry first published outside the United States. The book, *Elfenbeinzähne – ivory tusks*, appeared at Heidelberg, Germany, in 1956, and is bilingual throughout, with facing-page translations by Janheinz Jahn, the father of neo-African bibliography. As in all his early work, Allen used the pseudonym Paul Vesey for the book, and he also supplied a somewhat mythical background for the Vesey identity, which does not quite correspond to the character and reality of Sam Allen: born in 1913, reared in Michigan, itinerant worker (Ford amongst others) and self-educated in 'planlosen Abendkursen' – the classic pattern for the presentation of black writers since the twenties (in Japan they even now stick a jazz musician on the cover of Owen Dodson's novel in lieu of the author's portrait – obviously to the Japanese all blacks look alike). The whole thing reminds me strongly of Lucy Terry's lines: 'Young Samuel Allen, oh! lack-a-day, was taken and carried to Canada.' To confuse the issue further, Allen has published a second book of poems under an almost identical title (*Ivory tusks and other poems*, Poets Press 1968) but under his real name and with an almost wholly new selection of poems (only four are duplicated from the earlier book and the title poem appeared in the earlier book under an entirely different name!). In October 1969 the *Negro Digest* published a group of four recent poems and a book of hitherto unpublished poetry is scheduled to appear in the Heritage series, probably as *Paul Vesey's ledger*.

The staircase

'Abide with me
Fast falls the eventide
The darkness deepens
Lord, with me abide.'

The staircase mounts to his eternity –
the rotted floor, the dripping faucet
all now abide with him;
the cracked ceiling, the rusted bed in his dark squalid chamber
    abide with him now
in the hour that is upon him.

The balance is tenuous
as his twin comes running after

the infant he let go, unprotected –
   the hail of steel, stopped for a moment, lurks in the
   shadows.

The staircase turns and panting turns –
the completely vile woman assails him
throwing livid screams from her den
far up the dark filthy hallway
until she hears the twin come running after
   and falls sobbing and senseless to her knees.

A massive form stands out against the sky –
Come – Death – come!
Take me away.

The hail of steel begins . . .

Divestment

If I could know who held the cold iron there
and branded her in blood
and singed her hair with serpents singing
   coiling wraiths of flame
I could tell better where my father's shadow moans tonight
I could tell better where he moans.

If I could know where bird beaked span
   stretched huge from stone to monolithic stone
where died my mother's horrid thought in fright
upon the lumbering mountainside
I would know better where the sheath should drop
to spring the shimmering steel.

If I could tell in what dark closet, buffeted and tight
they locked my hope with monkey cock and snake
and what pale reason shrouds my soul tonight
I could then know
I could know what my need must know to feel.

Gwendolyn Brooks

is easily the most interesting of the early generation of female black poets. Both her work and her basic attitude to life and letters have remained remarkably constant. The gentle irony which pervades so much of her work and the ever-so-distant note on which she reads her poetry (a generous selection appeared on Folkways FP 91-1) seem like the outer defences of a total vulnerability and a warm and equally total generosity, which perhaps explain Miss Brooks's extraordinary dual position as the official 'poet laureate' of the state of Illinois (she succeeded Carl Sandburg in 1968) and as the militant mother of a whole generation of black poets (especially the women) in and around Chicago. A tributary anthology of work by pupils and admirers was published in 1971 as *To Gwen with love*.

Born 7 June 1917 in Topeka, Kansas, Gwendolyn Brooks has lived in Chicago all her life. She attended Englewood High until 1934, graduated from Wilson Junior College in 1936. She married Henry Blakely in 1939, and has two children, a son and a daughter. In 1940 she joined the poetry-writing class of Inez Cunningham Stark, but her writing had started long before that: she had been sending out poems since she was about twelve but 'not until I was twenty-one or twenty-two did I write any poems that I should want seen today'. Her first book of poetry, *A street in Bronzeville*, was published by Harper's in 1945. Book and author were a great success: the one won an award from the Academy of Arts and Letters, the other appeared as one of the ten 'women of the year' in Mademoiselle magazine. Before publication of the book Gwendolyn Brooks had already carried off four successive poetry awards from the Midwestern Writers Conference annual workshops, and these were but the beginning of a long list of honours, including two Guggenheim fellowships, and culminating in a Pulitzer for her second book of poetry, *Annie Allen*. Her next book was a novel called *Maud Martha* (1953), but after that only poetry has appeared, in an ever-growing number of periodicals, in broadcasts and personal appearances, and in five more books: *Bronzeville*

boys and girls in 1956; *The bean eaters* in 1960; the long narrative
compilation on life in a Chicago tenement, *In the Mecca*, in 1968;
and two books from Dudley Randall's Broadside Press: *Riot* in
1969 and *Family pictures* in 1970. Her *Selected poems* appeared in
1963. There are also several broadsides and single-poem pamphlets,
including *Blackstreet* and the much-quoted *We real cool* in Dudley
Randall's original series, and *In the time of detachment, in the time of
the cold* which appeared in a signed and limited edition in 1965.
In 1971 a bumper crop of Brooks material was released: *Jump
bad* (a Chicago anthology), *The world of Gwendolyn Brooks*,
Aloneness (a very slight illustrated juvenile), *A Broadside Treasury*
(fifty authors from Dudley Randall's stable), and the first issue of
her own semi-annual magazine *The Black Position*. The auto-
biography *Report from part one* has been announced for 1972.

During most of the last three decades Gwendolyn Brooks has
been teaching creative writing, in a succession of Chicago schools
(Columbia, Elmhurst, N. E. Illinois State College) and in her own
workshop for young black writers. She has instituted several
competitions (for which she invariably donates the cash prizes)
and by now the Gwendolyn Brooks Award has become a coveted
annual honour with a fair amount of publicity organized through
the Chicago-based *Negro Digest* (now *Black World*) magazine. In
1971 she commuted from Chicago to take up a teaching post at
the College of the City of New York. She is planning to edit an
annual compilation of 'fundamental statements' by black authors
under the title *Black position*.

Jessie Mitchell's mother

Into her mother's bedroom to wash the ballooning body.
'My mother is jelly-hearted and she has a brain of jelly:
Sweet, quiver-soft, irrelevant. Not essential.
Only a habit would cry if she should die.
A pleasant sort of fool without the least iron . . .

Are you better, mother, do you think it will come today?'
The stretched yellow rag that was Jessie Mitchell's mother
reviewed her. Young, and so thin, and so straight.
So straight! as if nothing could ever bend her.
But poor men would bend her, and doing things with poor
    men,
being much in bed, and babies would bend her over,
and the rent of things in life that were for poor women,
coming to them grinning and pretty with intent to bend and
    to kill.
Comparisons shattered her heart, ate at her bulwarks:
the shabby and the bright: she, almost hating her daughter,
crept into an old sly refuge: 'Jessie's black
and her way will be black, and jerkier even than mine.
Mine, in fact, because I was lovely, had flowers
tucked in the jerks, flowers were here and there . . .'
She revived for the moment settled and dried-up triumphs,
forced perfume into old petals, pulled up the droop,
refueled
triumphant long-exhaled breaths.
Her exquisite yellow youth . . .

Malcolm X

for Dudley Randall

Original.
Hence ragged-round,
Hence rich-robust.

He had the hawk-man's eyes.
We gasped. We saw the maleness.
The maleness raking out and making guttural the air
And pushing us to walls.

And in a soft and fundamental hour
A sorcery devout and vertical
Beguiled the world.

He opened us –
Who was a key.

Who was a man.

Myron O'Higgins

is a native of Chicago, born in 1918, who, after a very brief spell
as a writer and with only half a book to his credit, disappeared
out of the public eye and out of print altogether. He was educated
at denominational schools in Chicago and obtained an M.A. from
Howard where he studied under Sterling Brown and later taught
for a short while. He spent most of the Second World War in
the Army, and after that had a year on a Rosenwald fellowship
and a year as special research assistant at Fisk. In 1948 he published
a collection of poems together with Robert Hayden (who was
then teaching at Fisk): *The lion and the archer* became the first
volume in Hayden's Counterpoise series. After graduate work at
Yale, fellowships to the University of Mexico and to the Sor-
bonne, and extensive travel in Europe, Myron O'Higgins became
curator for a private art collection in the Midwest in 1958. His
poem 'Vaticide', occasioned by the assassination of Gandhi, is an
interesting early instance of identification with the broader issues
of what is now generally called the third world. It first appeared
in a special 'American Negro' issue of *United Asia* in 1953.

Vaticide

. . . he is murdered upright in the day
his flesh is opened and displayed . . .

Into that stricken hour the hunted had gathered.
You spoke . . . some syllable of terror. *Ram!*
They saw it slip from your teeth and dangle, ablaze
Like a diamond on your mouth.
In that perilous place you fell – extinguished.
The instrument, guilt. The act was love.

Now they have taken your death to their rooms
And here in this far city a false Spring
Founders in the ruins of your quiet flesh
And deep in your marvellous wounds
The sun burns down
And the seas return to their imagined homes.

Peter Abrahams

was born in Johannesburg, South Africa, in 1919, from an
Ethiopian father and a Cape-coloured mother. His middle name
of Henry he has long discarded, along with almost everything
else that at some stage or other he felt to be cluttering his path.
He attended St Peter's College for a while, but otherwise is largely
self-educated. In 1939 he decided to leave South Africa and go to
England; he took a job as stoker on a freighter, but due to the
outbreak of war it took him two years to reach his destination.
The rest of the war years he spent in London, where he married
a militant white socialist librarian. In 1945 he served as publicity
secretary to the Fifth Pan-African Congress held in Manchester
(George Padmore and Kwame Nkrumah were joint political
secretaries, Jomo Kenyatta their assistant).

Within a year of his arrival in England, Allen & Unwin pub-
lished Peter Abrahams's first novel, *Dark testament*, the beginning
of an astonishingly creative decade during which a succession of
novels and short stories (the latter still mostly unpublished)
gradually released the author's childhood pressures, political ideas
and social insights, to create the first consistent group of black
South African writing. *Song of the city* in 1943, *Mine boy* in 1946,
both published by Dorothy Crisp; *The path of thunder* and *Wild
conquest* from Harper's in 1948 and 1950; then *Return to Goli* and
Tell freedom from Faber's in 1953 and 1959. *A wreath for Udomo*
closed this volcanic period in 1956.

Since then, Peter Abrahams has published little, and nothing
that approaches the violent intensity of his earlier work. He left
his first wife, exhausted his first great fire, and abandoned the
grey mists of England for the more generous West Indies in 1957.
He served as a roving correspondent for several papers for a while,
then settled in Jamaica as editor of the West Indian *Economist*. His
travel sketches and mood pieces appeared in magazines like *Holiday*
and *Esquire*, and as early as 1957 he did a book on *Jamaica: an island
mosaic*. The only novels of this later period seem to be *A night of
their own*, in 1964, and *This island, now* in 1967.

While still in South Africa, in the dim years before 1939 (and consequently before his twentieth birthday), Abrahams had written poetry, and published two small books of it. The first one, *Here, friend*, I have never been able to trace: it is mentioned, however, in the preface to his second, *A blackman speaks of freedom!*, which appeared in Durban, probably in 1938, with a handsome, incredibly young and vulnerable portrait of the author, and a foreword by Ishmael Meer. It had a note saying, 'This stuff is copyrighted, but not for any worker, white or black, who might be able to make use of it in any way possible.' Ten years later, in some autobiographical fragments on his years in South Africa published in *Présence Africaine* (NS 5 and 6, 1948–9), Abrahams referred to his early verse as 'bad poetry but a true picture'. It is in that spirit that I have included the following fragment.

Fancies idle

iii

Mine dumps of the Rand.
These pyramids speak hands
Torn and bleeding,
Black, hard, rocky,
Like the black earth, wind-swept and touched by time
To leave
Torn nails and twisted thumbs
And missing spaces where the first and third fingers lived.
These pyramids speak eyes
Turned dim by gas and semi-blindness by day,
Deep, thousands of feet deep in the heart of the ocean-like
    earth,
Then daylight
And the hardness of the sun to turn them dim.
These pyramids speak lungs,

Tortured and touched with the coat of death,
Daily piling up layer upon layer
And wrecking the soul in a lung tearing cough,
Hour by hour with the passing of the night.
These pyramids speak bitterness
Of black men,
Thousands of black men, wrenched from their mother-earth,
And turned to gold-makers for the wealth of the earth
That grant them not the right of human thought.
These pyramids
Scattered over the body of the Rand,
Mighty in their grandeur and aloofness,
Monuments of the Twentieth Century Pharaohs,
Speak the world,
Not thousands of black men,
But millions of toilers,
Welded into a rock of firm aloofness,
Like them, made of the soul of suffering;
These pyramids are the symbol of revolt!

Ezekiel Mphahlele

is both compatriot and contemporary to Peter Abrahams; he, too, was born in South Africa (Pretoria) in 1919. He seems to have started life as a tribal herd boy, but attended St Peter's College in Johannesburg for three years, and finally obtained a teacher's certificate from Adam's College in Natal. For four years he worked as a clerk at a Johannesburg high school. He also worked for the remarkably successful *Drum* magazine, and gradually his ideas and articles developed to the point where he received the only government award of merit given to black writers: a ban from teaching. By that time his first collection of short stories had appeared under the title *Man must live* (1946).

In 1957 Mphahlele left South Africa with his wife and their three children. First he taught English at Ibadan University in Nigeria, later he moved to Paris where he ran the African programme of the Congress for Cultural Freedom. In 1966 he taught English literature at University College in Nairobi, and since 1967 he has been a lecturer in English at the University of Denver, Colorado, in the United States.

Meanwhile, several more books have appeared from his hand. *Down second avenue* (1959) is his much-translated autobiography. *The living and the dead* (1961) and *In corner B* (1967) contain more of his stories. *The African image* (1962) is a collection of political and literary essays. Mphahlele also edited a very rewarding anthology of *African writing today* for Penguin Books in 1967 and published a novel called *The wanderers* in 1971. *Voices in the wilderness* (1972) is another collection of essays.

Death

You want to know?
My mother died at 45
at 42 my brother followed.

You want to know?
She cleaned the houses of white folk,
and washed their bodily dirt
out of the baths.
One night a coma took her,
and he –
cancer hounded him two years
and rolled him in the dust.
You want to know?
My grandma left at 80,
she also washed her years away
and saw them flow
into the drain
with the white man's scum.
Many more from our tree have fallen –
known and unknown.

. . . and that white colossus
he was butchered by a man
they say is mad.

How often do I dream
my dearest dead stand across a river –
small and still I cannot traverse
to join them
and I try to call to them
and they wave and smile so distantly
receding beyond the water
that pulls me in
and spits me out into the dawn of the living.

. . . and he was butchered
like a buffalo
after overseeing many a negro's execution.

You want to know –
why do I say all this?
what have they to do with us
the ones across the water?
How should I know?
These past two decades
death has been circling closer
and beating the air about me
like a flight of vultures
in a cruel age
when instruments of torture
can be found with any fool and tyrant,
churchman, all alike,
all out to tame the heretic, they say.

. . . and they tell us
when that colossus fell
he did not even have a triple-worded
Roman chance.

And so to kill a bug
they set a house on fire
to kill a fire
they flood a country
to save a country
drench the land in blood
to peg the frontiers of their colour madness
they'll herd us into ghettoes
jail us
kill us slowly
because we are the Attribute
that haunts their dreams
because *they* are the blazing neon lights
that will not let us be

because we are the children of their Sin
they'll try to erase the evidence
because their deeds are howling from a fog
beyond their reach.

. . . and we laughed and danced
when news came of the death of that colossus
– the death of a beast of prey.

What can we do with the ashes of a tyrant?
who will atone?
whose blood will pay for those of us who went
down under the tanks of fire?
And voices cried, 'It's not enough,
a tyrant dead is not enough!'
Vengeance is mine and yours and his,
says the testament of man
nailed to the boulder of pain.

. . . and they say the butcher's mad
who sank the knife into the tyrant's neck
while the honourable men
who rode his tanks of fire
looked on
as if they never heard of giants die
as they had lived,
and all about the frog who burst
when he pushed his energy
beyond the seams of his own belly.

What if I go as the unknown soldier
or attended by a buzzing fly?
what if my carcass were soaked in organ music,
or my ancestors had borne me home?

I hear already
echoes from a future time of voices
coming from a wounded bellowing multitude
cry, 'Who will atone
Who will atone?'

You want to know? –
because I nourish
a deadly life within
my madness shall have blood.

Lance Jeffers

is the one most neglected figure in the generation of writers (Hayden, Brooks, Walker and a number of lesser talents) that came into its own at the beginning of the Second World War. He was born 28 November 1919 at Fremont in Nebraska, went to school at Stromsberg in that same state, and later in San Francisco. California seems to have remained his basic home ever since, although his teaching posts make it doubtful whether he has spent much consecutive time there. After serving as an officer during the war years Jeffers attended Columbia University from which he holds a B.A. (Honours) and an M.A. Since then he has been an influential teacher with an attendant in-cult following. At Howard he was the mentor of the Dasein group which (through Percy Johnston's perseverance) still hangs together around an occasional magazine: nine issues in as many years since 1961. It was Percy Johnston who first published a substantial number of Jeffers's poems, in his anthology *Burning spear* in 1963. Since that time Jeffers has taught at Morehouse in Atlanta, California State at Long Beach, at Indiana University (the Kokomo campus) and at Tuskegee. His poetry has appeared in magazines like *Phylon* and the *Tamarack Review*, and the continuing in-cult did, at least, result in two more groups of poems in anthologies: a very good group of five in Quincy Troupe's *Watts poets* of 1968; and a very large group which very nearly redeems the general dreariness of R. Baird Shuman's collection *Nine black poets*, also in 1968. Very belatedly, his first book of poems appeared towards the end of 1970 when Broadside published *My blackness is the beauty of this land*. Jeffers is now chairman of the English department at Bowie State College at Maryland.

Myself

My mother was stripped of her morning breasts,
my father's intestines leaked through the wound in his navel-
     door,
my grandmother was stern as a virgin upon the gallows,
my grandfather gathered whole counties in his arm,
     flung a million seeds of healing from his hand:
my slave greatgrandfather was grim upon his hoe,
     watched through eyes of hatred the livid whites,
my slave greatgrandmother was black and limp on her bed
     of snow:
     master stood over her as if she were a deer he had shot
     while he returned his penis to the holster at his hip

That woman rebuked and scorned

That woman who rebuked and scorned
washes dishes for a pittance in a restaurant kitchen
where her blackness and her hair short and kinky like a man's
will not be seen by the welldressed the wellspoken and the
     clean:
her face rough and mottled
her skirt and blouse cheap and stained
her face flat and thicklipped
her eyes red and her shambling walk along the sidewalk
her eyes startled pleading to be loved,

I stand before you in your bedroom,
silently I take your face between my hands:

to the unbelieving inquiry of your eyes I am silent:
I am the giver to your sweetness never courted,
your beauty this day I am bequeathed.

I lay the hardened layers of my skin down at your feet,
and when you slowly move my hand between your thighs,
in the spring of your astonished love I am reborn.

James A. Emanuel

(the A. stands for Andrew) is another Nebraskan, like Jeffers: he was born at Alliance on 14 June 1921, and completed his education there through high school. After school he became secretary to Brigadier-General Davis at the War Office, 1942-4, then spent the rest of the war in the Pacific service, until 1946. In the early forties he wrote some stories, and in the Pacific he wrote a few poems, but most of his early work he has since destroyed: a few poems survive in the *America sings* anthologies for 1946-9. By the time he received his B.A. from Howard (in 1950) he had completed a novel, which still remains unpublished. Emanuel married in 1950, and became a supervisor in the civil service of Chicago where he remained until 1952. The following year he took his M.A. at nearby Northwestern, then went to New York as an instructor at the Y.W.C.A. business school. Since 1957 he has been a lecturer in the English department at City College (now the City University), New York, breaking his run there for a year at Grenoble, France, from 1968-9.

A dissertation on the short stories of Langston Hughes, which obtained Emanuel's Ph.D. from Columbia in 1962, was later extended into the fuller study, *Langston Hughes*, which appeared shortly after its subject's death in Twayne's United States Authors series. Literary criticism has always been a favourite vehicle for the expression of Emanuel's ideas: he writes book reviews, he introduced the first course in negro poetry at City College, and it was announced some time ago that he would edit a series of studies in black literature for Broadside Press in Detroit under the title of *Broadside critics*. Broadside have already brought out his first book of poetry, *The treehouse*, in 1968. It is accompanied, as are several other books of that press, by a tape-recording of the author reading the entire contents of the book. In the same year, Emanuel and Th. L. Gross published an anthology entitled *Dark symphony: Negro literature in America*. A second book of poetry, *Panther man* (1970), is 'special for the reflection of personal, racially meaningful predicaments and events' – a new departure in

Emanuel's writing which needed the distance of the French Alps to come to the fore. 'Black humor' was one of its earliest expressions.

Black humor

for Etha

Outshouting bathwater,
whitefaced with soap,
behind me doorbursting,
'BOO!' right at my ear you jumped,
hopping to crouch and grin as
'DAMN!' went coffee sloshing.

'White folks scareya, hunh?'
Black only growled,
but soapface pranced and crowed
'think white!' 'think snow!'
till sip of coffee made the chuckle
'wash your face'
though dried to melancholy at the sign
of white so deftly brown again.

Final sip was 'All depends
which room you're in, I guess;
just don't come up behind me;
makes me nervous since the war';
    but didn't say when war began
    nor dare count all those faces,
    clean and white,
      that came up from behind.

Gabriel Okara

or, in full, Gabriel Imomotime Gbaingbaing Okara, was born in 1921 at Bumodi in the Ijaw country of the Niger delta – in that part of Nigeria which gained short-lived attention as Biafra. He was educated at the Government College at Umuahia, trained and practised as a bookbinder, later went into the civil service at Enugu. He is one of the most voracious readers among the writers of present-day Africa, and his studies are by no means confined to the literature of the West or of acculturation. His knowledge of Ijaw folklore, for instance, is wide and deep, and his translations are an important vehicle for making his native culture more accessible. He has been a regular contributor to *Black Orpheus* from the start of that magazine in 1957, and one of his poems in its first issue had previously won the main prize in the Nigerian Festival of the Arts in 1953. In number 13 of *Black Orpheus* he published a fragment of a novel, *Okolo*, which he called 'an attempt to translate Ijaw directly into English' – the problem of finding a way of adequately expressing African thought in the framework of the English language has long been a central theme in his experiments with language.

Okara writes plays and other features for Nigerian radio. His novel, *The voice*, was published in 1964. He has not yet collected any of his poetry into a volume of his own.

You laughed and laughed and laughed

In your ears my song
is motor car misfiring
stopping with a choking cough;
and you laughed and laughed and laughed.

In your eyes my ante-
natal walk was inhuman passing
your 'omnivorous understanding'
and you laughed and laughed and laughed.

You laughed at my song
you laughed at my walk.

Then I danced my magic dance
to the rhythm of talking
drums pleading, but you shut your
eyes and laughed and laughed and laughed.

And then I opened my mystic
inside wide like
the sky, instead you entered your
car and laughed and laughed and laughed.

You laughed at my dance
you laughed at my inside.

You laughed and laughed and laughed.
But your laughter was ice-block
laughter and it froze your inside froze
your voice froze your ears
froze your eyes and froze your tongue.

And now it's my turn to laugh;
but my laughter is not
ice-block laughter. For I
know not cars, know not ice-blocks.

My laughter is the fire
of the eye of the sky, the fire

of the earth, the fire of the air
the fire of the seas and the
rivers fishes animals trees
and it thawed your inside,
thawed your voice, thawed your
ears, thawed your eyes, and
thawed your tongue.

So a meek wonder held
your shadow and you whispered:
'Why so?'
And I answered:
'Because my fathers and I
are owned by the living
warmth of the earth
through our naked feet.'

The mystic drum

The mystic drum beat in my inside
and fishes danced in the rivers
and men and women danced on land
to the rhythm of my drum.

But standing behind a tree
with leaves around her waist
she only smiled with a shake of her head.

Still my drum continued to beat,
rippling the air with quickened
tempo compelling the quick
and the dead to dance and sing
with their shadows –

But standing behind a tree
with leaves around her waist
she only smiled with a shake of her head.

Then the drum beat with the rhythm
of the things of the ground
and invoked the eye of the sky
the sun and the moon and the river gods –
and the trees began to dance,
the fishes turned men
and men turned fishes
and things stopped to grow –

But standing behind a tree
with leaves around her waist
she only smiled with a shake of her head.

And then the mystic drum
in my inside stopped to beat –
and men became men,
fishes became fishes
and trees, the sun and the moon
found their places, and the dead
went to the ground and things began to grow.

And behind the tree she stood
with roots sprouting from her
feet and leaves growing on her head
and smoke issuing from her nose
and her lips parted in her smile
turned cavity belching darkness.

Then, then I packed my mystic drum
and turned away; never more to beat so loud.

Basil Clare McFarlane

is a Jamaican. He was born at St Andrew, on 23 April 1922, and, but for an interlude of two years from 1944–6 spent in the R.A.F. in England, he has lived his life on native ground. He attended Jamaica College and Calabar High – but briefly, so that he remained mainly self-educated. He was a journalist from 1939 to 1942 and a civil servant until 1954; his writing has included much film and art criticism. Since 1955 he has been a sub-editor on the Kingston *Daily Gleaner* and more recently a journalist for Radio Jamaica.

His poetry has been appearing, sporadically but regularly, in magazines like *Kyk-over-al*; Arthur Seymour's fabulous Miniature Poets series includes his only published volume, *Jacob and the angel* (May 1952). Janheinz Jahn later included almost the whole of that book in his anthology *Schwarzer Orpheus*, perhaps in an effort to show that there is more to Basil McFarlane than the fact that he happens to be 'the son of J. E. Clare McFarlane, founder of the Poetry League of Jamaica' (which was all his father managed to say in one of his own tedious anthologies).

Poem for my country

I am Jamaica –
And I have seen my children grow
Out of their separate truths;
Out of the absolute truth of me:
Out of my soil
Into false shadows
And I have wept
So
that the strangers with sunglasses
and red faces

who survey my passive sorrow
call me beautiful
and Isle of Springs
And God!
I have no voice
to shout out my disgust
When their vile trappings brush my skin
their filthy coppers reach my children's palms;
These palms: my flesh
my flesh beloved
But where, O where my spirit
where my self my fire?
Lost, I wander through a sunlit night
Beseeching beseeching my belly's result
to turn from other gods
to turn on me
the dawn
of their regard

Jan Carew

or, by his seldom used full name, Jan Alwin Rynveld Carew (a strong Dutch strain there somewhere), was born in Guyana in 1922, in a small village on the east bank of the Demarara River. He received his early instruction from a grandfather who 'ruled and instructed not only the school, but his family and the whole village too'. This redoubtable parent also possessed a large library: 'I read almost all the books in it, and I started writing stories.'

Carew left home at seventeen, just in time to catch the Second World War at slightly closer quarters. He continued his schooling in leaps and bounds throughout the United States and Europe. 'I studied at several universities' (including the one about which Martin Carter wrote so eloquently?) 'and have made my living by writing since. And all the time I have been travelling. I seem to need to travel in the way people need food.' London has served as his home base for most of his adult life, but in the late sixties he settled in Canada and since then he has been teaching at Princeton University in New Jersey.

The earliest publication by Carew that I have come across is his only collection of poetry, a small pamphlet called *Streets of eternity*, published in Guyana in August 1952. Later he became quite successful as a novelist, most of all with *Black Midas* of 1958 which is still being reprinted as a paperback. Also of 1958 is *The wild coast*, which has meanwhile been followed by *The last barbarian* (1961), *Moscow is not my Mecca* (1964) and *Green winter* (1968). The poem I am using here first appeared that last year, in the Marvin X edited issue of the *Journal of Black Poetry*. A new novel has been announced under the title *Cry, black power!*

Africa - Guyana

Labadi, on the Ghana coast
where palm fronds hiss like snakes
and moonlight cheats the dark
of its suzerainty;
palm-wine drinkards lean on moonbeams
listening to surf
roaring in their blood;
the beaches reel
before lips of rising tide edged with spume;
roots are white fangs
bared at the eroding wind and sea;
fisherman in long canoes
part high reefs of foam,
combing the manes of white horses with tridents;
A Fanti dance in a limbo of lagoons;
the stench of mud and crabs in the oleous breeze,
dancers swaying like kites
and Ewe drums talking.
High tide erases my footprints
from Labadi to the Angola coast
and north to El Jadida.
The middle-passage,
the reaches of Sargasso,
Atlantis of the legend,
are tombs for my ancestral bones.
Memories of two motherlands –
Africa – Guyana –
scrawled carelessly with broken spears,
and shattered gourds from which I once drank
buried their tribal secrets in the sand
before my parting.

Africa – Guyana!
Drunk as Boshongo Lords,
palm-wine drinkards chant,
'It was the same mangrove,
the same beaches with wreaths of amber foam,
the same sky, dyed a Berber-blue,
the same white clouds passing before the sun
like processions of marabouts.'

What language shall I speak to the lisping tides?
White worshippers of Kali
have long since tightened silken scarves
around ancestral throats.
Labadi is a name to conjure with.
Palm-wine drinkards sit in magic circles
incanting.
I hear the murmur of my beginnings,
talk to night winds, and tides,
fishermen,
dancing out of a bellows of sea and sky,
hear me speak.
'ABRUNI-MAN! And yet he has my cousin's face,'
they reply.
Our gourds are brimming over.
'I am your cousin's face three centuries away!'
'Where do you hail from again, my brother?'
palm-wine drinkards chorus drunkenly.
GUYANA! AFRICA – GUYANA, THREE CENTURIES AWAY.

Surf, lisping tides,
palm-wine drinkards,
and moonlight casting hard, communal shadows
on white sand
listen indifferently.

Abioseh Nicol

is the pen name of Davidson Sylvester Hector Nicol, who was born at Freetown in Sierra Leone in 1924 and went to the Government Model School and Prince of Wales School in that town. His university education took place in England: he did postgraduate work in biochemistry at Cambridge University from which he already held a medical degree, then took a research post at the London Hospital before going to Nigeria to lecture in physiology at University College, Ibadan.

Nicol has always successfully managed to combine the talents and activities of several people in one person. Since returning to Sierra Leone he has been senior pathologist in his country's medical service, director of the National Bank, and from 1960 the principal of Fourah Bay College which has since become the University College of Sierra Leone. He attended the Unesco conference in Boston in 1961, and has represented his country on several similar diplomatic missions before becoming its permanent representative to the United Nations.

Under his real and professional name, Davidson Nicol has published a lecture *On not being a West African* (1955) and *Africa: a subjective view* (1964). Under his pen name, Oxford University Press brought out two collections of stories in 1965: *The truly married woman* and *Two African tales*. His poems and articles also appear under that name, mostly in the *West African Review*. In 1956 he contributed a survey of West African literature to *Présence Africaine* (NS 8–10, pages 108–21) which ended with these telling sentences: 'Nearly all West African writers are intellectuals, not manual workers; and so their palms are soft. This characteristic and the colour of these palms are two of the things they share with most writers of every nation and race.'

from The meaning of Africa

So I came back
Sailing down the Guinea Coast.
Loving the sophistication
Of your brave new cities:
Dakar, Accra, Cotonou,
Lagos, Bathurst and Bissau;
Liberia, Freetown, Libreville,
Freedom is really in the mind.

Go up-country, so they said,
To see the real Africa.
For whomsoever you may be,
That is where you come from.
Go for bush, inside the bush,
You will find your hidden heart,
Your mute ancestral spirit.
And so I went, dancing on my way.

Now you lie before me passive
With your unanswering green challenge.
Is this all you are?
This long uneven red road, this occasional succession
Of huddled heaps of four mud walls
And thatched, falling grass roofs
Sometimes ennobled by a thin layer
Of white plaster, and covered with thin
Slanting corrugated zinc.
These patient faces on weather-beaten bodies
Bowing under heavy market loads.
The pedalling cyclist wavers by
On the wrong side of the road,
As if uncertain of his new emancipation.

The squawking chickens, the pregnant she-goats
Lumber awkwardly with fear across the road,
Across the windscreen view of my four-cylinder kit car.
An overladen lorry speeds madly towards me
Full of produce, passengers, with driver leaning
Out into the swirling dust to pilot his
Swinging obsessed vehicle along.
Beside him on the raised seat his first-class
Passenger, clutching and timid; but he drives on
At so, so many miles per hour, peering out with
Bloodshot eyes, unshaved face and dedicated look;
His motto painted on each side: Sunshine Transport,
We get you there quick, quick. The Lord is my Shepherd.

The red dust settles down on the green leaves.

I know you will not make me want, Lord,
Though I have reddened your green pastures
It is only because I have wanted so much
That I have always been found wanting.
From South and East, and from my West
(The sandy desert holds the North)
We look across a vast continent
And blindly call it ours.
You are not a country, Africa,
You are a concept,
Fashioned in our minds, each to each,
To hide our separate fears,
To dream our separate dreams.
Only those within you who know
Their circumscribed plot,
And till it well with steady plough
Can from that harvest then look up
To the vast blue inside

Of the enamelled bowl of sky
Which covers you and say
'This is my Africa' meaning
'I am content and happy.
I am fulfilled, within,
Without and roundabout
I have gained the little longings
Of my hands, my loins, my heart
And the soul that follows in my shadow.
I know now that is what you are, Africa:
Happiness, contentment, and fulfilment,
And a small bird singing on a mango tree.

Dennis Brutus

was born in Salisbury, Southern Rhodesia, 28 November 1924, of
South African parents who later went to live in Cape Province.
Dennis Vincent Brutus graduated from Fort Hare University
College and in the early sixties read law at the University of
Witwatersrand. From 1951 to 1961 he taught English and some
Afrikaans at the Government High School of Port Elizabeth. An
active sportsman, he got into trouble with the authorities over his
work as president of the South African Non-Racial Olympic
Committee: it is this work which became directly responsible for
the exclusion of South Africa from the Games. Banned from
gatherings and dismissed from his post in October 1961, Brutus
was finally arrested in 1963 but escaped while out on bail. When
he tried to leave Swaziland to attend the Olympic Committee
meetings at Baden-Baden he was arrested by the Portuguese and,
despite his Rhodesian passport, returned to the South African
security police. In an attempt to escape in Johannesburg he was
shot, recaptured, and sentenced to eighteen months hard labour on
notorious Robben Island. In 1966 he finally obtained an exit visa,
and moved with his wife and family of eight to England, where he
directed the World Campaign for the Release of South African
Political Prisoners. For the past few years he has been lecturing
at Northwestern University, Evanston, Illinois.

Dennis Brutus's poetry began to attract attention in the early
sixties. He won second prize in the Mbari poetry contest in 1962,
had the winning poems published in *Black Orpheus* 12 and in book
form as *Sirens knuckles boots* by Mbari in 1963. The poem 'Some-
how we survive' was printed in English and French in *Présence
Africaine* NS 50 (1964). Since coming to England he has published
a collection of poems dealing with his experiences on Robben
Island under the title *Letters to Martha* (1968). Another collection
appeared 1971 in Austin, Texas, as Occasional Paper no. 2 of the
African and Afro-American Research Institute of the University
of Texas. Its title is *Poems from Algiers*.

Somehow we survive

Somehow we survive
and tenderness, frustrated, does not wither.

Investigating searchlights rake
our naked unprotected contours;

over our heads the monolithic decalogue
of fascist prohibition glowers
and teeters for a catastrophic fall;

boots club on the peeling door.

But somehow we survive
severance, deprivation, loss.

Patrols uncoil along the asphalt dark
hissing their menace to our lives,

most cruel, all our land is scarred with terror,
rendered unlovely and unlovable;
sundered are we and all our passionate surrender

but somehow tenderness survives.

The sounds begin again

The sounds begin again;
the siren in the night
the thunder at the door
the shriek of nerves in pain.

Then the keening crescendo
of faces split by pain
the wordless, endless wail
only the unfree know.

Importunate as rain
the wraiths exhale their woe
over the sirens, knuckles, boots;
my sounds begin again.

Bob Kaufman

suffers a personality split, which one is tempted to call conceptual, over two conflicting minorities: he was born of a Jewish father and a black mother. That this happened in New Orleans in 1925 seems an insignificant statistic. Kaufman has coped with this heritage in a less spectacular way than, say, Sammy Davis junior – he has never been in the public eye, but private eyes have followed his career with enough interest to create a Bomkauf in-cult in a variety of places, American and other. This cult started fairly late, however, after Kaufman gave up the life of a merchant seaman which seems to have occupied all of his early years. In 1957 he settled (if that is the word) in San Francisco, and very soon got involved with the 'beats' of Ferlinghetti's City Lights bookshop. *Beatitude* magazine serialized his *Abomunist manifesto* which put some highly personal meat behind the vague surrealism of irritating people like Kenneth Rexroth. City Lights then published the whole text in 1959 as a fold-out pamphlet, which they followed up with two others, *Second April*, also in 1959, and *Does the secret mind whisper?* in 1960.

After this, Kaufman spent some time in New York: he wrote *Unhistorical events* there in 1961, and also the lyrics for Len Chandler's *Green green rocky road*. A novel, *Isolation booth*, written together with Lou Morheim, appeared in London in 1962. In 1965 New Directions brought out *Solitudes crowded with loneliness* which contains sixty pages of poems plus *Second April* and *Abo manifesto*. Mary Beach and Claude Pélieu then started to bring Kaufman to the sometimes remarkably receptive French: most of *Solitudes* appears, in their translation, in *L'inédit* vol. 10, no. 18 in 1966, and they also translated an early version of *Golden sardine* which, with a lot of other partly unpublished material and some photographs of Kaufman and his son Parker, appeared in a special issue of *L'Herne* (no. 9, December 1967) devoted to William Burroughs, Pélieu and Kaufman. The final version of *Golden sardine* also appeared in 1967, again from City Lights. Since then, Kaufman seems to have suffered the final indignities of mental disorder –

some years ago he already wrote, 'I no longer live in distress about my mind, I have learned to live without it' – but at the time I classed this line along with his other occasional statements like, 'I have but one life to give to my country, and billie holiday already gave it.' A great deal of Bob Kaufman's work remains unpublished.

Heavy water blues

The radio is teaching my goldfish Juijitsu
I am in love with a skindiver who sleeps underwater,
My neighbors are drunken linguists, & I speak butterfly,
Consolidated Edison is threatening to cut off my brain,
The postman keeps putting sex in my mailbox,
My mirror died, & can't tell if i still reflect,
I put my eyes on a diet, my tears are gaining too much weight.

I crossed the desert in a taxicab
only to be locked in a pyramid
With the face of a dog
on my breath

I went to a masquerade
Disguised as myself
Not one of my friends
Recognized

I dreamed I went to John Mitchell's poetry party
in my maidenform brain

Put the silver in the barbeque pit
The Chinese are attacking with nuclear
Restaurants

The radio is teaching my goldfish Juijitsu
My old lady has taken up skin diving & sleeps underwater
I am hanging out with a drunken linguist, who can speak
    butterfly
And represents the caterpillar industry down in Washington
    DC.

I never understand other people's desires or hopes,
until they coincide with my own, then we clash.

I have definite proof that the culture of the caveman
disappeared due to his inability to produce one magazine
that could be delivered by a kid on a bicycle.

When reading all those thick books on the life of god,
it should be noted that they were all written by men.

It is perfectly all right to cast the first stone,
if you have some more in your pocket.

Television, america's ultimate relief from the indian
    disturbance.

I hope that when machines finally take over,
they won't build men that break down,
as soon as they're paid for.

i shall refuse to go to the moon,
unless i'm inoculated, against
the dangers of indiscriminate love.

After riding across the desert in a taxicab,
he discovered himself locked in a pyramid
with the face of a dog on his breath.

The search for the end of the circle,
constant occupation of squares.

Why don't they stop throwing symbols,
the air is cluttered enough with echoes.

Just when i cleaned the manger for the wisemen,
the shrews from across the street showed up.

The voice of the radio shouted, get up
do something to someone, but me & my son
laughed in our furnished room.

Unhistorical events

APPOLLINAIRE

Never knew about Rock Gut Charlie
Who gave fifty cents to a policeman
Driving around in a 1927 Nash ...

APPOLLINAIRE

Never met Cinder Bottom Blue,
fat saxaphone player, who laughed
while playing, and had steel teeth ...

APPOLLINAIRE

Never hiked in papier mache woods and
had a scoutmaster who wrote a song about
Ivory soap, and had a Baptist funeral ...

APPOLLINAIRE

Never sailed with Riff Raff Rolfe
Who was rich in California, but
Had to flee, because he was queer.

APPOLLINAIRE

Never drank with Lady Choppy Wine,
Peerless female drunk who talked to shrubs
And made children sing in the streets . . .

APPOLLINAIRE

Never slept all night in an icehouse,
Waiting for Sebastian to rise from the
ammonia tanks
And show him the little unpainted arrows.

John A. Williams

(this time the A. is for Alfred) was born 5 December 1925 in Jackson, Mississippi, but grew up in Syracuse, New York, where, after his war service, he went to Syracuse University and its Graduate School. He has taught at City College, New York, and at the College of the Virgin Islands. In the early fifties he published some poetry in little magazines, but since then he has developed into one of America's most gifted novelists. 'He is precise and wastes no words; his plots are high architecture, his dialogue is fresh and contemporary, and he moves in and out of characters with the ease of a legerdemain artist' (according to Ishmael Reed in his *Necromancers* anthology). *The angry ones* (1960), *Night song* (1961) and *Sissy* (1963) were his first books, but his fourth, *The man who cried I am* (1967), is the one that established his reputation once and for all. It was written mainly in France and Spain, at the end of a long period of travel – throughout the States in 1963, in Africa the following year (he had already published *Africa: her history, lands and people* in 1962), then southern Europe in 1965. Back in New York by 1967, John Williams has been a lecturer at City College since 1968. *The man who cried I am* has since been followed by *Sons of darkness, sons of light* in 1969 and *The King God couldn't save* in 1970. The latter deals with Martin Luther King, and is the first of a series of projected biographical works of which *The most native of sons* (a juvenile on Richard Wright) has also come out. Williams has edited two anthologies of contemporary black writing called *The angry blacks* and *Beyond the angry blacks* (1966), and is one of the few editors to make good prose selections. He also edited the magazine *Amistad*, and the impressive first issues which appeared in 1970 and 1971 were again practically prose anthologies, not necessarily confined to new or recent work.

Safari west

The South Atlantic clouds rode low
in the sky; blue-fringed with rain that
would come later.
Popo Channel ran strong beneath its mud-green
undulating surface and the boatmen pointed
and told me
There were barracudas there. They swam in
from the ocean side, just to take a look,
hoping, perhaps
That slavery had returned and rebellious
and sick and dying blacks were being dumped
into the waters again.
Badagry, the town roofed over with rusted
tin and walled concrete hard mud, peddles a
view of its baracoon.
For a Nigerian pound; for two you can heft
old irons worn thin and tread the cells.
Ah, God!
Chains for the rebellious, the old, the strong;
chains for the weak, the children, all westbound,
all black.
And I raised each crude instrument to places
where gone, gone brothers had worn them,
the ankles,
Wrists, necks, and mouths, and did not wipe
my lips, hoping some terribly, dormant
all-powerful
Germ of saliva would dart quickly within
and shock awake memory, fury, wisdom
and retribution.
It did. And Nigerians drowsed in the heat

or floated through it, their voices truly
musical,
And wondered at this black man clothed in
the cloth of the West, his eyes swinging
angrily
Out over Popo Island and beyond, West,
West to the Middle Passage, eyes swinging
with wet anger.
There is an old one-pounder in the village;
it stands where a missionary, prelude to
Western armies,
Once had a church. When the ships rounded
Popo and stood swollen in the channel,
the missionary,
Forgetful of his role, fired the cannon to
warn his flock that the slavers had come.
Again.
As the vessels rode high in the channel
with light cargoes of cloth, trinkets and other
Western waste and
Lowered their sails in the humid wind,
the blacks ran and traitors ran with them
deep into the bush.
They could not run fast or far enough or fear
quite enough. The Badagry baracoon stands
today,
Somewhat maintained, I think, in the manner
in which Dachau is maintained in something of
greater degree.

Russell Atkins

was born 25 February 1927 in Cleveland, Ohio, where he still lives and where he was educated through high school and music school. He started to write at a very early age, his first works being short plays for puppets which he had also made himself. His first poems appeared in print when he was eighteen, and ever since then he has been a regular contributor to a large number of little magazines. Since 1950 he has been the most constant editor (with Caspar LeRoy Jordan) of *The Free Lance*, a magazine of poetry and prose which is not only (in his own words) 'the oldest black-bossed literary magazine' but by now one of the oldest surviving little magazines altogether. In its pages most of Russell's more important work has appeared, like his articles on 'A psychovisual perspective for "musical" composition' of the middle fifties, published in book form in 1958.

A restless experimentalist with a very high regard for craftsman-ship, Russell excels in anything 'dramatic' – whether it be poetry, radio play, or a production in which the protagonist is a luminous drop of blood. Through it all, he insists that he and his work are black – but the black community at large has a good deal of trouble with that, and we had a lot of fun when I brought out *Heretofore* in 1968 and one of the more compulsory-black re-viewers took me to task for misrepresenting Brother Atkins by excluding all his good meaty black-revolution type stuff – whereas actually Russell did the selection himself, very carefully, very deliberately, arranging ten poems and a play in chronological order (1945–61) to show that with each and every one of them he had anticipated ideas and techniques with which others had later made their reputations. Poor reviewer – what a chance missed for the glory of the revolution!

Before *Heretofore* Atkins had published three chapbooks: *Phenomena* in 1961, *Two by Atkins* (poetic dramas to be set to music) in 1963, and *Objects* in 1963. The poems used here first appeared in 1947 ('Christophe') and in 1959: 'Narrative'. In 1949 Atkins had been the youngest contributor to the Hughes and

Bontemps anthology, *The poetry of the Negro*. The rest of his work is to be found in the better of the small magazines and, as I have said elsewhere, 'before too long Atkins's scattered work will have to be collected in recognition of his being one of the most restlessly creative forces in U.S. poetry for two decades'. The collection of beautifully vicious sketches published in 1971 as *Maleficium* confirmed his range.

Narrative

I sat with John Brown. That night moonlight framed
    the blown of his beard like a portent's undivulged.
He came and said 'It's Harper's, men!'

Now Harper's was a place in which death thousand'd
    for us!
Already our faces, even as he told of how,
    sweated. And then suddenly, he,
with fierced spark'd eye – incredible heavens!

Horses dreadful appearance had of exhumed:
    our boots strode the ready. We dared off.

As generally seeming of the trail
    smooth – and so whist!
    i.e., save sounded thunder
    of us in a rush
    passed swift fierce "ft
    'ierce shsh!!
    'ss'd in a w'isk!
    'ierced passed "ft!
Harper's a !p !p !e !a !r !e !d!
    – into it we went in a dust!

"ft passed 'ierced
    " if 's, in, ss'd
    shsh "erced
    "ft
    "isk

Christophe

Upstood upstaffed
                passing sinuously away over an airy arch
   streaming where all th' lustres
   streaming
         sinuously shone
   bright
       where more sky
Upstood upstaffed
              th' sumptuously ready
   flags full –
   (th' shaded soothed an' blowing softly
   th' underlings smoothly
   with horses
          wavering with winds
   tangling with manly manners
               thick
   gathering th' steeds)
             that
   forthwith
   up up
   Christophe
   appearing in th' imminent
   an' th' passion overjoying the hour
   unfolded
        flaming
   Highly th' imperial sign
   shone in his glory!

Ellsworth McGranahan Keane

comes from St Vincent, one of the Windward Islands. He was born on 30 May 1927, attended St Vincent Grammar School and eventually worked as a teacher in that same school from 1948 to 1952. In his spare time he was the leader of an orchestra, and music ultimately became his profession. First, however, he went to England for further study at London University. During his early London years he became a frequent contributor to the B.B.C. Caribbean Series and after dropping out of university to concentrate on the trumpet, the only non-music job he would hold was that of producer of the series. This he did for one year, until 1959, by which time 'Shake' Keane had already become a well-known figure in the more avant-garde ranks of British jazz, often playing together with fellow West Indian saxophonist Joe Harriott, in the very early days of the Indo-Jazz Fusion.

Meanwhile Keane had published one fairly substantial book of poetry, *l'Oubli*, in 1950, and a smaller group appeared in the Miniature Poets series in September 1952 under the title of *Ixion*. These two remain his only book publications, but his poems occasionally appear in magazines like *Kyk-over-al* and *Bim*. For the past five years Keane has been a member of the Kurt Edelhagen band and transferred his residence to the band's headquarters, Cologne, in Germany.

Fragments and patterns

Once the sea
Said to the wind
I am sad
      Heed me
I am unwanted
      Need me

I am blind
       Lead me
And out of a pattern of tides islands became
(And out of the eater came forth meat)
Oh my islands
And out of a pattern of blood
Came forth we
          Came forth we

Oh my islands
Will the sins of the sea
Eventually
Find us out

You there
If you see Moses or Columbus
Tell him there is nothing here
That a person may not discover
In a glass of wine or the tint of a hair
Or the explosion of a little wave

(If you would commemorate anything . . .)

I talked once with one who was not dead
And he said
Why doesn't Chatoyer write home any longer
Out of a pattern of blood . . .

I walked with my lover near the cliff
In the clinging shadows
And she threw a flower out of the shadows
And we watched it settle on the silken sea
And she said

The sea grows nothing
The sea knows nothing to grow
The sea is sad
Is dry and unwanted

Once the water said
To the wind
I am unwanted
      Need me
I am unplanted
      Seed me
And out of the sweep of the wind's hands
Out of a pattern of tides
Came forth islands

Mountains remember our dawn
And rivers rumble of a time
Before Columbus
Before the bushed beards and red eyes
That spoke of a land long sea-days northward
And the little rippling efforts of memory
That make brows of our blue bays
Know with the wind
Tales of a ghost time's far telling

And time and her captains sailed west
Into a pattern of blood
By a pattern of tides possessed . . .

    Go to, Drake,
    Go to, Penn.
    Venables, go to.
    Rum and blood and the quake
    Of a thousand broadsides

(If you would commemorate anything)

Oh Abercrombie rides the flood rides the flood
Into a pattern of tides
Tides and blood
And the sins of the sea
That may eventually . . .

This was the temptation:
That they who daring the lips of the ocean
Had found Canaan without benefit of light
Or pillar of cloud
Should bring home the grape
And gorge without thanks

If you see Columbus or Cain
Or Philip of Spain
Tell him . . .
And this is the condemnation:
That they who gorged grape did not stop to consider
The shock of the vine, that they finding gold
Did not stop to consider the rock they had raped
That they making history did not stop to consider
The flesh they had undone . . .

I talked with the flower
That settled on the silken sea
And the flower said
I know the last brave cacique
Have known him head mountains and eyes tides
Have seen him ripples spreading
Out of tides
And out of a pattern of tides

Islands

And out of a pattern of blood
We
          Oh my islands . . .

And out of a pattern of tides and blood
History.

Martin Carter

was born in 1927, in Georgetown, Guyana, with the middle name of Wylde. He went to school at Queen's College in his home town, and eventually became a civil servant. But someone who writes 'I come from the nigger yard of yesterday/ leaping from the oppressor's hate/ and the scorn of myself' is bound to be a civil servant with a difference. Martin Carter's differences tend to be political, although he does not consider himself to be a particularly political animal. He did, however, become a member of the forcibly disbanded P.P.P. government, and as such was arrested in October 1953 and imprisoned until early in the following year. His first poetry pamphlets appeared in the years immediately preceding these events: *To a dead slave* and *The hill of fire glows red*, both in 1951 (the latter in Arthur Seymour's Miniature Poets series), followed the next year by *The kind eagle* and *The hidden man*. In 1954 a larger and stronger collection of poetry appeared in London as *Poems of resistance from British Guiana* – a fine book, very sloppily produced (as a comparison with a contemporary typescript has since taught me). It was reprinted in 1964 by the University of Guyana.

For a long time after his release, Carter steered clear of active politics. Until the mid-sixties he was the information officer for the Booker group of companies. In 1965 he became a delegate to the Guyana Constitutional Conference in London. During 1966 and 1967 he represented his country at the United Nations in New York; in the latter year he led its delegation as Minister of Information – a post he held until 1970. In 1966 his first new book in twelve years appeared under the title *Jail me quickly*. The *Poems of resistance* meanwhile appeared both in the U.S.S.R. and in China, and his poem 'University of hunger' has been translated and reprinted the world over.

Death of a slave

Above green cane arrow
is blue sky –
beneath green arrow
is brown earth –
dark is the shroud of slavery
over the river
over the forest
over the field.

Aie! black is skin
Aie! red is heart
as round it looks
over the world
over the Forest
over the sun.

in the dark earth
in cold dark earth
time plants the seeds of anger.

this is another world
but above is same blue sky
same sun –
below is same deep heart of agony,

cane field is green dark green
green with life of its own
heart of slave is red deep red
red with life of its own.

day passes like long whip
over the back of slave
day is burning whip
biting the neck of slave.

but sun falls down like old man
beyond the dim line of the River
and white birds
come flying, flying, flapping at the wind
white birds like dreams come settling down.

night comes from down river
like thief –
night comes from deep forest
in a boat of silence –
dark is the shroud
the shroud of night
over the river
over the Forest
over the Field.

slave staggers and falls
face is on earth
drum is silent
silent like night
hollow like boat
between the tides of sorrow.

in the dark floor
in the cold dark earth
time plants the seeds of anger.

Ancestor Accabreh

Was ancestor Accabreh
was ancestor himself
he stand up like a palm tree
his head touch the sky.

Was ancestor Accabreh.
He said no more the grey chimney no more
no more the cold wind no more no more.

He said, when I come back
O green shelter of long grass
hide me forever and ever.

He said, O woman face of earth
when I come back
let me lie down
kiss me to sleep.

He said when I come back
in the green shelter of darkness
let me lie down in peace.

Then he turned around
and he called them.
He pointed to the red sun
and said that is the field.
And the white birds over yonder
that is the chimney.
And the terrible cloud up there
that is our life
Not now but tonight
tonight in the darkness.

The Accabreh sat down
and they sat down around him
and he told them
he said, when we go the night will divide
like the sea for Moses.

And all chanted
Like the sea for Moses
Like the sea for Moses.

But suddenly night fell down from the green **roof**
and earth rose up like a young woman
and took off her clothes
to go to sleep.
And Accabreh murmured
O woman face of earth moving side by side
O green shelter of long grass hide me forever and ever.

The Accabreh rose up and crept softly through the jungle.
He walked with his bare feet on the bed of **Wikki**
on the cold bed of Wikki the black creek.
And all of them crouched down behind him
And crept softly over the bed of Wikki the black creek.
And the wall of the jungle
and the green wall of the night
opened for them, for all of them.

The great rough cayman with red eyes
and the shy agouti and the wild **tapir**
plunged in the scowl of the jungle
and dived in the soft banks of Wikki the black **creek.**

And down in the dark tunnel went **Accabreh**
down the dark tunnel of his time.
And behind him crept all of them
down the long tunnel of the dark.

Down in the tunnel
there is no star in the roof to follow
but only the sound of a foot like a drum.

Then they came to a hill of white sand
and searched the green darkness of the world
and the white moon was cold with rain
but nothing shifted in the green dream below them.

Then down in the jungle went again
and over the calm brown of the woman face of earth.
And when they came to the voiceless wail of freedom
Accabreh spoke and they listened to him.
He said, I come I come in the manner of a man
I shake darkness from my brow
with the fires of rebellion.

And night opened like a gate for him
and he went into the darkness of his doom.
And he took the parcel of night in his hands
and he loosened the knots that bound it
and held it up against the useless stars
and broke it into pieces
and scattered the lumps in the burning well of his life.

But those who engender the bleak night
they caught him they caught him
and tied a chain around his hands and feet
and took him to the far white god of grief.
But there was no darkness on his brow
only a laugh of scorn deep in his mouth.

When Accabreh laughed
his scorn was like thunder.
And when he cried
his tears were like rain.

Was ancestor Accabreh
ancestor himself.
At the door of his death
he looked far away
his heart it was beating
like high wind on fire.

Was ancestor Accabreh
His laughter is scorn
He stand up like a palm tree
His head touch the sky.

Then they took him and broke him on a wheel.
But before he died he laughed.
He said, O green shelter of long grass
O woman face of earth moving side to side
be naked for my children as for me
Accabreh! Accabreh!

Ellis Ayitey Komey

was born at Accra in 1927, a member of the Ga tribe. After his graduation from the Accra Academy he worked as a journalist. His first published poetry appeared in the Penguin anthology *Modern poetry from Africa*, in *Black Orpheus* and in Langston Hughes's *Poetry from black Africa*. A good deal of his other work has appeared in the *West African Review*. Komey toured the United States in 1962, after a long stay in London where he became involved with the now defunct magazine *Flamingo*: back in Accra, he served for some time as its African editor. Together with Mphahlel he has edited an anthology of *Modern African stories* which appeared in 1964.

The damage you have done

When I see blood pouring down the valleys,
Mahoganys trembling with fear
And palms drooping with disease,
I know you cannot stay with me
Nor hold a light across the land,
The damage you have done.

And when I remember how you looked
The first day you entered my hut,
A candle in one hand and a book in the other,
I know that your days are now gone
With the locust across the farm,
The damage you have done.

And when the first drop of rain
Manures the soil, now almost grey,

A hoe in one hand, wheat in the other
And a curse on the lips, I'll set to work
If the land is to recover
From the damage you have done.

John La Rose

was born on Trinidad, 27 December 1917. He first came to public
notice as a radical political activist during the 1950s in Port of
Spain, and from there throughout the West Indies including
Guyana. He held a variety of jobs in his earlier life, but not
necessarily the most predictable ones: he has been a building
worker, an insurance executive, and a secondary-school teacher.
As a journalist he became editor of *Freedom*, the official organ of
the West Indian Independence Party. For many years now he has
resided in London, and the bookshop he runs from his home in
one of the northern suburbs is a meeting ground for the intellec-
tuals and activists of the Third World. His stock of literature,
history, economics and politics of the Caribbean, Africa and
(more sparingly so far) Afro-America, is large but carefully
selected.

The name of the shop, New Beacon, also serves as an imprint
for John La Rose the publisher. His list is small and mainly
concerned with Caribbean affairs, but it shows the same careful
and purposeful selection principles. The *New Beacon reviews* are
'permanent collections' of articles which have previously
appeared in the kind of places where nobody would ever
remember them. John started the series in 1968, but we are still
waiting for volume two. Gentle, soft-spoken and very very slow –
but with strong convictions and an inner fire.

John La Rose has published two books of poetry, both by his
own press. The first, in 1966, was called *Foundations* and carried
his alternative first name Anthony La Rose. This book is the
source of the poem printed here. In 1971 John announced a new
collection, *Islets of truth within me*, but this still remains 'in
preparation'.

Not from here

You were not born here
        my child
        not here.

You saw daylight
among our islands
the sun was always there.

None could tap the light
from your eyes
or dictate roofs into space
        for your colour.

There in the middle of a hemisphere
you and I were born
        down there.

We were not in the exodus,
there was no Moses
and this was no promised land

You may not know this yet
        my son;
I sense that you sense it.

Yet what we leave
        we carry.
It is no mud
        we dry
on our boots.

The saliva we swallow
must ever dwell
        down there.

Kwesi Brew

or O. H. Brew as he seems to be more officially (Kwesi being a Twi day name for a child born on Sunday), was born in 1928 at Cape Coast, Ghana, of a Fante family. He was orphaned at an early age, but was lucky to have a guardian who looked after his welfare as well as anyone could have done. Brew went to school at Cape Coast, Kumasi, at Tamale and finally in Accra. He took a degree at University College, where he took an active interest in the drama group. He played the lead in its production of *Dr Faustus* and later appeared in several films made by the Gold Coast (afterwards Ghana) Film Unit. From 1953 he has been in the civil service, first as a government agent at Keta Krachi, later as assistant secretary in the Public Service Commission, and in the foreign service at Accra. He has served his country on diplomatic missions to India, the U.S.S.R. and West Germany, before becoming Ghana's first ambassador to Mexico. He now represents Ghana in Senegal.

Kwesi Brew belongs to the generation of African poets who found a voice in the post-war dawn of a new era, when independent states were emerging in quick succession and hopes were high. His own tribe, with its rich and interesting Twi language, has both an old and a new literary tradition, much of it recorded by Danish and German missionaries (the 'great' English missionary, Freeman, could not even speak Fante, although he worked on the Coast for forty years and was himself a 'man of colour'). Brew wrote poetry from an early age and won a British Council competition while still a student. He contributed poetry to the Ghana Broadcasting System throughout the fifties, and appeared (with 'A plea for mercy') in the first issue of Awoonor-Williams's magazine *Okeyeame* in 1961. His first volume of poetry, *The shadows of laughter*, was published by Longmans in 1968.

A plea for mercy

We have come to your shrine to worship
We the sons of the land.
The naked cowherd has brought
The cows safely home,
And stands silent with his bamboo flute
Wiping the rain from his brow;
As the birds brood in their nests
Awaiting the dawn with unsung melodies;
The shadows crowd on the shores
Pressing their lips against the bosom of the sea;
The peasants home from their labours
Sit by their log-fires
Telling tales of long-ago.
Why should we the sons of the land
Plead unheeded before your shrine?
When our hearts are full of song
And our lips tremble with sadness?
The little firefly vies with the star,
The log-fire with the sun
The water in the calabash
With the mighty Volta,
But we have come in tattered penury
Begging at the door of the Master.

Ancestral faces

They sneaked into the limbo of time.
But could not muffle the gay jingling
Bells on the frothy necks
Of the sacrificial sheep that limped and nodded after them;

They could not hide the moss on the bald pate
Of their reverent heads;
And the gnarled barks of the *wawa* trees;
Nor the rust on the ancient state-swords;
Nor the skulls studded with grinning cowries;
They could not silence the drums,
The fibre of their souls and ours –
The drums that whisper to us behind black sinewy hands.
They gazed,
And sweeping like white locusts through the forests
Saw the same men, slightly wizened,
Shuffle their sandalled feet to the same rhythms,
They heard the same words of wisdom uttered
Between puffs of pale blue smoke:
They saw us,
And said: They have not changed!

Ted Joans

was born on a riverboat, lying, at the time, at Cairo (Illinois, unfortunately). The event took place, not unnaturally, on the fourth of July. The year was 1928. His father was an entertainer – and so, in his own sweet way, is Ted. He plays the trumpet and the fool, he paints, adores making atrociously bad collages, and achieved early fame in the days of Greenwich Village beatery simply by being there ahead of everyone else. 'Like man, I came to the Village scene after doing the school bit in Indiana, Kentucky and Illinois, came here to paint and I did . . . got married and saw the birth of four masterpieces . . . after four years, divorce, blues, beat bread, then split for Europe, Middle East and Africa, fell in love with Tangiers and the European people and the African people, plan to take my love to Morocco with me and live there . . . I hate cold weather and they will not let me live democratically in the warm states of the United States, so I'm splitting and letting America perish.'

The school bit ended with a B.A. in Fine Arts from Indiana University in 1951. The wreck of the first marriage did not stop Joans from committing a second one, the mixed Nordic-Afric strain of the new 'masterpieces' being suitably expressed in names like Lars Kimani and Tor Lumumba. Ted spends most of the year in Africa and comes to the States only in the autumn. Most of his 'works in progress' of the early days are still in progress: of the poem 'Travelin', he said ten years ago that it 'will never be complete until I stop travelling', but *Spadework: the autobiography of a hipster* seems to have suffered the same fate for less obvious reasons. *Niggers from outer space: a Black Power novel* sounds like another fine title destined never to reach the bookstand. Two books did come out in 1961, however: *All of Ted Joans and no more*, a collection of poems and collages, went through two printings in that year (the autobiographical quotes, above, are from the post-script to the later one), and another book of collages provided a hilarious history of *The hipsters*. In 1969 Joans published what amounts to his collected poetry under the title *Black pow-wow*.

This was followed in 1970 by *Afrodisia: new poems*, and in 1971 a three-part collection of essay, poetry and reportage appeared as *A black manifesto in jazz poetry and prose*.

Je suis un homme

I am a man   I am a homo sapiens   I have never banged
  any one in the tail nor has anyone banged me
  I AM A MAN i am no homosexual

I am a man   I have hair on my face like Christ
  I am a terror and nightmare to razor blade
  salesmen I am a man I wear my beard proudly
  as your mother wears her permanent pubic hair

I am a man   I differ from other men because they're
  not me, I am the ONE, I am the real man and I'm
  authentic as hell, ask any anthropologist, they
  can give you diluvial egocentric facts about me
  and the tree from which I grew

I am a man   I am erotically in love with six women,
  one black, one white, one yellow, one brown, one
  pink, one purple and I have technicolored sex
  with all six each dawn at the dark entrance of
  the colored waiting room

I am a man   I wear my clothes until I outgrow them
  I don't support the fashions I am neither fat
  nor skinny tall nor short I am just a rightsized
  hipster who is out to destroy bigotry and old
  styled ignorance

I am a man   I am as healthy as the cum, I wear a
   wrinkled scrotum, I read poetry in the girl
   schools of America and I still refuse to read for
   no bread or circumcise my tool again

I am a man   I sleep sideways and I am more fluent in
   a bed I can make a Victorian Hen moist and I can
   love across the sea from the Halls of Montezuma
   to the shores of Tripoli

I am a man   I believe only in the poets musicians
   painters sculptors and hipsters and I continue to
   use deodorant between my fingers and toes and I
   shall remain an individual in the United States of
   ununited ideas of democracy

I am a man   I write sensual surrealist letters to
   young virgins and my best female companions who
   I continue to tell: women, Use ye not Tampax but
   make a Lipton Tea bag scene for double duty.

I am a man   I say to you the square Swingeth with me
   and ye too will learneth to dig

I am a man   my ideas are more important than the Naacp
   and White Citizens Council
   All men must be free now and this moment the chains
   should be broken

I am a man   I have read the Gettysburg address but I
   prefer the Ginsberg address and I continue the fight
   for freedom of everything except physical harm to
   my fellow man and never to stand in his way toward
   happiness

I am a man   I introduced democracy to Lil abner

I am a man   I kissed André Breton on Rue Bonaparte in
Paris and kissed Kaldis in front of the American
Express in Athens and Peter Orlovsky in the New
Years Eve dawn of New York, but I am still a man

I am a man   I saw maumau kicking santa claus underneath
Washington's Squarepark's arch last night and it was
then that I knew kangaroo shoes just don't fit
aardvarks and there should be a neon vagina on the
statue of liberty

I am a man   I know damn well what side the bread is
buttered on and where to plant contagious freedom
ideas into the oppressed people of the world
through jazz poetry, jazz painting and jazz music

I am a man   I have a head on my shoulder and her name
is your neighbor nextdoor

I am a man   I advocate the right for men to continue
pee standing and that all women should cop a squat
anywhere in a handbag or parking lot

I am a man   I have taken baths and showers all my life
I can not stand the dirt that you have in the corner
of your fisheyes nor can I tolerate the grime under
your fingernails and please remove that body of
yours out of my way and take your foot off of my
neck and that filthy hand out of my hardworking
pocket

I am a man   I am not lecherous like you and those that
   have joined the day-in-day-out rat race to get
   involved in the eternal payments for so called
   pleasures

I am a man   America I am a man I have had babies call
   me daddio I am a man I am a man I have held the
   hand of Elizabeth Taylor and the hand of Charlie
   Parker and the hand of Kwame Nkrumah and the hand
   of my mother who told me at the age of twelve that
   I was a man SO dig me American don't call me BOY!!!

Bobb Hamilton

comes from Cleveland, Ohio, where he was born 16 December 1928 and attended school right through Ohio State University, from which he obtained a B.Sc. (psychology and philosophy) in 1950. Since then he has made his home mainly in New York, where he has found more scope for his many-sided talents as an artist. For Bobb Hamilton is not just a versatile writer who can turn his hand with equal facility to reportage or poetry, he is just as adept in the visual arts as a painter, a sculptor, and a ceramist. He has actually taught art for a considerable time, in the New York City Welfare Department, and has used the experience in his work as therapist at a hospital. Since 1968 he has been instructor in black literature and history at Queen's College, New York. His involvement with the whole of the new movement in black art is deep and of long standing. Officially listed as its 'East Coast editor' or 'New York representative', it seems to be very much Hamilton who has, for nearly ten years, held together *Soulbook*, the 'quarterly journal of revolutionary afroamerica' with its early third-world commitment, emphasis on socio-economics, and surprisingly strong poetry sections (which range from Baraka and Kgositsile to Ho Chi Minh). More recently Hamilton has also become the editor of *Black caucus* for the Association of Black Social Workers.

'Brother Harlem Bedford Watts tells Mr Charlie where its at'

Man, your whole history
Ain't been nothing but a hustle;
You're a three card melly
Mother fucker.

You've even run the shell
And pea game on your own family.
I wouldn't trust you
As far as I could throw
A turd of
Gnat shit!
Let me run down
Just a little
            of my
Case against you
Chuck!
When you set your
Feet in our house,
Our troubles begun –
Yeah, we had our family fights,
But it took you
                to put
Shit in the game.
We thought you was sick
You looked so white and
Hairy, and we taken you
In like a brother
'Poor thing,' we said,

'He looks like one of our ghosts.

Look at his pinched up nose

And his little narrow

Pink lips. And that hair is a gas.

A lotta little brown

And blond strings

Hanging out of his head

His god must be poor

And don't have no wool – er else

Awfully stingy.'

And whilst we was
Wining and dining you.
And trying to put some Soul
In your poor pale frame,
You was casting
Your greedy gray eyes
Around, lusting after our
Shining black women, and
Our gold and silver
Yeah, and you even licked
Your fuzzy chops at our
Black bicepsed men!
You was scheming man.
Before we knewed it good,
We were took over.
Next thing we knowed
Ya'll had a squabble
Amongst yourselves
And divided up the whole
Country.
Old leopold run his
Cut like a game preserve
Chopping off hands and
Feets, plucking out eyeballs
Snatching off ears – He was
Swinging –
And when he got tired
He went home
Put on some silk drawers

Laid up in a
Big Belgian bed
Blew a fart and
Died.
The pope says he
Went to heaven.
Jeez man!
How dumb do you
Sombitches think we are?
What happened to
Your god's justice?
Speaking of justice
Your god is a fink
He let his own son get
Lynched over there in
Jerusalem Land.
If Shango had made
It with Mary,
He wouldn't a ever
Let his son
Lay in a stable
With all that
Oxshit and straw
Now man,
Mary woulda been
Set up in
The finest compound
With servants and good meals
And lots of
Palm wine!
And if Pontius Pilate
Had touched him,
His ass woulda popped
Like a motor boat

All the way back to
Rome!
And you got the nerve
To tell me, 'that was noble'.
You a jive cat
Charlie boy.
You paid off some
Rib picking Baptist Nigger preacher to
Go around telling us
To love you
            everytime
You kick our ass.
Let him do his Head-rag hop somewhere else
Cause if you ever kick me
You will make a
Dot and a dash
For footprints, cause you'll have
One peg and one shoe!
Help you fight in
Viet Nam?
Man, them's my folks
you fucking with over there,
Viet Cong
        or
Hong Kong
They is colored,
And I hope cuzz
Knocks a hole
In your ass
Big as the
Grand Canyon!
Man you been taking
One big piss
On me for

Four hundred years
And them
Calling me
Nasty!
Hell now
I ain't going
Nowhere!!

Derek Walcott

comes from the Windward Islands: he was born 23 January 1930 at Castries on Santa Lucia. Educated at St Mary's College on that island, he graduated in 1953 from the University College of the West Indies in Jamaica. He has since taught on Santa Lucia, Trinidad and Jamaica, worked as a journalist, travelled widely through Europe and spent some time in the United States, especially in 1957 when he was a Rockefeller Fellow on a grant 'to study the American theatre'. In 1958 he founded the Trinidad Theatre Workshop, which became the first touring ensemble of the West Indies. His own plays have been performed in London and New York. The B.B.C. used his *Henri Christophe: a chronicle in seven scenes* in 1950 (it was published in Barbados that same year) and *Harry Dernier* in 1951. *The dream on monkey mountain*, perhaps his best loved play, appeared in the Arts issue of the *Caribbean Quarterly* (vol. 14: 1–2) in 1968, together with a long article on 'Walcott and the audience for poetry', and an interview with Walcott.

Before that, Walcott had already published some of his earliest verse: his *25 poems* appeared in 1948, when he was barely eighteen, and *Epitaph for the young* followed in 1949. *Poems* in 1951 closed this earliest chapter, now usually forgotten (certainly in the official version which called *In a green night* 'a striking first collection' in 1962). During the later fifties Walcott continued to publish poetry only in magazines, but one cannot say that he went unnoticed; on the contrary, by 1961 (when he received the Guinness award for poetry) he had emerged as a firm favourite of what Walter Lowenfels would call 'the white poetry syndicate'. Blessed by Robert Graves and generally hailed in much the same patronizing manner as the French used to kill their own literate colonials like Senghor or Césaire, it is hardly surprising that Walcott carried off a succession of coveted prizes and distinguished reviews; it is more of a tribute perhaps that he was a very persistent second in the Dakar Festival of Negro Arts in 1966 (certainly his work and that of his successful competitor Robert Hayden bear more than a superficial resemblance).

The books of Walcott's second phase are *In a green night* (1962), *Selected poems* (1964), *The castaway* (1965) and *The gulf* (1969). Fortunately his handling English 'with a closer understanding of its inner magic than most (if not any) of his English-born contemporarie;' extends itself every now and then to the use of a truly Caribbean vernacular – as in *Tales of the islands* VI, on which John Figueroa wrote so illuminatingly in his anthology *Caribbean voices* II (pages 225–8). A sequence of long poems about life in Santa Lucia is scheduled for publication as *Another life*.

The glory trumpeter

Old Eddie's face, wrinkled with river lights,
Looked like a Mississippi man's. The eyes,
Derisive and avuncular at once,
Swivelling, fixed me. They'd seen
Too many wakes, too many cat-house nights.
The bony, idle fingers on the valves
Of his knee-cradled horn could tear
Through 'Georgia On My Mind' or 'Jesus Saves'
With the same fury of indifference
If what propelled such frenzy was despair.

Now, as the eyes sealed in the ashen flesh,
And Eddie, like a deacon at his prayer,
Rose, tilting the bright horn, I saw a flash
Of gulls and pigeons from the dunes of coal
Near my grandmother's barracks on the wharves,
I saw the sallow faces of those men
Who sighed as if they spoke into their graves
About the negro in America. That was when
The Sunday comics, sprawled out on her floor,
Sent from the States, had a particular odour;
Dry smell of money tingled with man's sweat.

And yet, if Eddie's features held our fate,
Secure in childhood I did not know then
A jesus-ragtime or gut-bucket blues
To the bowed heads of lean, compliant men
Back from the States in their funereal serge
Black, rusty Homburgs and limp waiters' ties,
Slow, honey accents and lard-coloured eyes
Was Joshua's ram's horn wailing for the Jews
Of patient bitterness or bitter siege.

Now it was that, as Eddie turned his back
On our young crowd out fêteing, swilling liquor,
And blew, eyes closed, one foot up, out to sea,
His horn aimed at those cities of the Gulf,
Mobile and Galveston, and sweetly meted
Their horn of plenty through his bitter cup,
In lonely exaltation blaming me
For all whom race and exile have defeated,
For my own uncle in America,
That living there I never could look up.

The royal palms

. . . *an absence of ruins*

i

Dispersing cupolas of cannon-smoke
Wreathed, like the wild parabolas of the sword
In this sea light, our islands' architecture.
The howling mouths, the startled hair,
Stunned when the iron thunder spoke
Were never petrified in praise
Of felons, cannibals and castaways.

Here there are no heroic palaces
Netted in sea-green vines, or built
On maize savannahs the cat-thighed, stony faces
Of Egypt's cradle, easily unriddled;
If art is where the greatest ruins are,
Our art is in those ruins we became,
You will not find in these green, desert places
One stone that found us worthy of its name,
Nor how, lacking the skill to beat things over flame,
We peopled archipelagoes by one star.

ii

And those who slew us, what was their disgrace?
They are our fathers just as those they slew,
A bastard composition like the race,
Conquistador, redleg, Sephardic Jew,
Cromwellian heretics, helots reeking gin,
With disinherited dukes drawn to the womb
Of weary Africa who had to let them in,
The bronze hue of her bastards is their tomb.

Since lust is not assuaged by statuary,
This should explain the absence of the arch;
Flesh fell so fast, the swiftest actuary
Cannot record the sword's triumphal march.
Flesh was the ravage of the phallic sword
That built its ruin in the conqueror's blood.

iii

Chained hands from exile lost whatever skills
They first possessed to pattern stone or bronze,

Knit ceremonial masks; from hand to mouth
Was the last way to share the tribal truth.
No arches praise those origins but the palms
With their Corinthian plumes and earthen plinth,
The columns of our racial labyrinth.

Tales of the islands

chapter v
'*moeurs anciennes*'

The fête took place one morning in the heights
For the approval of some anthropologist.
The priests objected to such savage rites
In a Catholic country; but there was a twist
As one of the fathers was himself a student
Of black customs; it was quite ironic.
They lead sheep to the rivulet with a drum,
Dancing with absolutely natural grace
Remembered from the dark past whence we come.
The whole thing was more like a bloody picnic.
Bottles of white rum and a brawling booth.
They tie the lamb up, then chop off the head,
And ritualists take turns drinking the blood.
Great stuff, old boy; sacrifice, moments of truth.

chapter vi

Poopa, da' was a fête! I mean it had
Free rum free whisky and some fellars beating
Pan from one of them band in Trinidad

And everywhere you turn was people eating
And drinking and don't name me but I think
They catch his wife with two tests up the beach
While he drunk quoting Shelley with 'Each
Generation has its *angst*, but we has none'
And wouldn't let a comma in edgewise.
(Black writer chap, one of them Oxbridge guys.)
And it was round this part once that the heart
Of a young child was torn from it alive
By two practitioners of native art,
But that was long before this jump and jive.

L. Edward Brathwaite

who, as the blurb of his first book so rightly said, is 'not to be confused with E. R. Braithwaite, author of *To sir with love*' but who is, instead, probably the finest English-writing poet the West Indies have so far produced, was born in Bridgetown on Barbados, 11 May 1930. He was educated mainly on his native island, but read history at Pembroke College in Cambridge from 1950 to 1954. His further career is briefly summarized: from 1955 to 1962 he taught in Ghana, where he started a children's theatre, and since 1963 he has been a lecturer in history at the University of the West Indies in Jamaica, breaking his engagement only for a year of research at the University of Sussex.

A regular contributor to the *Caribbean Quarterly* and long-time editor of *Bim* (which has been publishing his poetry since 1950), Brathwaite is succeeding rather spectacularly in an area where too many of his predecessors have all too signally failed: in laying the bridge to Africa as the true spiritual hinterland of the Caribbean experience, and in relegating the present main languages of the West Indies to the position of convenient vehicles which may have a past of their own but one that holds only a very limited validity for the New World writer. In three successive years Brathwaite published his great three-volume cycle of poems dealing with this development. *Rights of passage* in 1967, examining the condition of the black man in his contemporary surroundings, was largely concerned with the loss of Africa, *Masks* in 1968 explored the nature of that loss by examining aspects of ancient culture, and finally *Islands* in 1969 specifically dealt with the author's own Caribbean experience. In the words of yet another Oxford University Press blurb writer, the cycle 'confronts the New World Negro with his other self'. This other self is personified mainly by the Akan people, whose rhythms play an important part in the structure of *Masks* and whose proverb 'only the fool points at his origins with his left hand' was adopted as a motto for that same book.

Apart from the books already mentioned Brathwaite has

published *Four plays for primary schools* (1964) and a very strong selection of published and unpublished poetry in volume fifteen of the Penguin modern poets (1969). His researches into the West Indian slave and creole society are published as *The development of creole society in Jamaica* and *Folk culture of the slaves in Jamaica*. Since 1970 Brathwaite has been one of the editors of a fine new magazine called *Savacou* – he is also still an editor of *Bim*. His critical evaluations of the work of his fellow West Indian poets in *Contemporary poets of the English language* (1970) are among the best and most consistent contributions to a valuable reference book that manages to neglect Afro-American poets almost totally.

The making of the drum

i
The skin

First the goat
must be killed
and the skin
stretched.

Bless you, four-footed animal, who eats rope,
skilled
upon rocks, horned with our sin;
stretch your skin, stretch

it tight on our hope;
we have killed
you to make a thin
voice that will reach

further than hope
further than heaven, that will
reach deep down to our gods where the thin
light cannot leak, where our stretched

hearts cannot leap. Cut the rope
of its throat, skilled
destroyer of goats; its sin,
spilled on the washed gravel, reaches

and spreads to devour us all. So the goat
must be killed
and its skin
stretched.

ii
The barrel of the drum

For this we choose wood
of the *tweneduru* tree:
hard *duru* wood
with the hollow blood
that makes a womb.

Here in this silence
we hear the wounds
of the forest;
we hear the sounds
of the rivers;

vowels of reed –
lips, pebbles
of consonants,

underground dark
of the continent.

You dumb *adom* wood
will be bent,
will be solemnly bent, belly
rounded with fire, wound-
ed with tools

that will shape you.
You will bleed,
cedar dark,
when we cut you;
speak, when we touch you.

iii
The two curved sticks of the drummer

There is a quick
stick grows in the for-
est, blossoms twice year-
ly without leaves;
bare white branches
crack like light-
ning in the harm-
attan.

But no harm
comes to those who live near-
by. This tree, the
elders say, will never
die.

From this stripped tree
snap quick sticks for
the festival. Its wood,
heat-hard as stone,
is toneless as a bone.

iv
Gourds and rattles

Cal-
abash trees'
leaves

do not clash;
bear a green
gourd, burn
copper in the
light, crack
open seeds
that rattle.

Blind underground the rat's
dark saw-teeth bleed
the wet root, snap
its slow long drag of time,
its grit, its flavour; turn
the ripe leaves sour. Clash
rattle, sing gourd; never leave
time's dancers weary like this tree
that makes and mocks our music.

v
The gong-gong

God is dumb
until the drum
speaks.

The drum
is dumb
until the gong-gong leads

it. Man made,
the gong-gong's
iron eyes

of music
walk us through the humble
dead to meet

the dumb
blind drum
where Odomankoma speaks.

Jou'vert

i

He was a slave
To drums, to flutes, brave

Brass and rhythm. The jump-up saved
Him from the thought of holes, damp,

Rain through the roof of his have-
Nothing cottage. Kele, Kalinda-stamp,

The limbo, calypso-season camp:
These he loved best of all: the road-march tramp

Down Princess Street, round Mar-
Evale: Kitch, Sparrow, Dougla, these were the stars

Of his melodic heaven. Their little winking songs car-
Ried him back to days of green unhur-

Ried growing. The Car-
Nival's apotheosis blazed for two nights

Without fear or sorrow, colour bar
Or anyone to question or restrain his height-

Ened, borrowed glory. He walked so far
On stilts of songs, of masqueraded story. Stars

Were near. Doors of St Peter's heaven were ajar.
Mary, Christ's Christmas mother was there

Too, her sweet inclined compassion
In full view. In such bright swinging company

He could no longer feel the cramp
Of poverty's confinement, spirit's damp.

He could have all he wished, he ever
Wanted. But the good stilts splinter-

Ed, wood legs broke, calypso steel pan
Rhythm faltered. The midnight church

Bell fell across the glow, the lurch-
Ing cardboard crosses. Behind the masks, grave

Lenten sorrows waited: Ash-
Wednesday, ashes, darkness, graves.

After the bambalula bambulai
He was a slave again.

Folkways

i

I am a fuck-
in' negro,
man, hole
in my head,
brains in
my belly;
black skin
red eyes
broad back
big you know
what: not very quick

to take offence
but once
offended, watch
that house
you livin' in
an' watch that lit-
tle sister.

My puffy pink-
faced sin-
ful palms
are hands
that hit
hard, hold no
futures.
The precious life-
line readings there
outline no
ready fortunes.
Just hard hands,
man, spade hard
and licensed
with their blisters.

I am a fuck-
in' negro,
man, hole
in my head,
brains in
my belly;
steel
hits the rock
and the broad blade
shivers, eye
sockets bulge and
burn with the
shock, sweat
silvers the
back until I feel
bad, mother, I feel

like the sick

dog kicked from the
garbage, the snicked
hawk gripped in its tightening circle

of air. This is the hate
that makes my skin
stink, gives me my body
odour. And I feel

bad, mother, I feel
like a drum with a hole
in its belly, an old
horse lost at the hurdle.

But don't touch
me now, don't hold
me; for the good
God's sake, if you scheme-
in' now to relieve
me now, to sweet
talk me now, to support
me now, just forget

it now, please forsake
me now. Just watch
me fall in the mud
o' my dreams

with my face in the cow-
pen, down
at heart, down
at hope, down

at heel.

But bes' leh we get to rass
o' this place; out o' this
ass hole, out o' the stink o' this

hell.

To rass
o' this work-song singin' you singin'
the chant o' this work chain

gang, an' the blue bell

o' this horn that is blowin' the Lou-
eee Armstrong blues; keep them
for Alan Lomax, man, for them

swell

folkways records, man,
that does sell for two pounds ten. But get
me out'a this place, you hear, where my dreams are wet

as hell.

Tom

Under the burnt out green
of this small yard's
tufts of grass
where water was once used
to wash pots, pans, poes,
ochre appears. A rusted
bucket, hole kicked into its
bottom, lies on its side.

Fence, low wall of careful
stones marking the square
yard, is broken now, breached
by pigs, by rats, by mongoose
and by neighbours. Eucalyptus
bushes push their way amidst
the marl. All looks so left
so unlived in: yard, fence and cabin.

Here old Tom lived: his whole
tight house no bigger than your
sitting room. Here was his world
banged like a fist on broken
chairs, bare table and the side-
board dresser where he kept his cups.
One wooden only door, still latched,
hasp broken; one window, wooden,
broken; four slats still intact.
Darkness pours from these wrecked boards
and from the crab torn spaces underneath the door.

These are the deepest reaches of time's long
attack. The roof, dark shingles,
silvered in some places by the wind, the finger-
tips of weather, shines still secure, still
perfect, although the plaster peels from walls,
at sides, at back, from high up near the roof: in places
where it was not painted. But from the front,
the face from which it looked out on the world,
the house retains its lemon wash as smooth and bland as
    pearl.

But the tide creeps in: today's
insistence laps the loneliness of this

resisting cabin: the village grows and bulges:
shops, super-
market, Postal Agency
whose steel-spectacled mistress
rules the town. But no one knows
where Tom's cracked limestone oblong lies.
The house, the Postal Agent says,
is soon to be demolished:
a Housing Estate's being spawned
to feed the greedy town.

No one
knows Tom now, no one cares.
Slave's days are past, for-
gotten. The faith, the dream denied,
the things he dared
not do, all lost, if un-
forgiven. This house is all
that's left of hopes, of hurt,
of history . . .

James David Rubadiri

was born 19 July 1930 in Nyasaland, now the republic of Malawi. He was educated at King's College, and later at Makerere College, the inevitable school for generations of East Africans, both in Kampala in Uganda. He has since worked as a teacher and as a civil servant in the Ministry of Education. Detained during the 'state of emergency' in 1959, he went to England after his release and got his English Tripos at King's College, Cambridge. After his return to Malawi he has been principal of Soche Hill College at Limbe, and ambassador to the United States. In 1965 he joined the staff of Makerere College.

Some of his early verse appeared in the Makerere magazine *Penpoint* and scattered throughout various anthologies. The only larger group of his work now in print is in the *Poetry from Africa* volume of the Pergamon Poets series (1968) – the other poets represented in this volume are Okara, Gaston Bart-Williams, and Kwesi Brew: all four still belong very definitely to the rather troubled 'middle generation' of African English poetry, trying to reconcile a Western education and a white outlook with an African background and a black environment. The mixture, to them, is still uneasy – pride does not yet come naturally. Rubadiri is also a literary critic and the author of one novel, *No bride price*, reputedly published by the East African Publishing House in Nairobi.

Thoughts after work

Clear laughter of African children
Rings loud in the evening;
Here around this musty village
Evening falls like a mantle,

Gracing all in a shroud of peace.
Heavily from my office
I walk
To my village,
My brick government compound,
To my new exile.
In this other compound
I would no longer intrude.
I perch over a chasm,
Ride a storm I cannot hold,
And so must pass on quietly –
The laughter of children rings loud
Bringing back to me
Simple joys I once knew.

Mazisi Kunene

is a South African writer, born in 1930 in Durham with the first name of Raymond. He went to Natal University and obtained his M.A. there, won the Bantu literary competition in 1956, and came to London in 1959 to work on a thesis in Zulu poetry at the School of Oriental and African Studies. His own writing, which also includes plays, is mostly in Zulu but he is equally expressive in English. He is one of the truly new voices in African poetry – as was recognized as early as June 1966 in an article about him in the *New African* (vol. 5 no. 5). Kunene is now engaged both in political work and in writing an epic account of the Zulu tradition concerning the origin and purpose of life.

Avenge

How would it be if I came in the night
And planted the spear in your side
Avenging the dead:
Those you have not known,
Those whose scars are hidden,
Those about whom there is no memorial,
Those you only remembered in your celebration?
We did not forget them.
Day after day we kindled the fire
Spreading the flame of our anger
Round your cities,
Round your children
Who will remain the ash-monuments
Witnessing the explosions of our revenge.

Elegy

O Mzingeli son of the illustrious clans
You whose beauty spreads across the Tukela estuary
Your memory haunts like two eagles
We have come to the ceremonial ruins
We come to mourn the bleeding sun
We are the children of Ndungunya of the Dlamini clan
They whose grief strikes fear over the earth
We carry the long mirrors in the afternoon
Recasting time's play past infinite night.

O great departed ancestors
You promised us immortal life with immortal joys
But how you deceived us!

We invited the ugly salamander
To keep watch over a thousand years with a thousand
        sorrows
She watched to the far end of the sky
Sometimes terrorized by the feet of departed men
One day the furious storms
One day from the dark cyclone
One day in the afternoon
We gazed into a barren desert
Listening to the tremendous voices in the horizon
And loved again in the epics
And loved incestuous love!

We count a million
Strewn in the dust of ruined capitals
The bull tramples us on an anthill
We are late in our birth
Accumulating violent voices

Made from the lion's death
You whose love comes from the stars
Have mercy on us!
Give us the crown of thunder
That our grief may overhang the earth

O we are naked at the great streams
Wanderers greet us no more . . .

Chinua Achebe

born at Ogidi in Eastern Nigeria in 1930, is a third-generation-Christian Ibo, whose father taught school for a church missionary society. He went to school himself at Government College in Umuahia, later at University College, Ibadan, where he started as a student of medicine but soon switched to literature, obtaining his B.A. in 1953. The following year he started his career in broadcasting for the Nigerian Broadcasting Corporation at Lagos, and after independence he became its first director of External Broadcasting which he remained for five years. In 1966 he left the job to devote himself completely to writing, and in 1967 he started a publishing company with Christopher Okigbo at Enugu. In 1969 Achebe took part in a reading tour of American universities together with fellow-Biafrans Cyprian Ekwensi and Gabriel Okara. Together with 'Wole Soyinka and Ed Brathwaite he launched a new literary magazine, *Okike*, from Nsukka in 1972.

Meanwhile Achebe had made himself a considerable reputation as the first novelist of note to have come out of West Africa, and as the only one who consistently explored the contemporary African scene. 'It is clear to me that an African creative writer who tries to avoid the big social and political issues of contemporary Africa will end up being completely irrelevant.' His essays in *Transition* and *Black Orpheus* make it clear that Achebe will never become 'irrelevant', and the novels he has published so far do not leave his creativity in doubt. His first book, *Things fall apart* (1958), is already occupying a rightful place as one of the few undisputed classics of the new African literature. It won the Margaret Wrong prize, and it inaugurated the paperback African Writers Series which Heinemann started with such success in 1962 (Achebe is now general editor of the series). By that time another novel had appeared, *No longer at ease*, in 1960, followed by a collection of stories called *The sacrificial egg* in 1962. *Arrow of God* was the next novel, in 1964, and *A man of the people* appeared in 1966 alongside the juvenile *Chike and the river*.

There are already two major studies of Achebe's writing, both published in 1969: G. D. Killam's *The novels of Chinua Achebe* and Arthur Ravenscroft's *Chinua Achebe*. His novels have been translated into sixteen languages. A bibliography of his original work appeared in the first issue of the *Africana library journal* in 1970, and the *Studies in Black Literature* devoted vol. 2 no. 1 to his work early in 1971.

Mango seedling

to the memory of Christopher Okigbo

Through glass window pane
Up a modern office block
I saw, two floors below, on wide-jutting
Concrete canopy a mango seedling newly sprouted
Purple, two-leafed, standing on its burst
Black yolk. It waved brightly to sun and wind
Between rains – daily regaling itself
On seed-yams, prodigally.

For how long?
How long the happy waving
From precipice of rainswept sarcophagus?
How long the feast on remnant flour
At pot bottom?
    Perhaps like the window
Of infinite faith it stood in wait
For the holy man of the forest, shaggy-haired
Powered for eternal replenishment.
Or else it hoped for Old Tortoise's miraculous feast
On one ever recurring dot of cocoyam
Set in a large bowl of green vegetables –
    These days beyond fable, beyond faith?
      Then I saw it
Poised in courageous impartiality

Between the primordial quarrel of Earth
And Sky striving bravely to sink roots
into objectivity, mid-air in stone.

I thought the rain, prime mover
To this enterprise, someday would rise in power
And deliver its ward in delirious waterfall
Toward earth below. But every rainy day
Little playful floods assembled on the slab,
Danced, parted round its feet,
United again, and passed.

It went from purple to sickly green
Before it died.
    Today I see it still –
Dry, wire-thin in sun and dust of the dry months –
Headstone on tiny debris of passionate courage.

Sun-Ra

(whose real name has long been forgotten) must have been born about 1930. In the very early fifties he formed a group of multi-instrumentalists (he plays piano and any other percussion instrument himself) into what became variously known as his Arkestra, Solar Arkestra, Myth-Science Arkestra, or Astro-Infinity Music. Originally based in Chicago, the arkestra has been working in New York since 1960. A remarkably steady nucleus including the reed players John Gilmore, Pat Patrick and Marshall Allen has at times been expanded from its standard ten-to-fifteen size to the giant 100-plus who played the summer 1970 concert at the Mall in Central Park. Starting point of the whole venture is Sun-Ra's 'cosmic equation poetry', which he considered better suited for translation into pure sound-structures working directly on the brain than for the imprecise form of the printed word with its overload of obstructing references. His first record, *Super-sonic sounds*, appeared in 1956 on his own label, Saturn Records, and with a long poetic manifesto on the sleeve. Since that date, he has released at least twenty-five albums, of which the two-record set *Heliocentric worlds* of 1966 (on ESP) remains my favourite. Very few of Sun-Ra's poems ever appear in print except on record sleeves, but the 1967 *Umbra* anthology featured a strong if small group of them.

The visitation

In the days of my visitation,
Black hands tended me and cared for me ...
Black minds, hearts and souls loved me ...
And I love them because of this

In the early days of my visitation,
Black hands tended me and cared for me;

I can't forget these things
For black hearts, minds and souls love me –
And even today the overtones from the fire
    of that love are still burning

In the early days of my visitation
White rules and laws segregated me . . .
They helped to make me what I am today
And what I am, I am.
Yes, what I am, I am because of this
And because of this
My image of paradise is chromatic black.

Those who segregate did not segregate in vain
For I am,
And I am what I am.

Lloyd Addison

was born 10 March 1931 in Boston, Massachusetts, but went to school first in Virginia, later in New York, finally at Brooklyn College and the University of New Mexico. He served in the Air Force, mainly in the Pacific, went through two unsuccessful spells of marriage and now lives with his twelve-year-old son in Harlem where he works for the Welfare Department.

Addison has written half a dozen lengthy novels, some plays, a number of prose poems, a score of short stories, and a considerable body of poetry (again much of it unfashionably long). Practically all of this remains unpublished, and the exceptions are confined to poetry only. Some of his poems appeared in the first issue of the New York magazine *Umbra*, and indeed the group took its name from another of Lloyd's works. In 1965 he published a small brochure called *Rhythmic adventures beyond jazz into avowal sound streams*, the title being as succinct a summing-up of his central preoccupation as one can hope to arrive at. He was poet-in-residence to Harlem's Afro Arts summer festival in 1967 and editor of its souvenir programme, and has recently published several issues of his own magazine, *Beau-Cocoa*, mainly devoted to such long poems as 'Black in search of beauty' (written 1956–7) for which no editor has ever found a place. Some of his more accessible work appeared early in 1970 in the Heritage volume *The aura & the umbra*.

After MLK: the marksman marked leftover kill

Until deaf-dumb bullet self-improved comi-tragic time
deathdrops suicidally from error of unimproved trajectory
towards humankind's disintegrating vestpocket protest
    suitability,
and its ex-it disappear-ring of steel rearbounds

for vain deathproof namesake gods,
watch the little black hole
in the new world order undeliver-rated life-space;

if execution equals solution, let beforesight exceed
where mass meetings equal civilly engineered rights
obversely proportional to wishfountainpen power,
and anti-rights-bodies equal ten/time square
by the co-efficient light minus the magnetic exponential . . .

and if the short straight pigskin pass between All-American
        equals
the short straight bullet line pass to Other-Americannots –
on an elect/rode day-o shootout in atomic space-limited
        time –
into how many bullblooded pointillistic pigments
will the first canvass camped war of the worlds explode
        awry?

Hereby youth articles of war a unifying field threat
to destruct distrust-overlapping generations past
to inherit their time of health to live,
or run on sentence-structured fellowship.mad theme antics,
ordering inapt peeled evil bitterthick
to eat the beauty fall indigestion limbo, Armageddon Eve,
a surfeit's indefinite period . . .

and THOU SHALT NOT not KILL ROYALTY

was here latrined behind these walls where maddog stood,
and dog said let there be muzzle velocity
and there was a ballistics report of delight,
enriched, the eye-witness to the creation of death said,
man his tri-vestry of cloth – skintightrope walked
when he should have crawled – will vindicate me . . .

Whether in Kings or Psalms or Ecclesiastes,
never blink . . . in Acts or Revelation . . .
by goods the goodbye contract of the little black hole.

As for the law of inertia,
concern with condition will electric quote status obtain
warrants for the arrears rest of perpetual motion aliases
until delight year of overfunny.

So now rhetoric unpacked good physics call forth over-
      coming
uni-lateral-field anti-hymns of Ptolemaic tickled bylaws,
with march-on strike for ghetto respect for labor,
in Copernican accounting for a new toned iron sting in graft
      itch
before the picture of muzzle simultaneity develops
to mass spree-the-corpuscle of dropout entropic delight . . .
to wRap-trap white might wind in a Brown paperbag for
      sailing . . .

Calvin C. Hernton

was born at Chattanooga in Tennessee, on 28 April 1932 – 'the precise day after Hart Crane went home'. He studied sociology at Talladega (B.A. 1954) and at Fisk (M.A. 1956), then taught history at Benedict College, Columbia, South Carolina, and at Alabama A. & M. in much-misnamed Normal, Alabama. His first poems appeared in 1954, in the Atlanta University magazine *Phylon*, but he had in fact been writing since he was thirteen – 'out of a feeling of loneliness, rejection'. He has written several plays, two of which were produced at Waters College, Jacksonville, Florida, during a teaching spell there. Hernton also spent several years in New York, working for the Welfare Department as a social worker for children, and as a sociology instructor. During his New York period he became one of the founders of the *Umbra* group, with Tom Dent and David Henderson. The group produced two fine issues of a magazine in 1963 and 1964, and a remarkable anthology in 1967. By that time, Hernton was listed as 'editor in exile': he had left America in 1966, and has since spent most of his time either in London or teaching in Lund (Sweden), with brief visits back to the States.

The 'Communiqué' first appeared in the *Umbra* anthology, which also carried a beautiful photograph of Hernton at a reading, and his four-page essay on 'Blues for Mr Charlie' which remains the only sensible piece anyone seems to have written about that much-reviled play. Earlier, Hernton had published 'an epical narrative of the South' called *The coming of Chronos to the House of Nightsong* (1964) which will eventually become recognized as one of the major achievements of the new black literature. His two books of essays, *Sex and racism in America* (1964) and *White papers for white Americans* (1965), both published by Doubleday and in paperback by Grove Press, probably contributed to the necessity of exile. In the *White papers* he elaborated on his earlier analysis of Baldwin, and an expanded version of this essay appeared in 1970 in *Amistad* I. Also in 1970 Hernton returned to the States as writer-in-residence at Central State College,

Wilberforce, Ohio, and published a new book, *Social struggle and sexual crisis*. The novel *Scarecrow people* seems still to be just as much 'in progress' as ever, and Hernton's latest appearance in print was in 1971 with a collection of five essays called *Coming together*. On the album 'New jazz poets' edited by Walter Lowenfels (BR 461, published by a subsidiary of Folkways Records in 1967), Hernton reads his often-anthologized poem 'Jitter-bugging in the streets'.

An unexpurgated communiqué to David Henderson: London - 1966

If you are qualified it is legal to be a dope addict in London
It is allright to go mad, plenty people do, especially feeble
    minded people
I, for instance, want to have faith in the world like I used
    to have
Oh, I want to gratify all of my pathological desires!
I want to make love to every man and woman I see
I want to run up to little girls on the street and take
    their young bodies into my mouth
When I pass the playground and see the little boys swinging
    in the swings and playing football in the park
I want to be the child that I never was
I want to have dirty hands and scratches on my knee where
    the band aid keeps slipping off;
    and shining in my eyes, among the garbage cans
    of the ghetto,
The clear light of sunrise!

But I am in this country illegally
In fact in fucked to fetus accident

I cannot sit or stand or lie down in peace because the red
      hair of the panther is woven into my green garment
Spaded and shaded
By a candle in the moon so dim
I crouch over the ocean injecting ink into the lives
      of my contemporaries
Bootlegging feats of sheer witchcraft for crude bread and
      such –
Judging and waiting
It is astounding how thoroughly policed the skin forged
      boundaries are –
From Notting Hill Gate to Piccadilly Circus
The West Indians work on the buses

                             any more fares please

The prime ministers of the white world are perpetrating
      sodomy on the destiny of humanity in the bath houses
      of Atom Bombs
And scribbled on the underground subway advertisements,
      it is not *la rouge baiser* that makes Frenchwomen
So French
      it is 'nigguh filth'
King Kong
Mau Mau
Liver Lip Ape
Rhythm Blues and Jazz
From Alabama to the Congo to Glasgow
Night train is the RIGHT train

                             any more fares please

If you are in the You Know Who it is easy to cop out in
      Europe
It is allright to drill a hole in your skull and avant garde
      back into childfoolery and senility

Plenty people do, especially babies, and once upon a time
who sang a protest song
William Blake, for instance, will refuse to read his best poems
naked in Hyde Park this summer
little daddy Trocchi says he is going to kick the junk out of
his brain, into the cosmos (just for a change!)
Jevtusjenko has promised to pay his dues to the Jews at some
unknown date in the newclear future – (thank you,
comrade!)
But I will never abandon the suffering of the suffering people!
Bessie Smith dying on the Alabama pavement when blood
of my mother's womb spewed out the witch that is my
name
Oh, I am in this world without a passport to humanity!
Spaded and shaded
I smoke hashish everyday and walk the streets with ears full
of eyes, *a love supreme, a love supreme*
Every night I get stoned in the Seven Stars among the
wretched of the earth
and plot the downfall of empires

from The coming of Chronos to the
House of Nightsong

ii

I, Eleanor Nightsong, am God
This house, built by my father's father and preserved to this
day by me, is my Rock –
And when the morning sun walks up this hill like a natural
man and sets my window ablazing with the flaming
serpent of creation
I will be One Hundred Years Old

Oh, praise the Lord!
Oh, praise my soul!
I am going to live forever!
This house and this land will stand against all change
These values founded on ancestor creed and God's natural
    law will never perish
Oh, praise the bones of my progenitors, lined across three
    centuries back to the pits of England, the siege of
    Cromwell, back to Ireland, to my mother's womb and
    dead fish bellies

Like refugee ants, my ancestors came to this continent one
    by one
The wilderness rose up to meet them,
The savage tribes with their painted bodies danced against
    the sun
The sun itself was hostile, the extremities of the seasons
    swept upon them without warning
But my people – the Nightsong Lineage – were fired with
    a vision
They were superior people, they were the best of Caucasian
    stock
My father's father received his commission from the great
    Duke of Hamiltonshire
My mother's mother was of rich blood leading back to the
    Tribune of Richard himself
For miles and miles as far as eyes could see, their property
    stretched across the highlands of Georgia, as if it were
    never going to end
Slowly, by dying and suffering, by killing and sweating,
    through hard times and bull-dog persistence
The great deed was accomplished
This land was cleared and planted, cotton and tobacco were
    harvested, women were married and babies born

Season after season
Negras were imported and domesticated to serve in the
     enterprise of our building
And as nights and days exchanged faces, as mill wind turned
     mill wheel
The House of Nightsong rose
Stone on stone, this house rose like a fortress
Rose on this hillside to tower over this community in the
     same aspect as a great sentinel of the irrefutable stability
     of blood and custom

Yes, I testify to you, the ethos of Nightsong rose, spread and
     stamped itself upon the Southland like the hide of a
     mammoth buffalo
There were magnolias, azaleas and honeysuckle in every
     garden, cotton blooming in the fields, fried chicken on
     the tables, peace, prosperity and contentment became
     the inherent properties of our way of living in the
     Southland of America

Oh, praise my bones!

iii

I am in my rooms now
And it all seems so long ago
Yet, inextricably, the good days of the past stir in my blood

What is the soul
The past is a living thing –

Pigeons roost in my hair
Sparrows make nests in the folds of my ears, they sing there
The wind moves when I wave my hands

My fists rise in anger: stars go out, planets explode
My voice whispers a prayer: old men fall asleep, wombs of
    women issue forth lilac and daffodil

I repeat – what is it to be a woman, and know the burden
    of being all the good things on earth?

I wish to speak about my children, my daughters and sons
    the issuance of my womb

I wish to recall my youth, the hot heat of men upon my body,
    riding me down to plasm and photosynthesis
The joyous, fulfilling agony of stretching my legs,
    the pull on the anal muscles
    the prolonged vaginal thrust
The mystic emergence of a head, arms, a torso,
    naked, slimy, filmy-eyed
    the total body of a living thing oozing out of your womb
    still strapped to your entrails
    yet set free forever!

This is the way my children were born, one by one – Cleola,
    Jeffery, Horace, Brenda, Eleanor, John, Nathan
On and on they kept coming, one by one through the years
    until there were nineteen, and then Robert, my baby,
    the last of Nightsongs, the ghost, the mysterious scare-
    crow of my conscience
Oh, yes, the guilt, the immorality
Should I have told him, ever should I have whispered in his
    ear why his nose was so broad and hair coarse and
    unruly

Oh planets explode!
Oh stars go out!
Oh pigeons fly in and out of my mouth!

Oh sparrows flutter and soar like jets in my womb!
Oh how the black seed swells in my loins, lifts me
     boomerangs my white flesh
Lets me down to serene disaster
Naked and complete

Should I hate the soul
Should I hate lilac and daffodil
Should I hate the touch of wooly hair
Should I hate monstrosity
And should I know what it is to be lily flower and bear the
     burden of my fathers' crimes

I wish only to speak about my children, my daughters and
     sons
To speak about the indestructable glory of this great house

Hush! –
Who goes, in the dark of night, upon that lonesome hill!

iv

I may be dead before sun walks over the mountains
How does it feel to stand without and look on the inside
How will we recognize the hands of our clocks if they break
     loose and walk up to us and shake us awake!

The soul is more than a retroactive dream

That is the way Cyril died, my first husband, in a dream
That must be horrible, or easy, to die in sleep . . . dreaming
Or is it the inability to know how it is that makes it seem
     terrible
Dying *is* a dream
We believe our dreams while we are dreaming them

Cyril gave me five children, and I was thirty seven when he
    sauntered into his dream that summer evening and
    never walked from it

I wonder is it still the same sunny evening for him
Is he still dreaming that dream, whatever it was

There was a smile on his face
I wonder if he was dreaming of the splendor of this great
    house
      the magnificence of the plantation
      the cotton, tobacco and indigo stretching everywhere
      the negras singing in the fields
      the almost endless expanse of our property where one
        could ride from sun-up to sundown and never
        exhaust this great estate
      the gentry and the eloquence, the magnitude of our
        social affairs, the lily ladies and wellbred families;
      the lean mulatto wenches in their huts, the one in our
        kitchen

Perhaps not ! – for I discovered a trace of agony on his lips
    before he slipped into oblivion
No dream is totally *only* dream
Perhaps the nightmare of that war loomed in Cyril's sleep
    like a runaway scarecrow stalking the fields Northward
    the iron-chiseled musculature of Abe Lincoln shouting
    down intrusion upon our way of life
    the dying and starving, the rape and pillage
    and that pyro-maniac general, marching, burning,
    collecting negras in his ranks, marching and burning
    all the way from Charleston through Atlanta, Mobile,
    clear to the Gulf of Mexico !
    leaving behind everywhere ashes and brimstone

Oh, what a cruel wrath!
Down from Chicago, New York, Maine, Boston, New
    Hampshire, the Yankee dogs came
      erecting schools, building churches, setting up ballot
      boxes
      promising forty acres and a mule to every black nigger
And the niggers believed, the stupid niggers! –
Like eunuchs suddenly illusioned with the dream of
    unlimited potency, the niggers ran from the fields, from
    the big houses
The darkies ran from the people who had loved and protected
    them; ran, screaming *freedom*; ran into the arms of
    traitors, carpetbags and filthy opportunists

Oh, how cruel the wrath!
The era of Black Domination, like a mammoth plague, fell
    upon the Southland
There were niggers voting, niggers holding political office,
    niggers governor, niggers senators, niggers district
    attorney, rampart niggers prowling the streets and
      raping white women
Riot and Armageddon ensued everywhere

These were hard days for the House of Nightsong, for the
    whole Southland
But we were not put down for long by these darkies
A superior people, linked by blood and skin, will never
    submit to domination and tyranny
By the help of God Allmighty, the white people struck back
    at the negra race and their filthy consorts from the North
And, like a mighty white sheet, we rose up in one great Klan
We put the niggers in their places again, drove the Yankees
    out and established peace and harmony and democracy
    in the Southland once more

But Cyril never lived to rejoice in this
By then I was wedded to Franklin, a distant cousin to the
    great John Calhoun –

Dying and living are names for stability of creed and ethos

Frank Kobina Parkes

whose early contributions to anthologies and magazines were signed F. E. K. Parkes (for Francis Ernest Kobina – the latter name indicating that he is of the Akan tribe and Tuesday's child), was born at Korle Bu in what is now Ghana, in 1932. His parentage was mixed (if one may use the term in a black context without giving offence) – a Ghanaian mother, a Sierra Leonean father, and a West Indian grandfather. The different backgrounds of the parents are reflected in Parkes's childhood surroundings: from 1935 he lived in Freetown, from 1941 in Accra where he promptly ran away from school to find odd jobs at the military camp at Wineba. The next year he went back to high school, however, and in 1944 transferred to Adisadel College from which he graduated in 1949. He has since worked as a junior reporter on the *Daily Graphic*, as a clerk, as the editor of two short-lived Cape Coast papers (the *Monitor* and the *Eagle*), and from 1955 in radio as a writer and producer.

His work, which includes short fiction and essays as well as poetry, is scattered through dozens of ephemeral publications – which is a pity, for in the dead-seriousness which characterizes so much of his generation of African writing, his gently ironic voice is a positive joy. His 'translation' of Frank Imoukhuede's pidgin poem, 'One wife for one man' was a discovery of Langston Hughes, who included it in his *Poems for black Africa* in 1963. By that time Parkes had moved to England, where London University Press published his only book of poetry in 1965 under the title *Songs for the wilderness*.

African heaven

Give me black souls,
Let them be black
Or chocolate brown

Or make them the
Colour of dust –
Dustlike,
Browner than sand.
But if you can
Please keep them black,
Black.

Give me some drums;
Let them be three
Or may be four
And make them black –
Dirty and black:
Of wood,
And dried sheepskin,
But if you will
Just make them peal,
Peal.

Peal loud,
Mutter.
Loud,
Louder yet;
Then soft,
Softer still
Let the drums peal.

Let the calabash
Entwined with beads
With blue Aggrey beads.
Resound, wildly
Discordant,
Calmly
Melodious.

Let the calabash resound
In tune with the drums

Mingle with these sounds
The clang
Of wood on tin:
Kententsekenken
Ken-tse ken ken ken:

Do give me voices
Ordinary
Ghost voices
Voices of women
And the bass
Of men.
(And screaming babes?)

Let there be dancers,
Broad-shouldered negroes
Stamping the ground
With naked feet
And half-covered
Women
Swaying, to and fro,
In perfect
Rhythm
To *Tom shikishiki*
And *Ken*,
And voices of ghosts
Singing,
Singing!

Let there be
A setting sun above,
Green palms

Around,
A slaughtered fowl
And plenty of
Yams.

And dear Lord,
If the place be
Not too full,
Please
Admit spectators.
They may be
White or
Black.

Admit spectators
That they may
See:
The bleeding fowl,
And yams,
And palms,
And dancing ghosts.

Odomankoma,
Do admit spectators
That they may
Hear:
Our native songs,
The clang of woods on tin
The tune of beads
And the pealing drums.

Twerampon please, please
Admit
Spectators!
That they may

Bask
In the balmy rays
Of the
Evening Sun,
In our lovely
African heaven!

A thought

They said:
Wherever you sit to chew tigernuts
It is tigernuts that you chew
It's the chewing
(And what it is we chew) that counts
Forget the scene. Reck not the time

They added:
No matter the colour of the object
To which we dab on black man's paint
The object will (try as it can
To fight against this law) take on
The colour of the clay

And then they mused:
The colour of clay is endeavour's mark
So striving will leave its mark
No matter how dark the hearth
Striving will gain its end
No matter where we live
Our teeth can chew the nuts
For the red clay of the earth
Can make the black spot red
And wherever we sit to chew tigernuts
We surely will chew nuts
Surely.

Christopher Okigbo

was an Ibo born at Ojoto near Onitsha in Eastern Nigeria in 1932. Like most of the members of his tribe who went for a totally European education he attended first Government College at Umuahia, then University College at Ibadan where he read classics. In 1956 he became a ministerial secretary, two years later he went to teach at Fiditi near Ibadan, and after a further two years he joined the library staff of the University of Nigeria at Nsukka. He was also the West African editor of Rajat Neogy's magazine *Transition*, which in the early sixties became the most important journal of African letters. It was in *Transition* that Okigbo first printed most of the poetry that eventually went into his three books published by Mbari: *Heavensgate* in 1962, *Limits* in 1964, and *Silences* in 1965. In 1967 Okigbo joined forces with his fellow-countryman Achebe in a publishing venture that was to have concentrated on new African writing. A few months later, caught up in the Biafra scandal, he was killed in action with the Biafran army.

In the African Writers Series of which he is now the editor, Achebe has brought out Okigbo's collected verse in a volume called *Labyrinths, with Path of Thunder*: the last-named section contains six hitherto unpublished 'poems prophesying war'. The 'Elegy for slit drum' stems from that group. Paul Théroux, a young lecturer at Makerere College, wrote an early and sensitive appreciation of Okigbo's work in *Transition* 22 (May 1965).

Limits

i

Suddenly becoming talkative
      like weaverbird

Summoned at offside of
        dream remembered

Between sleep and waking,

I hang up my egg-shells
To you of palm grove,
Upon whose bamboo towers hang
Dripping with yesterupwine

A tiger mask and nude spear . . .

Queen of the damp half light,
        I have had my cleansing,
Emigrant with air-borne nose,
        The he-goat-on-heat.

ii

For he was a shrub among the poplars
Needing more roots
More sap to grow to sunlight
Thirsting for sunlight

A low growth among the forest.

Into the soul
The selves extended their branches
Into the moments of each living hour
Feeling for audience

Straining thin among the echoes;

And out of the solitude
Voice and soul with selves unite
Riding the echoes

Horsemen of the apocalypse

And crowned with one self
The name displays its foliage,
Hanging low

A green cloud above the forest.

iii

Banks of reed.
Mountains of broken bottles.

& the mortar is not yet dry . . .

Silent the footfall
            soft as cat's paw,
Sandalled in velvet,
      in fur
            So we must go,
Wearing evemist against the shoulders,
Trailing sun's dust saw dust of combat,
With brand burning out at hand-end.

& the mortar is not yet dry . . .

            Then we must sing
Tongue-tied without name or audience,
Making harmony among the branches.

And this is the crisis point,
The twilight moment between
   sleep and waking;
And voice that is reborn transpires
Not thro' pores in the flesh
   but the soul's back-bone.

Hurry on down –
   Thro' the high-arched gate –
Hurry on down
   little stream to the lake;
Hurry on down –
   Thro' the cinder market –
Hurry on down
   in the wake of the dream;
Hurry on down –
   To rockpoint of CABLE
   To pull by the rope
   The big white elephant . . .

& the mortar is not yet dry
& the mortar is not yet dry . . .

and the dream wakes
   and the voice fades
In the damp half light,
   like a shadow,

Not leaving a mark.

vi

He stood in the midst of them all
       and appeared in true form,
He found them drunken, he found none
       thirsty among them.

Who would add to your statue,
Or in your village accept you?

He fed them on seed wrapped in wonders;
They deemed it a truth-value system,
       Man out of innocence,
And there was none thirsty among them.

They cast him in mould of iron,
And asked him to do a rock-drill –
       Man out of innocence –
He drilled with dumb-bells about him.

And they took the key off
And they hid the key of . . .
That none may enter.

And they took the hot spoils off the battle,
And they shared the hot spoils among them:

Estates, among them;
And they were the chosen,
       mongrel breeds,
With slogan in hand, of
       won divination . . .

And you talk of the people:
There is none thirsty among them.

viii

But the sunbird repeats
Over the oilbean shadows:

'A fleet of eagles,
      over the oilbean shadows,
Holds the square
      under curse of their breath.

Beaks of bronze, wings
      of hard-tanned felt,
The eagles flow
      over man-mountains,
Steep walls of voices,
      horizons;
The eagles furrow
      dazzling over the voices
With wings like
      combs in the wind's hair

Out of the solitude, the fleet,
Out of the solitude,
Intangible like silk thread of sunlight,
The eagles ride low,
Resplendent . . . resplendent;
And small birds sing in shadows,
Wobbling under their bones . . .'

x

And to us they came –
Malisons, malisons, mair than ten –
And climbed the bombax
And killed the Sunbird.

And they scanned the forest of oilbean,
Its approach; surveyed its high branches . . .

And they entered into the forest,
And they passed through the forest of oilbean
And found them, the twin-gods of the forest . . .

And the beasts broke –
Malisons, malisons, mair than ten –
And dawn-gust grumbled,
Fanning the grove
Like a horse-tail-man,
Like handmaid of dancers,
Fanning their branches.

Their talons they drew out of their scabbard,
Upon the tree trunks, as if on fire-clay,
Their beaks they sharpened;
And spread like eagles their felt-wings,
And descended upon the twin gods of Irkalla

And the ornaments of him,
And the beads about his tail;
And the carapace of her,
And her shell, they divided.

xi

And the gods lie in state
And the gods lie in state
Without the long-drum.

And the gods lie unsung,
Veiled only with mould,
Behind the shrinehouse.

Gods grow out,
Abandoned;
And so do they . . .

Elegy for slit-drum

with rattles accompaniment

CONDOLENCES . . . from our swollen lips laden with
                                                    condolences:

The mythmaker accompanies us
The rattles are here with us

condolences from our split-tongue of the slit drum
                                                    condolences

one tongue full of fire
one tongue full of stone –

condolences from the twin-lips of our drum parted in
                                                    condolences:

the panther has delivered a hare
the hare is beginning to leap
the panther has delivered a hare
the panther is about to pounce –

condolences already in flight under the burden of this
                                                    century:

parliament has gone on leave
the members are now on bail
parliament is now on sale
the voters are lying in wait –

condolences to caress the swollen eyelids of bleeding
                                                    mourners.

the cabinet has gone to hell
the timbers are now on fire
the cabinet that sold itself
ministers are now in gaol –

condolences quivering before the iron throne of a new
                                                    conqueror:

the mythmaker accompanies us (*the Egret had come and gone*)
Okigbo accompanies us the oracle enkindles us
the Hornbill is there again (*the Hornbill has had a bath*)
Okigbo accompanies us the rattles enlighten us –

condolences with the miracle of sunlight on our feathers:

The General is up ... the General is up ... commandments ...
the General is up the General is up the General is up –

condolences from our twin-beaks and feathers of
                                                    condolences:

the General is near the throne
an iron mask covers his face
the General has carried the day
the mortars are far away –

condolences to appease the fever of a wake among tumbled
                                                    tombs

the elephant has fallen
the mortars have won the day

the elephant has fallen
does he deserve his fate
the elephant has fallen
can we remember the date –

Jungle tanks blast Britain's last stand –
the elephant ravages the jungle
the jungle is peopled with snakes
the snake says to the squirrel
I will swallow you
the mongoose says to the snake
I will mangle you
the elephant says to the mongoose
I will strangle you

thunder fells the trees cut a path
thunder smashes them all – condolences . . .

THUNDER that has struck the elephant
the same thunder should wear a plume – condolences:

a roadmaker makes a road
the road becomes a throne
can we cane him for felling a tree – condolences . . .

THUNDER that has struck the elephant
the same thunder can make a bruise – condolences:

we should forget the names
we should bury the date
the dead should bury the dead – condolences

from our bruised lips of the drum empty of condolences:

trunk of the iron tree we cry *condolences* when we break,
shells of the open sea we cry *condolences* when we shake . . .

Lenrie Peters

was born at Bathurst in Gambia, 1 September 1932, of parents who came from Sierra Leone. He went to school first at Bathurst, and from 1949 at Freetown in Sierra Leone, where he finished his high school training before going to England in 1952. At Trinity College, Cambridge, he obtained a medical degree in 1959, then went to Guildford to specialize in surgery. He still lives in England, practising as a surgeon, but finding relief from his profession in writing (which he calls 'painful but necessary') and in a somewhat surprising shadow career as a broadcaster and singer in the Overseas Service. At Cambridge he was president of the African Students Union, and his interest in politics has a firm Pan-African basis.

The Nigerian publishing house Mbari brought out Lenrie Peters's book of *Poems* in 1964; some of these had earlier appeared in *Black Orpheus*, and later, twenty-one of them made up slightly less than half of his second book, *Satellites*, which appeared in the West African Writers series in 1967. In 1965 Peters published a novel called *The second round*.

We have come home

We have come home
From the bloodless war
With sunken hearts
Our boots full of pride –
From the true massacre of the soul
When we have asked
What does it cost
To be loved and left alone?
We have come home,
bringing the pledge

Which is written in rainbow colours
Across the sky – for burial
But it is not the time
To lay wreaths
For yesterday's crimes
Night threatens
Time dissolves
And there is no acquaintance
With tomorrow
The gurgling drums
Echo the star
The forest howls –
And between the trees
The dark sun appears.

We have come home
When the dawn falters
Singing songs of other lands
The Death March
Violating our ears
Knowing all our lore and tears
Determined by the spinning coin.

We have come home
To the green foothills
To drink from the cry
Of warm and mellow birdsong.
To the hot beaches
Where boats go out to sea
Threshing the ocean's harvest
And the harassing, plunging
gliding gulls shower kisses on the waves.
We have come home
Where through the lightning flash

And thundering rain
The Pestilence, the drought
The sodden spirit
Lingers on the sandy road
Supporting the tortured remnants
Of the flesh
That spirit which asks no favour
Of the world
But to have dignity.

Eugene Perkins

was born 13 September 1932 in Chicago, Illinois, and eventually attended George Williams College there, obtaining a B.Sc. for group work and an M.Sc. for group work administration. Group work is what he has remained active in, as a member of the Catalyst cultural committee, as convenor of the writers' workshop of the South Side community art centre. For one of these workshop projects, a programme called 'On the beach' which was organized by Youth Action, Perkins later edited the anthology *Black expressions* (1967), which included some remarkable work by young people of eight to fifteen. An important participant in the Youth Action projects is the Metropolitan Chicago Y.M.C.A. where Perkins is instructor in black literature.

His own work has appeared in *Negro Digest*, *Freedomways* and *Liberator* magazines, and in a little book called *An apology to my African brother* (1965) which was reprinted in 1969 by the Free Black Press of which Perkins is the editor. The press has also published his broadside, *Poem for niggers*, a book with photographs by Roy Lewis called *West wall* and his latest books of poetry, *Black is beautiful* (1968), which is dedicated to the late Conrad Kent Rivers, and *Silhouette* (1970). The poem used here, 'Diary of a Bronzeville boy', is remarkably close to one of Rivers's most popular poems, 'Four sheets to the wind'.

Diary of a Bronzeville boy

As a small boy
I wandered through the jungle of Bronzeville
Carrying a jagged knive to conquer my enemies.
I was a soldier before puberty.

    To be born in Bronzeville
    Was to be born without justice

At twelve, I knew the violence of manhood
And the excitement of sleeping with women.
Once I jackrolled a crippled old man
Who sold pencils near the corner drugstore.

My father died when I was fifteen
Shot down by a cop's blinded emotions.
Mother became a whore and I sold newspapers.
We were on relief and the precinct captain
Gave food baskets on Jesus' birthday.
I never did see a black Santa Claus

School was a bore.
I couldn't understand what made Hamlet mad
Or why George Washington told the truth
When he chopped down that damn cherry tree.

War came.
Pearl Harbor was attacked during holy communion
I had thought all people respected God.
In Europe, Jews were being persecuted
While Bronzeville was promised a new deal.
I became a soldier again

    In battle I learned how to live
    I already knew how to die

War ended.
The Third Reich had collapsed at Normandy
Hiroshima swallowed by a burning monster.
I never learned why the Jews were persecuted
I journeyed home to Bronzeville, with a lousy
Medal to compensate for a shattered leg.
I searched for the American dream

But I was betrayed.
The hatred didn't die in Germany
America still had segregated cemetaries.
(I finally learned why Jews were persecuted)

    Instead of guns there were signs
    Instead of a bomb there hung a rope

But no justice
For a Bronzeville boy.

Dollar Brand

is a South African jazz musician. Born in Cape Town about 1933, he grew up in 'district six' where he went to Trafalgar High School. As a pianist and composer he worked mainly around his native town and in Johannesburg until 1960, when he led a small combo on a tour to Switzerland and Scandinavia. His earliest verse seems to date from that period. From 1965 until 1968 he worked in the States, but afterwards went back to South Africa where he is married to singer Bea Benjamin. An appreciative article about his work appeared in the magazine *Transition* (no. 24).

from Africa: music

iii
spiritual

> when i get to heaven gonna play on my harp
> gonna play all over god's heaven
>
> but only with the cats who can make the changes

iv
western influence

> my baybee eesah cryink baa baa
>   forra me
> i geef her de mango
> i geef her de banana
> but she's stillah cryink baa baa
>   forra me

v
rhythm afrique

   joey had the biggest feet
   so he played tenor

vi
blues for district six

   early one new year's morning
   when the emerald bay waved its clear waters against the
     noisy dockyard
   a restless south easter skipped over slumbering lion's head
   danced up hanover street
   tenored a bawdy banjo
   strung an ancient cello
   bridged a host of guitars
   tambourined through a dingy alley
   into a scented cobwebbed room
   and crackled the sixth sensed district
   into a blazing swamp fire of satin sound

   early one new year's morning
   when the moaning bay mourned its murky waters against
     the deserted dockyard
   a bloodthirsty south easter roared over hungry lion's head
   and ghosted its way up hanover street
   empty
   forlorn
   and cobwebbed with gloom

Etheridge Knight

is without a doubt the strongest of the new black poets who have gathered under Dudley Randall's Broadside imprint – just as the Broadside imprint is the strongest among the (in recent years suddenly numerous) small series devoted to the poetry of the 'black revolution'. Knight was born 19 April 1933 at Corinth in Mississippi. He trained as a medical technician, and put his training to use in the army, seeing active service in Korea, less active in Guam and Hawaii.

'I died in Korea from a shrapnel wound & narcotics resurrected me. I died in 1960 from a prison sentence & poetry brought me back to life.' Like at least one other contributor to this anthology, Etheridge Knight started to write while serving a prison sentence. In 1968, Broadside brought out his *Poems from prison*, an astonishing first book in which another silent minority suddenly found its voice. 'It is certainly male – with formidable austerities, dry grins, and a dignity that is scrupulous even when lenient. But there are centers of controlled softness too. And there is blackness, inclusive, possessed and given; freed and terrible and beautiful,' said Gwendolyn Brooks in her preface. Later in 1968 Knight recorded all the poems in the book on a tape which was made available in a limited edition. A year later, he was released from Indiana State Prison.

Since then, Etheridge Knight has been married to Sonia Sanchez, thus, for an all too brief spell, making up the most formidable team in black letters. He now teaches black studies at the University of Pittsburgh. He is writing a novel on the early South Carolina slave revolt led by Denmark Vesey, and has edited an anthology, *Black voices from prison*, with writings by himself and other inmates of Indiana State Prison. He is poetry editor for *Motive* magazine, a remarkable methodist journal published in Nashville.

The idea of ancestry

i

Taped to the wall of my cell are 47 pictures: 47 black
faces: my father, mother, grandmothers (1 dead), grand
fathers (both dead), brothers, sisters, uncles, aunts,
cousins (1st & 2nd), nieces, and nephews. They stare
across the space at me sprawling on my bunk. I know
their dark eyes, they know mine. I know their style,
they know mine. I am all of them, they are all of me;
they are farmers, I am a thief, I am me, they are thee.

I have at one time or another been in love with my
mother, 1 grandmother, 2 sisters, 2 aunts (1 went to the
asylum), and 5 cousins. I am now in love with a 7 yr old
niece (she sends me letters written in large block print, and
her picture is the only one that smiles at me).

I have the same name as 1 grandfather, 3 cousins,
3 nephews, and 1 uncle. The uncle disappeared when he
was 15, just took off and caught a freight (they say). He's
discussed each year when the family has a reunion, he
causes uneasiness in the clan, he is an empty space. My
father's mother, who is 93 and who keeps the Family
Bible with everybody's birth dates (and death dates) in it,
always mentions him. There is no place in her Bible for
'whereabouts unknown.'

ii

Each Fall the graves of my grandfathers call me, the brown
hills and red gullies of mississippi send out their electric

messages, galvanizing my genes. Last yr / like a salmon
quitting the cold ocean – leaping and bucking up his
birthstream / I hitchhiked my way from L.A. with 16 caps
in my pocket and a monkey on my back. and I almost
kicked it with the kinfolks. I walked barefooted in my
grandmother's backyard / I smelled the old lands and the
woods / I sipped cornwhiskey from fruit jars with the
men / I flirted with the women / I had a ball till the caps ran
out and my habit came down. That night I looked at my
grandmother and split / my guts were screaming for junk /
but I was almost contented / I had almost caught up with
me.
(The next day in Memphis I cracked a croaker's crib for
a fix.)

This yr there is a gray stone wall damming my stream,
and when the falling leaves stir my genes, I pace my cell
or flop on my bunk and stare at 47 black faces across the
space. I am all of them, they are all of me, I am me, they
are thee, and I have no sons to float in the space between.

He sees through stone

He sees through stone
he has the secret
eyes this old black one
who sits under prison skies
sits pressed by the sun
against the western wall
his pipe between purple gums

the years fall
like over-ripe plums
bursting red flesh
on the dark earth

his time is not my time
but I have known him
in a time now gone

he led me trembling cold
into the dark forest
taught me the secret rites
to take a woman
to be true to my brothers
to make my spear drink
the blood
of my enemies

now black cats circle him
flash white teeth
snarl at the air
mashing green grass beneath
shining muscles
ears peeling his words
he smiles
he knows

the hunt   the enemy
he has the secret eyes
he sees through stone

For black poets who think of suicide

Black Poets should live – not leap
From steel bridges (like the white boys do).
Black Poets should live – not lay
Their necks on railroad tracks (like the white boys do).
Black Poets should seek – but not search too much
In sweet dark caves, nor hunt for snipes
Down psychic trails (like the white boys do).

For Black Poets belong to Black People. Are
The Flutes of black Lovers. Are
The Organs of Black Sorrows. Are
The Trumpets of Black Warriors.
Let all Black Poets die as trumpets,
And be buried in the dust of marching feet.

Conrad Kent Rivers

was born in Atlantic City, New Jersey, on 15 October 1933. He went to school in Pennsylvania, Georgia, Ohio (where he graduated from Wilberforce University), in Illinois (Chicago Teachers College) and Indiana (University). He served in the army in Maryland and Kentucky. While in high school in Georgia he won the Savannah State poetry prize in 1951; he was three times included in the *America sings* college verse annuals. Casper LeRoy Jordan, who was the Wilberforce librarian when Conrad studied there, published him in *Free Lance* magazine and acted as godfather to his early literary career: under the *Free Lance* auspices he brought out his first three books, *Perchance to dream, Othello* in 1959, *These black bodies and this sunburnt face* in 1962 and *Dusk at Selma* in 1965. The Heritage anthology, *Sixes and sevens*, featured a strong group of his poems in 1962, together with a 'statement' on his reason for writing and the place of 'race' in his work. This statement has been reprinted as often as his more popular poems.

In the middle sixties, living in Chicago and teaching in its industrial suburb Gary (over the Indiana state line), Rivers and others – like novelist Ronald Fair, journalist David Llorens and Gerald McWorter – formed an active and lively discussion group out of which, through tortuous byways, was born the Organization of Black American Culture (O.B.A.C.), still an active force in Chicago's black arts scene today. Conrad Rivers, however, saw little of its realization: he died a senseless and avoidable death on 24 March 1968, just three weeks before publication of a new book of poetry, *The still voice of Harlem* (volume five in the Heritage series).

Rivers was a writer with a great deal to say, on an interesting quest for ways in which to say it. One of the recurring themes in his work is the question of the black writer's position and responsibility, and his ambiguous relations with his dual audience. Much of this particular motif found expression in a series of poems addressed to, or occasioned by, Richard Wright: eight of these, dating from as many different years right up to their author's untimely death, have been published, with an introduction by Ronald Fair, as *The Wright poems* (Heritage series, 1972). The stories and other fiction, and the dramatic work (including a play on the life of Paul Laurence Dunbar) have so far remained unpublished.

The still voice of Harlem

Come to me broken dreams and all,
bring me the glory of your wayward souls;
I shall find a place for them in my garden.

Weep not for the golden sun of California,
think not of the fertile soil of Alabama,
nor of your father's eyes, your mother's
body twisted by the washing board.

>   I am the hope
>   and tomorrow
>   of your unborn.

Truly, when there is no more of me
there shall be no more of you . . .

Watts

Must I shoot the
white man dead
to free the nigger
in his head?

For Richard Wright

(Paris, 1963)

Your white bright city meets my discontent
    she sells her soul for symbols.
Your first grave leads me home to white America
    our roots grow dry and spent:
Too far lies Europe and I forget my hate.

Your grave, the city and my rooted discontent
    leads me home where Paris is not
and I leave your black Adonis spirit here
    in time your land shall bring you up
where green grass and sun-burnt soil
    returns the native son of God.

And here where garçons come and go
    one finds it difficult to remain free;
America spreads herself so very thin
    and France embraces greed and mediocrity.

We who walk the bright streets of Paris
    dreaming of space in another time
should shake the dying roots of our own land
    to live like men or die like lions.

Audre Lorde

or by her full name Audre Geraldin Lorde Rollins, was born 18 February 1934 in New York City, and, but for a few short spells, has lived in the city all her life. She attended Hunter College from 1951 to 1959 (with a year at Mexico University in the middle) and followed her B.A. in English and philosophy with an M.Sc. in library service from Columbia. During her college years she held a variety of jobs from ghost writer to X-ray technician. She later became young adult librarian in Mount Vernon and for the last few years she has been teaching creative literature in New York at City College and 'the black experience' at Lehman ('neither replaces writing or being black'). She also conducts classes for white teachers working in ghetto areas. In the spring of 1968 she was poet-in-residence at Tougaloo College in Mississippi and edited a small anthology of class work: 'Poets must teach what they know, if we are all to continue being.' Her first published poem appeared early in 1949, she has since had work in a variety of little magazines, a major selection in the anthology *Sixes and sevens* in 1962, and two books of her own: *The first cities* was published by Diane Di Prima in 1968, and *Cables to rage* appeared as volume nine in the Heritage series in London in 1970. A group of eight poems appeared early 1972 in *Transatlantic Review* no. 41.

Coal

I
Is the total black, being spoken
From the earth's inside.
There are many kinds of open.
How a diamond comes into a knot of flame
How a sound comes into a word, coloured
By who pays what for speaking.

Some words are open
Like a diamond on glass windows
Singing out within the crash of passing sun
Then there are words like stapled wagers
In a perforated book – buy and sign and tear apart –
And come whatever wills all chances
The stub remains
An ill-pulled tooth with a ragged edge.
Some words live in my throat
Breeding like adders. Others know sun
Seeking like gypsies over my tongue
To explode through my lips
Like young sparrows bursting from shell.
Some words
Bedevil me.

Love is a word another kind of open –
As a diamond comes into a knot of flame
I am black because I come from the earth's inside
Take my word for jewel in your open light.

'Wole Soyinka

whose name is an affectionate abbreviation of the full Akinwande Oluwole Soyinka, is a Yoruba from Abeokuta in Western Nigeria, where he was born 13 July 1934. After attending the inevitable Government College and University College at Ibadan, he went to England. He graduated from Leeds University (English honours) in 1958, then taught in London, and for a while worked in the experimental Royal Court Theatre where his first short verse play, *The lion and the jewel*, was produced in 1966. For although he is a fine and much-anthologized poet, Soyinka is first and foremost a man of the theatre, both as actor and as playwright. Since his return to Nigeria in 1960 his influence on the emerging and rapidly developing theatre movement there has been great and beneficial. *A dance of the forests*, his other verse play, was produced for the Nigerian independence festivities in October 1960. Mbari, in 1963, published *Three plays* and Oxford University Press, in 1964, did *Five plays*. The following year Soyinka published a novel called *The interpreters*, had his satirical revue *Before the blackout* performed at Ibadan, and wrote a new play, *The road*, which won the main drama prize of the Dakar Festival of Negro Arts in 1966. The same festival saw the premiere of Soyinka's most successful play to date, *Kongi's harvest*, which has subsequently been played in England and in the United States: in 1969 the Negro Ensemble Company at St Mark's Theater in New York produced it, and in 1970 it was filmed by Ossie Davis's independent production company. *Three short plays* appeared in 1969.

Soyinka is one of the editors of, and an occasional contributor to, the remarkably long-lived magazine *Black Orpheus*, founded in 1957 by the indefatigable Ulli Beier and ubiquitous Janheinz Jahn. He has published two substantial collections of poetry (*Idanre* in 1967 and *A shuttle in the crypt* in 1972), and a small pamphlet published in London in 1969 contains two *Poems from prison* written when the Nigerian government had stuck its leading author in jail (August 1967 to October 1969) for expressing his doubts about the Biafran affair. Until his imprisonment Soyinka had been senior lecturer in African literature at the University in Lagos; after his release he became director of drama at Ibadan. During 1970 he toured the United States with a production of his latest play, *Madmen and specialists*, performed by his own company.

Abiku

In vain your bangles cast
Charmed circles at my feet
I am Abiku, calling for the first
And the repeated time.

Must I weep for goats and cowries
For palm oil and the sprinkled ash?
Yams do not sprout in amulets
To earth Abiku's limbs.

So when the snail is burnt in his shell,
Whet the heated fragment, brand me
Deeply on the breast. You must know him
When Abiku calls again.

I am the squirrel teeth, cracked
The riddle of the palm. Remember
This, and dig me deeper still into
The god's swollen foot.

Once and the repeated time, ageless
Though I puke; and when you pour
Libations, each finger points me near
The way I came, where

The ground is wet with mourning
White dew suckles flesh-birds
Evening befriends the spider, trapping
Flies in wind-froth;

Night, and Abiku sucks the oil
From lamps. Mothers! I'll be the
Suppliant snake coiled on the doorstep
Yours the killing cry.

The ripest fruit was saddest;
Where I crept, the warmth was cloying.
In the silence of webs, Abiku moans, shaping
Mounds from the yolk.

The immigrant

Knowing
(Though he will deny it)
That this equation must be sought
Not in any woman's arms
But in the cream-laid
De-Odo-ro-noed limbs
Of the native girl herself,
He scans the gaudy bulbs
(For the fiftieth time)
Of dancing Hammersmith Palace.
Then, desperately
(Although his swagger belies it)
He tries his manhood
On the triteness of –
'May I . . . ?'

And waits upon the languor of
Her bored appraisal.
They would have paired each other
To an even point
(Even though her stare confounds it)
Her gown, fashion wise
But body foolish,
Beggars his flashy
Incredible tie.
Her face exchanges
Vulgarity
For his uncouthness.
And the plumb of their twin minds
Reads Nil.
And yet her answer, given negative,
Was barbed with
(Albeit ill-fitting) contempt.
Without
Even the usual paliative
False-bottom smile,
Her eyes had said,
'You? Not at any price!'
He felt the wound grow septic
(Hard though he tried to close it)
His fingers twitched
And toyed with the idea,
The knife that waited on the slight,
On the sudden nerve that would join her face
To scars identical
With what he felt inside.
The blade remained
In the sweat-filled pocket.
He ran a gauntlet of milling couples
And they all seemed

To know
To jeer at his defeat.
He knew now the fatality
Of his black, flattened nose,
– Not at any price? –
The fingers shift
From blood
To feel the folded
Shrewish savings of his menial post.
His little brain seeks
Factual negation of her estimate
Seeks
Quick revenge
Lusts for the act
Of degradation of her sex and race.
Failing to find
A difference in the street-lamp faces
(He had sought the very best)
He makes his choice at random
Haggles somewhat at the price,
Then follows her, to pass
The night
In reciprocal humiliation.

Henry Dumas

was born on 29 July 1934, in the incredibly-named village of Sweet Home, Arkansas. He was shot and killed by police on 23 May 1968, on the Harlem Station (125th Street) platform of the New York Central Railroad. No explanation of the event has ever been offered, and certainly no one who knew him as one of the gentlest and least demonstrative of people has ever been able to think of a reason why anyone should want to kill him. Perhaps being black, being gentle, and writing poetry was enough, perhaps it could be spotted across a subway platform and engender rage.

Dumas had come to Harlem at the age of ten. He went to City College, then to Rutgers, spent three years in the Air Force (including a year in Arabia), and at the time of his death was teaching at Hiram College in Ohio. He was on the editorial staff of the *Hiram Poetry Review*, and was deeply involved in the Southern Illinois University's 'experiment in higher education' programme at East St Louis. He was also married, and had two children. His poetry had appeared in *Umbra* and *Freedomways*, and he had completed a novel. In 1970 Southern Illinois University Press brought out a posthumous two-volume edition of his work, edited by Hale Chatfield and Eugene Redmond: *Poetry for my people* (a large collection of verse – 176 pages) and *Ark of bones and other stories*.

Knock on wood

i go out to totem street
    we play
      neon monster
        and watusi feet

killer sharks chasin behind
    we play hide
    siren !
        and out-run cops
they catch
    willie
    and me
        splittin over fence
they knock
    in willie's head
    hole
they kick me watusi
    down
        for dead
like yesterday
    runnin feet in my brain
    won't stop willie lookin blood
        beggin me
cut off blackjack pain

so whenever you see me comin
    crazy watusi
        you call me watusi
i keep a wooden willie
    blade and bone outa that fence
a high willie da conqueror
    listen ! up there he talkin
wooden willie got all the sense

i go out to siren street
    don't play no more
me and willie beat a certain beat
    aimin wood carvin shadows

sometimes i knock on wood
    with fist
me and willie play *togetherin*
    and we don't miss.

A. B. Spellman

was born 7 August 1934 at Elizabeth City, North Carolina; he was christened Alfred by his schoolteacher parents but has for countless years been addressed as 'A.B.'. He went to Howard University in 1952 and remained there following his B.A. in political science and history to do graduate work in the Law School until 1958. For the following ten years he lived in New York, where he became a well-known Village personality through years of work in the Eighth Street Bookshop. His early work appeared in magazines like *Yugen* and *Kulchur*, but it was especially through his jazz reviews and broadcasts that Spellman attracted attention. He became a regular contributor to *Downbeat* and *Metronome*, writing with considerable insight and sensitivity about contemporary black music. With LeRoi Jones and Larry Neal he eventually became the editor of a new 'black music bulletin' called *The Cricket*. His book *Four lives in the bebop business* (1967) is, despite its title, one of the very few basic books on a musical development which has gone a remarkable length beyond the days of Parker.

In 1964 the Poets Press, run by Diane Di Prima, published Spellman's first collection of verse, *The beautiful days*, with an introduction by Frank O'Hara. In 1968 Spellman left New York for the South; in 1968–9 he was writer-in-residence at Moorehouse College in Atlanta, and afterwards he stayed in Atlanta as co-editor of the Centre for Black Revolutionary Art. He has recently been the first (and presumably last) black judge in the white poetry syndicate's American Literary Anthology farce. He has also started a new magazine, *Rhythm*, 'committed to revolutionary Pan-African nationalism'.

Untitled

when black people are
with each other
we sometimes fear ourselves
whisper over our shoulders
about unmentionable acts
& sometimes we fight & lie.
these are somethings we sometimes do.

& when alone i sometimes walk
from wall to wall fighting visions
of white men fighting me
& black men fighting white men
& fighting me & i lose my
self between walls &
ricocheting shots & can't say
for certain who i have killed
or been killed by.

it is the fear of winter passing
& summer coming & the killing
i have called for coming
to my door saying
hit it a.b., you're in it too.

& the white army moves like thieves
in the night mass producing beautiful
black corpses & then stealing them away
while my frequent death watches me
from orangeburg on cronkite &
i'm oiling my gun & cooking my food
& saying 'when the time comes'
to myself, over & over, hopefully.

but i remember driving from atlanta
to the city with stone & featherstone
& cleve & on the way feather talked
about ambushing a pair of klansmen
& cleve told how they hunted
chaney's body in the white night
of the haunted house in the mississippi
swamp while a runaway survivor
from orangeburg slept between wars
on the back seat.
times like this
are times when black people
are with each other & the strength flows
back & forth between us like
borrowed breath.

Ameer Baraka

was born 7 October 1934, in Newark, New Jersey, under the name of LeRoi Jones. He was processed by the public school system in his rather uninviting home town, then went to Howard University where he obtained his B.A. in 1954. During the next three years he served in the Air Force, much of the time in Europe, Africa and the Middle East. In 1957 he went to Columbia University, got an M.A. in philosophy, and stayed for post-graduate work before going over to the New School for Social Research (where he eventually returned as a teacher of creative writing).

During these late fifties, when Jones was in his early twenties, he began to attract attention both as a writer and as an uncommonly able editor. He and his wife Hettie Cohen edited *Yugen*, which ran to seven issues by 1961 as the undisputed leading magazine of the beats and the avant-garde – both at that time as white as snow. In 1960 Jones also became assistant editor of *Kulchur*, another of the legendary magazines of the period, and in 1961 Corinth Books (for whom he was poetry editor) brought out his first book, *Preface to a twenty volume suicide note*. From 1961 to 1963 he edited *The Floating Bear*, with Diane Di Prima. In 1963 LeRoi Jones affirmed his versatility once and for all, by adding a novel called *The system of Dante's hell* (published bit by bit in a variety of magazines, like Joyce's *Work in Progress* of *Transition* days, but not released in book form until 1965), a book on 'negro music in white America' called *Blues people*, and an anthology of work by *The moderns* (fourteen authors among whom Jones is still the only black) to the rapidly growing canon of his published work. The next year he branched out into the theatre; *Dutchman* opened off-Broadway in March and promptly carried off the Obie award for the season, and *The slave* opened in the autumn of the same year. His second book of poems appeared under the title *The dead lecturer*. The most popular piece from that collection, 'Black dada nihilismus', is featured, read by its author, on the New York Art Quartet's 1965 album (ESP-Disk 1004).

At this stage it was quite clear that a major new talent had burst on the American literary scene – in such a way and in such company that it never occurred even to his fiercest detractors (and they have been an envious many right from the start) to dismiss him the easy way, as merely another black author: a beatnik, one of those beardies – yes – but one of *them*? oh surely not. And this is the point at which LeRoi Jones turned a leaf and started out on the road which led to Ameer Baraka. The search for self, for meaning and for a place, which occupies a central place in all of his work, was narrowed down, defined. Identification, the necessity to find a cause, became the motive force. 'We are on the streets, we are somewhere in the world' – but also, painfully: 'When I walk in the streets, the streets don't yet claim me, and people look at me, knowing the strangeness of my manner, and the objective stance from which I attempt to "love them".'

In 1964 Jones moved to Harlem and there founded the Black Arts Repertory Theatre and its school, attracting people like Ed Bullins, Charles Patterson, Ben Caldwell, Clarence Reed, and eventually, through Bullins, sparking off a Black Arts West in California. But in Harlem certainly the streets did not yet claim him, and before too long he moved back to his native Newark, there to start Spirit House and its attendant publishing venture, Jihad. Spirit House and the Committee for a Unified Newark are more than just another community centre for the arts, they are a political organization aiming at total community involvement – not an easy task in an industrial ghetto. Political persuasion, the vital voters' registration drive, and the growth of civic pride among the blacks of Newark did not go without violent opposition – violence of a brutal physical nature – nor did it come about without making the gulf between the revolutionary leaders and their chosen people painfully plain. Black was still an acquired taste, hard to accept as a matter of fact, and therefore to be screamed out every minute of the day.

Meanwhile the books kept coming. *The baptism* and *The toilet* continued the theatrical success, even if their subject and setting confined them to the smaller more experimental stage. *Home: social essays* and *Black art* (a small collection of poems) both appeared in 1966; *Tales* and a short 'self-defence' play for the Spirit House theatre called *Arm yourself or harm yourself* followed in 1967. Then, on 4 January 1968, Le Roi Jones was sentenced to three years' imprisonment on a dubious arms charge, and the case made history because the contents of his work were cited by the judge as part of the motivation for the sentence. By that time, however, the author was no longer 'the alienated ex-Village poet but a dynamic black philosopher and Sunni Muslim soothsayer, concerned not only with lambasting whitey, but with reconstructing the political, cultural, and spiritual identity of the emerging Black Nation' – as Askia Muhammad Touré put it in the *Journal of Black Poetry* 10 (autumn 1968). The interview printed in that same issue revealed a quiet and balanced conviction, a great inner peace that one is glad to see happen. It is fitting that such a rebirth should be accompanied by the assumption of a new name.

During 1969 Ameer Baraka visibly put his house in order, even to the point of collecting seven years of poetry in the three-part *Black magic poetry*, and as many years as a dramatist in *Five black revolutionary plays*. Since then, only two fairly small pamphlets have appeared, both in 1970 and from the Third World Press in Chicago: *It's nation time* contains three long poems; *A black value system* reprints an essay that originally opened the first issue of *The black scholar* magazine. A collected edition of essays written after 1965 appeared in 1971 as *Raise race rays raze*.

Notes for a speech

African blues
does not know me. Their steps, in sands
of their own
land. A country
in black & white, newspapers
blown down pavements
of the world. Does

not feel
what I am.
       Strength
in the dream, an oblique
suckling of nerve, the wind
throws up sand, eyes
are something locked in
hate, of hate, of hate, to
walk abroad, they conduct
their deaths apart
from my own. Those
heads, I call
'my people'.
       (And who are they. People. To concern
myself, ugly man. Who
you, to concern
the white flat stomachs
of maidens, inside houses
dying. Black. Peeled moon
light on my fingers
move under
her clothes. Where
is her husband. Black
words throw up sand
to eyes, fingers of
their private dead. Whose
soul, eyes, in sand. My color
is not theirs. Lighter, white man
talk. They shy away. My own
dead souls, my, so called
people. Africa
is a foreign place. You are
as any other sad man here
american.

A poem some people will have to understand

Dull unwashed windows of eyes
and buildings of industry. What
industry do I practice? A slick
colored boy, 12 miles from his
home. I practice no industry.
I am no longer a credit
to my race. I read a little,
scratch against silence slow spring
afternoons.

        I had thought, before, some years ago
that I'd come to the end of my life.

           Water color ego. Without the preciseness
a violent man could propose.

         But the wheel, and the wheels,
won't let us alone. All the fantasy
         and justice, and dry charcoal winters
All the pitifully intelligent citizens
         I've forced myself
to love.

    We have awaited the coming of a natural
phenomenon. Mystics and romantics, knowledgeable
workers
of the land.

But none has come.
(REPEAT)
        but none has come.
Will the machinegunners please step forward?

I substitute for the dead lecturer

> *What is most precious, because*
> *it is lost. What is lost,*
> *because it is most*
> *precious.*

They have turned, and say that I am dying. That
I have thrown
my life
away. They
have left me alone, where
there is no one, nothing
save who I am. Not a note
nor a word.

        Cold air batters
the poor (and their minds
turn open
like sores). What kindness
what wealth
can I offer? Except
what is, for me,
ugliest. What is
for me, shadows, shrieking
phantoms. Except
they have need
of life. Flesh,
at least,
        should be theirs.

The Lord has saved me
to do this. The Lord
has made me strong. I
am as I must have

myself. Against all
thought, all music, all
my soft loves.

       For all these wan roads
I am pushed to follow, are
my own conceit. A simple muttering
elegance, slipped in my head
pressed on my soul, is my heart's
worth. And I am frightened
that the flame of my sickness
will burn off my face. And leave
the bones, my stewed black skull,
an empty cage of failure.

Beautiful black women

Beautiful black women, fail, they act. Stop them, raining.
They are so beautiful, we want them with us. Stop them,
    raining.
Beautiful, stop raining, they fail. We fail them and their
    lips
stick out perpetually, at our weakness. Raining. Stop them.
    Black
queens, Ruby Dee weeps at the window, raining, being
    lost in her
life, being what we all will be, sentimental bitter frustrated
deprived of her fullest light. Beautiful black women, it is
still raining in this terrible land. We need you. We flex our
muscles, turn to stare at our tormentor, we need you.
    Raining.
We need you, reigning, black queen. This/terrible black
    ladies

wander, Ruby Dee weeps, the window, raining, she calls,
     and her voice
is left to hurt us slowly. It hangs against the same wet
     glass, her
sadness and age and the trip, and the lost heat, and the
     grey cold
buildings of our entrapment. Ladies. Women. We need you.
     We are still
trapped and weak, but we build and grow heavy with
     our knowledge. Women.
Come to us. Help us to get back what was always ours.
     Help us, women. Where
are you, women, where, and who, and where, and who,
     and will you help
us, will you open your bodysouls, will you lift me up
     mother, will you
let me help you, daughter, wife/lover, will you

For Tom Postell, dead black poet

i

You told me, you told me
a thousand years ago. And the white man thing
you screamed on me, all true, and the walk
across from dead Trujillo, who grinned at us
into yr dead room. Only the winebottles lived
and sparkled and sailed easily for completion. You
screamed and slobbered on me, to hear you. And I
didn't. Shacked up with a fat jew girl. Talking about
Shakespeare, I didn't hear
you brother. Pussy Eater, you said, and another nigger

said the same, and the blood flowed down my face, and Lear
laughed at his new fool. I wallowed in your intestines,
brother, stole, and changed, your poems. And rode was
    rode
by the cows and intelligent snakes of the age. While they
killed you, while they ran you down third avenue, 'talking
through your mouth', I didn't understand. You had your
    hand
clapped tightly on your lips. Your eyes rolling rolled up
Sanpaku dying. 'The jews are talking
through my mouth.' And I was horrified so niggerish and
unheroic was your death. And jews talked through my
    mouth,
and I used your wine fume soul. I laughed among the beasts
and meateaters. I strode with them, played with them,
    thought myself
one with them, and jews were talking through
my mouth. I had not the sense to stop them.
A thousand years ago you told me. Horrified beyond
    breathing. Stiff
with terror at the kikish evil pulling at your lips. I should
    have screamed
for you, brother. I should have climbed to the tops of the
    buildings and
screamed and dropped niggerbombs on their heads. For my
    dead. For my
dead brother. Who told me. A thousand years ago.

ii

Now I know what the desert thing was. Why they fled
    from us
into their caves. Why they hate me now. Why Martin
    Duberman (what

kind of man . . .) A *Duber* man, dobiedoo . . .
   Why they hate me,
having seen them as things, and the resistance to light, and
   the
heart of goodness sucked off, vampires, flying in our midst,
      at the
corner, selling us our few horrible minutes of discomfort
      and frus
tration. Smile, jew. Dance, jew. Tell me you love me, jew.
      I got
something for you now though. I got something for you,
      like you dig,
I got. I got this thing, goes pulsating through black
      everything
universal meaning. I got the extermination blues, jewboys.
      I got
the hitler syndrome figured. What that simpleton meant.
      He can't
stand their desert smell, their closeness to the truth. What
Father Moses gave them, and lifted them off their hands. A
      Magic
Charm. A black toe sewn in their throats. To talk, to get up
off their hands, and walk, like men (they will tell you.
So come for the rent, jewboys, or come ask me for a book,
      or
sit in the courts handing down yr judgments, still I got
      something
for you, gonna give it to my brothers, so they'll know what
      your *whole*
story is, then one day, jewboys, we all, even my wig
      wearing mother
gonna put it on you all at once.

Ed Spriggs

was born Edward S. Spriggs in Cleveland, Ohio, in 1934, but seems to have lived in Harlem for most of his life. He has been an active member of the Spirit House group, and more recently became the editor of *Black Dialogue*, an utterly committed magazine on all aspects of black life in the United States. He is also a corresponding editor of the *Journal of Black Poetry*. His own publications are few and far between, but he has a genius for sparking off others and for raising important if often uncomfortable questions. In 1968 his decision to 'boycott' Clarence Major's anthology, *The new black poetry* (because it would be handled by a white publisher), sparked off a heated discussion on the responsibilities of the writer and the possibilities of black publishing ventures. For poetry, several ventures exist, but for anything more ambitious the establishment is still virtually the only outlet. 'le Roi the terrible, baldwin the goodie gum drop, malcolm the irreplaceable, and all the rest of us git compromised just because we want to git our things out there. it's weird. black publishers and the would be ones stand in the shadows subsisting on broadsides, throwaways, rubberstamps and other trivia because black writers won't give them a decent play, but we scream "Black Power".'

For black Newark: 1968

begin
here
with us
here
on these shores
weary beginning
of NATION, but with us
here begins here.

on these shores
hold tightly to
the cord, crossing the sea
the LAND, the cord, the LAND.
the cord, the sea, the cord, the LAND
with blood filled memories of MOTHER.
the cord is taut
and rhythms re bound
as rhyming waves continually
come to shore and sink down
within the drum-head of our being
on all the shores
of the sun and our vision.

Pending solemnization

Olórun is winking
He is talking above the drums
And in the intervals
Our ancestors agree
Among themselves.

He is talking above the drums
And they accept our gifts;
The white flowers, the pigeons
the cocoanuts and rum,

Tomorrow
Obàtálá and Yémàjá
Will grant us our wish.
They will receive us in New Oyó.
We offer the dark rooster

And the white hen and our ancestors talk
Above the drums.
They say our houses are to be one, Ebun.
They say our houses are to be one!

Ed Bullins

has emerged as the leading playwright of the black revolution, and one of the most imaginative and forceful spokesmen for the black theatre in general. He was born in Philadelphia in 1935, but his breakthrough to general public recognition did not come until 1968, when his triple presentation under the general title *The electronic nigger*, produced at the American Place Theater, was the only thing worth seeing in New York. Long before that, however, Bullins had already become an active force on the black home front. He was involved in LeRoi Jones's venture into Harlem and after that had co-founded its offshoot, the Black Arts West in San Francisco's Fillmore district. He has been the cultural director of the Black House, San Francisco headquarters of the Panther party, and a frequent contributor to all the more militant black magazines. Bullins writes stories and essays, and occasionally poetry, some of which appeared in the *Journal of Black Poetry* and in the *Negro Digest*. Woodie King junior presented Bullins alongside Jones, Ronald Milner and Ben Caldwell in *A black quartet*, and in 1969 *Five plays by Bullins* included the successful *Electronic nigger* plays. Most of the plays are one-acters, the latest to appear is *We righteous bombers*. The one I like best is the *Short play for a small theatre* which took up only one page in the April 1971 issue of *Black World*. In 1970 Bantam Books published in paperback Bullins's anthology of *Plays for the black theatre*. In the same year the New Lafayette Theater in Harlem, where Bullins has been resident playwright since his return from the West Coast, put out his fine pamphlet of ritual poetry, *To raise the dead and foretell the future*. In 1971 Bullins published a collection of 'early writings' under the title *The hungered one* and a 'black love fable in four movements' called *The duplex*.

When slavery seems sweet

When slavery seems sweet
its scent is Chanel
and rustles Sachs silk
upon an ivory slide
that presses
your Black balls
like Burgundy grape

When slavery seems sweet
it wakes you with a
listerine kiss
& sends you to the
corner to its father,
Saul
(six eggs
your morning meal,
dear)
& please don't read
the paper before coffee,
darling,
you know how the
news of Mississippi
gets you up on the
wrong side of the
morning

When slavery seems sweet
it has a history
buried in the caves of
Germany, Russia, Poland,
Great Britain . . . and re-
members a grandfather, a

junk peddler,
in St Louis,
spoke nothing 'cept
Yiddish

When slavery seems sweet
You wallow within
its colorless
flesh, seep through
its skin
(a slug, you are)
your eyeball sweating
hate of yourself
& when you come
inside that form
you scream & dream
of the creamy Eunuchs
that will one
day noose the barbed
wire about
your Black throat . . .

> singing
> daddy
> daddy
> daddy

Kofi Awoonor

is a Ghanaian, born George Awoonor Williams at Wheta in the Togo region, on 13 March 1935. His mother came from Togo, his father was a Sierra Leonean. He was educated at Keta ('the flood town, with the sea in my ears'), at Achimota and finally at the University in Legon, where he later returned to work in the Institute of African Studies (1960–64). His speciality: vernacular poetry. In 1961 he founded the literary magazine *Okeyeame*, in which he published some of his own stories. In 1964 Mbari brought out his volume of verse, *Rediscovery*. A novel, at that time described as 'in a shapeless manuscript', seems not to have materialized – unless it contained the material for *This earth my brother*, 'an allegorical tale of Africa' published in 1970. By that time, Awoonor had left Africa for a year of further study in London where he is now chairman of the Comparative Literature Program, and after that to teach at the State University of New York. Earlier he took an active part in Ghana's nascent film industry and became the chairman of the Ghana Film Corporation (1964–7). He has also worked as an actor, and written for radio. Together with Geormbeeyi Adali-Mortty he edited the anthology *Messages: poems from Ghana*, published in 1970 in Heinemann's African Writers Series. A new book of poetry, *Night of my blood*, appeared in 1971.

My god of songs was ill

Go and tell them that I crossed the river
While the canoes were still empty
And the boatman had gone away.
My god of songs was ill
And I was taking him to be cured.
When I went the fetish priest was away

So I waited outside the hut
My god of songs was groaning
Crying.
I gathered courage
I knocked on the fetish hut
And the cure god said in my tongue
'Come in with your backside'
So I walked in with my backside
With my god of songs crying on my head
I placed him on the stool.
Then the bells rang and my name was called thrice
My god groaned amidst the many voices
The cure god said I had violated my god
'Take him to your father's gods' he said in my tongue
So I took him to my father's gods
But before they opened the hut
My god burst into songs, new strong songs
That I am still singing with him.

I heard a bird cry

There was a tree which dried in the desert
Birds came and built their nests on it
Funeral songs reached us on the village square
And our eyes were filled with tears
The singing voice which the gods gave me
Has become the desert wind
Talk, my heart, talk
Talk and let me hear,
And I will ask you how
How they avoided the sacred rams.

Your tears are running like flood river,
They are as bitter as the waters of the sea.
Why are your eyes so red?
Do you cover your head with your hands
And tremble like the orphan child by the road-side?
I shall leave you
So that I go to perform the rites for my Gods
My father's Gods I left behind
Seven moons ago.

I shall weave new sisal ropes
And kill two white cocks
Whose bloods will cleanse the stools.
The bitterness of your tears,
Still lingers on my tongue
And your blood still clings to my cloth.

Do you remember that day,
When I saw you
And asked whether you too
Believed in the resurrection of the living?
Remember that the greenfields
Are waiting for the feet of the striving.

Hush, I heard a bird cry!

The winds of the storm have blown,
Destroying my hut
Goats came and did a war dance
On the fallen walls of my father's house
What happened before the vulture's head is naked?

Swear to me that you saw the widows
Who beat the funeral drums
And put tears in the eyes of the orphans by the road-side.

Jay Wright

was born on 25 May 1935, at Albuquerque in New Mexico, spent most of his childhood in San Pedro, California, near the shipyards. He has had a rather chequered career. He played professional football with the Mexicali Eagles in the Arizona–Texas league, and for Fresno in the California State league. He also studied chemistry at the University of New Mexico – for two months. He served three years in the Army Medical Corps, mostly in Germany. He obtained a B.A. from the University of California in 1961, then entered Union Theological Seminary, which he stuck for one whole semester. Wright tutored for S.A.V.E. in Harlem, and at the Teachers-Writers Collaborative run by Columbia. In 1966 he received his M.A. in comparative literature from Rutgers University. During 1967 he went on a reading tour through the South. Towards the end of 1968 he became poet-in-residence at Tougaloo, and the year after he held the same position at Talladega College. Since then he has left the States for the warmth of Jalapa in Mexico and more recently for the cold of Midlothian.

One of Wright's main interests, as a writer, is in the theatre. His thesis at Rutgers was on Calderón, and some of his own short plays were produced at the Exodus Coffee House in San Pedro (*The doors*), and by the Playwright's Workshop at Berkeley (*Welcome, black boy*). One longer play, *Balloons*, was printed in Baker's Plays series – half a dozen others remain unpublished. Wright has published only one small collection of poems, *Death as history*, in 1970, but is beginning to attract a considerable in-cult. The first anthology appearance I can trace is in Langston Hughes's *New Negro poets: USA*, of 1964: his is the opening poem, a very accomplished piece of work for an eighteen-year-old football player.

An invitation to Madison County

I ride through Queens,
out to International Airport,
on my way to Jackson, Tougaloo, Mississippi.
I take out a notebook,
write 'my southern journal', and the date.
I write something,
but can't get down the apprehension,
the strangeness, the uncertainty
of zipping in over the Sunday streets,
with the bank clock flashing the weather
and time, as if it were a lighthouse
and the crab-like cars mistook it
for their own destination.
The air terminal looks
like a city walled in, waiting for war.
The arrivals go down to the basement,
recruits waking at five A.M. to check out their gear,
to be introduced to the business end of the camp.
Fifteen minutes in the city,
and nothing has happened.
No one has asked me to move over
for a small parade of pale women,
or called me nigger, or asked me where I'm from.
Sure only of my destination, I wait.

Now, we move out through the quiet city,
past clean brick supermarkets,
past clean brick houses with nameplates
and bushy lawns, past the sleepy-eyed
travelers, locked tightly in their cars.
No one speaks. The accent I've been
waiting to hear is still far off,

still only part of that apprehension
I had on the highway, in Queens.

The small campus springs up
out of the brown environment,
half-green, half-brown, covered over
with scaly white wooden houses.
It seems to be fighting this atmosphere,
fighting to bring some beauty
out of the dirt roads, the tense isolation of this place.

Out to Mama's T's, where farmers, young instructors
and students scream for hamburgers and beer,
rub each other in the light of the jukebox,
and talk, and talk. I am still
not in Jackson, not in Mississippi,
still not off that highway in Queens,
nor totally out of Harlem, still
have not made it into this place,
where the tables creak, and the crickets
close up Sunday, just at evening,
and people are saying goodnight early.
Afraid now, I wonder how I'll get into it,
how I can make my hosts forget
these impatient gestures, the matching socks and tie
I wonder how long I'll have to listen
to make them feel I listen, wonder
what I can say that will say,
'It's all right. I don't understand
a thing. Let me meet you here, in your home.
Teach me what you know,
for I think I'm coming home.'

Then I meet a teen-aged girl,
who knows that I can read.

I ride with her to Madison County,
up backroads that stretch
with half-fulfilled crops,
half-filled houses, half-satisfied
cows, and horses, and dogs.
She does all the talking,
challenging me to name the trees,
the plants, the cities in Mississippi, her dog.
We reach her house,
a shack dominated by an old stove,
with its smoky outline going up the wall
into the Mississippi air, mattresses tossed
around the table, where a small piece of cornbread
and a steaming plate of greens wait for her.
Her mother comes out, hands folded before her
like a madonna. She speaks to me,
moving step by step back into the house,
asking me to come again,
as if I were dismissed,
as if there were nothing more
that I could want from her, from Madison County,
no secret that I could ask her to repeat,
not even ask about the baby resting there on her belly,
nor if she ever knew anyone with my name
in Madison County, in Mississippi.

Since I can't, and will not, move,
she stays, with her head coming up,
finally, in a defiant smile.
She watches me sniff the greens,
look around at the bare trees
heaving up out of the bare ground.
She watches my surprise
as I look at her manly nine-year-old

drive a tractor through the fields.
I think of how she is preparing him
for death, how one day he'll pack
whatever clothes remain from the generations,
and go off down the road,
her champion, her soldier, her lovable boy,
her grief, into Jackson, and away,
past that lighthouse clock,
past the sleepy streets,
and come up screaming,
perhaps on the highway in Queens,
thinking that he'll find me,
the poet with matching socks and tie,
who will tell him all about the city,
who will drink with him in a bar
where lives are crackling, with the smell
of muddy-rooted bare trees, half-sick cows
and simmering greens still in his nose.

But I'm still not here,
still can't ask any easy question,
or comment on the boy, the bright girl,
the open fields, the smell of the greens;
can't even say, yes, I remember this,
or heard of it, or want to know it;
can't apologize for my clean pages,
or assert that I must change, after being here;
can't say that I'm after spirits in Mississippi,
that I've given up my apprehension
about pale and neatly dressed couples
speeding past the lighthouse clock,
silently going home to their own apprehensions;
can't say, yes, you're what I really came for,
you, your scaly hands, your proud, surreptitious

smile, your commanding glance at your son,
that's what I do not search, but discover.

I stand in Madison County,
where you buy your clothes, your bread,
your very life, from hardline politicians,
where the inessential cotton still comes up
as if it were kind, and belonged to you,
where the only escape is down that road,
with your slim baggage, into war,
into some other town that smells the same,
into a relative's crowded house
in some uncertain city, into the arms
of poets, who would be burned,
who would wake in the Mississippi rain,
listening for your apprehension,
standing at the window in different shadows,
finally able to say, 'I don't understand.
But I would be taught your strength.'

The father comes down the road,
among his harness bells and dust,
straight and even, slowly, as if each step
on that hard ground were precious.
He passes with a nod,
and stands at the door of his house,
making a final, brief inventory
all around and in it.
His wife goes in, comes out with a spoon,
hands it to you with a gracious little nod,
and says, 'Such as . . .'

'Such as . . . ,' as I heard
when my mother invited the preacher in,

or some old bum, who had fallen off
a box-car into our small town
and come looking for bread-crumbs,
a soup bowl of dish water beans,
a glass of tap water, served up
in a murky glass.
'Such as . . . ,' as I heard
when I would walk across the tracks
in Bisbee, or Tucson, or El Paso, or Santa Fe,
bleeding behind the eyes,
cursing the slim-butted waitresses
who could be so polite.
'Such as . . . ,' as I heard
when I was invited behind leaky doors,
into leaky rooms, for my loneliness,
for my hunger, for my blackness.
'Such as . . . ,' as I hear
when people, who have only themselves to give,
offer you their meal.

John Pepper Clark

was born in 1935 in the Ijaw country of the Niger delta in Nigeria. He went to the Government College at Wari and later to University College at Ibadan, where he founded the literary magazine *The Horn*. His schooling completed, Pepper Clark made his living from writing in one form or another. From 1960 onwards he worked as a journalist at Ibadan and Lagos, and after his return from Princeton University (where he spent 1962 as a graduate student on a fellowship) he became the leading editorial writer on the staff of the Lagos *Daily Express*.

His literary work, like that of several of his contemporary countrymen, is divided between poetry and the theatre. His play, *Song of a goat*, published by Mbari in 1962, has proved popular with Nigerian audiences – it was produced first at Ibadan, later at Enugu by Michael Echeruo. In 1964 Oxford University Press brought out *Three plays* by Clark, and in 1966 another play, *Ozidi*. Meanwhile his American observations had been put down in the documentary *America, their America*, in 1964. John Pepper Clark's poetry, much of which has appeared in *Black Orpheus*, was collected in three volumes: *Poems* by Mbari in 1962, *A reed in the tide* in 1965, and most recently in *Casualties: poems 1966–68*. In 1965 Clark also contributed a very interesting article to *Présence Africaine* (NS 54) on 'Thèmes de la poésie africaine d'expression anglaise'. A collection of essays on African literature appeared in 1970 under the title *The example of Shakespeare*.

'Abiku', the title of one of Clark's poems given here (and also of the 'Wole Soyinka poem, appearing a few pages back), is a Yorubu word meaning 'a child born to die': a spirit child, borne by a human mother, who wants to return to its spirit companions. The mother tries to make it stay by the use of herbs, charms, stigmata: unless the child can be made to stay, it will be born again and again to the same mother. The dead child is marked in the hope that it will be recognized on its next appearance, for recognition will force it to stay and grow up normally. The implications of this theme for the modern African are endless

and these two poems are by no means the only ones on the
theme.

Ivbie

i

Is it not late now in the day
Late late altogether late,
Turning our doubled backs upon fate.
To pluck out of honey
Fresh milk fangs?
Is it not late, so awfully
Late, fingering sun-dried husks and
Shells on whose live-sap suckling,
We stifled our initial pangs?

You who from far-fabled country
Reached into our virgin jungle
Passing thro' like therapeutic rays
Muscles tangled-torn out of roll
Has the fire stopped riding the wind
The fire you lit cigarettes on behind?

Walk as on your tarmac our occult groves
With alien care and impunity
Walk in abandon ahead tourist droves
Eyes so big like sailors
        Ranging mirage distance
To where God in heaven plunges to earth
How can they in the fixity
And delirium of a glance

How can they catch the thousand intricacies
Tucked away in crannies
And corners perhaps known only to rats?
How can they tell the loin-cloth
Cast away in heat of desire
The bits clanging in the wind
    Now groins want oiling?
The sanctuary of things human is swathed
In menstrual rags, not in the market-place.

. . .

ii

In the irresolution
Of one unguarded moment
Thereby hangs a tale
A tale so tall in implications
Universal void cannot contain
The terrible immensity
Nor its permanence dissolve
In the flux-wash of eternity:

Those unguent gums and oils
Drawn in barrels off to foreign mills
The soil quarried out of recognition
As never would erosion
    another millenium
The blood crying for blood spilt free
From keels away on frothing sea
The dark flesh rudely torn
And grafted on to red fetid sore
Breeding a hybrid lot
To work the land of sunset –

Sweet Mrs Gamp, not a coward,
Followed her man into the wild
And wiping gentle hands on her eyes,
Without bias,
Delivered amid cries in the mission ward
A wisdom-teethed child
Is it truce or ruse
That Peace which passeth all understanding
O big brother in heav'n!

iv

Say, you communal gods at the gate,
Has yon whiff of carrion crept
Past your bars while you slept?
Did it roll-blowing gain the village
And without even as a fight
From you? Say, did he brow-beat
Bribe-beat you into our plight?
A man is a man for a that
So when fallen upon in the dark
Why bleat, oh why bleat!

Come into the house
Go in to bed O children
Who falls in mud
Need not smear another's blood
So come in children.

An unlaid ghost
Has come into village
Tonight out of the coast
I hear his wings flapping in the twigs

I smell the dank sweat
Brine of his breath
Heavy on plantain leaves and palm
They crinkle dry up and die
Yes I Oyin in times
Before farm-maids walked home
Upon the rainbow in fog climes
Had lived the fear frou-froued in fronds
The loud despair out in the dark
We have been through all before.

Fear him children O fear the stranger
That comes upon you
When fowls have gone to roost
Fear him his footfall soft light
As a cat's shadow far darker
Than forest gloom or night
And flimsy like matter in the mist
O fear the dragon-smoke-cloud
That hangs bloat-floating over
Roof-thatch mangoes and lime
Fear him that wreath-curling fetish-tree
Seeth-writhing beyond lofts
It turns out no less than he:

A snake-bird fell down early flat
In the market-place
Clinging quick to earth on his belly
Digging with his bristle fangs
Open communal graves
                    Amid confused clangs
Of race and riot
Fear the poison passed out or spat
Straight on our ancestral seat

Fear it tho' a trickle or dot
Fear it the corruption
That dissolving, will deluge all the earth
Fear the flood, children
On whose repulsive waves
Two life-buoys alone bob –
'Dirt and death, death and dirt . . .'

'Dirt and death'
And all along only the owl
Safe in her magic cowl
Saw all
I the white bearded woman
Of night fame saw all
But men heeded not my hooting
Placed instead penalty in warning
And finality in brief omen.

v

When you and I were young
Oyin bade us hold our tongue
Bade us note 'things dont stand
Looking into . . . so why trouble
Our heads,' and later in our moments
Of expansion, both on the cricket field and
          At the office desk,
We clapped ourselves on the back;
So well-fed on sweet quotations and wine
Were we, with pride, we said;
'Forget O forget . . . to forgive is divine.'

Yet in my father's house I can not sleep
Nor shut myself up in peace

But loud knocks,
Absorbed in thick of shocks,
Come beating back on my door
Crying: 'Sleep no more!'

I can not sleep I can not sleep
Though not acting
Fierce flood-lights flush-focus me
Our fathers rightly or wrongly
Heavily drugged slept at least
And you say I ought to on this cup of tea
But all night I walk to and
Fro dung-polished floors
Unable to shut a little slit
That fast should fringe like flash at flies
Balancing the right and wrong of it –
For does not the Holy Writ
Loud peddled abroad
To approve imperial flaws and fraud
Does it not say true:
'Knock and it shall be opened unto you?'

And if I open unto them in haste
That cry out of a violated past
Shall ancient bones
          Safe laved in seas
Not crush-crash on crags
And if I fail
Shall bars not lifting burst of their own?

Talk then round the point Hamlet
          Do talk on
               The Niger, long ago,
Faced with similar lot,

Hedged round and till tomorrow
Will go spinning whirlpools.

The cocks begin again to crow
The night is old
And I am cold
        So cold I know
Right in my bones the fear
Electrical in her breast
        As new kites appear
Swooping in from the west.

In can not sleep nor act
And here I pace, her bastard child,
A toy twirled on by complexity
'Gnawing at my finger-tips deep perplexity'.

Abiku

Coming and going these several seasons,
Do stay out on the baobab tree,
Follow where you please your kindred spirits
If indoors is not enough for you.
True, it leaks through the thatch
When floods brim the banks,
And the bats and the owls
Often tear in at night through the eaves,
And at harmattan, the bamboo walls
Are ready tinder for the fire
That dries the fresh fish up on the rack.
Still, it's been the healthy stock
To several fingers, to many more will be

Who reach to the sun.
No longer then bestride the threshold
But step in and stay
For good. We know the knife scars
Serrating down your back and front
Like beak of the sword-fish,
And both your ears, notched
As a bondsman to this house,
Are all relics of your first comings.
Then step in, step in and stay
For her body is tired,
Tired, her milk going sour
Where many more mouths gladden the heart.

Frank Abiodun Aig-Imoukhuede

is a Yoruba contemporary of Soyinka, born in 1935 at Edunabon near Ife in Western Nigeria. His real home is in Benin province, but his early life was unsettled – he attended at least fifteen primary schools before going to Ibgodi College and finally graduating from University College, Ibadan. At college, where he majored in English, Frank wrote two plays for campus production, and drama has remained one of his favoured outlets. Most of his later plays were written for broadcasting rather than for stage production. His early verse appeared in Pepper Clark's magazine *The Horn*, and later poems were published in *Black Orpheus*. After graduation, Aig-Imoukhuede worked first in Broadcasting House in Lagos, then as a reporter on the city's *Daily Express*. In the early sixties he moved to Ibadan where he works for the Ministry of Information.

Aig-Imoukhuede comes from a family where an interest in letters was inevitable. His father, a clergyman, worked on a translation of the *New Testament* into Ora, a widely-spoken branch of the Bini language group, but died just before finishing it. His son was the first of the younger Nigerian writers to use the vernacular pidgin-English which, much more than 'proper' English, forms the lingua franca of the common people of West Africa. As Langston Hughes put it: 'Its dialect possesses an urban folk flavour full of earth humour, but it is difficult for foreigners to understand.' Langston seems to have been the first to print the poem 'One wife for one man' together with its fine line-by-line translation by Frank Kobina Parkes.

One wife for one man

*italicized line-by-line translation from West African pidgin-English
by Francis Ernest Kobina Parkes*

I done try go to church, I done go for court.
I've tried the altar, I've tried the court-room.
Dem all dey talk about di *new culture*
All both of them talk about is this 'new culture'.
Dem talk about *equality*, dem mention *divorce*.
They talk about 'equality' and proclaim 'divorce'.
Dem holler am so-tay my ear nearly cut;
They shout it so much my ear-drums nearly burst:
One wife for one man.

My fader before my fader get him wife barku.
My father's father had plenty of wives.
E no' get equality palaver; he live well
He did all right without all this 'equality' humbug.
For he be oga for im own house.
And he was the boss in his own house.
Bot dat time done pass before white man come wit im
But since then the white man's come with this stuff about
One wife for one man.

Tell me how una woman no go make *yonga*
Tell me how a man can keep a woman from being bossy
Wen'e know say na 'im only dey,
When she knows well she has no lawful rival.
Suppose say-make God no 'gree-'e no born at all.
Suppose it is God's will she has no offspring at all.
A' tell you dat man bind dey craze wey start
I tell you the man must've been crazy who suggested
One wife for one man.

Jus' tell me how one wife fir do one man?
Just tell me how one wife can be enough for a man?
How man go fit stay all time for him house,
What can make a man stay home all the time
For when belle done kommotu.
When his one wife is pregnant as she can be?
How many pickin, self, one woman fir born
After all, how many children can one woman bear
When there's just one wife for one man?

Suppose self, say na so-so woman your wife dey born;
Suppose your wife's womb houses only females;
Suppose your wife sabe book, no' sabe make chop;
Suppose your wife is educated and doesn't know how to cook;
Den, how you go tell man make 'e no go out
Then how can you tell a man not to run around –
Sake of dis divorce? Bo, dis culture no waya o!
*Or he'll be threatened by divorce. Man, this 'new culture' is
    awful:*
Just one wife for one man!

Sonia Sanchez

is probably the most powerful of the black women poets of today, although she lacks the craftsmanship of Audre Lorde and will ultimately be more limited in scope than Nikki Giovanni. Her work has the fierceness and directness of street poetry, but was never itself 'of the streets' in the way much of the fashionable whitey-baiting was.

Born 9 September 1935 in Birmingham, Alabama, she obtained a B.A. from Hunter College in New York in 1955 and afterwards went to the New York University writing courses. She has taught creative writing herself, in the black studies programme of San Francisco State College for two years, and she has also taught fifth graders in New York. She is the mother of three children, two of them still very young, and has been the wife of fellow-poet Etheridge Knight. Together they moved first to Indianapolis, then to Pittsburg, where in 1969–70 they both taught in the black studies programme of the municipal university. The next academic year saw Sonia Sanchez, alone again, teaching black literature at Rutgers.

Apart from poetry (which has appeared in predictable magazines like *Soulbook*, *Librator*, *Negro Digest* (*Black World*) and the *Journal of Black Poetry*, as well as unpredictable ones like the *Transatlantic Review*), Sonia Sanchez also writes one-act plays. All her published books are collections of poetry: *Homecoming* appeared with an introduction by Don Lee (and accompanied by a complete tape recording read by the author) from Broadside Press in 1969. The same press brought out *We a baddDDD people* in 1970: the ill-considered spelling of this title (just try and SAY it that way) is indicative of what Don Lee has since come to regret as Sonia's 'pre-1968 bag', a regrettable reluctance (or incapability?) to look at circumstance and presentation with the fresh and inquisitive eye that makes a poet distrust old formulas and invent new concepts. *It's a new day* (1971) contains 'poems for young brothers and sisters', and these youngsters are given their own voice in *360° of blackness comin at you*, the anthology Miss Sanchez edited out of her experience with the workshop she conducts at the Harlem branch of the New York Public Library. Her one-act play *Sister Sonji* was performed at the opening of the Black Folks Theater of Northwestern University in 1971.

Indianapolis/summer/1969/poem

like.
    i mean.
             don't it all come down
to e / co / no / mics.
                  like. it is fo
money that those young brothas on
illinois &
            ohio sts
                allow they selves to
be picked up
            cruised around
                  till they
asses open in tune
            to holy rec / tum /
                    dom.
& like. ain't it
          fo coins
                that those blond /
wigged / tight / pants /
                wearen / sistuhs
open they legs / mouths / asses
                fo wite / dicks
to come
        in tune to
              there ain't no

asses
    like blk / asses.
                 u dig?
and i mean.
           like if brothas
programmed sistuhs fo love
instead of
             fucken / hood
                 and i mean
if mothas programmed
             sistuhs fo
good feelings bout they blk / men
and i
    mean if blk / fathas proved
they man / hood by
               fighten the enemy
instead of fucken every available sistuh.
and i mean
       if we programmed /
                loved / each
other in com / mun / al ways
             so that no
blk / person starved
          or killed
              each other on
a sat / ur / day nite corner.
then may
      be   it wud all
come down to some
            thing else
like RE VO LU TION.
          i mean if.
              like.   yeh.

TCB

wite/motha/fucka
wite/motha/fucka
wite/motha/fucka

        whitey.

wite/motha/fucker
wite/motha/fucker
wite/motha/fucker

        ofay.

wite/mutha/fucka
wite/mutha/fucka
wite/mutha/fucka

        devil.

wite/mutha/fucker
wite/mutha/fucker
wite/mutha/fucker

        pig.

wite/mother/fucker
wite/mother/fucker
wite/mother/fucker

        cracker.

wite/muther/fucka
wite/muther/fucka
wite/muther/fucka

        honky.

               now.   that it's all sed.
let's get to work.

Right on: white america

this country might have
been a pio
            neer land
once.
   but.   there ain't
no mo
       indians   blowing
custer's mind
                with a different
image of america.
                        this country
might have
            needed shoot/
outs/ daily/
            once.
                    but. there ain't
no mo real/ white/   allamerican
                                bad/guys.
just.
   u & me.
            blk/ and un/armed.
this country might have
been a pion
            eer land.   once.
                            and it still is.
check out
            the falling
gun/shells   on our blk/ tomorrows.

James Washington Thompson

was born in Detroit on 21 December 1935. He was schooled in his home town, and from his high school days he trained as a dancer. He appeared professionally from 1953 on, and left his native city in 1955 when he choreographed an ice act for the Fairbanks (Alaska) winter carnival. The travelling phase of his life lasted to 1959, when it was cut short by ill health. A forced stay back in Detroit saw the gradual change to a life in which writing became his principal creative outlet.

James Thompson's first published poem appeared in June 1958 and two years later he was included in the national anthology *America sings*. The first major presentation of his work came in the Heritage anthology *Sixes and sevens* in 1962, and since then his work has been decidedly under-exposed. This is partly a by-product of Thompson's fiercely high standards, which have also kept him from issuing a book of his poems (until at last a compromise was reached by issuing his 'early work' in the Heritage volume *First fire: poems 1957–1960*) and which are on another level the cause of the state of continual unemployment in which he has since 1964 been living in New York. 'Survival sustained by my own criteria is most important to me' – fine, but when one lives in an equally continual struggle for health, life is at times barely tolerable and being the self-styled 'Georgia Douglas Johnson of First Avenue' provides but meagre sustenance.

Thompson was to have edited the third issue of *Umbra* magazine after the original editors fell out over the question of whether or not to publish Ray Durem's attack on president Kennedy in the wake of the latter's assassination. The issue never came to be, and it is typical of the paranoid situation around Thompson that he appeared as 'editor emeritus' on only a few of the copies of the later *Umbra* anthology. When that anthology finally appeared, the disputed editor was travelling in Europe. At present he is working with Richard Bruce Nugent on a history of *Harlem: a cultural capital*. He has recently issued a few of his poems as broadsides, including the one printed here.

You are alms

for Cecil Taylor

You are alms – love
  – all lilting legs
     lending light
  in shadowed streets;
    strolling benificent
beneath star's steel, morning's mauve,
      noon's amalgamate frenzy;
rain wind and the rage of raucous Rotarians
realing to unwind from the stupor of acquisition
      in an alcohol-acquired feel
        of ready red-bloodedness
and rage; rage for your alms, your acquisition
      being the essential (yourself)
        not bi-leveled rooms
          attached
          entombed.

You are alms – love
  – the lyricism of the living,
    unfettered even in your needs
      strolling benificent
        lending light
to pallid thugs hunched on corners
      hopping in frantic step:
the brown posture – clutching, anguished,
    at their acquisition of manhood
      (not being men but postures to penises attendant);
in envy without knowledge of need which makes being
    vital, and acquisition – an attendant factor
      of living –
        not itself a life;

without knowledge of why the language of African
   or Red Indian – wedded in a mellow mouth
      raised an idiom
         and an esthetic felt,
            formulated through the ritual
of maintaining life in the outrageous streets of the settlers.

You are alms – love
  – raised in an idiom and an esthetic
     felt and formulated
       before the brain could record the feeling
          in the introspective isolation of intellect
    to art, attending:
           yours is the art and record of itself
and though time visits the vital with remonstrances
    art is the living – not the dead.

Mbella Sonne Dipoko

was born in 1936 at Dawala, the main port of the Cameroons. He spent most of his childhood on his grandfather's farm at Missaka on the Mungo river which forms the border with West Cameroon. His primary schooling also took place in West Cameroon, then he moved further west again and attended secondary school in Eastern Nigeria from 1952 to 1956. He worked in Cameroon for a while, then joined the news staff of Radio Nigeria in Lagos in 1957. Since 1960 Dipoko has lived in Paris, where he read law and studied journalism and worked for some time for the *Présence Africaine* organization. After 1968 he travelled widely through Europe and North Africa.

Présence Africaine published his earliest works: a short story in 1962, poems in 1963 and 1964 (issues 48 and 51). He has remained a regular contributor ever since, but in later years has written mainly prose. His novel *A few nights and days*, which appeared in 1966, is to be the first part of a trilogy. *Because of women* came out in 1968. That same year the B.B.C. produced his play *Overseas*. The volume *Black and white in love* (1972) is a 'collected poems 1963–1971' and contains a new and shorter version of 'Our Destiny', the long poem of 1965 which represents Dipoko in this anthology.

Our destiny

i

Anthems and flags
Medals of gold
Say, lively voice
Who are these innovators
Inheritors of past kingdoms?

The night will not reply
In its pre-occupation with tomorrow
Living the centuries
Not knowing the years.

And we sang our memory
Ritual rags lacquered with blood
In the passion of naked night
Obeying an incarnate instinct
To link the real with the unknown
Multiform in the universe

ii

We are the progeny of a persecuted achievement
We are the progeny of an infinite past
Naked in love and in hatred naked
Creating in blood and dying in blood.
Crimson blossom of shattered virginity
Bleeding wound in the Amazon's heart
Bleeding wound in the warrior's breast
And behind
In the villages and towns
The sinewy lines of the mind's creation
The order of ruler and the ruled
Served by the throaty voice of drums
Served by the thoughtful, less buoyant music of strings
And all the time
God of the gods
Creating the glory of masks
Laying the landmarks of the spirit.

iii

We are the moderns in time
Working for tomorrow
Shying away from the naked kingdoms of history
Trying to build new cities
In a world of clean flags

That is not progress
It's all falsehood.
The causes remain the same
The rituals have only gone into trenches
And sacrificial blood flows in pipe-lines.
Things are being done in secret which were done in public
We become like all mankind
Decent without
Indecent within
Scaling the years on the misery of others.

iv

Evening.
The sun is falling into a cloudy horizon
Like a lighthouse into a surfy sea.

We had fixed our destination at the distant rim of the ocean
And our eyes were turned towards the skyline.
So did we falsify our ideal which we saw alighting before us;
So did our enchantment become the stylized gaze of a mask.

The sky has still not touched the ocean
So that the treasures of the illusory heights may pile at your
     destination.

v

We lose our authenticity in its quest
And to thinkers more than three times in the morning
And to thinkers more than three times in the evening.

I opt for something else
Not for the naked city.

But make its glories eternal
While our thoughts like travellers overtake our hesitations
Heading for the distant tomorrow
Cultivating our memory
Creating the unknown
Remembering without aping
Our great grand parents in the valley of drums and rivers
Our great grand parents in the dance of blood.

vi

See,
Nimbus clouds!
Listen,
Festival drums!
What is being celebrated?

The ruler appears
The drums are frenzied
Women sing and clap their hands
While in the adjoining forest echoes of glory play
Songs of a millenary repertoire
On the xylophone of fallen trees

Soon, we shall be sitting around the conference table
Priest worker pagan and sorcerer
Sitting there to draw up the plan of our days
And then it will be time to glorify you, life
Manifest in God
Manifest in hunger
Manifest in the end-of-the-village tree
Manifest in the forces that kill
And palavering we shall defend our respective visions of you
Virgin greenness that yellows and fades away with time
Virgin greenness vulnerable to the prospector's knife.

vii

Not for their ears
The story of growth
Not for their eyes
The becoming.

Deaf in the depth of departure
Dumb in death.

Not for their joy
The new colours.

And the elephants lumbered in
Bulldozing the graves away
So do the mortal mighty of an affluent breed despoil
The monuments of departure
Leaving behind egocentric tracks of vanity.

viii

Never again will it rise
The old flag
Artificial rainbow that dried the sky of rain
Pompous drunkard draped in wind-borne colours.

And the oppressed freed themselves
And the oppressors killed themselves

Glory of our struggle
Dressed in the uniform of hope.

Exile

In silence
The overloaded canoe leaves our shores

But who are these soldiers in camouflage,
These clouds going to rain in foreign lands?

The night is losing its treasures
The future seems a myth
Warped on a loom worked by lazy hands.

But perhaps all is not without some good for us
As from the door of a shack a thousand miles away
The scaly hand of a child takes in greeting
The long and skinny fingers of the rain.

Okogbule Wonodi

was born at Diobu, near Port Harcourt in Eastern Nigeria, on 23 August 1936. From an early age he had to act as breadwinner for his family: his father died in 1945. This, of course, interrupted his school education, but in 1956 he managed to train as a teacher and thereafter to work as a teacher until he went to the Nigerian College of Arts, Science and Technology at Enugu in 1960. The following year he went to the University of Nigeria at Nsukka, from which he graduated in June 1965 with an honours degree in English. His poems had by then appeared in several Nsukka magazines, and he had become a regular contributor to *Transition*. For his first book of poems, *Icheke*, published by Mbari in 1964, he still used the full version of his name and the older spelling of his surname (which has since become a pain for bibliographers): Glory Okugbule Nwanodi. Wonodi did a year at Iowa University to obtain his M.A., and joined Paul Engle's writers' workshop there, as had Gwendolyn Brooks before him.

'Laments for 'Shola' ('Shola was a nephew of the poet who died when only one year old) clearly demonstrates Wonodi's absorbing interest in folklore, tradition and proverbs. Much of his work, as for instance the seven-part title poem in his published book, is concerned with the conflict of generations and the clash of opposing cultures.

Laments for 'Shola

i

When the dust came I sought shelter
Under a canopy of thick grown palms,
I raised my voice,
Half-speaking, half-singing,

Above the rustle of winds,
Far from our fathers' barns.
I have heard your response,
Half-laughing, half-chattering,
Fondling my name;
Flattered, I have hung my songs
A foot too low
That you and Tony and Toddy
May from them weave
Scenes too distant for your birthcry.
But you are gone,
Gone with morning dews on your head,
You have left before the first rays
Have lighted the swallows' ways.

ii

We sang through white horns
At the sprouting in the farms,
But the fruit falls unripe,
Our barns thin and rust
Yet their keepers keep no words
That were theirs on earth.
Only, I wait for the rains
And speak to them:

>   You've left us to ourselves
>   In our season of drought;
>   We have come handsfull
>   And have made our mouth taleful
>   Between drought and new yams,
>   But you have left your hold
>   And your seeds fall unripe

I am alone
And the murmur of my lips,
Carry song and tears homewards
From a plain away from home.

    And when the rains come, you fathers,
    Who will run and laugh under your houses?

Gerald Jackson

was born in Chicago on 30 December 1936, and lived there long
enough to go through the public school system and eventually to
the Art Institute. Moving to New York, he continued his art
training at the Brooklyn Museum school. He is primarily a
painter, but has been writing poetry off and on for a number of
years and is at present trying to combine both interests in the
production, together with his bookbinder friend Richard Minsky,
of a small group of books with illustrations in various techniques
(including original paintings). His earliest publication was in the
Umbra anthology of 1967, and that same year he read one of his
poems on the New Jazz Poets record edited by Walter Lowenfels
and Art Berger. Since then he has also written a play, and more
work has appeared in the anthology *Expanded poetry*.

The song

for Kevin

So many centuries dried and blown away –
The sun wind and sea turn red,
Italian swiss colony port,
   We drink and sing the song, Oh red.

Out of the starting gate stumble leap –
burning too fast to run is a feather in your cap –
like a motor you, and rest –
then on to the filling stop, Oh red.

At the post bucking foam arms yea swing –
   and tear armpits out,

eye rounding drop daze, drop; Run, red,
calls feel me hot:
can't feel no pain

                  can't-feel-no-pain.

The light shows the track at night
   small blue green yellow noises
cheer for head to see pennies into air
kicking their legs apart:
thumpings meet wail dazzled cures to split boys and girls
alike down the middle
   white and black America yes or no.

There are so many hippy dips around giving their fathers
     hell
   Fuck you, fathers, I ain't going to be president
and fuck you fathers, I am going to be president.

Velvet underpants give t.v. father pot
   put t.v. father down

oh, yes, that was good news; oh, yes yes

red rain is possible I say to you fathers
   and some of hip America
Why wasn't Cleopatra mother of our Country instead of
     Aunt Jemima?

In case you teeter totter at this point
   the velvet underpants fall down
and there are still babies with two heads
   faces and franks with bags and bags of bits
pieces of residue
That drink wine like their fathers on the Bowery
   that wonder to thrill at kicks in any

evenings find them talking of best ways;
I mean to say, of marrying the president's daughter.

Golden eyes run smooth along regretting
my own wondering why the bop galloping lips sound
    unsteady
Golden head turns over my skinny frame.
Inside the golden brain counts my life
outside the same smile crosses the country face of home
    crosses leaving tracks or long red peppermint haircuts
or black snotty noses broken teeth white black –

Stale tits along after midnight
and our best R&B R&R C&W R&B P&R cannot change
    her.

The hanging tree still stands
Our European our Britannia as funny
as being Japtized by black ghetto patriots
    dressed as imagined white G.I. gallants

Or Negro Americans singing the song of the Green Berets
at house parties.
and sing because we happy
and sing because we are sad
    and sing because it all runs down to the sea
And the sky turns red, Oh red.

Clarence Major

was born on 31 December 1936 in Atlanta, Georgia, but spent most of his childhood in Chicago where he went through all the usual 'educational channels', winding up at the Art Institute in 1954, the year he published his first collection of poems *The fires that burn in heaven*. The year after that he went into the Air Force from which he emerged again in 1957 to become a welder in an Omaha (Nebraska) steel plant. From 1958 to 1961 he edited his own literary magazine, the *Coercion Review* – he has since become associated with the *Journal of Black Poetry*, compiling its twelfth issue in 1969 as guest editor. That same year he also edited an anthology called *The new black poetry* which consisted of single poems by seventy-six 'new' authors who showed signs of permanence.

Major has been involved in various experiments aimed at using creative writing as a teaching aid. His work for the Harlem Education Program resulted in the 1967 *Writers' Workshop Anthology*. At the Pennsylvania Advancement School in Philadelphia, at Macomb's junior high, and at Brooklyn College, Major has conducted similar creative writing classes. He now lives in New York City, where his wife, Sharyn Skeeter, is fiction and poetry editor for Gordon Parks's glossy magazine, *Essence*.

Major's published work shows an unusual versatility (unusual also in the high and professional standards he maintains, even in 'minor' details like presentation). His early collections of poetry were private publications: *Love poems of a black man* (1964) and *Human juices* (1965) both bear the Coercion imprint. *Swallow the lake*, however, was done by the Wesleyan University Press in 1970. His novel *All-night visitors* was an Olympia Press book in 1969 and has also appeared in German and Italian. A new novel *No* is scheduled for publication this year. Meanwhile a steady stream of poems, short fiction, and non-fiction articles has gone into anthologies and magazines, most recently and regularly into *Nickel Review*, Walt Sheppard's marvellous 'pulp art form'. The *Dictionary of Afro-American slang* appeared in 1970.

A great believer in the diversification of his talent, Clarence Major planned to have three poetry books out in 1971: *Symptoms & madness* is done by Ted Wilentz at Corinth, *Private line* has already appeared as volume fifteen in my own Heritage series and only *The Cotton Club*, which is on the Broadside programme, has not yet materialized.

For her, the design

Even though the music and it's harmony
Works into one area of my boredom,
There remains the stale air.
And the house, and the things around
My brain cells: the little things
You never come to terms with;
No matter how more difficult
The neighbors task is.
I am tired of filledup ashtrays.
The apartment is too dull a place
To think in. But it will all come
Down to this: the time of day, the night
Sharper each year.
When there was no idea at all
That you would last even this long.

Surrounded myself with alien things;
because I feel the distance between us.
But there are left still a few belongings
Of my ancient life: the Ibo woman with a shrunken leg,
The Yoruba woman with a jug, and there are a few
Dancing kings. My dear, nothing has changed
In my paradox.
If I were writing a letter to you I would say

They worry about Mao Tse-Tung these days. Small talk,
You know.
I remember your perfumed body used to comfort
Me in the terror filled nights & I didn't think
Of you as a white stranger then. I was blind;
Deft, and dumb. And maybe a little bit still.
In the cold rooms in which a mocking laugh
Rattled inside the walls and the planks of the house
Whined like a dozen sick kittens.

Well, let me tell you a little bit about my new lady.
She belongs to the World.
It is not proven yet, but this most exalted
Creature is a coddle for a fool's pride.
And pleasure. Contemporary moments in America
And undignified designs, exist thru her presence.
She has to come down front, baby.

They say the important thing is her virtue;
And her sins, *and* the building she lives in.
And the country she lives in.
She lives in 'security' but one day
Gothic and modern chaos with very dry wood
Will burn her down. The roots of destruction are in her
    now.

Let me tell you I always enjoyed your ability
To look into your cracked mirror.
This new hustler can't do it: she has to go on missions.
To save people from killing Her.

The tongue of the water does not wake her,
But it has not let me sleep yet.

And when the water runs low, there is fire
To fight. Sometimes I sleep like an old man.
Sometimes I even watch class B movies on TV.
I think, at times, I am losing my touch;
I faced rough walls while my poor family watched.
I can tell you about these things
Because I *know* you. Scared into intelligence
By the terrible minutes in which we know less.

I stop to think what a weekend would be like
If I were to pick up a little man on the road
With real goat legs.

The churp of small birds in Chinese poems,
The clamor of nordic fear & hunger to EXPLOIT
& the peaceful people in ancient villages
Would quickly make sense, all together in harmony
If I saw, really faced my little goat man.
Something for a change would be too lovely
And terrible to endure.

For her, these capsules by the millions;
She cannot really lose, none of us can.
Aspects of the metropolitan excuse for not thinking.
Persist like the dying sun.

I told her sternly one day that women were sound
Because of the capacity for motherhood.
Abstractions. I was inactive for long whiles
Until with all I have of courage I got to my feet
To force myself like a commercial sunrise
Forces itself from a post card sent to you from Florida.

I suppose it is not important to you;
Nor to her. I remember when I first met her.

I said, Come into this black purple house of blues.
That night she had so much cold in her
She could hardly speak, but she came in.
She was a sick civilization all right.
She told me back in those days that there would be
A funeral, perhaps right on the sidewalk of her city.

Author of an attitude

(with one's ass on one's shoulder)

guess i was imper-
sonal as you, can. be
my back, standing
at the red bar, liquor of
the year;

        in that year in the middle
        of the day. but then you
        were real cool. and, could, &
        did Speak. spoke to people be-
        fore they spoke

                to you. you weren't famous
                then. you saw you were
                a bitch, last time i saw
                nothing, so busy. glossy eyes,
                so blackeyed. we ate blackeyed
                peas, from paperplates dug your
                spoon through. don't think

you even recognized me.
so busy watching your-
self. trying to protect
your own ass, i guess

Lebert Bethune

was born at Kingston in Jamaica in 1937, and went to schools on his native island. Having completed his education as far as high school, he left Jamaica to join his family who were already living in New York's Queens borough. Bethune then attended New York University to obtain a B.Sc., and later went to France to complete his studies at the Sorbonne in Paris. He has travelled extensively in Europe and the Middle East, and worked in East Africa as writer and co-director of documentary films for the Tanzanian government. Some of his poems appeared late 1965 in number 55 of the magazine *Présence Africaine*. Later in the same year one of this group became the title poem of his first book, *Juju of my own*, privately published in Paris with a cover by cartoonist Siné.

In the preface to *Juju* the author wrote that his poetry centres on 'the experience of a man living in the Western world, cut off by slavery and colonialism from the cultural well-spring of his motherland – Africa'. Certainly the theme of alienation is much more dominant in Bethune's work than is usual with West Indian poets, who have on the whole rather veered in the somewhat opposite direction, towards nostalgia.

Apart from poetry and film scripts Bethune has written plays, a number of essays and articles, and a novel called *Skate's dive*. During the 1970–71 academic year he taught courses on the black experience at Columbia University Teachers College.

A juju of my own

To make a Juju of my own
For I was tired of strange ghosts
Whose cool bones
Lived on the green furnace of my blood

Was always my destiny
So she warned me – my grandmother,
And now and now
When I kindle again her small eyes with their quick lights
Darting ancient love into my infancy
And when I break through to her easy voice
That voice like the pliant red clay she baked
She sings the only lullaby she sang me

'Me no care for Bakra whip
Me no care fe fum-fum
Come Juju come'

So I am fashioning this thing
My own Juju
Out of her life and our desire
Out of an old black love
I am baking my destiny to a lullaby –

'Me no care fe Bakra whip
Me no care fe fum-fum
Come Juju come . . .'

To strike for night

The man with the blood in his sight
with the knife in his voice
and nothing to lose but that life
which in living like them
comes to death – is me

The man with the children on fire
his women with panthers for titties
and something to hate like that love
which in loving like them
comes to nothing but death – is me

The man who will win is me
the man who cant die anymore
the man who forged behind patience and smiles
a long black gun of justice
that man is me

I'm Dedan
I'm Toussaint, I'm Garvey
I'm names that in dying for life
make life surer than death

Yes
The man with the blade poised
to strike for my night
that black man is me.

Larry Neal

whose full name is Lawrence P. Neal, was born in Atlanta, Georgia, on 5 September 1937, but reared in Philadelphia where he went to the Roman Catholic high school. He graduated from Lincoln University in 1961, then did post-graduate work at the University of Pennsylvania. Married, he now lives in New York where he was the education director of the Panther party. In 1971 he went to Haiti on a Guggenheim fellowship.

In a number of his more public ventures Larry Neal seems to have been moving in the shadow of LeRoi Jones – but this is an altogether deceptive appearance. His wide knowledge of contemporary literature, a lightning intelligence which has no place for irrelevancies, and a very practical view of the realities of the revolution have made Neal, in LeRoi's words, 'bright and Black and always in front and on top of what's happening'. Together with Jones he edited the giant anthology *Black fire* (1968) which contains fourteen essays, ten theatre pieces, seven stories or fragments of novels, and the work of no less than fifty-six poets. It will undoubtedly be the definitive record of its chosen decade – and Larry Neal's afterword will survive most of the other contents, it really is a bitch. The real difference between Neal and Jones is perhaps best illustrated by their respective comments on N.A.A.C.P. secretary Roy Wilkins: where Jones in his Black Art period launched his famous promise to 'stick half my sandal up his ass', Neal contented himself with the far more deadly observation that 'Wilkins got scabs on his head from scratching so much!'

A frequent contributor to such magazines as *Black Dialogue*, *Soulbook*, *Liberator* (of which he was the arts editor for some time), Larry Neal has so far published only one book of his own: *Black boogaloo*, subtitled 'notes on black liberation', is a collection of poems which ends on this short and almost hidden statement of Neal's realism in revolutionary poetics: 'Poems are ways into things, the opening of the natural spirit in us. Poems do not shoot guns; they are spiritual cohesives, tightening us up for the future war, if there be one, and giving us the strength to build a nation.

These are dimensions of our consciousness; ourselves extended as far as current possibilities allow.' A new book, *Hoodoo hollerin' bebop ghosts & other versions* has been announced.

Black boogaloo was published in 1969 by the *Journal of Black Poetry* Press. A year earlier, Neal had turned the ninth issue of that miraculous Journal into a model anthology of new poetry. His plays remain unpublished and, as far as I know, unperformed. He has also been working on a biography of Richard Wright (which would seem unlikely to obtain the blessing of Wright's widow who appears to hold strong views on which parts of the myth she wants preserved at all costs), and with Evans Walker on the screenplay for Pharr's novel, *The book of numbers*.

The summer after Malcolm

The Summer after Malcolm, I lost myself in a jet stream of mad words, acts, bits of love-memory. Like that. It was a cold bitch. the pain. All Summer, I could see Malcolm's face drifting with the sound of Harlem children: old men played checkers on the blocks running between Seventh and Eighth: and there was a moan in the Summer air. the wine smells and hallways were screaming women. Mine gone. Missed her smell and awkwardness. the walk. the soft spots in the dark of her. a still clinging that robbed sleep on hot nights.

Under the beat, we made love, reaching for something beyond the music, made love well into the morning. Hot Summer bodies sliding against the flesh, and the sudden come draining us leaving us wet with love-slime.

That was the Summer after Malcolm. The end and the con-

tinuation of a Black Dream. Marks my era. Marks my phase
in time. After Malcolm, the seasons turned stale; there was a
dullness in the air for awhile. And you had gone, and there
was a lingering beauty in the pain. Now there are scraps of
you here and there in the backwash of my mind. Stuck
between odd pages in a book, your handwriting in red ink.

Malcolm X – an autobiography

I am the Seventh Son of the Son
who was also the Seventh.
I have drunk deep of the waters of my ancestors
have traveled the soul's journey towards cosmic harmony
the Seventh Son.
Have walked slick avenues
and seen grown men, fall, to die in a blue doom
of death and ancestral agony,
have seen old men glide, shadowless, feet barely
touching the pavements.

I sprung out of the Midwestern plains
the bleak Michigan landscape wearing the slave name –
Malcolm Little.
Saw a brief vision in Lansing, when I was seven, and in
my mother's womb heard the beast cry of death,
a landscape on which white robed figures ride, and my
Garvey father silhouetted against the night-fire, gun in hand
form outlined against a panorama of violence.

Out of the midwestern bleakness, I sprang, pushed eastward,
past shack on country nigger shack, across the wilderness
of North America.

I hustler. I pimp. I unfulfilled black man
bursting with destiny.
New York city Slim called me Big Red,
and there was no escape, close nights of the smell of death.
Pimp. Hustler. The day fills these rooms.

I am talking about New York. Harlem.
talking about the neon madness.
talking about ghetto eyes and nights
about death oozing across the room. Small's paradise.
talking about cigarette butts, and rooms smelly with white
sex flesh, and dank sheets, and being on the run.
talking about cocaine illusions, about stealing and selling.
talking about these New York cops who smell of blood and
        money.
I am Big Red, tiger vicious, Big Red, bad nigger, will kill.

But there is rhythm here. Its own special substance:
I hear Billie sing, no good man, and dig Prez, wearing the
        Zoot
suit of life, the pork-pie hat tilted at the correct angle.
through the Harlem smoke of beer and whiskey, I under-
        stand the
mystery of the signifying monkey,
in a blue haze of inspiration, I reach for the totality of Being.
I am at the center of a swirl of events. War and death.
rhythm. hot women. I think life a commodity bargained for
across the bar in Small's.
I perceive the echoes of Bird and there is gnawing in the
        maw
of my emotions.
and then there is jail. America is the world's greatest jailer,
and we all in jails. Black spirits contained like magnificent
birds of wonder. I now understand my father urged on by
        the

ghost of Garvey,
and see a small black man standing in a corner. The cell, cold.
dank. The light around him vibrates. Am I crazy? But to
     under-
stand is to submit to a more perfect will, a more perfect
     order,
to understand is to surrender the imperfect self,
for a more perfect self.

Allah formed man, I follow
and shake within the very depth of my most imperfect being,
and I bear witness to the Message of Allah
and I bear witness – all praise is due Allah!

Julia Fields

is one of the few black poets of note to not only come out of the deep South but to actually, and voluntarily, still live in its rural areas. Born 21 January 1938, at Uniontown in Alabama, she was one of the younger of eight children in a farmer's family. After completing her secondary schooling at Hatch High School, she graduated from Knoxville College in Tennessee with a B.Sc. in 1961. She attended the Bread Loaf writers' conference in New England in 1962, and went to summer school at the University of Edinburgh, Scotland. Julia Fields taught for some time at a Birmingham, Alabama, high school and at Hampton Institute, and spent the mid-sixties in New York. She married Lloyd Lawrence, a storekeeper and filling station attendant, almost (if that were possible) as beautiful as she is herself – they made their home, which now includes two children, in Scotland Neck, North Carolina.

For several years, even before she went to New York, Julia Fields had become an in-cult through the anthologies of Rosey Pool and through personal appearances of great charm and force at several black writers' conferences. In 1968 the Poets Press in New York brought out her book of *Poems*, and in that same year Julia had a National Council on the Arts grant, a major share (with twelve poems) in the otherwise undistinguished collection *Nine black poets* edited by R. Baird Shuman, and an appointment as writer-in-residence at Miles College in Birmingham. Apart from poetry she writes short stories, which have appeared in *Negro Digest* and in the anthology *Black fire*; and plays, one of which, *All day tomorrow*, was produced in May 1966 at her old school, Knoxville College. During the 1969–70 academic year she returned to Hampton Institute, this time as writer-in-residence.

For Malcolm X

The voice has gone
Out of the wilderness
Out of the carnage kingdom
Out of the mire.
And without his eloquence
We are mute
And rocks and stones break in the soul
The world winds
On its frozen axis
The dizzy oceans churn our pain.
All needed storms abate
Themselves. Moons freeze the rain.

Gone. Delivered.
So piteous there were
The stolid and the dumb
So piteous as not to mourn
So piteous, so many
The stolid and the dumb.
Gone. Delivered.
He has gone up, delivered.

His eyes were mirrors of our agony.
They are closed.
His lips were testaments of our hunger.
They are closed.
His ears were circuits for our cries.
They are closed.
His hands were petitioners against our bondage.
They are closed.
When shall such another
Pierce and sting this land?

When shall such another
Herald this land?
Gone. Delivered.

They have shut the eyes of
The father
Before the risen womb
Over the tears of the wife
They have shrived him for the tomb
They have sent death
For the father
With the swords
And with the merciless
Voices of the guns.
They have hidden the father's death in words
And god has ceased from giving them sons
Everywhere in the vacuum land.

Toussaint! Dessalines! Marcus! Patrice!
Behold this man.
Gone. Delivered.

And we are here
With his deliverers.

If the million voices could cry 'reason' –
So piteous there were
The stolid and the dumb
So piteous as not to mourn
So piteous, so many
The stolid and the dumb.
Gone. Delivered.

Ishmael Reed

was born 22 February 1938 at Chattanooga in Tennessee, and is fond of explaining that 22 is 'the most powerful number in hoodoo numerology'. Beyond these basic facts, to which can be added that he attended the University of Buffalo, Ish would much prefer to remain obscure – 'too much of that stuff clutters, you know'. Patient observers have noticed, however, that his passing usually has consequences. In 1967 he went to California, where he has been teaching black studies practically ever since.

'Mr Reed is a member of the American metaphysical night-flying squad along with Cecil Brown, Steve Cannon, Calvin Hernton, Glenn Myles and Joe Overstreet and other young American painters and writers: astro-soul detectives closing in on the Fiend about to tap his shoulder as signal for arrest.' Mr Reed is also a very successful novelist, whose extravaganzas called *The free-lance pallbearers* (1967) and *Yellow-back radio broke-down* (1969) met with enormous critical success. *The rise, fall, and . . . ? of Adam Clayton Powell* also appeared in 1967, under the name Emmett Coleman. *Mumbo Jumbo Kathedral* has been announced as his next novel.

Reed's stories, articles and poems have appeared in a varied number of periodicals, of which Hoyt Fuller's *Negro Digest* was the least, and Walt Sheppard's *Nickel Review* ('a pulp art form'), the most endearing. His prose anthology *19 necromancers from now* (1970) 'omitted White writers. Examining the many exclusionary American anthologies that flood the market, I somehow feel that they will get by.' Reed's only book of poetry appeared in 1960 in the Heritage series: *Catechism of d neoamerican hoodoo church* ('may the best church win. Shake hands now and come out conjuring – '). He reads one of the poems in this book on the Broadside (Folk-ways) album *New jazz poets*.

Catechism of d neo-american hoodoo church

iii

   i do not write solicitd
   manuscripts. oswald spengler said
   to joseph goebbels when askd to make a
   lie taste like sweet milk.

because they wrote d way they saw it, said
their prayers wrong, forgot to put on their number in d
a.m., got tore dwn in d streets & cut d fool:
men changd their names to islam & hung up d phone on
    them.
meatheaded philosophers left rank tongues of ugly mouth on
their tables. only new/ark kept them warm that summer. but
now they will pick up d tab. those dear dead beats who put
our souls to d wall. tried us in absentia before
some grand karate who hd no style. plumes on garveys hat
he was.

iv

word of my mysteries is getting around. do not cme
said de dean / invite cancelld to speak in our chapel
at delaware state. we hv checked yr background. u make
d crucifixes melt. d governor cant replace them.
stop   stop   weird customer.

v

i am becoming spooky & afar you all. i
stir in my humfo, taking notes. a black cat

superstars on my shoulder. a johnny root dwells
in my purse. on d one wall: bobs picture
of marie laveaus tomb in st louis #2. it is
all washd out w/ x . . . s, & dead flowers &
fuck wallace signs. on d other wall:
d pastd scarab on grandpops chest, he was
a nigro-mancer frm chattanooga. so i got it
honest. i floor them w/ my gris gris. what
more do i want ask d flatfoots who patrol d beat
of my time. d whole pie? o no u small fry
spirits. d chefs hat, d kitchen, d right
to help make a menu that will end 2 thousand yrs
of bad news.

vi

muhammed? a rewrite man for d wrong daily
news. messenger for cons of de pharaohs court.
perry mason to moses d murderer & thief. pr man
for d prophets of SET. as for poets? chapt
26 my friends – check it out. it is all there in
icewater clear.

Norman Jordan

comes from West Virginia. He was born at Amsted, 30 July 1938. Years later he became what is now known as a high school drop-out, and after that he spent four years in the Navy. Ever since then he has lived in Cleveland, Ohio. He worked there with students at the Muntu workshop, read at Karamu, and founded O.D.A.C.B.A., a sort of Cleveland offshoot of Chicago's O.B.A.C. Married, with two children, Jordan works as technical writer for a Cleveland business firm. In 1970 he was writer-in-residence at Karamu, with a special brief to start a literary magazine and develop the theatre. He writes plays as well as poetry, and in both injects a healthy dose of sceptical realism into the ideals of the revolution to which he is obviously deeply committed. His first book of verse, *Destination: ashes*, was published in 1970, and the next, *Above Maya*, appeared in 1971.

The second plane

I have
watched
them try
to fill
your empty
Black pocket
your empty
Black belly

Come
with me
I will
fill
your empty
Black mind.

Black warrior

At night while
whitey sleeps
the heat of a
thousand African fires
burns across my chest

I hear the beat
of a war drum
dancing from a distant
land
dancing across a mighty
water
telling me to strike

Enchanted by this
wild call
I hurl a brick through
a store front window
and disappear.

Keorapetse Kgositsile

is a South African from Johannesburg, where he was born 19 September 1938, and where he spent the first twenty years of his life. He graduated from Madibane High School, and left South Africa for good in November 1961. He worked for a while at Dar-es-Salaam for the now defunct *Spearhead* magazine, and late in 1962 made his way to the United States where he has since attended various universities (Lincoln, New Hampshire, Columbia). From Columbia's creative writing workshop he went to the New School for Social Research, being sponsored by the African American Institute. He is now on the staff of *Black Dialogue* under its new editor Ed Spriggs.

Kgositsile's articles and poems have appeared in the *Negro Digest* (*Black World*), *Soulbook*, *Liberator*, and of course *Black Dialogue*. The poem 'My people no longer sing' was published in number twenty-three of the African magazine *Transition* in 1965. Early in 1967 Kgositsile's work was featured in *Présence Africaine* 62. His first book of poetry, *Spirits unchained*, put out by Broadside Press in 1969, won him the second Conrad Kent Rivers Award. He has since published two further collections: *For Melba* (his wife) in 1970, and *My name is Afrika* in 1971.

Kgositsile has been accepted with alacrity by his contemporaries in militant black American letters, and at first one could not escape the impression that he was being used more or less as a mascot, at best as an ambassador from a motherland with which for many years it seemed almost impossible to establish tangible relations. The quality of his work and the intensity of the person behind it have quickly dispelled any further fears.

Like the tide: cloudward

    Turning here
  Or returning there
A fractured rhythm from
The distant past makes demands
Or the image summoning
The existence of things
Or exploding the core of
The sinister rot our minds must vomit
When the cloudward flood screams
And some panting and fear-ridden
Wish to have been born without as
Much as a teaspoonful of brain
           Soldiers or architects
We might have been. But here we stand torn
Between academic masturbation and splitting
Or chiselling words leaving the air unreddened
Where for humanity a little wrench
Would have sufficed for salvation. But
Words, be they elegant
As verse or song
Robust and piercing as sunshine
Or hideous memories of our
Cowardice in bondage are meaningless unless
They be the solid coil around our desire and method
Or the most 'competent rememberer'. May we

    Turn here
  Or return there
Where a fractured rhythm from
  The distant past moves us.

My people no longer sing

Remember
> When my echo upsets
> The plastic windows of your mind
> And darkness invades its artificial light
> The pieces of your regrets hard to find
>
>   Remember
> I shall only be a sighing memory then
> Until you look in the fiery womb of sunrise
> Retrieving songs almost aborted
> On once battered black lips

Remember
> When you get sickandtired
> Of being sick and tired
> To remind the living
> That the dead cannot remember.

Sam Cornish

is one of those amazing people whose trail one crosses wherever one goes: I have met friends of Sam's in every corner of America without ever meeting him. He was born Samuel James Cornish on 22 December 1938, in West Baltimore, Maryland, and has lived in Baltimore most of his life. He dropped out of Douglas High School after one semester in 1952, and from the age of fourteen has been self-educated.

Cornish seems to have been writing poetry for most of his life. By 1967 he had published four small, undated, and mostly mimeographed pamphlets of verse: *Angles, Generations, In this corner, The shabby breath of yellow teeth*. A fifth book, with a photo-cover, contains poems dated 1963. It is called *People beneath the window*, and the introduction says that 'this is Sam's Spade book' – meaning it tries to sort out what it means to be black (and 'the only way to know is to be born that way', as Waring Cuney said several decades back). Cornish has an oblique but devastatingly honest approach to life and the things he finds meaningful in it. In his work for the Enoch Pratt Free Library 'community action' programme it was, in the words of his supervisor, 'his imagination, closeness to the lives of the people in Baltimore's inner city, and poetic gifts that transformed the idea' into a workable reality. He started a magazine for the 'young voices from the black ghetto': the first issue of *Chicory* appeared in November 1966, and it continued to be published every four to six weeks for years. Sam edited it for a year, then went to Boston University for the academic year of 1967–8. His next book of poetry, *Winters*, appeared at Cambridge, Massachusetts, in 1967, and his most recent collection, *Generations*, is dated Boston 1971. He has also published two children's books: *Sam* in 1969 and *Your hand in mine* in 1970. After Boston, Cornish joined the Central Atlantic Regional Education Laboratory in Washington, D.C. as a consultant in methods and techniques of teaching reading and writing to elementary school pupils.

Harriet Tubman

harriet tubman you are so
black
you make my mother
cry

go from door to northern
door black is black your
skin is deeper
than the dust
in your throat
your skin
is a dark place
you live in

Lord while I sow earth

lord while i sow earth
or seed   the sun go down

my only mother on a dirt
floor dying

her mouth open on straw
and black soil

the smell of chicken
or stew in a pot

her only memories
i think

of her children
made in her and sold

too old on the land
unable to walk
the dry hair falling from the skull
she moves when my silent feet
come in from the fields

i think she knows
i live her life

what passes from the mother
kills   child

lord you hide behind books
and words

i sing to hide
the sounds of my feet

dance to conceal
the pistol under my apron

Joseph Waiguru

is a Kenyan born in 1939 at Nyeri, about sixty miles north of Nairobi, in the shadow of Mount Kenya. He was educated at Kangaru Secondary School, and in 1959 went to Makerere College in Tanzania from which he graduated in 1964 in English, economics and political science. His earliest poems appeared in the college magazine *Penpoint* which was started in 1958. 'The round mud hut' appeared in 1965 in David Cook's Makerere anthology, *Origin East Africa*.

The round mud hut

The round warm hut
Proud to the last
Of her noble sons
And daughters
Stands besieged.

Of late, stones,
In tripartite agreement,
Guarded a fire.
And then a pot,
A large hot pot
Which nurtured
Black, black children.

Near the door
Stands a thin-necked pot,
Guard to the entrance,
Hiding cold, cold water,
Water cold
As the morning dew.

Three thick gourds
Firm on the floor
Near the wall
Have in them something,
Something sour-sweet,
Which, three days past,
Was tasteless.

That is a mat tray,
The work of a skilled hand;
Abundant with food,
Yes, ten round lumps,
It's generous to all.

There's a shelf,
Masterpiece to a carpenter
Specialized in wood and string,
On it rests
Calabashes large and small.
Their sum who knows?

See five stools,
Three three-legged,
Two four-legged,
Worn smooth through use.

Up there,
A high, high shelf,
Higher than man standing,
Covered with soot,
A story strange it tells;
Fires have burnt, and burnt.

And there's a bed,
No, more than one:
Many goats have died
To make the bedspread.

The bleating sheep
And the horned goat,
Calves cud-chewing
At that end penned,
Share the warmth
Of the round mud hut.

All this and much more,
Slowly and slowly disappears:
Slowly and slowly iron appears,
Lays a siege on the roof
And takes prisoner the pot and the gourd.
The plate, the cup, the lamp,
What's this but a change
To the new oblong house?
The round mud hut is no more.

Al Young

hails from Ocean Springs, Mississippi. He was born there 31 May 1939, but went to Detroit when still a child and there evinced his first literary aspirations by editing a journal in junior high school: *The krazy krazette* was devoted to hectographed humour. He was at that time already writing science fiction and detective stories, and later edited a more literary magazine called *Generation* at the University of Michigan. Young graduated from the University of California at Berkeley, and won a fellowship which enabled him to enrol in the Stanford University creative writing course in 1966–7 (he returned to it in 1970, but at that time in a teaching capacity). From the spring of 1965 on, his life has been governed by 'a remarkable and continuing series of (non-drug-induced) mystical experiences' from which he has drawn much of his inspiration to write. 'For me the writing of poetry is a spiritual activity. The poem, when it is for-real, expands us to the level of our quintessential selves where we are nothing but spirit and light. It is, therefore, functional. It serves a purpose in the very highest sense.'

From his university days Al Young has lived in San Francisco. He is a professional musician as well as a disc jockey, has taught Spanish and worked at almost any job imaginable. His poems have appeared in the Mexico-based *Corno Emplumado*, the *Evergreen Review*, *Umbra* and the *Journal of Black Poetry*. His first collection, *Dancing*, appeared in 1969, and his first novel, *Snakes*, followed in 1970. His new book *Who is Angelina?* should also be out by now.

Birthday poem

First light of day in Mississippi
son of laborer & of house wife
it says so on the official photostat

not son of fisherman & child fugitive
from cottonfields & potato patches
from sugarcane chickens & well-water
from kerosene lamps & watermelons
mules named jack or jenny & wagonwheels,

years of meaningless farm work
work Work WORK WORK WORK –
'Papa pull you outta school bout March
to stay on the place & work the crop'
– her own earliest knowledge
of human hopelessness & waste

She carried me around nine months
inside her fifteen year old self
before here I sit numbering it all

One day I'll know more about the old man
but I only got to see him once

How I got from then to now
is the mystery that could fill a whole library
much less an arbitrary stanza

But of course you already know about that
from your own random suffering
& sudden inexplicable bliss.

Julius Lester

grew up at Pine Bluff in Arkansas, where he lived with his grandmother, but was born in 1939 at St Louis in Missouri. He graduated from Fisk in 1960, and left the South the year after to settle in New York – he still lives there, a married man with two children, and runs a weekly radio programme for W.B.A.I. He is also a field secretary for S.N.C.C., a photographer, and an accomplished folk singer and song writer. He started singing and playing the guitar relatively late, at twenty, in college. His first record, called simply *Julius Lester*, was brought out by Vanguard in 1965, followed by *Departures* in 1967. Lester's own illuminating notes on the sleeves were an early indication that his writing skill could be applied to fields other than songwriting, and he has since proved his versatility in a small collection of poetry *The mud of Vietnam* written during a stay in Hanoi early in 1967, as editor of the folk-song magazine *Sing-out*, with a powerful and remarkable history of the 'black power' concept in America (*Look out, whitey! black power's gon' get your mama!* 1968) and as the compiler of an anthology of writings by W. E. B. DuBois. Lester's other books include *To be a slave* (1968, a documentary compiled from slave narratives and interviews), *Revolutionary notes*, and *Search for the new land: history as subjective experience* (1969) which is a fascinating attempt at compiling contemporary history from carefully selected 'faits divers'.

Through his ancestry (his father was a pastor) and his active researches into folk material from slavery days on, Lester has a deep awareness of roots, in a much wider sense than usual, and a very personal philosophy of his own place in space and time. 'Once upon a time being Negro was a burden added to all other burdens of life. Now my color does not rest heavily on my shoulders. It has become an added dimension of my life, relieving the burdens and adding spice to the joys. The past is helping me and many young Negroes to illuminate the present and, in so doing, it will carry us into the future.' This is the concluding paragraph of his sleeve notes for his first record in 1965 – in a note to the songs he personalized this into three lines: 'Someday, my present will be someone else's past. I am indebted to those in my past who have given me so much. I would like to add whatever I can and give it to someone else.'

On the birth of my son, Malcolm Coltrane

(at the time of the Newark Rebellion 12 July 1967)

Even as we kill,
let us
not
forget
that it is only so we may be
more human.

Let our
exaltations not be
for the blood that
flows in the gutters,
but for the
blood that
may more freely flow through our bodies.

We must
kill
in order to live,
but let us never
enjoy the
killing
more than the
new life,
the only reason for the killing.

And if we forget,
then those who come
Afterward
will have to kill us
(will have to kill us)
for the
life that we,
in our killing,
failed
to give them.

Norman H. Pritchard

is a native New Yorker born 22 October 1939. His education included the Cathedral Choir School of St John the Divine, St Peter's School (Jacob's Hill), Washington Square College, the Institute of Fine Arts, and Columbia University. He was one of the original members of the *Umbra* group in the early and middle sixties, he conducted a poetry workshop at the New School for Social Research and is poet-in-residence at the Friends' Seminary of New York.

His poetry is essentially a poetry of sounds and rituals, and although some of the more conventional ones have appeared in magazines (from the *East Village Other* to *Liberator*), Pritchard's work is better represented on two long-playing records read by himself: Power Tree LP 2501 called *Destinations*, which contains the work of four contemporary American poets, and the Broadside (Folkways) album BR 461 *New jazz poets*. In 1970 Doubleday published his first book *The matrix: poems 1960–1970*, a beautiful piece of production of which there exist some exquisite copies 'hand-coloured by the artist'.

O

uou who uou   who who uou
uou who uou   who who uou
who uou uou   uou who uou
uou uou who   who uou who

uou who uou   who who uou
uou who uou   who who uou
who uou uou   uou who uou
uou uou who   who uou who

                    uou who uou who
                    who uou who uou
                    who uou who uou
                    uou who uou who

who who uou   uou who uou
who who uou   uou who uou
uou who uou   who uou uou
who uou who   uou uou who

uou who uou   who who uou
uou who uou   who who uou
who uou uou   uou who uou
uou who uou   who uou who

                    who uou who uou
                    uou who uou who
                    uou who uou who
                    who uou who uou

                    uou who uou who
                    who uou who uou
                    uou who uou who
                    who uou who uou

                    uou uou who uou
                    uou uou who uou
                    who uou uou who
                    who uou uou who

                    uou who uou who
                    uou uou who uou
                    uou uou who uou
                    uou who uou who

uou uou who who
who uou uou who
uou uou who who
who uou uou who

uou who who uou
who who uou uou
uou who who uou
uou uou who uou

uou who uou who
who uou who uou
who uou who uou
uou who uou who

Dennis Scott

is a Jamaican, born 16 December 1939, who, in contrast to most
of his writing compatriots, does not seem to have left the West
Indies for even the briefest of European 'exiles'. Educated at
Jamaica College and the University of the West Indies, he has
since made teaching his main career. He was assistant master at
Presentation College in Trinidad, and served on the staff of
Jamaica College. He has, however, also pursued various vocations
outside education: a brief spell in public relations, frequent radio
and television work, the assistant editorship of the *Caribbean
Quarterly*. Scott is also an actor and theatre director, and a member
of the National Dance Theatre Company of Jamaica. His poetry
has long been popular in his native island; it has won him several
awards and was finally collected in a privately published book
called *Journey and ceremonics: poems 1960–1969*. This proved to be
the springboard from which Dennis Scott's reputation is suddenly
taking off: in 1971 he was strongly represented in the anthologies
Seven Jamaica poets published in Kingston, and *Breaklight* edited
in London by Andrew Salkey.

Epitaph

They hanged him on a clement morning, swung
between the falling sunlight and the women's
breathing, like a black apostrophe to pain.
All morning, while the children hushed
their hop-scotch joy and the cane kept growing,
he hung there, sweet and low.

                              At least, that's how
they tell it. It was long ago.

And what can we recall of a dead slave or two,
except that, when we punctuate our island tale,
they swing like sighs across the brutal
sentences, and anger pauses
till they pass away.

Ahmed Akinwole Alhamisi

sometimes uses as a middle name the 'slave name' of Le Graham under which he was born 18 February 1940 at Savannah in Tennessee. Alhamisi grew up in Oak Ridge, where he attended high school, then went to Tennessee Agricultural & Industrial State University. After obtaining his B.Sc. there in 1962 he went on for an M.Sc. from Stout State University in 1963. That year he entered the army, where he stayed for nearly three years, the last one being spent at an education centre in Germany. The end of 1965 found him in Amsterdam, working on a so far unpublished autobiographical novel provisionally called *& on this night*.

Back in the States Alhamisi developed in two main directions: as a writer and editor, and as an applied artist and sculptor. He is associate editor of *Soulbook*, contributing editor of *Black Dialogue*, corresponding editor of the *Journal of Black Poetry*. As a playwright, mainly of one-acters, Alhamisi remains unpublished, but his first book of poetry, *The black narrator*, was brought out in 1966 by Vaughn's Book Store, the militant black book shop on Dexter Avenue in Detroit (where Alhamisi has lived since his return from Europe). This first book appeared under the name Le Graham, but not so his second, *Black spiritual gods*, of 1968. By 1970, for the pamphlet *Guerilla warfare: newer pomes*, his name had grown to Ahmed Akinwole Alhamisi. In the years of his first books Alhamisi also showed his work as a sculptor, first at the Black Arts festival of which he was one of the most active organizers, and in 1968 at the University of Detroit during its 'racism in education' conference. In 1969 the Black Arts festivals resulted in a collection of essays, poems and photographs called *Black arts: an anthology of black creations*, edited by Alhamisi and Harun Kofi Wangara. Alhamisi's most recent book is *Holy ghosts* of 1972.

Look for me dear mother

behold a prophet will bring plans of liberation in the world
  again
revolutionize your mind
that you may be in harmony with the youth of your soul

look for me dear mother

look for me
dear mother
look for me
but only when you shall see me coming

*look for me dear mother look for me, but only when you shall see
  me coming*
attention. attention.   attention. attention
by orders of the american army if the persons responsible for
  the destruction
of the american dream have not been turned over to the
  military authorities
by friday night then all black people will be killed shot to
  death for aiding the enemy
attention. attention. attention
by orders of the navy.   by orders of the c.i.a.   by orders of
  white and black
americans.   by orders of the constitution.   by orders of
  animals for a sane
society.   we repeat. all black people will be shot to death.
we repeat. we repeat.   we repeat. we repeat.   we repeat.
  we repeat.   we repeat.

look for me dear mother.   but only when you shall see me
  coming

mulingu. god. creator of trees. mountains. grass.
    flowers. lakes. rivers. the sky. look for me.
in black people. lovely people
drinking palm wine. providing insight for centuries yet.
to come. look for me

look for me dear mother
look for me. but only when you shall see me coming
histories. pulling. words. the voice of kofi. are paths.
leading to the shores of africa. asia. and latin america.
look for me
i'm still in the ruins of north america. and
there is nothing to hold me. the people i use to know
are tilted bricks. are falling soon. tomorrow i won't
    know them with their dusty faces. scattered in night
    winds.

look for me dear mother. look for me
animals are chained in prisons. buildings suck life from
    trees. truth is
only a word. concrete covers the ground. everyday
    people are dying. in spilt
wine. behind lunch counters timed to death. everyday.
    everyday. hanging.
from cars. searching for quiet moments. waiting for
    the right gal. probe.
the agony of thots. the four yrs. spent in factories for a
    job you now
hate. deal. the struggle to teach truth. look. people are dying
    in parked
drunks. on world war II pensions. in the mist of 10 per cent
    sir tax eating
at both ends. feel. bricks falling and crushing black babies.
    housed in

churches. run. from schools of 20th century thots.   know.
    black earth is
turning to concrete.   trees are used for paintings.   there
    is no place for children to play.
but don't worry about me.
burning buildings give the light.   from the weather i
    fashion my weapons.
the floor sleeps me.   from the sun i tell the time of day.
    and we own the night.
but look for me dear mother.   look for me.

look for me dear mother.   look for me
but only when you shall see me coming
we will meet again someday.
the gods are with me. nature is with me, bird hunting
is a thang of the past. nigger hunting is the task.
we love now, cept when people come together. unity
    meetings kills us with polluted air.   arguments are
    knives. people are bleeding, and
there are no doctors around.
we have black films. a projector. but no one to operate them.
music from the streets never move pass iron doors. white
    thots.
we cannot understand our role.   like we don't play
    checkers. no more.

so look for me dear mother. look for me
nothing to hold me here.   nothing.   especially when
    yesterday u.s.a. sent her away. in mechanical words.
    spreaded
like rusty earth creaks
swallowing her beautiful body. with streets as mouths.
look for me. no love. no love. now
and it was by chance we met

tht i dug your black smiling face
in a contemplating mind at first. now within my throbbing
      heart.
rather than to continue loving you
maybe it is better to become
a stature of ebony and never feel the hardships of love
but tonight i will think of her. so look for me
there are no bright moments. i stand here in the mist of time.
      my buzzer don't sound right any more. the typewriter
      types
nonsense poetry.
and the trees. so green
have taken on a newer look.
sadness. all around from torn pages. 45pms. desk drawers.
      slipping
from lips of brothers. sisters
all up and down the streets of black creators. sucking dead
thots from skull faces.
i speak of sadness. of beautiful women. hanging
smoke. painting
our reality. we die fast. moving pass our thots. we talk.
      long range.
nothing to save me. nothing
                              especially since her beauty lies
      on display
in streets leading nowhere.
probe. think man. probe. into your life. probe. now. probe.
      probe. probe.
flash. my name is johnson and i like it. he said. flash. i like
      soul
food. in western definitions. probe. cut the pig loose my eye.
      she said.
flash. i revolutionary. now. let's burn the honky. probe.
      if we cain't

run for president of america. they said. flash. lets take the
    car. hell
we don't have to know how to drive. their children. all
    their children said.
look for me dear mother
screaming sirens hollering from the ghetto.
i wander bout my passport. bout what my friends will say.
if the pomes dedicated to them is ashes.
i go to school. and teach slow grinning death to black
    children. i don't want to be a killer. now i peep behind
    afro signs. looking
at people dying. in their mind. and there mind. and there
    ain't a thang i can do
but maybe bring in nature. it wd be very easy. i could hide
    some in my pocket without telling nobody. cept the
    sister that feels
her hands in my trousers.
but look for me dear mother. look for me
there is nothing really important anymore. not to matter
pomes. only a possibility in natural hair. long legs. and
    poetry
running down her thighs. keeping me alive.
now i sit here. sitting. searching for myself in hurried
pomes. of a future lover. i cain't leave it to people cause
    people
i use to know. are tilted bricks. are falling soon. tomorrow i
won't mean a thang. in all their liquid dusty perfume. i will
    never know them. just like that.
yeah. somewhere out there alone. gotta keep on looking
    momma dear i feel delayed and alone. nobody to drop
    my thots on.
o k h a d i d r a o k h a d i d r a
our brothers are dying. our sisters are dying. the whole
    world is

dying. and we sit. sitting. listening to the agonies of those
    before us
o m o t h e r a f r i c a
o you lost souls of african kings and queens
of histories unknown. to human minds. in these tired times.
    panthers
  lurking on niggers at night. the creakers
  on brothers at day. in dying
times. with staggertooth niggers. spitting at their images.
children playing hopscotch. inches from their door
on creaked sidewalks. leading no where.
momma praying. papa laying. down. round. dead. faggot
    clowns. doing
stiff. mechanical steps. to rock and roll musick.
o you b e a u t i f u l c h i l d r e n
still standing. staggering in this unfaithful world of sinning
faggot. priests. and apostles of hypocritical robots called
    nuns.
o k h a y i y a k h a d i d r a. o baby. o all you
    beautiful black
women of hope, you future creators of beauty in all this
    ugliness
let there be warriors
marching from your womb. scattering brains of white
    beasts
all over this planet earth.

o let there be warriors marching. marching. marching.
    marching. marching. marching. on
into the motherland. so look for me dear mother
look for me
but only when you shall see me coming

Carl Wendell Hines

was born in 1940 at Wilson in North Carolina, but has lived most of his life in Indianapolis. He studied at Tennessee Agricultural & Industrial State University, at the same time as Alhamisi, graduating in science education in 1962. He has since put this training to practical use in various places, and at present teaches both mathematics and a course under the black studies programme at Marshall High School in Indianapolis. A semi-professional musician, he plays the piano and leads his own combo on weekend gigs. The rhythms and structures of jazz in its late-fifties incarnation (Indianapolis was, after all, the town of Wes Montgomery) are evident in many of his poems.

Now that he is safely dead

        Now that he is safely dead
let us praise him
                build monuments to his glory
        sing hosannas to his name.

        Dead men make
such convenient heroes: They
                cannot rise
        to challenge the images
                we would fashion from their lives.

        And besides,
it is easier to build monuments
        than to make a better world.

So, now that he is safely dead
we, with eased consciences
            will teach our children
    that he was a great man . . . knowing

        that the cause for which he lived
is still a cause
    and the dream for which he died
            is still a dream,
        a dead man's dream.

Fred Bradford

contributed his poem 'Death of a nigger' to the third issue of the *Journal of Black Poetry*, in the winter of 1966. He lived in Los Angeles at that time. I have never seen anything else by him, and have not succeeded in tracing his whereabouts.

Death of a nigger

I saw you die today
I saw you bend your bald head toward
The window and yell and yell
As long and hard as you could moan
Something to leave bitter memories
And someone said should we call an
Ambulance and I said yes
For someone to go into your dirty
Hotel room and pick you up,
A dead nigger.

When I saw you dying there
When I saw them bring you down

Dead, I knew you were always afraid of death
And it came like you feared it would
When you were alone in your room.

And I promised myself I would never go down like that.

Tonight (and every night now)
I think of trees turned over, roots in the air

Knives and guns, huge gashes in the earth, and rivers
Run over . . .
A storm
To leave them bitter memories for all their coming years.

Alice H. Jones

is another writer about whom I know nothing – except that at one time she lived in Buffalo, New York. 'For Sapphire' first appeared in the *Negro Digest* poetry issue of September–October 1968, and it remains this author's only published work that I have so far come across.

For Sapphire, my sister

Woman with hoe in hand, and baby on your back,
Sorrow-sated and tired to apathy,
My sister:

I oil your skin, manicure your feet, take hookworm from your
Children,
Your man takes back his spear.

I turn your sweat into perfume and your breasts into onyx-
tipped
Fruit.
I erase the erosions of childbearing from your stomach
And the robbers of your teeth have replaced them with pearls
And the scent of honeysuckle.
I give desire again, when your man comes
And if immortality slips, screaming, from your loins,
I give you joy to replace despair.

The river gives its many-tongued kisses as you bathe;
It does not hide the crucified body of your brother.

The rope holds clothes and draws water from the well;
It does not hold the dead and blackened fruit, that once was
Your neighbor.
The fire warms your home and the bones of your old:
It does not roast your screaming son under the sign of Jesus.

I give you handmaidens, not a boss lady;
Bodyguards, not the Klan.
I give you a castle, with peacocks in the garden:
You will never know of shacks with flies or tenements with
        rats.
I give you incense, hummingbird tongues in honey,
Sandals of beaten gold and bracelets of ivory.

I give you jewels and crowns for your velurial hair
And rings for your ebon hands.
I give you the Kings of Benin at your feet
And lands to the rim of the world.

Woman with hoe in hand, and baby on your back,
Sorrow-sated and tired to apathy,
My sister:
I oil your skin, manicure your feet, take hookworm from
        your
Children,
Your man takes back his spear.

Barbara Malcom

lives in Louisiana and has published one slim volume of verse
(from which both poems printed here have been taken) called
I want me a home. It appeared in 1969 under the Nkombo imprint
of the Free Southern Theater in New Orleans. As Nayo the author
had been a member of the Nkombo writing and acting workshop.

Bedtime story

Hey Mama, what's revolution?
      It's war, son
War where soldiers fight huh?
      Yeah baby soldiers fightin and killin 'n' dyin
We gonna have a war gainst whitefolks huh?
      Yeah baby I guess so
But why we haf to have a war Mama?
      Cause the white devils tricked us
          tricked us in to be slaves
Are we slaves now Mama?
      Yeah – might as well be
But I don't wantta be a slave Mama
      I know son – I know we won't be
      much long – go to sleep now honey
Cause of the revolution huh Mama
      Yeah son, cause of the revolution
          now hush chile and go to sleep

Hey Mama when we gonna have the revolution
      soon son – soon as we can

But – Mama we ain't got no army
      Boy did I tell you to go to sleep
      we'll make a army alright, don't you **worry**
Will it take long time to make a army Mama?
      Naw son, I hope not
Who's gonna be in the army Mama?
      oh I guess ya Daddy and ya **uncles**
      and a whole lot o' black folks
      and boy hush and go to sleep

And me Mama – kin I be in the army when I git big?
      Boy you ain't gonna be fit for no army
      and nothin else if you don't shut your
      mouth and go t'sleep. Soldiers
      haf to be strong, ya can't be strong
      if ya stay wake all night
      Now here – take ya gun and the
      nation's flag – sleep wit it and
      dream bout it – you satisfied
Yes mam – g'night Mama
      night son.

The men are all away

The men are all away
    they are yet away
    and there is much to be done

The men are away
    to war and will **not**
    let the foe near

to hunt for beast and fowl
        for the storehouse
to tend the business matters
        of the land
they are yet away

The men are away
        to barrooms and poolhalls
                and gambling dens
        to the houses
                of leisure bodies
        to steal the goods
                of the Master
they are yet away

The men are away
        in chain gangs, stockades
                and in fugitive states
        in work house
                prison cells
        and on death row
they are yet away

Will they return
        for harvest time
        or when the young are born
        or when the old grow cold

The men are all away
        they are yet away
        and there is much to be done

Yetunde Esan

is a young Nigerian whose first published poetry appeared in the Ibadan University College magazine *The horn* and in the 1960 anthology *Nigerian student verse*. By 1966 she had become the headmistress of a secondary school. Further information I have not been able to obtain.

Ololu – an Egungun

Seven skulls he carries on his back
Blood drained wild eyed, a baleful look.
    If any man tries
    To see him rise,
He loses all, his heart, his head.

His regalia – so the story goes –
Is steeped in the very devil's blood.
    He does not know
    His family,
Must not be seen by a woman's eye.

Long long ago, so the story adds
He walked out once in full array,
    His daughter ran
    To say, 'Baba'
And dropped down dead! 'Poor girl! How sad!'

The crowd thronged him as he moved along,
And shouts of 'Olu' could be heard.
    In rushed the women,

All doors were locked,
'Ololu, Ololu is passing by.'

I peeped out – a great crowd, all men,
I looked again – what did I see:
    A tall thin man,
    In plain pyjamas,
Barefooted, bareheaded, marks on his face.

And suddenly I wished I were back
In the good old days when Ololu was
    A semi-god,
    With seven skulls,
Not – no one in particular.

Eseoghene Barrett

better known, until very recently, as C. Lindsay Barrett, was born in Jamaica in 1941, spent all of his early youth and school time on the island, worked for the *Daily Gleaner*, but left in 1961 and seems to have no intention of ever returning home. In fact, he is one of the relatively few New World negroes who have successfully made that other 'return home', the transition to Africa.

After leaving Jamaica he spent about a year in England, working for the B.B.C. and the Transcription Centre, then a longer period in France, mainly as a journalist and writer of occasional features. Early in 1966 he went to Dakar for the First World Festival of Negro Arts, and from that time he has worked his way ever further south along the West African coast. First he lectured at University College in Fourah Bay, Sierra Leone, then he taught in Ghana, and eventually he became guest lecturer at the University of Ibadan in Nigeria, with 'the roots of African and Afro-American literature' as his special subject. He was the head of the Information Department for East Central State at Enugu during all of the Biafran crisis – 'I served in the ultra-bureaucratic capacity out of a conviction that no matter the rightness of the Biafran grievance, there could be no justification for the Biafran cause which was 'separation' of ideals and ideas in a specific Black community, the Nigerian one.'

Barrett's first books were a collection of essays and three poems called *The state of black desire*, privately printed in France in 1966, and a novel *Song for Mumu* which came out in London in 1967. Several other novels remain unpublished, although at least one of them, *Leap skyward*, has at some time been announced. His short stories and essays have appeared in several magazines on both sides of the Atlantic, but he seems to have published very few poems. The one used here was written in Paris in May 1963 and appeared exactly one year later in *Daylight* magazine. Barrett's main creative interest now lies in the theatre. He has had several plays produced in Nigeria, mainly by Soyinka's company, and he has married one of the country's leading actresses, Beti Okotie.

In my eye and heart and all about the same blood

i

And I say Alabama again without a thought
This year they loosened dogs with four feet
On my heart
Baring their own fangs whiter than ever before
And wherever I trudge my black skin goes with
Me
And the stench of their fear follows me and
I lay my tongue upon the block without my
Stony fear
And I say Alabama again.
Who said centuries and centuries have passed
Since the terrible shrieks of Arawaks
Gorged by hounds belled atop night who said all
This has passed I dream the Arawaks have walked
Into my father's soul
Father father do I hear you screaming Alabama again
Or Johannesburg!
Yes. Wherever I go my black skin trudges with me

ii

She was six years old and the white tongue
Told her stand back and she said
O no you ain' my daddy and I don't like
You and he said as white in his power as
White
As white in his knowledge he was within
The whiter law he said go get them dogs

And let them loose
But dogs will inspire dogs to bark or bite
Or snap about the air they fear to lose!
But then here again we stand
And do you think your fangs will kill this wish
O no!
And I say Alabama again eat the flesh of their fear
Father!

iii

Sometimes I feel and then I don't
And sometimes I weep and the clouds alone
Believe but this is too much and there is
No way to say just what is here!
A feeling falls about my head and I scream
Tell me . . .
Tell me how the time is here and not to come
And the time has passed not to be lamented
For if pain is pain it kills and who am I
To die beneath the terrible pain a white-ness
Leaks within me . . .

A Negro dies within my dream each night and
You say pray? pray? pray?
I have these fingers do you know them
They have scratched too many walls and now
They hunger for a whiter grip!
A throat alive upon my blood will do!
An eye will do and when I have plucked the ball
From the head
I will explore the gaping socket!
These fingers hunger to rip the very bowels

From the carcasses whose power alone has
Threatened my bowel to uselessness!
Do you know this?
Last night I ran about the streets of my
Soul
Blood covered and afraid for myself.
Today I wait to kill all Alabama
For wherever I trudge my blackskin moves with me!

iv

And I say Alabama again, who whispers the false word
Wait! in my ear?
I waited three hundred years in the night.
I watched the morning bleeding by.
O yes I have waited and won't wait forever!
(I heard the twelve tribes of Israel have waited longer)
And if I stand among crowds so long
If I look up so long and watch and wait
If I bleed so long my wounds uncovered
If I do this Alabama,
If I do this Johannesburg,
If I do this and the names swell up and up
In my brain
If I do this I die
And I don't want to die
And as your dogs sent dogs to chew our rights
Invisible
The death I see sends murder to my brain
In my defense!
In my defense I stand about to kill you!
In my defense I only wait to eat your balls
To plunge my teeth into your heart!
In my defense I cup a blue revenge!

Frank John

was born 14 November 1941 on Trinidad, and lived on the island until 1967, when he came to London. There he has lived ever since, pursuing nobody quite knows just what kind of work, writing a great deal but publishing very little, a quiet unassuming and incredibly thin man who seems to get most of his enjoyment of life out of helping others and promoting causes. Soon after his arrival in England he started publishing the poetry of his friends and political speeches (C. L. R. James) in small mimeographed pamphlets which he not only produced but also sold himself – in the streets, at readings, at meetings. It is at readings that one gets the true measure of his work – and of him. There is a subtle transformation as Frank starts 'jumpin up in de husa band in he own mind', and a superb entertainer emerges. The keen ear for rhythms and speech patterns, which one has been only dimly aware of seeing in his poem on the dead page, is exploited to the full and his affinity with the newer African writing (with its rediscovery of oral rather than literary traditions) becomes instantly clear.

The only one of Frank John's private publications to contain any of his own work is *Black songs* of 1968 – it formed the basis of a book published late the next year under the same title. The book has a short but important introduction defining the tasks of the black poet. 'I write to help put me right, to re-create myself, to help put other black people right. I am tormented to write because of the blackness of my skin, and because of the blackness of my situation of despair, and because of the hope to bring about a complete change in all the black societies of the world.' A larger collection of poems and play-sketches has been announced by Bogle-l'Overture in Jamaica as *Black waves*. In August 1972 Frank produced his poem *Freedom* as a very handsome poster designed by Rolph Webster – the first in what promises to become a regular series.

Down

for Rachel

      Push it down
             burn it down
                        hammer it down
                                    deep down

I'm bleedin
      push it down
             burn it down
                        hammer it down
                                    deep down

I'm dying
      push it down
             burn it down
                        hammer it down
                                    deep down

Seein freedom
      push it down
             burn it down
                        hammer it down
                                    deep down

Livin song
      push it down
             burn it down
                        hammer it down
                                    deep down

BLACK FOLKS
      push it down
             burn it down
                        hammer it down
                                    deep down

Push it down
        burn it down
                hammer it down
                        deep down
      UHURU
           UHURU

Don L. Lee

was born in February 1942 in Little Rock, Arkansas – then just another little southern town, as yet without echoes in the international press. The L. of his middle initial stands, I think, for Luther. He was raised in Detroit, went to school in Chicago, then worked for a while at Margaret Burroughs's museum, now called the Du Sable Museum of African American History. During the last five years Don has become the poet of the revolution, easily the most widely read, certainly the most consistently sold, of the younger black poets who emerged from the 'rioting sixties'. His first book, *Think black* (1967), was a small pamphlet privately printed in 700 copies: it sold out in a few weeks. Reprinted by Broadside Press, it has been selling at about the same rate ever since, its total printing reputedly well over fifty thousand by now. Equally high on the Broadside best-selling list were his later books, *Black pride* (1969), *Don't cry, scream* (1969) and *We walk the way of the new world* (1970). The four books have lately appeared in a volume of 'selected and new poems' called *Directionscore*, the only really handsome volume Broadside have so far produced.

Directionscore, which includes the text of some broadsides and pamphlets as well as the books, gives an opportunity of taking the true measure of Don Lee as a writer, and he comes over much stronger than from any of the individual pieces. His early work I have always found painfully bad: one could see, or rather hear, how some of the ideas and odd phrases might work with a mass audience when read by their author, but the whole remained street poetry in the worst rather than in the (now happily acknowledged) good sense of that term. The last collection is much stronger, and Gwendolyn Brooks's technical influence seems to have taken root, or grown branches even. Don's portraits especially are sure and often devastating – be their subjects as far apart as Sun House, 'Big Momma', Ted Joans or Sammy Davis. His gift for observation is at last matched by a quiet control of his words – as he puts it, it is 'louder but softer'.

'Don Lee wants/a new nation/under nothing;/a physical light

that waxes; he does not want to/be exorcised, adjoining and
revered;/he does not like local garniture/nor any impish onus in
the vogue;/is not candlelit/but stands out in the auspices of fire/
and rock and jungle-flail;/wants/new art and anthem; will/want
a new music screaming in the sun': Gwendolyn Brooks's ap-
praisal, buried in the book-length narrative of her *In the Mecca*.
Don, for once, says it better and simpler: 'If you can't stop a
hurricane, be one.'

Don Lee was poet-in-residence at Cornell at the time of the
'riots' there; he has taught Afro-American literature and history
at Roosevelt University and Columbia College (both in Chicago),
and more recently at Northeastern Illinois State College and the
University of Illinois (at Chicago Circle). He is a book reviewer
for *Black World*, and has compiled a two-volume evaluation of
black poetry in the sixties called *Dynamite voices*. Haphazard in its
choice of subjects (probably because it uses some published articles
as a backbone), this book is nevertheless the most balanced account
available of new trends and personalities, and will obviously
become the main textbook for this particular phase in all 'black
studies' programmes. Some of the poets and poems which gain
special commendation in his book can also be found in the Pan-
African issue of the *Journal of Black Poetry* which he edited in
1971.

A long critical evaluation of Don Lee's work appeared in
Amistad 2. Two of the Broadside books have also been released on
tape, read by the author, but the impact of his personality is con-
veyed more clearly by the long-playing record *Rappin and readin*
released in 1971. In the autumn of that year Don Lee became
writer-in-residence at Harvard University: it was there that he
wrote the introduction to *Black Spirits*, the anthology which
resulted from Woodie King's 'Festival of new black poets in
America' (1972). For several years Don has run the interesting
Third World Press in Chicago, which has published much of the
new black literature emanating from that city.

Nigerian unity, or, little niggers killing little niggers

for brothers Christopher Okigbo and 'Wole Soyinka

suppose those
who made
wars
had to fight them?

it's called blackgold.
 & you,
my brothers / former warriors
who use to own the nights
that
knew no boarders
have acquired strings on yr/minds
 & have knowingly sold yr/our/mothers.
there are no more tears.
tears will not stop bullets.
the dead don't cry,
the dead just grow; good crop this year,
wouldn't u say.

it's called blackgold
 & u fight blindly,
swinging at yr/own mid-nights,
at yr/own children of tomorrow.

come   one   come   two
against the middle is
a double feature starring the man from u.n.c.l.e.
with a nigger on his back
who played ping-pong with christ
and won.

little niggers
killing
little niggers: ontime/intime/outoftime
             theirtime/otherpeople'stime as
             niggers killed niggers everytime.

suppose those
who made
wars
had to fight them?

blackgold is not
the newnigger:
with a british accent
called me 'old chap' one day,
i rubbed his skin
it didn't come off. even him surprised.

him
another pipe-smoking faggot
who lost his balls in
a double-breasted suit
walking thru a nadinola commercial
with a degree in european history.
little nigger
choked himself with a hippy's tie
his momma didn't even know him/
             she thought he was a TWA flashback or
             something out of a polka-dot machine.
he
cursed at her in perfect english
called her:
Mother-Dear.

WANTED   WANTED
    black warriors to go south
    to fight in Africa's mississippi.
go south young man.

everybody missed that train,
except one sister.
she wanted to fight the realenemy
but
she was 'uneducated',
wore the long-dress
talked the native tongue
& had a monopoly on blackbeauty.
when we met – she smiled & said: 'i'm the true gold,
                            i'm the real-gold.'

suppose those
who made
wars
had to fight them?

the real blackgold
was there before the drill,
before the dirty-eyed,
before the fence-builders,
before the wells,
before the british accent,
before christ,
before air condition,
before the cannon,
the real blackgold: was momma & sister; is momma &
    sister.
was there before the 'educated',
before the pig-eaters,
before the cross-wearers,

before the pope,
before the nigger-warriors.
the real blackgold
was the first warrior.

go south young man.

little niggers
killing
little niggers.
the weak against the weak.
the ugly against the ugly.
the powerless against the powerless.
the realpeople becoming unpeople
& brothers we have more in common
than pigmentation & stupidity.
that same old two-for-one
was played on 47th & ellis –
invented on 125 & lenox
and now is double-dealing from
the mangrove swamps to the savannah grassland;
2 niggers for the price of nothing.

newnigger
lost his way
a whi-te girl gave him direction
him still lost
she sd whi-te / he thought bite
been eating everything in sight
including himself.

suppose those
who made
wars
had to fight them?

the lone ranger got a new tonto
he's 'brown' with a Ph.D. in
psy-chol-o-gy
& still walks around with
holes
in his brain.
losthismind.
saw him the other day
with his head across some railroad tracks –
tryin to get an untan.
will the real jesus christ
please stand up
and take a bow;
u got niggers tryin to be trains.

trained well.
european-african took a
double
at oxford.
wears ban-lon underwear & whi-te socks,
has finally got the killer's eye,
join the deathbringers club
& don't want more than two children.

the real blackgold
will be crippled,
raped,
and killed
in
that
order.

i will miss
the joy

of calling her
sister

go south young man.

suppose those
who made
wars
had to fight you.

To be quicker

for black political prisoners on the inside & outside – real
to my brothers & sisters of O.B.A.C.

clamb ape mountain backwards
better than the better u thought u had to be better than
jump clean.   cleaner.
jump past lightning into field-motion, feel-motion, feel mo
feel mo than the world thought u capable of feelin.
cd do it even fool yr momma, jim ! fool yrself, hunh –

goin ta be cleaner,   hunh.
goin ta be stronger,   hunh.
goin ta be wiser,   hunh.
goin ta be quick to be quicker   *to be.*

quick to be whats needed to be   what's needed:
quicker than enemies of the livingworld,
quicker than cheap smiles of a cadillac salesman,
quicker than a dead junky talkin to the wind,
quicker than super-slick niggers sliding in the opposite,
quicker than whi-te-titty-new-left-what's-left suckin
     niggers,
quicker to be quick, to be quick.

u wise brother.
u wiser than my father was   when he
talked the talk   he wasn't suppose to talk.

quicker to be quick, to be:

a black-African-fist slapping a wop-dope pusher's momma,
a hospital a school anything workin to save us to pull us
closer to Tanzania to Guinea or Harlem to the West Indies to
closer to momma to sister to brother closer to closer to
FRELIMO to Ras Tafari to us to power to running run
        to build
to controllifelines to Ashanti to music to life to Allah closer
to Kenya to the black world to the rays of anti-evil.

clamb ape mountain backwards   brother
feel better than the better u thought was better
its yr walk brother,
lean a little, cut the smell of nasty.
jump forward into the past
to bring back

goodness.

Big momma

finally retired   pensionless
from cleaning somebody else's house
she remained home to clean
the one she didn't own.

in her kitchen where we often talked
the *chicago tribune* served as a tablecloth
for the two cups of tomato soup that went
along with my weekly visit & talking to.

she was in a seriously-funny mood
& from the get-go she was down, realdown:

> roaches around here are like
> letters on a newspaper
> or
> u gonta be a writer, hunh
> when u gone write me some writen
> or
> the way niggers act around here
> if talk cd kill we'd all be dead.

she's somewhat confused about all this *blackness*
but said that it's good when Negroes start putting them=
    selves
first and added: we've always shopped at the colored stores,
> & the way niggers cut each other up round
> here every weekend that whiteman don't
>   haveta
> worry bout no revolution specially when
>   he's
> gonta haveta pay for it too, anyhow all he's
> gotta do is drop a truck load of *dope* out
>   there
> on 43rd st. & all the niggers & yr
>   revolutionaries
> be too busy getten high & then they'll turn
>   round
> and fight each other over who got the
>   mostest.

we finished our soup and i moved to excuse myself.
as we walked to the front door she made a last comment:
    now *luther* i knows you done changed a lots but if
    you can think back, we never did eat too much pork
    round here anyways, it was bad for the belly.
i shared her smile and agreed.

touching the snow lightly i headed for 43rd st.
at the corner i saw a brother crying   while
trying to hold up a lamp post,
thru his watery eyes i cd see big momma's words.

at sixty-eight
she moves freely, is often right
and when there is food
eats   joyously with her own
real teeth.

F. J. Bryant jnr

(who used to be f. j. bryant, but either way is named Frederick
James and called Rocky) was born in Philadelphia, 6 July 1942.
After his secondary schooling he went into the Navy, and
remained there until June 1963. During the next four years he
attended Lincoln University in Pennsylvania – he was its 'poet
laureate' for 1966. After his graduation the next year he went
back to Philadelphia where he is a caseworker for the state of
Pennsylvania.

His poetry first appeared in the Jones-Neal and Major antholo-
gies of 1968, and that same year he had his first book out, a collec-
tion of 'life poems' called *While silence sleeps*. His brother wants
to illustrate his next collection, and Fred himself, who is a keen
and good photographer, dreams of adding his pictures to a book
by his friend Ron Welburn (who can be found elsewhere in this
anthology). Fred Bryant has also completed a novel which was
several years in the making and has as yet not found a publisher.
One of his one-act plays was produced at Lincoln in 1967.

Patience of a people

It is our hand, the
Deepness of our eye, legs
Taut as a springboard
    That they forget

It is ridiculed curls,
Grim nights without moons,
Love, a family, arbitrary consent,
    That they forget

It is death at early ages,
Shabby homes with walls of fear,
The lie of our carefree ways
    That they forget

It is wide-eyed sight,
A silence that is not theirs, a
Fall bonfire in summer that only
    Lets one eye sleep

David Henderson

born in Harlem in 1942, is a poet, a novelist, an actor and generally one of the most beautiful people of his generation (as the back jacket of his latest book of poetry makes reasonably clear). He received his training at Hunter College and the New School for Social Research – the one institution that crops up with greatest regularity in these biographical notes. Since then, he has been teaching. For the academic year 1968–9 he joined a teachers' and writers' collaborative in Ocean Hill; the next year saw him at City College (now the City University of New York), and during 1970 he went to the University of California at Berkeley.

Henderson was one of the founder-members of the *Umbra* workshop, together with Tom Dent and Calvin Hernton. Rolland Snellings (now Askia Muhammad Touré), Norman Pritchard and Ishmael Reed were among the early members. By the end of 1963 the group had produced two issues of a magazine which made it clear that their twofold aim was no mere slogan: '*Umbra* exists to provide a vehicle for those outspoken and youthful writers who present aspects of social and racial reality which may be called 'uncommercial' but cannot with any honesty be considered non-essential to a whole and healthy society ... We will not print trash, no matter how relevantly it deals with race, social issues, or anything else.' In 1967 the group, now led by Henderson (with Hernton in Sweden and Tom Dent in New Orleans directing the Free Southern Theater), produced an anthology. Singer Len Chandler, dancer Asaman Byron, and the painters Gerald Jackson and Joe Overstreet had further extended the group's scope. Late in 1970 David Henderson managed to revive the magazine, now in a newspaper format with fine art work by Glenn Myles.

Meanwhile Henderson's own work has appeared in magazines like *Freedomways* and the *East Village Other*, and in 1967 Diane Di Prima published his first book of poems, *Felix of the silent forest* (a black cat in the asphalt jungle), with an introduction by Le Roi Jones which says a deal more about Jones than about

Henderson. In 1970 a massive collection of Henderson's poems
appeared under the title *De Mayor of Harlem*.

Pentecostal Sunday

> *(It aint the father*
> *It aint the son*
> *Its the holy ghost*
> *yall)*

they boys from philadelphia
calling
       our lady St Guadalupe
       Saint Martin
       Saint Expedite
             do it now!

he was cripple in the aisle
walking with a cane
the preacher broke his cane
the preacher spit fire on the **man**
the man burn up
the sisters sang
the music played
the man danced in the aisle
     HOW MANY PEOPLE HERE SAW
         GOD!
     LIFT THIS MAN UP OFF HIS
         CANE!
PENTECOSTAL Sunday
north africa to rome
en route a donkey and a coffin
within

the original christian church
the original
christian ritual
the holy ghost
the holy spirit

>   within the spirit in the dance
>   within the spirit in the dance
>   in the getting of the spirit
>   in the body of the dancer
>   in the sweat gyrations head falling off
>   heat body sweat power of the atom
>   grows a breast back in Spanish Harlem

power to drink blood and whiskey mixed
power to handle snakes
power to be what you want to be
the spirit on the temple floor
writhing and screaming
jumping and shouting
getting happy
the spirits have come
doing the jackleo and the boogaloo
fear no fear in memphis
fear no fear in dallas
fear no fear in atlanta
fear no fear in the original christian church
north africa and reverend ike
glory glory

>   he say

>   put your hand on the radio
>   repeat after me

> *it cost money to be on the air*
> *but everybody got something*
> *and it took sacrifice to get it*

yusef rahman say /'yeah them preachers talking bout the
real thing
when Rev. Ike say put God on the spot
when you in
trouble he's saying put yourself yusef on
the spot.
Put God on the spot, he'll surely get you
out.
Can't run away. Got to deal with it. Let
God get you out. Put God on the
spot for you.'

the ritual is black
the ritual is in the storefront temple
on the corner
the drum and organ the guitar and tambourine
glory glory glory
bid the preacher to teach
cause the shit is deep

baptist preacher
man of god
strong man of the tongue and heart
ptah of egypt lay source to osiris
the corn in earth heart
next to the water
the river spirits/ good people
the crossing over
a wash basin and wooden raft
take me over
dance upon Nile Delta
isis mourning.

Among the whites

(Throggs Neck, Bronx, New York)

My mother among the whites
the Negroes / same & oldening
                              year after year
We should have never
                    left Harlem
magical Hamilton Terrace
                              140th Street
to College Avenue Bronx
                              we discovered the Jews
in their seales coffins
                    stone structured
                              along the Grand Concourse
          silent   sunning
                              people/fat disease
Yr environment 50% yr
                    mind
Yr energy directly related
                              to yr neighbors/
                    white   oldening   same
                    stasis in suburb
Better the foul-aired city / of Harlem
the funk & flesh
than no life at all/
in Throggs Neck
                    angry neighbors Italian Irish Edgewater
                              Silver Beach
                    housing project
those structures
                    of the future pink/
self-enclosed
wind-buffeted

fire-proof
coffins
of a silent
culture coming
existing
      in boyhood dreams
             sights
of eerie structures
balanced on clouds
front   blue sky
and sun
      silence
          buffets
   storm
      silence

Arthur K. Nortje

is a South African, born at Port Elizabeth in the Cape Province in
1942. He grew up in his native town and eventually went to the
University College of Western Cape, the segregated college for
Cape coloureds, from which he graduated in 1964. His first
published poems appeared three years earlier, in the twelfth issue
of *Black Orpheus*, and in 1962 Nortje won third prize (after
Echeruo and Brutus) in the Mbari poetry competition. His work
has since appeared in a few anthologies, with a more generous
selection in the collection *7 South African poets: poems of exile*
collected and selected by Cosmo Pieterse (Heinemann's African
Writers Series 1969).

After leaving school Arthur Nortje taught English for about a
year, then left South Africa, first for Jesus College, Oxford, where
he read English, and from there in 1967 for Canada where he has
settled as a teacher. Dennis Brutus, who was once his teacher,
commented in *Protest and conflict in African literature* on the
'tremendous freedom' Nortje's poetry had acquired since he had
come to accept the fact of permanent exile, without the restraint
put on his writing by the thought that anything else would mean
prison if ever he returned to his homeland.

Autopsy

i

My teachers are dead men. I was too young
to grasp their anxieties, too nominal an exile
to mount such intensities of song;
knowing only the blond
colossus vomits its indigestible
black stepchildren like autotoxins.

Who can endure the succubus?
She who had taught them proudness of tongue
drank an aphrodisiac, then swallowed
a purgative to justify the wrong.
Her iron-fisted ogre of a son
straddled the drug-blurred townships,
breathing hygienic blasts of justice.

Rooted bacteria had their numbers
swiftly reduced in the harsh sunlight of arc-lamps,
the arid atmosphere where jackboots scrape
like crackling electric, and tape recorders
ingest forced words like white corpuscles,
until the sterile quarantine of dungeons
enveloped them with piteous oblivion.

In the towns I've acquired
arrive the broken guerrillas, gaunt and cautious,
exit visas in their rifled pockets
and no more making like Marx
for the British Museum in the nineteenth century,
damned: the dark princes, burnt and offered
to the four winds, to the salt-eyed seas. To their earth
unreturnable.

       The world receives
them, Canada, England now that the laager
masters recline in a gold inertia
behind the arsenal of Sten guns. I
remember many, but especially one
almost poetic, so undeterrable.

ii

He comes from knife-slashed landscapes:
I see him pounding in his youth across red sandfields
raising puffs of dust at his heels,
outclassing the geography of dongas
mapped by the ravenous thundery summers.
He glided down escarpments like the wind, until
pursued by banshee sirens
he made their wails the kernel of his eloquence,
turning for a time to irrigate
the stretches of our virgin minds.

Thus – sensitive precise
he stood with folded arms in a classroom
surveying a sea of galvanized roofs,
transfixed as a chessman, only
with deep inside his lyric brooding,
the flame-soft bitterness of love that recrudesces;
O fatal loveliness of the land
seduced the laager masters to disown us.

36,000 feet above the Atlantic
I heard an account of how they had shot
a running man in the stomach. But what isn't told
is how a warder kicked the stitches open
on a little-known island prison which used to be
a guano rock in a sea of diamond blue.

Over the phone in a London suburb he sounds
grave and patient – the years have stilled him:
the voice in a dawn of ash, moon-steady,
is wary of sunshine which has always been
more diagnostic than remedial.

The early sharpness passed beyond to noon
that melted brightly into shards of dusk.
The luminous tongue in the black world
has infinite possibilities no longer.

Christina Ama Ata Aidoo

is one of Ghana's most promising younger writers. Born in 1942, she established her reputation as a playwright as early as 1965, when Longmans published her first play, *The dilemma of a ghost*, which has since rivalled Soyinka's work in popularity. Before this, she had been known primarily as a writer of short stories: she won third prize in the Mbari contest for 1962, and published stories in *Black Orpheus*, *Okyeame*, the London-based *Flamingo*, and in Mphahlele's anthology of African writing. In 1964 she obtained her B.A. from the University of Ghana at Legon, then took an 'advanced creative writing' course at Stanford University in California. She travelled the States widely, gaining friends wherever she went and making a great impression as a person, as a writer, and as a beautiful black woman militant enough to get on the editorial board of *Soulbook*. Back in Ghana she became a research fellow at the Institute of African Studies at Legon. She has published a volume of short stories under the title *No sweetness here*. Her second play, *Anowa*, appeared in 1970. Poetry has so far been a relatively minor part of her writing and its appearance in print has been limited to magazines like *Okyeame*.

Poem

My spirit Mother ought to have come for me earlier.
Now what shall I tell them who are gone? The daughter of
slaves who come from the white man's land.
Someone should advise me on how to tell my story.
My children, I am dreading my arrival there
Where they will ask me news of home.
Shall I tell them or shall I not?
Someone should lend me a tongue
Light enough with which to tell

My Royal Dead
That one of their stock
Has gone away and brought to their sacred precincts
The wayfarer!

They will ask me where I was
When such things were happening.
O mighty God!
Even when the Unmentionable
Came and carried off the children of the house
In shoals like fish,
Nana Kum kept his feet steadfast on the ground
And refused to let any of his nephews
Take a wife from a doubtful stock.

Nikki Giovanni

is, to me, the most consistently interesting of the under-thirties using their often powerful voices in the expression of what we now seem to be calling 'the black experience'. From her earliest work on she has deployed a range, both in choice of subject matter and depth of individual exploration, that few of her generation can yet muster. Easily as 'committed' as Don Lee, she combined the raw strength of Sanchez with the aloof professionalism of Gwen Brooks – no mean achievement at twenty-five.

Born at Knoxville, Tennessee, 6 July 1943, she spent most of her childhood at Lincoln Heights, the black suburb of Cincinnati, Ohio. She went to Fisk in 1959, studied writing under Killens, and put S.N.C.C. on the campus. There are persistent references to her having been 'kicked out of Fisk', but she seems to have graduated all right in 1967. In June of that year Nikki Giovanni organized the first Black Arts Festival in Cincinnati, and as an offshoot of that, established The New Theater. During 1968 her first books of poetry appeared: *Black feeling black talk* was privately printed at Wilmington, Delaware, where she then lived (and where she started a Black History group), and later *Black judgment* came out in New York. A combined edition of these two books was published by Morrow in 1971. Meanwhile Nikki had another collection out, *Re:creation* (Broadside 1970), and she had also edited an (indifferent) 'anthology of black female voices' called *Night comes softly*. With Ed Spriggs and a few others she edits the new incarnation of *Black Dialogue* – at the other end of the scale she is a regular contributor of very good interviews and articles to the women's glossy *Essence*. Her most recent poetry pamphlet is the *Poem of Angela Yvonne Davis* written in October 1970.

Nikki Giovanni has been living in New York for the last few years, dividing her attention between *Black Dialogue*, a small son, her writing, a course of black poetry at Rutgers University, and a growing number of very well attended readings. Her record, *Truth is on its way*, released by Right On records in 1971, contained her own reading of ten poems with some fairly indifferent gospel music in between – it was a surprise hit which made best-seller charts, a fact which one finds reflected in the growing amount of publicity her new publishers are giving her *Gemini* (1972), subtitled 'an extended autobiographical statement on my first twenty-five years of being a black poet'.

Nikki – Rosa

childhood remembrances are always a drag
if you're Black
you always remember things like living in Woodlawn
with no inside toilet
and if you become famous or something
they never talk about how happy you were to have your
    mother
all to yourself and
how good the water felt when you got your bath from one
    of those
big tubs that folk in chicago barbecue in
and somehow when you talk about home
it never gets across how much you
understood their feelings
as the whole family attended meetings about Hollydale
and even though you remember
your biographers never understand
your father's pain as he sells his stock
and another dream goes
and though you're poor it isn't poverty that
concerns you
and though they fought a lot
it isn't your father's drinking that makes any difference
but only that everybody is together and you

and your sister have happy birthdays and very good
  christmasses
and I really hope no white person ever has cause to write
  about me
because they never understand Black love is Black wealth
  and they'll
probably talk about my hard childhood and never
  understand that
all the while I was quite happy

My poem

i am 25 years old
black female poet
wrote a poem asking
nigger can you kill
if they kill me
it won't stop
the revolution

i have been robbed
it looked like they knew
that i was to be hit
they took my tv
my two rings
my piece of african print
and my two guns
if they take my life
it won't stop
the revolution

my phone is tapped
my mail is opened

they've caused me to turn
on all my old friends
and all my new lovers
if i hate all black
people
and all negroes
it won't stop
the revolution

i'm afraid to tell
my roommate where i'm going
and scared to tell
people if i'm coming
if i sit here
for the rest
of my life
it won't stop
the revolution

if i never write
another poem
or short story
if i flunk out
of grad school
if my car is reclaimed
and my record player
won't play
and if i never see
a peaceful day
or do a meaningful
black thing
it won't stop
the revolution

the revolution
is in the streets
and if i stay on
the 5th floor
it will go on
if i never do
anything
it will go on

The geni in the jar

for Nina Simone

take a note and spin it around spin it around don't
prick your finger
take a note and spin it around
on the Black loom on the Black loom
careful baby
don't prick your finger

take the air and weave the sky
around the Black loom around the Black loom
make the sky sing a Black song sing a blue song
sing my song make the sky sing a Black song
from the Black loom from the Black loom
careful baby
don't prick your finger

take the geni and put her in a jar
put her in a jar
wrap the sky around her
take the geni and put her in a jar
wrap the sky around her

listen to her sing
sing a Black song our Black song
from the Black loom
singing to me
from the Black loom
careful baby
don't prick your finger

Carolyn M. Rodgers

is a native of Chicago, born about 1943. She attended the schools of her home town, including Hyde Park High, the University of Illinois (Navy Pier) and finally Roosevelt University where she majored in English and did graduate work in psychology. After that, she became a social worker. She has been writing since the age of nine – 'but *seriously* only since the middle sixties'. A veteran of the O.B.A.C. Writers Workshop and the Gwendolyn Brooks Workshop, she first attracted public attention in June 1968 when she won the first Conrad Kent Rivers award. In the same year her first book appeared: *Paper soul*, published, as were her later ones, by the Third World Press.

Carolyn Rodgers is one of the best of the younger Chicago writers, and the strongest independent talent to survive the Workshops. 'I want to write a novel and at least one good play. I want to ultimately write like Smokey sings, or 'Trane plays.' She has been getting nearer at least the first of these ideals in writing, with verse published in the *Negro Digest* (*Black World*), *Nommo* and the *Journal of Black Poetry*, in a 1969 pamphlet called *2 love raps* and a book of the same date called *Songs of a black bird*. She has also been increasingly engaged in teaching creative writing, conducting seminars at Columbia College, Chicago, in 1969, at the University of Washington in the summer of 1970, at Xavier and Albany in 1971–2. As a lecturer in Afro-American literature she has blitzed Fisk, Howard, Cornell and many other places. Her four articles on black poetry in *Black World* (1970) were among the earliest expressions of a new black criticism. Also in 1970 she edited an anthology, *For love of our brothers*.

Jesus was crucified, or, it must be deep
(an epic poem)

i was sick
and my motha called me
tonight yeah, she did she
sd she was sorri
i was sick, but what
   she wanted tuh tell
me was that i shud pray or
have her (hunky) preacher
pray fuh me. she sd. i
had too much hate in me
she sd u know the way yuh think is
got a lots to do
wid the way u feel, and i
agreed, told her i WAS angry a lot THESE days
and maybe my insides was too and she sd
   why it's somethin wrong wid yo mind girl
that's what it is
                 and i sd yes, i was aware a lot
lately and she sd if she had evah known educashun
woulda mad me crazi, she woulda neva sent me to
school (college that is)
she sd the way i worked my fingers to the bone in
this white mans factori to make u a de-cent some-
bodi and here u are actin not like decent folks
   talkin bout hatin white folks & revolution
& such and runnin round wid Negroes
  WHO CURSE IN PUBLIC!!!! (she sd)
THEY COMMUNIST GIRL!!! DON'T YUH
   KNOW THAT???
DONT' YUH READ THE NEWSPAPERS?????
        (and i sd)

i don't believe – (and she sd) U DON'T BELIEVE IN
     GOD NO MO DO U?????
u wudn't raised that way! U gon die and go tuh HELL
and i sd i hoped it wudn't be NO HUNKIES there
and she sd
what do u mean, there is some good white people and some
bad ones, just like there is Negroes
and i says i had neva seen ONE (wite good that is) but
she sd Negroes ain't readi, i knows this and
deep in yo heart you do too and i sd yes u right
Negroes ain't readi and she sd
why just the utha day i was in the store and there was
uh negro packin clerk put uh colored woman's ice cream
in her grocery bag widout wun of them 'don't melt' bags
  and the colored ladi sd to the colored clerk
'how do u know mah ice cream ain't gon tuh melt befo I
git home.'

    clerk sd. 'i don't' and took the ice cream
    back out and put it in wun of them 'stay hard'
    bags,
and me and that ladi sd see see, ne-groes don't treat
nobody right why that clerk packin groceries was un
grown main, acted mad. white folks wudn't treat yuh that
way. why when i went tuh the BANK the otha day to
deposit some MONEY
this white man helped me fast and nice. u gon die girl
and go tuh hell if yuh hate white folks. i sd, me and
my friends could dig it . . . hell, that is
she sd du u pray? i sd sorta when i hear Coltrane and
she sd if yuh read yuh bible it'll show u read genesis
revelation and she couldn't remember the otha chapter
i should read but she sd what was in the Bible was
happnin now, fire & all and she sd just cause i didn't
believe the bible don't make it not true

                              (and i sd)
    just cause she believed the bible didn't make it true
and she sd it is it is and deep deep down
in yo heart u know it's true

                              (and i sd)

    it must be deeeep

she sd i gon pray fuh u tuh be saved. i sd thank yuh.
    but befo she hung up my motha sd
      well girl, if yuh need me call me
i hope we don't have to straighten the truth out no mo.
i sd i hoped we didn't too
                    (it was 10 P.M. when she called)
she sd, i got tuh go so i can git up early tomorrow
and go tuh the social security board to clarify my
record cause i need my money.
work hard for 30 yrs. and they don't want tuh give me
$28.00 once ev'ry two weeks.
          i sd yeah . . .
don't let em nail u wid no technicalities
            git yo checks . . . (then i sd)

    catch yuh later on jesus, i mean motha!

          it must be
                  deeeeep . . .

It is deep

(don't never forget the bridge that you
crossed over on)

Having tried to use the
witch cord

that erases the stretch of
thirty-three blocks
and tuning in the voice which
    woodenly stated that the
    talk box was 'disconnected'

My mother, religiously girdled in
her god, slipped on some love, and
laid on my bell like a truck,
blew through my door warm wind from the south
concern making her gruff and tight-lipped
    and scared
that her 'baby' was starving,
she, having learned, that disconnection results from non-
    payment of bill(s).

She did not
recognize the poster of the
grand le-roi (al) cat on the wall
had never even seen the book of
Black poems that I have written
thinks that I am under the influence of
    'communists'
when I talk about Black as anything
other than something ugly to kill it befo it grows
    in any impression she would not be
considered 'relevant' or 'Black'

                        but
there she was, standing in my room
not loudly condemning that day and
not remembering that I grew hearing her
curse the factory where she 'cut uh slave'
and the cheap j-boss wouldn't allow a union,
not remembering that I heard the tears when

they told her a high school diploma was not enough,
and here now, not able to understand, what she had
been forced to deny, still –

she pushed into my kitchen so
she could open my refrigerator to see
what I had to eat, and pressed fifty
bills in my hand saying 'pay the talk bill and buy
some food; you got folks who care about you . . .'

My mother, religious-negro, proud of
having waded through a storm, is very obviously,
a sturdy Black bridge that I
crossed over, on.

Mukhtarr Mustapha

was born on Christmas day of 1943, at Freetown in Sierra Leone. He is the son of Muhammed Sanussi Mustapha, who has in turn been Minister of Works, of Natural Resources, of Finance, Deputy Prime Minister from May 1960, and at all times the 'exceptionally able and widely respected' representative of the country's powerful Muslim community as well as the head of a prosperous import-export business.

Mukhtarr attended Prince of Wales School, but owes much of his 'education' (he would probably prefer to call it training) to an uncle who has remained in close touch with the varied patterns of the family's ancestral heritage – combining Yoruba and Woloff backgrounds and a 'motherland' which is in no way defined by, or confined to, present political boundaries. This unique background, of deep and natural roots in various cultures combined with the international ramifications of business, is noticeable in Mukhtarr's work – which is, I hope, typical of what the 'third generation' of African writers is going to contribute to its own heritage, to the dialogue between conflicting cultures, and to world literature. At last it is becoming possible to write without explanation, self-consciousness or cross-reference.

Since he started to write poetry, at the age of fifteen, Mukhtarr has considerably broadened his already unusual background and experience. The family business has made it possible for him to travel widely: he has been to Australia, travelled in India, and visited the United States where he lectured and read at Rutgers University. Pursuing more personal interests he has journeyed the length and breadth of West and North Africa, lived with the Berbers and become a 'griot', similar to a wandering minstrel. He reads exceedingly well, plays tambur, gongs and drums, has made a number of recordings for the B.B.C. West African service. His writing is, almost inevitably, all-embracing: poetry, at least four plays, short stories, a completed novel and one in progress, articles and essays. His latest development is the writing of long 'scrolls' integrating poetry, painting and, where possible, sound patterns.

His first book of poetry, *Thorns and thistles*, has appeared in the Heritage series. Another collection of his poems will appear opposite the etchings of Alabama-born artist Lev Mills.

Dalabani

I will dance for grief
and hate
I will dance for joy
and love
I will dance for plenty
and rain
I will dance to stop the unknown
and mysterious
I will dance for vodoo – wunde – Poro – Soko
and Kolomashi
I will look at my raw black skin
and dance
I will shut my eyes to plenty
and dance.
I will dance and dance till I
destroy you
I will dance till you choke and give in
give in
I will dance till the dying man
staggers and coughs
I will dance my dance till
I suck you up – Ghee!
I will dance now and stop
the running water – Zim!
I will dance for the new born
till it talks – Bam!

I will dance for the snakes
I will dance for the leopards
I will dance for the alligators
I will dance for the lion
I will dance for the big Iroko tree
I will dance and make your mouth
twist and fold
I will dance and put my curse on you
I will dance for my mother, gone beneath,
beneath the ground
And raise the dead to full height
And rid the earth every corner of it
of evil spirits.
I will dance and circumcise
and initiate the innocent
I will dance, I swear to God
And end you. I will.
Dance is me.
The only property you can't have.
I want to dance
And dance for days
    Daily without food
Or rest until the crisis
Comes to my door
    To dispose of
My victim's rabied remains
Then I will
Fall to the ground
Like a noble Palm tree struck
By white lightning
With only the whites
Of my withered eyes
Showing my special song.
My special drum   My special wind

My special song   My special spirit
My special woman   My special fit
        My special gestures
        My special grimaces
        Rolling on the ground
        Then eat the earth
        My special single dance
        My special couch drum
Spasmodic!
Single!
Starting!
Stopping!
Stooping!
        I cannot hear the
        Rhythm without dancing
        Dancing till I get
          Out of range
        The song is a
        Strange curious pantomine
        It awakens me from sleep
        And stretch my arms
          And my eyes
          And my head
          And my tongue
        My purple black tongue
        I will open my eyes
          with my forefingers
        Then my ears
        Then my nose
        Next to my mouth
        Now I will
        Focus on nothing
        This nothing which
        Is all thing and

Everything and nothing
Remove me by force
Use ARMS
Use ARROWS made
Of ARROW roots
NOT ME
I can no longer hear
Nor see the ordinary
My heart is ordained
With the blood
Of an amputated Ram.

Dance hysteria! Dance erotica!
Dancing with a verve
What nerve
Expressing emotion
True in primitive – motion – meant – movement
Dancing to devouring drums
                    and
Drenching the clan's blood
Dancing with gnawing anxiety
Dancing with the psyche in delightful daylight
Dancing to loose the physical strength necessary to
Dance.
Drum and dance in different tones imperceptable to human
        eyes
Dance!
Dance is our lives
Dance erotica! Dance and grace.
Dance! First place. Dance!
Drum and Dance and alter the rhythm I will
Dance
                Drum and dance
                beyond all octaves,
                in whole scales, I will dance

Dance in the voiceless forests and pour your woes
Dance and appeal for rain it shall be granted
Dream your trance in Dance
Dambala!
Din – Din – Kedin – Din
Daimba!
Dumike!
Nga – Kane!
Dansokoh!
Dance! destiny in dance to passtime
       to avert calamity

    'Dance'.

Gbassay – 'blades in regiment'

Push a porcupine quill into
My quaint eyes
Then plunge an assagai into
My fibroid face
Then slash my neck and stain
The tortoise back rich with my blood.

Force a rug needle into my narrow
nose; force it right into my
Indigo marrow.

Lift my tongue and tie it
With a rope from a tethered goat
Lacerate my lips with deep sanguine
gutters splattering blood like a
Bellow in full blaze – blazing yellow

Disembowel my belly and feed the
Hawks that hover there hourless –
timeless black blue sky
And inside a crater bury
My ears.
        'Is it death?'

Ron Welburn

(his full name is Ronald G.) was born on 30 April 1944 at Bryn Mawr in Pennsylvania, but was educated mainly in the schools of Philadelphia. He came out of high school in 1962, then took up employment as an I.B.M. clerk for two years, first in New York, later back in Philadelphia again, before going on to Lincoln University. At Lincoln he edited several students' magazines and yearbooks, received (twice) the coveted Edward Silvera prize for poetry (his friend Rocky Bryant had it next), and spent the last two years as the school's 'poet laureate'. He graduated in 1968 and stayed on to teach English in summer school. Later in the year he moved to the University of Arizona at Tucson, for graduate study in creative writing. By the middle of 1970 Ron moved to Syracuse, where he teaches Afro-American literature and where he was one of the pillars of Walt Sheppard's *Nickel Review*.

By now, the volume of Ron Welburn's poetry has assumed quite considerable proportions, but very little of it has been published. He has several groups ready for publication, including one of what he calls 'older poems, of a protest nature'. He also writes short stories, and has in the last few years developed into one of the most articulate of young black literary critics. His book reviews appear regularly in *Black World*, *Liberator*, and the *Nickel Review*. He is equally interested in music (as a composer, performer and critic) and plays chess at tournament level.

Wayman, as a driven star

Moonstricken country roads.
Orbits. You found yourself
growing more frustrated, so uneasy
living in your home where

all this heavy existence
        becomes a geneology, lost into
a random list of journeys. The service
to Ciotti's/ 8-balls roll
into the end of silent street with no money,
nothing to scratch against yr thighs.
Streetlamps. The watchers of bitter shadows,
like mine. Like us. Coming down from the
corner on a cold night in March
or day, afternoons
of chess thought in NY or Philadelphia
            (once every year
        we get older. understand each
          other more sharply. the mind.
Craft or industry.
Churchmen's sons. Their economy, politics, social
experience hustling death. Then
            walking, riding home
5 times in a decade/ Those shadows.
Fingers on the weedy earth.
Bats. Winged features of the night/
You go home. I go home.
    We sleep in our memories.
    Our shoes. You think about
the grass growing green one more time.
        one more chance at transcience;
no jail, or rain. Cities
even get sick in my face.
              my people
more numerous than hair, more real
than life itself. more terrible,
those lives
        in church-pews,
        at communions and their lies:

The last time I tasted the wine.
                    Or you, the wine. Our religion
              wherever we are. wherever it is.
with lovers, musicians, & other foul names of people
          who aint shit)
                              Yr sister, who loves you,
        knows this
        but she'll never understand.

Marvin X

was born under the 'slave name' Marvin Jackmon on 29 May 1944, at Fowler in California. He went to high school at Fresno, later to Oakland City College (where he worked for a sociology degree) and to San Francisco State College. With Ed Bullins he founded the Black Arts West and the San Francisco Panther establishment known as Black House. On 7 December 1967 he publicly renounced his U.S. citizenship, and settled in Toronto. He has since migrated back to the States and lived in Harlem for a while. In 1969 he was recommended as lecturer at Fresno State College: this caused an administrative/political crisis which led to the college president's resignation. The last few years Marvin has been living in Fresno again, where he runs a small publishing house called Al Kitab Sudan. From this press his first book of poetry, *Fly to Allah*, appeared in 1969; later that same year Broadside published a collection of 'poems and proverbs' called *Black man listen*. Earlier, some of his work had appeared in the *Journal of Black Poetry* of which he is a contributing editor (he did the selection for its tenth issue in the autumn of 1968, making it probably the most militant one they have yet produced) and in a few pamphlets published by the Journal's printer, Julian Richardson Associates. Most of his early work appeared under the name Nazzam al Fitnah or Nazzam al Sudan.

Apart from poetry Marvin X has written several plays, a 'parable for black children' (*The black bird*) published as an attractive illustrated broadside by Al Kitab Sudan in 1968, and a number of exceptionally good interviews (in the *Journal*, *Black Dialogue*, *Soulbook* and similar magazines) which he hopes to publish in book form under the title *Black dialogue*. His Broadside book has also been released on tape, read by its author.

A soul on ice

for e. c.

We came
And the virgins came
We took them in
Raised them
And they were submissive
For a time

The people came
Danced from door to door
Searching for peace
And found it
And didn't want to leave
Til the sun came up
There was music in the air
Drummers everywhere
And righteous food
The people begged for more

Young brothers came
Without their fathers
We fathered them
Taught them truth
Though they were young
And in the end rebelled

Devils came
Searching for Blood
They beat him in the backyard
We let them
For a time

High people came
Low people came
We loved them all
Prayed for them
Told them the truth

And then we heard the thunder
Yacub was back
Dressed in black
A panther.

Al asil suddi – the origin of blackness

Sudan La al lawn
Black is not a color.
Lawn kuli min sudan
All colors come from Black.
Sudan al harakat
Black is a rhythm.
Al marna tambura
A drum beat.
Anata
Ancient.
Assi
Primitive.
Al awwal sudan kalam
The first word was Black.
Al awwal rajuli sudan
The first man was Black.
Allah sudan
God is Black.
Sudan ilmi akhi

Black knows its brother.
Anta mufail mashay min sudan
You can't run from Black.
Anta mufail ghaybay min sudan
You can't hide from Black.
Ka umma sudan
Your mother is Black.
Ka abu sudan
Your father is Black.
Ka burka sudan
Your shadow is Black.
Al atun ra'a wa sami sudan
The things you see and hear are Black.
Al atun mufail ra'a wa sami sudan
The things you can't see and hear are Black.
Sudan al asil
Black is reality.
Wahabi, hurriya, adil, masawati
Unity, freedom, justice, equality.

Charles Cobb

is probably better known as one of the most active and powerful of S.N.C.C. field secretaries than as a poet. Born in 1944, he went to Howard University in 1961, but soon dropped out to go and work for S.N.C.C. in Mississippi – there are numerous 'anecdotes' about this phase of his life in Julius Lester's fine history *Look out, whitey!* As a field secretary, based in Washington, Cobb has been developing the concept and practice of 'liberation schools' through the South, and of a Center for Black Education on the lines of the Malcolm X Liberation University at Durham in North Carolina.

Cobb's earliest published collection of poetry, *Furrows*, appeared in 1967 as a very well produced private pamphlet illustrated with his own photographs (taken, as the poems were written, during 1965–6 in Los Angeles, Atlanta, Mississippi and Hanoi). The book includes some remarkable verse portraits of the leaders of the Lowndes County movement (where the Panthers originated), especially Stokely Carmichael. In 1970 Cobb toured East Africa and eventually settled in Tanzania. The next year the Third World Press brought out his new book of poetry, *Everywhere is ours.*

L.A.: the order of things

iv

Says a man
standing
in
his black

with his together black

and in the flickering

fire red
white bled
black dead
night:

You

gave me the bottle
and taught me
to

empty

its burning inside my body.

I

gave it back
Stuffed

with the rags you made me wear

Kerosened
with my sweat

Lit

with the match
of your oppression

Burning baby
burning

i feel the fire
burn

baby
burn

feeling froggy
got
got

to

leap.

Mekonsippi

Yeah,
the mississippi
runs into the mekong
get the boat at harlem
sail red rivers
black seas

or walk
from cotton to rice
from cement to silt

Vietnam
and
Amsterdam

avenues of whitey's wars
Mekonsippi

the 17th isn't parallel

doesn't
divide.

D. L. Graham

whose first name was Donald but who published under the simple
if somewhat unfortunate name of Dante, was born in 1944 in the
black suburb of Chicago known as Gary, Indiana. He studied at
Fisk until 1968 and there published three books of poetry: *Black
song* appeared in 1966 with a foreword by John O. Killens; the
two others, called *Soul motion* (I and II), were 'written and
illustrated in partial fulfilment for the B.A. degree in art'. Dante
also worked on a novel, which has not been published. After
graduating from Fisk he went back to live in Gary. Some of his
best poetry has appeared in *Umbra* and the *Journal of Black Poetry*.
Much of it is about (and has affinities with) the music of Coltrane,
Rollins, Dolphy, Shepp – significantly all of them versatile horns
with an emphasis on the tenor. Graham died in an automobile
accident near Nashville in the spring of 1971.

A portrait of Johnny Doller

> lady, lady
> why do you holler
> ain't nobody seen your
> johnny doller

i

Piss
   ain't never smelled sweet
johnny whispered and
                        walked away
walked away tired of
greasy pillow cases
and dirty house coats

and manny fat again
beggin   again
– johnny don't go –

        screaming from the window won't
        bring your johnny back

Hey brother can i help you
he'd say to some
piece for a price
and
judy would shake
her beauty
if the face was pale
enough

        Pacing   won't
        bring him back

ii

Though times are hard
i saw johnny at the Era
drinking hundred pipers
thru a straw
no more pimp talk/ talks
about guns pineapples 'n
white cherries busted loose
for his brother   torn
from his television set
             torn
by a shot gun blast

        Crying won't bring him back

Nobody remembers that **i**
turned somersaults and
bled under the moon
johnny said/ then
sing a song brother
sing a song about
a thirteen year old
who died in the streets
sing/ cause you do that best

> Pacing 'cross the floor
> won't bring your johnny
> back

Tony get the boys

old man / man black man
what do you know about a
molotov cocktail
can you run / can you crawl
can you duck / can you kill
you got no gun
you'll stumble in the dark
can you kill / huh can you kill
don't want no old man going
with me –
where were you when
your daughter cried
on a piece-work-blood-stained
                pallet
were you in that same dark
shack or did you hide somewhere
                outside

dont pray come sunday
bring bottles gas rags
 & cutty sark to help our aim
yeah, help our aim old man
go home

the street lights are on /
tony get the boys

Stanley Crouch

is a Californian born in 1945 in Los Angeles, where he eventually attended East Los Angeles City College. He has since taught at Claremont City College where, apart from literature and black drama, his courses have included one in music appreciation. Music, in fact, is his first love. He is a practising and professional musician, playing the drums in his own group, Stanley Crouch and the Black Music Infinity. Some of his earlier poems appeared in *Watts poets*, the 1968 anthology edited by Quincy Troupe, a member of the original Watts Writers' Workshop. Stanley Crouch had himself been active at the Watts Happening Coffee House ('an abandoned furniture store that the young people of the area have transformed – industriously and ingeniously – into an art center') and in the Watts Repertory Theater Company. Later he became a frequent contributor to the *Negro Digest*, *Liberator* and *Black Dialogue*. His first book of poetry was published by E. P. Dutton in 1971 as *Ain't no ambulances for no niggers tonight*. He is under contract with Harper & Row to finish his first novel, *The music*.

Up on the spoon

That horn chased me
like a hound
and I hid
in spoons
and I boiled
and my insides
turned black
like the bottom of that
spoon beneath that match:

All the darkness,
coming down off bennies
my knees about to split
my dick shrivelled
and disappearing inside my stomach
as my insides scrapped together
like a parody of the belly rub
and my horn sucking out all my sadness
like my veins sucked all that smack
out of needles:
            Then pee pees
plenty of em,
I'd beep my horn and there they'd be:
Nothing sweet anywhere,
just the freakishness of
white women following me from club to club
whispering in corners
about giving up head
while I sipped my ice water
and that water
that water turned into the world
when I was sick
had the jitters, the chills
balled up like a rotten loaf of pawn
tickets I couldn't eat
Me: Blasphemer
Me: Bastard
Me: Vandal tearing apart my flesh
and memory,
lynching my music with strings
just for fix money,
for another chance to drop a cigarette
on a new suit,
sticking needles full of blindness

into my eyes everyday.
WHAT ELSE CAN I TALK ABOUT BUT MY
    SICKNESS
Stick your foot up my ass, please,
outside a tinsel music hall named
after me:
Birdland, the Valley of the Long Distance Runners.

Hug me in the corner mama
and tell me that I'll get well.

Leumas Sirrah

was one of the earliest Watts poets to drift into Bud Schulberg's empty Writers' Workshop, towards the end of 1965. He appeared as 'a mysterious eighteen-year-old who had dropped out of Jordan High School in his junior year, the same year he had left the home of his stepmother and ten half-brothers and sisters, living thereafter from hand to mouth with many meals not passing from hand to mouth for many days'.

Leumas Sirrah was born in Watts in 1947. From the day he left his family and started to fend for himself he has been accorded the treatment usual for unemployed black males in many towns, North, South or West: he has been bounced in and out of jail cells so often he has lost track – but his arrest record grows with every new charge, even if they are usually dropped before the case is ever brought to court, until convictions become automatic and the chance of employment dead zero. Eventually he and his cat Thought found the shelter of Frederick Douglass House, the commune that grew out of the Workshop. Meanwhile the *Los Angeles magazine* had printed his and Johnie Scott's poetry, he had appeared in the television documentary *The angry voices of Watts*, in the anthologies *From the ashes* (1967) and *Watts poets* (1968). And Leumas Sirrah continues to weld the inferno of Watts into metaphysical verse.

Me – I'm black

I'm black
I'm black
I can't change the fact
Understanding I don't lack
I'm me – I'm black.

I'm me
I'm me
I can't change that
Today is black
Tomorrow, yesterday
I wasn't promised.
I am what I am –
That's all that I am
I'm me I am
I'm black
I'm black.

Day off the street

Mornings of interrupted dreams
   by noise of doors and then
   lights.
Dreams, erupt, escape and
   vanish as I among other lifeless
   bodies move out to collect that
   starting meal of the day.
As dawn comes over the horizon
   I watch an unsuitable vision
   of the sun where even the
   chickens can't see.
Imagination engulfing me as I
   try to decide what
   to do best for that day.
Doing one's time becomes one's
   torture once one realizes there's nothing
   but time if there's no portrayal of freedom.
Absentmindedly not linking those

forever promises forever promises of not
 returning along with the same savage mistake
 of how it is I'm here.
I'm black.
I find slumber my only answer
 of that short past of thoughts,
 as well as what to do advice
 which is very troublesome.
Now laying back I still try
 to find that deep satisfaction
Of freedom, my truth with
 love, though now it's the age of
 the age of day dreaming and solitude.

Johnie Harold Scott

is another original member of the Watts Writers' Workshop, but he is not a native of Los Angeles: born 8 May 1948 at Cheyenne in Wyoming, he only came to Watts a full ten years later. He went to school in Watts, and persevered to graduate from Jordan High ('hated Jordan High especially, for what it had done to him: nothing'). A 'troubled year' at Harvard, ending in June 1965; the Workshop from early 1966, and after that a teaching course at Douglass House: the tribulations and motivations of these early years are candidly and potently set out in his essay 'The coming of the hoodlum' which, with a generous selection of poems, was his contribution to *From the ashes*, the 1967 Workshop anthology.

His appearance in the *Angry voices* television programme led to a commission for two N.B.C. 'experiment in television' scripts. Scott's interest in the media is great, he is attending Stanford University on a scholarship, wants to go to its School of Communications, Broadcasting & Film. As a research assistant at Stanford he has worked under St Clare Drake on an Afro-American studies programme; he directs the Black Studies Workshop in creative writing. His second play, *David*, was performed at Stanford early in 1970.

Chaos in a ghetto alley

I am a little girl playing in my yard.
My mother is calling me into the house.

I am a little boy who is walking through the projects.
My mind is calling me into incinerators to make love.

We are the two who are one
we are male and female

whose genitals match perfectly
and whose fruits are ugly statistics.

I am the son of the other man
whose face was not blurred in the water,
whose mind was not lost in the mirror,
whose soul was not lost in the fires of August.

We are the sons of hate
We are the daughters of love
whose mothers have always called us,
whose desires have always called us,
whose need for father has always called us.

We were never children of the sun
who might bask beneath golden rays and burn red.
We were never children of darkness
whose mists shroud the stealing of thieves
or a whore-slaying Jack the Ripper.

Why do we lose the sounds out of our throats
and remember aimless dogs whose only needs
are for offspring and phone poles and fire hydrants?

We are night and today creatures
breathing in yesterday
whose minds have left today
to die in the foul clutches of tomorrow.

We are yesterday people
who cannot live in tomorrow.
What must be done must be done by our children.
And they burn fires in the alleys.

D. T. Ogilvie

lived in Washington, D.C. and was born (there?) around 1948. Several years ago I came by the typescript of a large collection of her poetry, called *Sketches in black*: the three short poems used here are from that collection. Meanwhile everybody seems to have lost track of her.

Black thoughts

i
Dudu ni dudu

Once you are black
you can never be
blacker
than your black
brother

ii
Enikeni le sero

it takes all kinds of people
with all kinds of talents
to make a revolution work.
so what's your excuse?

iii
Gangan

black people in America
must establish
a talking-drum
with their African brothers

Victor Hernandez Cruz

represents a relatively new addition to the racial melting pot of New York letters: the Puerto Rican who has taken the speech of the city rather than the tongue of his island as his working medium. Born at Aquas Buenas in Puerto Rico in 1949, Cruz came to New York City in 1954 and has lived in East Harlem for most of his life. He went to Franklin High School (where he is reputed to have conducted 'voodoo demonstrations') until 1967, and the next year opened the East Harlem Gut Theater on East 104th Street. He has also worked for the Parks Department (to whose offices much of the popular culture of the city seems to be designated), for the ubiquitous Teachers–Writers Collaborative, in Herbert Koch's teaching experiments, and in readings for the Academy of American poets. At present he teaches in the English department of the University of California at Berkeley.

Victor Cruz's first book of poetry, *Papo got his gun* (which I have never seen), is said to have been published in 1966 with the financial aid of his neighbours. A much larger collection, *Snaps*, was issued in 1969 by Random House. Other poems have appeared in the *Journal of Black Poetry*, *Umbra*, *Ramparts* and *Evergreen Review*.

Two way

& look how they waste that guy
in afternoon gator shoes
to the head
                    a hole in the fence
makes life faster
                    ancient bottles
one time alive with alcohol
                              turn red
stepping feet for many a year
                    head

smiles against the brick, red
water around the neck
                           someone is named
Gypsy
        who is bad
        who is bad
laughter chokes the throat
                              saigon
saigon/ saigon
                  section of lexington
ave.
     saigon
              section of the mr. mac
hine
     they ran together with the
wind
       into the hallway
                          coming out
on the street
                  throw the knife away
put it down
                  the people ran into the
mountains
              ran thru the hole in the
fence
     blood made a trail to the place
of silence
              the guy was loud
              fucken loud
              so we did him in
              kick his ass on fire
the avenue jumps in front
                              the little
girl ate watermelon beer cans crushed

against the curve
                    drums shake the air
dancing
            floors pleading
            pretty corner ladies
            the movement of bodies
the children brothers of mine
                              wasted against
a door / in the dark of a world
in the middle of
                    soldiers murder in saigon
king size smoke brightens the night
the police was naked in the middle
of the avenue according to old
puerto rican tale blowing his whistle
 & scratching his ass it was 12 noon

a guy came round with all that shit/ so they
gonna give him a break/ but before he left
he got so loud so they hit him with pipes
 & shit
          an enemy lies pass 3rd avenue
the village was calm after the jets
bombed it all up
                    americans   the mountains
were on fire & cries went to the sky
                                        the
police came round looking for dirty hands
or dirty looks
                  americans/ americans
                              & look
how they waste the guy
                        new york.
                        new york.

Musu Ber

is a native of Tennessee: she was born in Memphis in 1950 and continued to live in that city until 1967 when she left for Lincoln University 'which is in semi-seclusion somewhere between 1856 and 1971 on Pennsylvania route 1'. She graduated from Lincoln in 1971 and then moved to Philadelphia where she had already been a part-time teacher during her own last year at college. The poem 'Peaches' first appeared under the more revealing title 'And so I am gentle' in an anthology of black Philadelphians published in 1970 by the Black History Museum (and Library), an institution which proudly recalls the days of the Philadelphia Reading Room Society which was founded in 1828 as the first library for free blacks in America. In that anthology Musu Ber was still using the slave name Carol Luther; shortly after she became Mrs Carol Johnson. I think her work holds the right kind of promise to end this book with.

Peaches

peaches in open markets
in brownsville, bed-stuy &
the east village
remind me of summers in
memphis
where peaches grew on trees
and we shook them down

and my mother was a girl
who worked in some nice white
woman's house who
gave us hand-me-downs
and called my mother girl

even though
she had two children
older than hers and a
husband

who was a man
even though he was 6'2"
and weighed 200 pounds
and was jet black
ebony, it's called

in memphis where peaches grew
on trees
my aunt killed chickens
in the backyard
of the house we rented
from the jewish lady
down the block
and i couldn't eat them
cause i saw them runnin
around with their necks all bloody
and their heads on the
ground dead
and my aunt would laugh
and give me banana pudding
instead

you can still buy live chickens
in the market in brooklyn
but now the white man
kills them for you

summer was going to the
company picnic

and being black
and sitting at the tables
with the other black families

and smiling when the white men
who drove a freight truck like
my father
but got paid more money
came over and patted you on
your straightened nappy head
and my mother would offer them
slices of peach pies
made from the big red ripe peaches
off the tree in our backyard

our peaches were
bigger and redder than anybody's
especially the ones in
new york
until we climbed the tree
to reach the juiciest peach
in the whole world
and the limb broke
and the peach tree died

then my mother came home
early
and told us that she was going to college
and become somebody
and a woman instead
of a girl

with the peach tree dead
the summers passed slowly

until we went to graduation
for my mother
on the great green grassy lawn
of the negro college
and i saw my mother cry
because she got the paper
bound in real leather
that said she was a woman
and all i saw was
the letters b.a. and with honor
in greek or latin

and after summer we moved
to the good negro neighborhood
where there was
a barbeque pit
and the boy next door had
a built in swimming pool
and we got a black and brown
chihuahua
but nobody had a peach tree
or chicken coop
and the people across the street
had a maid that they didn't call
girl

the summers kept going by
slowly and
finally i went up north
to college
and i met people
and loved people
and found out that there is
more to life than

peach trees that die
if you climb them
people die
especially your boyfriend
and it leaves you empty
and your mother doesn't understand
much   or enough

and james brown
sings, grinds, and shouts
to honkies up north
the same day
your boyfriend dies
and there you are
trying to relate
and hold on to
your sanity
because life
is beginning to be too much
too fast

and going home to memphis
and my sister married
and my parents
moving 'up north'
to jew town
getting whiter
while i got blacker
and no longer being able to
relate to me

and running, running
running, always
and meeting people who

are always running
not knowing where
we run,
never stopping
running,
remembering peaches
that grow on trees and
trees
and people and places that
change or die

Paul Breman

was born 19 July 1931 at Bussum, a dormitory village south of Amsterdam, in Holland. There he went through all the usual schools until graduation in 1948, then spent a year reading Greek and Latin (to no great effect) before enrolling at Amsterdam University and attending just enough lectures to drop out before anyone had noticed he was there. He handled public relations for an Amsterdam art gallery for about two years, running an extensive programme of concerts, readings and happenings, but in 1954 he 'drifted into the antiquarian book trade' and has remained there ever since. From 1959 he has been living in London, where since 1968 he has been running his own business.

Shortly after the Second World War he decided ('because of an interest in the poetic discipline of the blues') to collect what was then known as negro poetry. His first translations appeared in 1948 – mercifully they also remained his last, with the exception of a bilingual (Dutch-English) anthology edited together with Rosey Pool and called *Ik zag hoe zwart ik was* (1958). In 1960 his interest took a slightly different form when he edited, for a Dutch bibliophile society, the first book of Waring Cuney, a Harlem Renaissance poet whose work had previously been scattered through countless periodicals. The next year Breman's own book on secular negro folk music called *Blues en andere wereldlijke volksmuziek van de noordamerikaanse neger* was published in Holland as a paperback. This is the only part of his own writings that he still likes (with the exception of a few antiquarian catalogues cryptically known as 'Goldschmidt 126, Weinreb 14 and Breman 5 or 11') and consequently it must be gratifying that it is still in print.

During the early sixties another sideline of his collecting activities developed out of persistent attempts to interest publishers in the work of Robert Hayden – who, Breman thinks, is the only black American poet to range with Damas, Césaire, Senghor, Lima and Guillén. These attempts all failed ('the response from T. S. Eliot is a minor classic') but resulted, eventually, in a new series of black poetry books edited and published by Paul Breman and inaugurated in April 1962 with Robert Hayden's 'A ballad of remembrance' which was to win the Grand Prix de la Poésie at the Dakar Festival of Negro Arts in 1966.

The Heritage series has since proved to be durable: after a hard start (four volumes in as many years) it seems to have settled down to a steady four books a year, has survived to be the oldest such series still in production, and bridges the gap between the 'negro poets' and the 'black revolution' more successfully than anyone would have thought possible.

The present anthology Breman sees as an end result of his collecting and publishing activities, a chance to communicate the fun of discovery and acquisition. Fun is an operative concept in virtually everything he undertakes – a personal euphemism, probably, for the more pretentious 'joys of living'. It underlies his refusal ever to write articles or take part in academic discussions – there is no fun in being an authority.

When (once) that rule was broken, with an article on 'Poetry in the sixties', the result was startling enough (in an otherwise wholly predictable collection of weighty essays) to be called 'a perfectly silly piece of ranting' by the earnest editor of *Black World*. 'When I saw that I laughed – it's good, every once in a while, to find it confirmed that one's not yet a fossil.'

Indexes

Alphabetical Index

Geographical Index

(entries for each country or state are in
chronological order of authors' birth)

Acknowledgements

Acknowledgements

Peter Abrahams — 'Fancies idle' (iii) from *A blackman speaks of freedom*, Durban, *c.* 1938

Chinua Achebe — 'Mango seedling' from *Biafra revisited*, American Committee to keep Biafra alive, New York (1969)

Lloyd Addison — 'After MLK' from *The aura & the umbra*, Paul Breman, 1970 (first published in *Beau-Cocoa*, autumn 1968)

Christina Ama Ata Aidoo — 'Poem' from *Nouvelle somme du poésie du monde noir*, Présence Africaine, Paris, 1966

Frank Aig-Imoukhuede — 'One wife for one man' from *Modern poetry from Africa*, Penguin Books, Harmondsworth, 1963

Ahmed Alhamisi — 'Look for me dear mother' from the *Journal of Black Poetry* no. 14, San Francisco, 1971

Samuel Allen — 'The staircase' and 'Divestment' from *Ivory tusks and other poems*, Poets Press, New York, 1968 (originally published under the pseudonym Paul Vesey)

R. E. G. Armattoe — 'Deep down the blackman's mind' from *Deep down the blackman's mind*, privately published, 1954

Russell Atkins — 'Narrative' and 'Christophe' from *Heretofore*, Paul Breman, 1968. 'Christophe' first appeared in *View Magazine* 1947, 'Narrative' in *Hearse* 1959, *Objects* 1963, *Fine Arts* 1966

Kofi Awoonor — 'I heard a bird cry' from *Black Orpheus* no. 15, Ibadan, June 1961; 'My god of songs was ill' from *Rediscovery*, Mbari, Ibadan, 1964

Ameer Baraka 'Notes for a speech' from *Preface to a twenty volume suicide note*, Totem-Corinth, New York, 1961; 'A poem some people will have to understand' and 'For Tom Postell, dead black poet' from *Black magic poetry*, Bobbs-Merrill, Indianapolis, 1969; 'I substitute for the dead lecturer' from *The dead lecturer*, Grove Press, New York, 1964; 'Beautiful black women' from *Black art*, Jihad, Newark, 1966

Eseoghene Barrett 'In my eye and heart and all about the same blood' from *Daylight* magazine, May 1964

Vera Bell 'Ancestor on the auction block' from *The independence anthology of Jamaican literature*, Ministry of Development, Kingston, 1962

Musu Ber 'Peaches' from *Black poets write on, an anthology of Black Philadelphian poets*, Black History Museum Committee, Philadelphia, 1970

Lebert Bethune 'A juju of my own' and 'To strike for night' from *Juju of my own*, Lebert Bethune, Paris, 1966; by permission of the author

Peter Blackman 'My song is for all men' (fragment) from *My song is for all men*, Lawrence & Wishart, London, 1952

Arna Bontemps 'Southern mansion' and 'A black man talks of reaping' from *Personals*, Paul Breman, 1963

Fred Bradford 'Death of a nigger' from the *Journal of Black Poetry* no. 3, San Francisco, 1966

Dollar Brand 'Africa: music' (iii–vi) from *Journal of the New African Literature and the Arts*, Stanford, 1967

Edward Brathwaite 'The making of the drum' from *Masks*, Oxford University Press, London, 1968; 'Folkways' (i) from *Rights of passage*, Oxford University Press, 1967; 'Jou'vert' (i) from *Islands*, Oxford University Press, 1969; 'Tom' from *Penguin modern poets* no. 13, Penguin Books, 1969

Kwesi Brew	'A plea for mercy' and 'Ancestral faces' from *The shadows of laughter*, Longmans, London, 1968
Gwendolyn Brooks	'Jessie Mitchell's mother', copyright © Gwendolyn Brooks, 1960; 'Malcolm X', copyright © Gwendolyn Brooks Blakely, from *The world of Gwendolyn Brooks*, 1971
Sterling Brown	'Long gone' from *Southern road*, Harcourt Brace, New York, 1932; 'Old Lem' and 'An old woman remembers' by permission of the author
Dennis Brutus	'Somehow we survive' and 'The sounds begin again' from *Sirens, knuckles, boots*, Mbari, Ibadan, 1963; by permission of the author
F. J. Bryant jnr	'Patience of a people' by permission of the author
Ed Bullins	'When slavery seems sweet' by permission of the author, associate director at The New Lafayette Theater, editor of *Black Theater Magazine*
Jan Carew	'Africa-Guyana' from the *Journal of Black Poetry* no. 10, San Francisco, 1968
Martin Carter	'Death of a slave' from *Kyk-over-al* no. 22, Georgetown, 1957; 'Ancestor Accabreh' from manuscript (originally intended for *Poems of resistance*, Lawrence & Wishart, London, 1954)
John Pepper Clark	'Abiku' and 'Ivbie' (i, ii, iv & v) both from *Poems*, Mbari, Ibadan, 1962
Charles Cobb	'L.A.: the order of things' (iv) and 'Mekonsippi' from *Furrows*, Flute Publications, Tougaloo, 1967
Sam J. Cornish	'Harriet Tubman' and 'Lord while I sow earth' both from manuscript by permission of the author
Stanley Crouch	'Up on the spoon' from *Watts poets*, Quincy Troupe, Los Angeles, 1968

Victor Hernandez Cruz	'Two way' from the *Journal of Black Poetry* no. 9, San Francisco, 1968
Countee Cullen	'Heritage' from *On these I stand*, by Countee Cullen, copyright © 1925, Harper & Row, New York Publishers Inc., renewed 1953 by Ida M. Cullen; 'Caprice' from *Color*, by Countee Cullen, copyright © Harper & Row, Publishers Inc., 1925, renewed 1953 by Ida M. Cullen
Waring Cuney	'No images' from *Puzzles*, De Roos, Utrecht, 1960; 'Hard time blues' from manuscript, by permission of the author
Raymond G. Dandridge	'Time to die' from *The book of American negro poetry*, Harcourt Brace, New York, 1922
Margaret Danner	'The slave and the iron lace' from *To flower*, Hemphill Press, Nashville, 1963
Mbella Sonne Dipoko	'Exile' from *Modern poetry from Africa*, Penguin Books, Harmondsworth, 1965; 'Our Destiny' from *Black and white in love*, Heinemann, London, 1971, reproduced by permission of the publishers
Owen Dodson	'For Edwin R. Embree' from manuscript, by permission of the author
William Edward Burghardt duBois	'The song of the smoke' from *Selected poems*, Ghana Universities Press, Accra, 1964
Henry Dumas	'Knock on wood' from *Black fire*, William Morrow, New York, 1968
Paul Laurence Dunbar	'An ante-bellum sermon' and 'We wear the mask' from *Lyrics of lowly life*, Dodd Mead, New York, 1896; 'The haunted oak' from *Lyrics of love and laughter*, Dodd Mead, 1903
Ray Durem	'To all the nice white people', 'The saddest tears' and 'Broadminded' from *Take no prisoners*, Paul Breman, 1971

James A. Emanuel	'Black humor' from *Panther man*, Broadside Press, Detroit, 1970, copyright © James Emanuel, 1970, reprinted by permission of Broadside Press
Yetunde Esan	'Ololu – an Egungun' from *Nigerian student verse*, University Press, Ibadan, 1959
Iulia Fields	'For Malcolm X' from *For Malcolm*, Broadside Press, Detroit, 1967; reprinted by permission of the author
Nikki Giovanni	'Nikki – Rosa' and 'My Poem' from *Black judgment*, Nikki Giovanni, New York, 1968 (distributed by Broadside Press), copyright © Nikki Giovanni, 1968; 'The geni in the jar' from *Re: creation*, Broadside Press, Detroit, 1970, copyright © Nikki Giovanni, 1970
D. L. Graham	'A portrait of Johnny Doller' and 'Tony get the boys' from *Soul motion II*, Fisk University, Nashville, no date
Bruce Grit	'The black man's burden' from *Cullings from Zion's poets*, Mobile, 1907
Bobb Hamilton	'Brother Harlem Bedford Watts tells Mr Charlie where it's at' from *Black fire*, William Morrow, New York, 1968
Robert Hayden	'A ballad of remembrance', 'Middle Passage', 'The ballad of Nat Turner' and 'Frederick Douglass' from *A ballad of remembrance*, Paul Breman, 1962, and from *Selected poems*, copyright © Robert Hayden, 1966, reprinted by permission of October House Inc. 'Locus' from *Words in the mourning time*, copyright © Robert Hayden, 1970, reprinted by permission of October House Inc.
David Henderson	'Pentecostal Sunday' from *De mayor of Harlem*, Dutton, New York, 1970; 'Among the whites' from manuscript, by permission of the author

546 Acknowledgements

Calvin C. Hernton   'An unexpurgated communiqué' from *Umbra* anthology, New York, 1968; 'The coming of Chronos' (ii–iv) from *The coming of Chronos to the House of Nightsong*, Interim Books, New York, 1964

Carl Wendell Hines   'Now that he is safely dead' was published originally in *Hold fast to dreams*, ed. Arna Bontemps, Follett Publishing Co., 1969

Israel Kafu Hoh   'Baby' from *Voices of Ghana*, Ministry of Information, Accra, 1958

Langston Hughes   'The Negro speaks of rivers' from *The weary blues*, Knopf, New York, 1926; 'Red silk stockings' from *Fine clothes to the Jew*, Knopf, New York, 1927; 'My people' from *The dream keeper*, Knopf, New York, 1932; 'Lenox Avenue mural' from *Montage of a dream deferred*, Henry Holt, New York, 1951; 'Junior addict' from *The panther and the lash*, Knopf, New York, 1967

Gerald Jackson   'The song' from manuscript, by permission of the author

Lance Jeffers   'Myself' and 'That woman rebuked and scorned' from manuscript, by permission of the author, chairman of the Department of English, Bowie State College, Bowie, Maryland

Ted Joans   'Je suis un homme', copyright © Ted Joans, 1961, reprinted by permission of the author's representative, Gunther Stuhlmann. All rights reserved

Frank John   'Down' from manuscript, by permission of the author

James Weldon Johnson   'The white witch' from *Saint Peter relates an incident*, Viking Press, New York, 1935

Alice H. Jones   'For Sapphire, my sister' from *Negro Digest*, September–October, 1968

Norman Jordan   'The second plane' and 'Black warrior' from
Destination: ashes, Norman Jordan, Third
World Press. Copyright © Norman Jordan,
1971; reprinted by permission of Norman Jordan

Bob Kaufman   'Heavy water blues' and 'Unhistorical events'
from *Golden sardine*, City Lights, San Francisco,
1967, copyright © Bob Kaufman, 1967

E. McG. Keane   'Fragments and patterns' by permission of the
author

Keorapetse   'Like the tide: cloudward' and 'My people no
Kgositsile   longer sing' from *My name is Africa*, Keorapetse
Kgositsile, copyright © Keroapetse Kgositsile,
1971, reprinted by permission of Doubleday &
Co. Inc.

Etheridge Knight   'The idea of ancestry' and 'He sees through
stone' from *Poems from prison*, Broadside Press,
Detroit, 1968, copyright © Etheridge Knight,
1968; 'For black poets who think of suicide'
from *Broadside Poster* no. 1, copyright ©
Etheridge Knight, 1969. Reprinted by permission
of Broadside Press

Mazisi Kunene   'Elegy' from *Modern poetry from Africa*, Penguin
Books, Harmondsworth, 1965; 'Avenge' from
manuscript

John La Rose   'Not from here' from *Foundations*, New Beacon
Publications, 1966

Don L. Lee   'Nigerian unity' from *Don't cry, scream*,
Broadside Press, Detroit, 1969, copyright ©
Don L. Lee, 1969; 'Big momma' from *We
walk the way of the new world*, Broadside Press,
Detroit, 1970, copyright © Don L. Lee, 1970;
'To be quicker' from *Directionscore*, Broadside
Press, Detroit, 1971, copyright © Don L. Lee,
1971. All reprinted by permission of Broadside
Press

Julius Lester	'On the birth of my son, Malcolm Coltrane' from *Soulscript* anthology, Zenith Books, New York, 1970
Audre Lorde	'Coal' from *The first cities*, Poets Press, New York, 1968
Basil C. McFarlane	'Poem for my country' from *Jacob and the angel*, Georgetown, 1952
Claude McKay	'The tropics in New York', 'The Harlem dancer' and 'Outcast' from *Harlem shadows*, Harcourt Brace, New York, 1922, and from *Selected poems* by Claude McKay, copyright © Bookman Associates Inc., 1953
Roger Mais	'Men of ideas' from *The independence anthology of Jamaican literature*, Ministry of Development, Kingston, 1962
Clarence Major	'For her, the design' from *Swallow the lake*, copyright © Clarence Major, 1970, by permission of Wesleyan University Press; 'Author of an attitude' from *Private line*, Paul Breman, 1971, copyright © Clarence Major, 1971, reprinted by permission of the author
Barbara Malcom	'Bedtime story' and 'The men are all away' from *I want me a home*, Blkartsouth, New Orleans, 1969
Ezekiel Mphahlele	'Death' from the *Journal of New African Literature and the Arts* no. 3, Stanford, 1967
Mukhtarr Mustapha	'Dalabani' and 'Gbassay – "blades in regiment"' from *Thorns and thistles*, Paul Breman, 1971
Larry Neal	'The summer after Malcolm' and 'Malcolm X – an autobiography' from *Black boogaloo*, Journal of Black Poetry press, San Francisco, 1969
Abioseh Nicol	'The meaning of Africa' (fragment) from *A book of African verse*, Heinemann, London, 1964

Arthur K. Nortje   'Autopsy' from *7 South African poets*, Heinemann, London, 1970

D. T. Ogilvie   'Black thoughts' from the manuscript *Sketches in black*

Myron O'Higgins   'Vaticide' from *United Asia*, international magazine of Asian affairs, June 1953

Gabriel Okara   'You laughed and laughed and laughed' from *Negro verse*, Vista Books, 1964; 'The mystic drum' from *Modern poetry from Africa*, Penguin Books, Harmondsworth, 1963

Christopher Okigbo   'Limits' (i–iii, vi, viii, x & xi) and 'Elegy for slit-drum' from *Labyrinths*, Heinemann, London, 1969, reproduced by permission of the publishers

Dennis C. Osadebay   'Who buys my thoughts' and 'Young Africa's plea' from *Africa sings*, privately published, 1952

Frank Kobina Parkes   'African heaven' and 'A thought' from his anthology *Songs from the wilderness*, University of London Press Ltd, 1965

Eugene Perkins   'Diary of a Bronzeville boy' from manuscript

Lenrie Peters   'We have come home' from *Poems*, Mbari, Ibadan, 1964

N. H. Pritchard   'O' from *The Matrix poems 1960–1970*, Doubleday, New York, 1971, copyright © Norman H. Pritchard jnr

Dudley Randall   'The southern road' from *Poem counterpoem*, Broadside Press, Detroit, 1966, copyright © Dudley Randall, 1966, reprinted by permission of Broadside Press

Ishmael Reed   'Catechism of d neo-american hoodoo church' (iii–vi) from *Catechism of d neo-american hoodoo church*, Paul Breman, 1970, copyright © Ishmael Reed, 1968, 1969, 1970

Conrad Kent Rivers	'The still voice of Harlem' and 'Watts' from *The still voice of Harlem*, Paul Breman, 1968; 'For Richard Wright' from *The Wright poems*, Paul Breman, 1972
E. M. Roach	'I am the archipelago' from *Kyk-over-al* no. 22, Georgetown, 1967
Carolyn M. Rodgers	'Jesus was crucified' and 'It is deep' from *Songs of a blackbird*, Third World Press, Chicago, 1969, reprinted by permission of the author
David Rubadiri	'Thoughts after work' from *Poetry from Africa*, Pergamon Press, 1958, reprinted by permission of the author
Sonia Sanchez	'Indianapolis/summer/1969/poem', 'TCB' and 'Right on: white America' from *We a baddDDD people*, Broadside Press, Detroit, 1970, copyright © Sonia Sanchez, 1970, reprinted by permission of Broadside Press
Dennis Scott	'Epitaph' from *Breaklight*, London, 1971
Johnie Scott	'Chaos in a ghetto alley' from *From the ashes: voices of Watts*, Meridian Books, New York, 1969
A. J. Seymour	'First of August' from *Kyk-over-al* no. 22, Georgetown, 1957, reprinted by permission of the author
Philip M. Sherlock	'Jamaican fisherman' from *Ten poems*, Miniature Poets series, Georgetown, 1953
Leumas Sirrah	'Me – I'm black' from *From the ashes: voices of Watts*, Meridian Books, New York, 1969; 'Day off the street' from *Watts poets*, Quincy Troupe, Los Angeles, 1968
'Wole Soyinka	'The immigrant' from *Black Orpheus* no. 5, Ibadan, 1959; 'Abiku' from *Idanre & other poems*, Methuen, 1967; reprinted by permission of the author

551 Acknowledgements

A. B. Spellman	'Untitled' from the *Journal of Black Poetry* no. 10, San Francisco, 1968
Ed Spriggs	'For black Newark' and 'Pending solemnization' from the *Journal of Black Poetry* no. 9, San Francisco, 1968
Sun-Ra	'The visitation' from *Black fire* anthology, William Morrow, New York, 1968
Harold M. Telemaque	'In our land' from *Kyk-over-al* no. 22, Georgetown, 1957, by permission
James W. Thompson	'You are alms' from manuscript, by permission of the author
Melvin B. Tolson	'Mu' section from *Harlem gallery, Book I, The curator,* Twayne, New York, 1965
Jean Toomer	'Reapers' and 'November cotton flower' from *Cane,* Boni & Liveright, New York, 1923
Joseph Waiguru	'The round mud hut' from *Origin East Africa,* Heinemann, 1965
Derek Walcott	'Tales of the islands' (v & vi) from *In a green night,* Jonathan Cape, London, 1962; 'The glory trumpeter' from *The castaway and other poems,* Jonathan Cape, 1965; 'The royal palms' from *Negro verse,* Vista Books, 1964
Margaret Walker	'For my people' from *For my people,* Yale University Press, New Haven, 1942; 'For Mary McLeod Bethune' from *United Asia,* international magazine of Asian affairs, June 1953
Ron Welburn	'Wayman, as a driven star' from manuscript, by permission of the author
John A. Williams	'Safari west' from manuscript, by permission of the author
Okogbule Wonodi	'Laments for 'Shola' from *West African verse, an anthology,* Longmans, London, 1967

Jay Wright 'An invitation to Madison County', Corinth Books, New York, copyright © Jay Wright, 1971

Richard Wright 'Between the world and me' from *The poetry of the Negro 1746–1749*, Doubleday, New York, 1953; 'In the falling snow' first published in *Ebony*, February 1961, p. 92, reprinted by permission of Paul R. Reynolds & Son

Marvin X 'A soul on ice' from the *Journal of Black Poetry* no. 10, San Francisco, 1968; 'The origin of blackness' from *Black man listen*, Broadside Press, Detroit, 1969; reprinted by permission of the author

Al Young 'Birthday poem' from manuscript, copyright © Al Young, 1969, by permission of the author

Penguinews and
Penguins in Print

Every month we issue an illustrated magazine,
Penguinews. It's a lively guide to all the latest Penguins,
Pelicans and Puffins, and always contains an article on
a major Penguin author, plus other features of
contemporary interest.

Penguinews is supplemented by *Penguins in Print*, a
complete list of all the available Penguin titles – there
are now over four thousand!

The cost is no more than the postage; so why not write
for a free copy of this month's *Penguinews*? And if
you'd like both publications sent for a year, just send
us a cheque or postal order for 30p (if you live in the
United Kingdom) or 60p (if you live elsewhere), and
we'll put you on our mailing list.

Dept EP, Penguin Books Ltd,
Harmondsworth, Middlesex

Note: *Penguinews* and *Penguins in Print*
are not available in the U.S.A. or Canada

A Pelican Book

Because They're Black

Derek Humphry and Gus John

Because They're Black, first published as a Penguin
Special is the winner of the 1972 Martin Luther King
Memorial Prize. Its two authors (one of them is a black
social worker and the author of the Handsworth report)
have managed to get black people in England to 'tell
it like it is'. The major part of their book, which the
Tribune called 'admirable', describes in detail, through
individual case histories, what it feels like to be on the
receiving end of discrimination in our society.

The authors then examine the way out. Integration
is discussed and shown for what it is: the desire to
convert black men into white men. Black power,
different in kind from its U.S. counterpart but equally
strong, is seen as a humanizing necessity for black and
white alike; and political conflict and struggle are
essential if we are to change ourselves and our society.
As the *Guardian* wrote: 'It is an exhilarating development
and this pugnacious little book will speed it along.'

A Volume in the Penguin African Library

Modern Poetry from Africa

Edited by Gerald Moore and Ulli Beier

This modern 'poetical geography' of Africa is unique. It draws on sixteen countries to present the work of black poets writing in English, French, and Portuguese, although all the poems, many of which appear for the first time here, are presented in English. As a sample of contemporary African writing they reveal an interesting blend of public and personal statements.

Poetry composed in African languages has been left out, because no two editors could possibly have covered the enormous field. This omission, however, does not impair the clear picture of emotional, social and political pressures (fashionably termed *Negritude*) as they are reflected by Africa's imaginative and committed poets today.

Return to My Native Land

Aimé Césaire

Cahier d'un retour au pays natal (translated in this volume by John Berger and Anna Bostock) was written thirty years ago but seems to belong very much to our own time. Its theme is the future of the Negro race, expressed in the spirit of Frantz Fanon or Malcolm X or the Olympic athletes who raised blackgloved hands in Mexico. Nevertheless this is no political tract, but a poem of remarkable lyricism and probably the most sustained to have been inspired by the French Surrealist movement.

Césaire's life and work is discussed at length in an introduction which has been written for this edition by the South African poet, Mazisi Kunene.

Poet To Poet

In the introductions to their personal selections from
work of poets they have admired, the individual editors
write as follows:

Crabbe Selected by C. Day Lewis

'As his poetry displays a balance and decorum in its
versification, so his moral ideal is a kind of normality
to which every civilized being should aspire. This, when
one looks at the desperate expedients and experiments
of poets (and others) today, is at least refreshing.'

Henryson Selected by Hugh MacDiarmid

'There is now a consensus of judgement that regards
Henryson as the greatest of our great makars. Literary
historians and other commentators in the bad period of
the century preceding the twenties of our own century
were wont to group together as the great five:
Henryson, Dunbar, Douglas, Lyndsay, and King James I;
but in the critical atmosphere prevailing to day it is
clear that Henryson (who was, with the exception of
King James, the youngest of them) is the greatest.'

Herbert Selected by W. H. Auden

'The two English poets, neither of them, perhaps, major
poets, whom I would most like to have known well
are William Barnes and George Herbert.

Even if Isaac Walton had never written his life, I think
that any reader of his poetry will conclude that George
Herbert must have been an exceptionally good man, and
exceptionally nice as well.'

Whitman Selected by Robert Creeley

'If Whitman has taught me anything, and he has taught
me a great deal, often against my own will, it is that the
common *is* personal, intensely so, in that having no one
thus to invest it, the sea becomes a curious mixture
of water and table salt and the sky the chemical formula
for air. It is paradoxically, the personal which makes
the common in so far as recognizes the existence
of the many in the one, In my own joy or despair, I am
brought to that which others have also experienced.'

Wordsworth Selected by Lawrence Durrell

'Wordsworth almost more than any other English poet
enjoyed a sense of inner confirmation – the mysterious
sense of election to poetry as a whole way of life. He
realized too that one cannot condescend to nature – one
must work for it like a monk over a missal which he
will not live to see finished.'

Tennyson Selected by Kingsley Amis

'England notoriously had its doubts as well as its
certainties, its neuroses as well as its moral health, its fits
of gloom and frustration and panic as well as its
complacency. Tennyson is the voice of those doubts
and their accompaniments, and his genius enabled him to
communicate them in such a way that we can understand
them and feel them as our own. In short we know from
experience just what he means. Eliot called him the
saddest of all English poets, and I cannot improve on
that judgement.'

Some Recent Penguin Anthologies

The Penguin Book of Victorian Verse
Edited by George MacBeth

... of the Forties*
Edited by Robin Skelton

The Penguin Book of Restoration Verse
Edited by Harold Love

Twentieth-Century German Verse
... Bridgwater

The Penguin Book of English Romantic Verse
... by David Wright

... Penguin Book of Satirical Verse
... by Edward Lucie-Smith

The Penguin Book of Welsh Verse
... by Anthony Conran

The Penguin Book of Animal Verse
... by George MacBeth

The Penguin Book of Elizabethan Verse
Edited by Edward Lucie-Smith

The Mid-Century English Poetry 1940–60*
... Wright

... Book of Japanese Verse
... Geoffrey Bownas and Anthony Thwaite

... Thir...*
... Skelton

... the Nineties
... K. R. Thornton

*Not for sale in the U.S.A.